I0781227

DISSONANCE

Volume IV: Relentless

AARON RYAN

In 2045, gorgons don't give up easily, and now they know who their enemy is.

Published in 2024, Edition 1.

Paperback ISBN # 9781965372043. Hardcover ISBN # 9781965372036. eBook ISBN # 9781965372029. Audiobook ISBN # 9781965372050.

Gorgon creature by Rodrigo Vivedes. Man and spacecraft by Guadalupe del Rio.

Edited by Denouement Editing and CM LLC. Published independently.

This is a work of fiction. Any similarities to persons living or dead, or actual events is purely coincidental.

For Sweeps, Bren & AJ:
my true loves.

You've helped me to survive.

I CHAPTERS

"The greatest enemy to human souls is the self-righteous spirit which makes men look to themselves for salvation."

- Charles Spurgeon

I NOTE ON AI

We live in an age of AI. Every day, more and more services spring up promising revolutionary and innovative results using artificial intelligence. The authoring industry is not immune to this.

I want every one of my readers to know that not once did I employ, nor will I *ever* employ, the use of AI to sculpt any part of any of my stories. Those who know me know that I am staunchly and adamantly opposed to such cheats.

I'm very proud to be a verified human. The ability to create is a gift that I was endowed with by my Creator, and I will never forfeit that nor set it aside to propagate something synthetic and imitative.

Everything you've read by me in this saga, and in my other works, is 100% entirely created by me, the genuine article. I'm a verified human, and always will be.

To my fellow authors, I urge you to preserve the sacred gift of human creation and never stoop to such lows. Always cherish this gift you've been given. If you encounter writer's block, take a break. Don't cop out. Don't take the road more traveled by. Don't cheat. Toe the line for all of us, and keep creation – *true* unadulterated creation – alive.

Long live humanity.

Sincerely,

Aaron Ryan,
Verified Human

I NOTE ON FAITH

I am a Christian author. What does that mean exactly? It means I worship Jesus, and I serve my God in Heaven. That implies certain standards should be upheld, and that my life should be lived in certain ways, with certain morals, by certain convictions, and with a sense of honoring God in all I do and in all I write. I seek to tell **true** and inspiring stories.

One thing I've always strived for is verisimilitude. I've wanted my books to be on par with what we read out there in the world: to be adventurous escapism, to provide a gritty sense of reality, and to provide a real glimpse into the ebbs and flows of the struggles that humanity faces. That means that life isn't always glimpsed through rose-colored stained-glass windows. It means that with the good comes the gory. With the sheer valor comes the shock value. With the awe comes the awful. Does that then mean that I will ever drop an F-Bomb or take my Lord's name in vain in my works? **Never**. But does it mean that I will bury my head in the sand

and pretend that we humans down here don't talk a certain way, walk a certain way, act a certain way? **<u>Never</u>**.

I want my works to reflect the real, genuine authentic struggles that humans face, and as such I want the real, genuine, authentic reactions that come with being human. If an alien is going to eat you, you might not say "Oh, shucks." You might say something, hmm, *a bit more colorful.* But I want my readers to know that I've always struggled with this, and do not mean to offend anyone with material some might find objectionable. I'm a Christian, but I'm also an artist, and artists seek to stretch themselves and strive for truth and reality in their works. That does **<u>not</u>** mean that I need to go overboard and pepper you with revolting material or words that Christians have no business engaging or indulging in. As such, I want all of my faith-based readers to know that I am highly conscious of what I put out there into the world, and am constantly checking it against my spirit before I do so. Nothing you'll read in my novels is much different from what we experience on this ball in space, and I trust you'll see that I've walked a fine line here, and I ask for your forgiveness if I've offended you in any way.

I pray this work of mine provides you with an awesome and incredible odyssey of escapism and adventure. I pray you are moved at times by the Holy Spirit as you read. I pray that you understand God better, and that you know that God knows my heart, and I tried my best to tell a **<u>real</u>** story, understanding that we're all down here, **<u>all</u>** of us, just trying to do our very best in creating what we feel led to create. I thank you **<u>so</u>** much for reading my novel.

In Jesus' Name,

Aaron Ryan

I PREFACE

Recap from all previous volumes:

Dissonance Volume Zero: Revelation

The year is 2026. Andrew Shipley, a firefighter and EMP, is just like the rest of humanity, going about his business and providing for his family. He and his wife Melissa attend Mount Pleasant Baptist Church in Blue Spring, Kentucky, with their young children Cameron, Adelynn, aka 'Sissy,' and Wyatt, aka 'Rutty.'

In early June 2026, cellular service begins to be disrupted. Lightning storms afflict the earth. Satellite communications are affected, and all oceanic satellites cease transmission. Shortly thereafter, their Jack Russell Terrier, Jack, exhibits strange behavior. His ears bleed, and he howls in pain. He, along with all the other canines and animals with sensitive hearing, is suddenly afflicted with high frequencies. Jack recovers, but the ominous development frightens the family.

The family enjoys a church picnic where they meet fellow parishioners, eat BBQ, and play frisbee, etc. While there, Melissa meets Anya Mayfield, her husband, Justus, and their 2-year-old son, Liam.

The family then heads to Seattle to visit Andrew's mother and father. His father is in failing health with dementia. The visit is restorative, but Andrew's dad, Jim, has good and bad days. Following their return, the older kids head off to a weeklong camp.

On June 6, 2026, while Andrew and family join best friend Mick and family on the lake, they see them. The aliens descend down from the sky, silently, hovering at a geostationary orbit over our planet, remaining there, virtually motionless, for three months. There are hundreds, and then thousands, and then hundreds of thousands of them, still coming down, falling ominously into position across the entire globe.

No country is immune. No one knows what they want, nor why they are here. Some think they are angelic messengers. People fly drones up to them to investigate. They don't move or react. In the heat of summer, they sweat. On the backs of the necks of each hovering alien seems to be implanted some kind of small green gemlike device, like a chemotherapy port.

The stock market dives. Individuals take matters into their own hands, and shoot at the aliens. When the aliens are struck, they rise back up in the sky, and three more take their place. Humanity realizes such action is futile. In an effort to quell the panic, the President holds a State of the Union address where he assures the American people that we have the best scientists and technologists developing a formidable defense, and construction companies have begun developing underground bunkers should the aliens' intentions prove hostile. These bunkers are known as 'Blockades.' They will be finished within a few months' time all over the globe, using underground automated drills and excavation teams. Blockades will be equipped with sanitary needs, food, hydroponics, and heat. They are walled in by massively tall gun towers: the only known defense against the aliens. In a thin attempt at humor, the President assures the American people that life will go on, despite our living like moles.

Three months later, on September 3rd, 2026, as Andrew and his older children, Cameron and Sissy, participate in a fun church-sponsored marathon, the aliens suddenly activate and begin hunting down all of mankind. In the terror and pandemonium, Andrew witnesses the aliens' horrifying ability to paralyze humans where they stand, consuming them at their leisure. Andrew and his kids escape and take refuge in a small office on a nearby property. Meanwhile, Mick's entire family is killed, leaving him to attempt a desperate escape into that same small office. Despite his best friend's anguished pleading, Andrew refuses to let him in, terrified for his own children's safety, and hears Mick's final moments through the door. He texts a frantic message to Melissa to lock herself in the attic with their youngest, Rutty. He assures her that he'll come home with the older kids and fills her in on what happened during the race. Melissa shares what she's seen on the news.

After sunset, the aliens move on for the night. A brave citizen drives through the macabre scene and searches for survivors after the aliens have moved on to kill others. The man's name is Hudson, and he is in a hybrid vehicle, and the silence of the engine provides them the ability to return home. Once home, they reunite with Melissa and Rutty. Aliens invade their home and attempt to access the attic ladder but become distracted by other noises and leave. Mercifully, Jack – who can barely hear anymore – doesn't bark, and the kids sleep through the ordeal.

They escape with the help of Hudson, in their own hybrid vehicle and his. Hudson and his wife, Andrea, equip them with armament and weapons, and they all head for a Blockade they hear has been constructed in Clarksville, Tennessee, south of them. Hudson and Andrea are behind the Shipley family and distract aliens who have set upon them, dying in the process. The Shipley family flees to the Blockade and begins their long, slow life of hiding.

By December 2026, eighty-five percent of humanity is dead. No one knows what to do, and no one can fight back. Soon, all of humanity learns the Number One Rule as it pertains to aliens: *You just... don't... look.* Mankind ends up calling them 'gorgons' due to their unique ability to, with just one look, paralyze us.

Andrew joins up as a soldier on recon missions for food, ammunition, and straggling survivors. The missions are physically and emotionally grueling with several team member casualties. Andrew blames himself but perseveres. Eventually, he is promoted up to First Lieutenant.

One day in 2034, Cameron and Rutty steal out to hunt a deer, thinking they could bring it back to the Blockade and be regarded as heroes for providing much-needed meat and protein. In the process, they are pursued by their teacher, Christopher Jackson, who is killed by a gorgon while trying to shepherd them back to the Blockade. They are terrified. Andrew and his fellow soldier, Ray, rescue the boys, successfully bringing them back to the Blockade.

Melissa's smoking has had long-term effects, and she has developed lung cancer. On July 22nd, 2035, she succumbs to her cancer with Andrew, Cameron and Rutty by her side.

Cameron eventually enlists at age 18, and on October 20th, 2037, he heads out on his first mission. He and the team, along with Andrew Shipley, Captain Stone and two others, are sent on a recon mission for food, supplies, and survivors up to the old zinc plant nearby. While there, they are set upon by gorgons. Andrew throws himself in between a gorgon and Cameron, saving his son's life and dying in the process.

Dissonance Volume Up: Rising

The year is 2037. Told from the perspective of four key figures: Rosalita Campion, Miguel Monzon, Allison Trudy, and Joe Bassett.

Andrew Shipley is dead. He was killed after being frozen by a gorgon while defending his son's life. His fading body is brought back to medical at DN436, with his sons Jet and Rutty by his side. Nurse Ferro's father, Ray, also loses his life.

Jet and Rutty grow up under the shadow of darkness in the Blockade and are 'adopted' by a new father figure, Captain Maurice Stone, who becomes their 'Dad.' Rosie counsels them through their trauma.

Meanwhile, in Nashville, First Lieutenant Miguel Monzon is serving under the watchful eye of President Jean Graham. His contact, Vance Cardona, has been expelled and restationed at Mammoth Cave, which proves to undermine Graham, as he is able to recruit members of the Resistance far and wide out from under her nose. Graham begins to amass military vehicles and equipment. Two captured gorgons are held in a special lab where scientists test new sound technology they hope will prove lethal to the captives.

The test is successful. However, infuriated by these new technological sound attacks, the gorgons assault both Nashville Airport and the Embassy. A conspiracy is then unmasked to assassinate Graham.

Simultaneously, hundreds of miles away in Alpharetta, GA, a young soldier named Trudy, serving in the science department at Blockade DN282, develops new mask technology that can withstand the gorgons' powerful telepathy. Her supervisor, Staff Sergeant Joe Bassett, took her, years earlier, under his wing as a mentor and father figure.

Back at DN436 in Clarksville, the boys continue to grow up underground, with Private Jet Shipley serving and being promoted to Corporal. He eventually requests that his younger brother, Rutty, be disallowed from enlisting. Stone grants his request.

Trudy is promoted to Lieutenant, leapfrogging Staff Sergeant Bassett, due to her incredible development of the mask technology, which, along with the new DTF sound technology, has afforded mankind a tangible way to finally defend themselves against the gorgons. She meets Steph, Bassett's kid sister.

Colonel Cartwright, the conspirator who attempted to assassinate Graham, is discovered and thwarted. Graham orders the killing of the would-be assassin. At the same time, Captain Vance Cardona, Miguel Monzon's contact, has journeyed in secret from Mammoth Cave to the Embassy to visit Monzon. He is caught on camera. The President frames him for Cartwright's murder, setting up an inevitable assassination directive on his life.

The President summons Monzon to aid her with his Air Force knowledge, providing her with valuable information on how to conduct aerial sweeps with focused DTF technology to hem the gorgons into a specific kill zone. The information proves highly valuable and successful, and First Lieutenant Miguel Monzon is promoted to Captain.

At DN436, Rutty graduates and desires to enlist, only to discover that his older brother has made a deal with Captain Stone to bar the younger brother from enlisting. A violent altercation ensues, ending in redemptive confession on the part of Jet that he could not stand to lose his younger brother, his only remaining family member.

At the directive of the President, mobilization has begun, and both DTF and mask technologies are being manufactured en masse, with plans for their distribution underway.

At DN282 in Clarksville, Trudy has an argument with Steph, Joe Bassett's kid sister, who has been through much trauma and encourages Trudy to cling to hope: the one thing that they all have left.

Rutty finally enlists. On a mission back at DN436 in Clarksville, he is out with his older brother Jet, Sarah Ferro, Alex Santella, and Markus Jentzen. They make a grisly discovery in D-Range: bodies upon bodies frozen together in a church, trapped and murdered by the gorgons long ago. Jet is still protecting his younger brother and shielding him from painful realities. He is confronted by Pastor Rosie, who encourages Jet to let his younger brother mature.

On a later mission out in the field, Alex Santella is killed while they are fleeing from the gorgons. The rest of the team survives and discovers that the gorgons cannot telepathically freeze them underwater.

The gorgons that were captured for the DTF testing in Nashville were killed during that research. Therefore, the President issues a directive for a team to wrangle a gorgon. She chooses the science team and recon patrols from Alpharetta because they have the mask technology to defend themselves. The gorgon is to be analyzed. During the wrangling operation, Steph is killed along with another soldier. Her older brother, Joe, is devastated.

In Nashville, the President frames Vance Cardona for Cartwright's murder and issues an order to kill him. Miguel Monzon is charged with that order. She is also experiencing cabin fever and plans on journeying to multiple Blockades and bases now that they can move under the protection of the DTF emitters. Miguel accompanies her to said bases; he is overjoyed that one such base is DN436 in Clarksville, where his wife, Rosie, lives and serves.

In Clarksville, Rutty and Jet are out on a mission at the zinc plant, when they are cut off from the rest of their team members. Jet manages to distract the gorgons and lure them away from his brother. Jet eventually makes it back to the Blockade. Rutty is pinned down overnight but returns safely the following morning. Jet realizes he can trust his little brother's tactical and survival skills. Rutty proved to him and everyone at the Blockade that he is a diehard.

The President travels up to Wright-Patterson base in Dayton, Ohio, to ready her Air Force fleet. She then returns to Nashville and journeys up the Cumberland under DTF protection with Miguel Monzon, stopping at various marine bases and stations to rally her troops. They are on their way to Clarksville.

On what was to be a simple recon patrol, Jet and Rutty are stranded once again at the zinc plant for seventeen days. Markus and his team search for the brothers and are also ambushed by a massive group of gorgons. However, Markus' team is freed and delivers a broken amulet to Jet and Rutty to bring back to the Blockade. Markus Jentzen and Shannon Hickey do not make it back, but their other two team members do. Finally, Jet and Rutty are given the cautious all-clear from Command that it should be safe to return to the Blockade. They attempt to flee and are briefly pinned down in the alleyway at the plant. The brothers must make some strategic decisions in order to be able to return home.

Dissonance Volume I: Reality

The year is 2042. Sergeant Cameron "Jet" Shipley and his brother, Private Wyatt Rutledge, aka "Rut" Shipley, are part of a military Blockade in Clarksville, Tennessee. Under fortified towers, the unit provides solace, shelter, hydroponics, education, and training for military reconnaissance missions to find survivors, food, and ammunition.

The brothers eventually make it home from their mission, and they are issued a new mission: head up to Austin Peay University and investigate thermal signals indicating possible survivors. On their way, they encounter a mass of gorgons at the Cumberland River, where newcomer, Staff Sergeant Joseph Bassett, employs a manual trigger and detonates something akin to an EMP: what the military is calling a "DTF," or *Dissonant Tidal Flood.*

This new technology operates similarly to an EMP, but on audio frequencies lethal to the gorgons' sensitive hearing, sending them fleeing or killing them outright in close proximity. The news of this unannounced technology catches both Shipley brothers by complete surprise.

On this same mission, while taking shelter at Austin Peay University's Harvill Hall, they are given a new assignment: they must lojack a gorgon, installing a tracker to monitor its movements. During this dangerous assignment, Private Shipley is tragically and violently killed by a berserker gorgon. Berserkers are variants of the gorgon species that are far more aggressive and lethal than the gorgons previously encountered. Lieutenant Allison Trudy and Joseph Bassett provide aid, comfort and friendship to a now devastated Cameron Shipley.

For their journey back to the Blockade, they are joined by three recruits from Harvill Hall: Jesse, Liam, aka 'Foxy,' and Vera. The team takes shelter from the gorgons at Madison Street United Methodist Church in Clarksville, only to be preyed upon both by gorgons and a lone octogenarian striving for survival who has resorted to lethal desperation.

Vera and Jesse are killed, and Foxy is wounded. The team battles their way out and is rescued by a tank squadron that employs another DTF before escorting them back to an encampment on the Cumberland River. What's left of the team realizes then, to their surprise, that military operations have been underway for quite some time now.

The revelations are bittersweet. Mankind is finally on the precipice of launching a major counteroffensive, but the technology has existed for some time now, causing Sergeant Shipley to question why it wasn't deployed sooner, perhaps sparing the life of his brother.

Captain Stone, whom Cam had previously trusted as a father, lets slip that the lojack mission was only a test, directed by President Graham herself, in cooperation with Stone and others. Confronted with this news, realizing that Rutty's death was in vain at the hands of operations founded upon lies, Cameron is overcome by emotion and attempts to assault the Captain. He is brought down by Stone's guard and knocked unconscious.

He awakes to find himself in the Blockade brig. Joe Bassett visits the newest prisoner and informs him that the President is coming to their very Blockade. Thus, Cameron's thirst for vengeance is ignited, and his quest for revenge begins.

Dissonance Volume II: Reckoning

Eventually freed, Shipley meets with Pastor Rosie, who reveals some long-honored truths to him about justice versus revenge. He is then able to meet and confront President Graham for her role in his brother's death. Somewhat convinced of her professed good intentions, Cameron is reinstated in his service role and promoted to Lieutenant. He is assigned to Mammoth Cave, northeast of their Blockade, to train the new recruits stationed there.

Preparing to leave, Cameron and Bassett meet with Pete Beckinsale, a member of Halcyon Crew at Blockade DN436. Pete reveals to them that little Nevaeh, a child the team encountered outside Madison Street United Methodist Church, is now at the encampment. The encampment, now called *Base One*, came under attack recently, but Nevaeh survived.

However, Rebecca "Meemaw" Burgess from Harvill Hall was also at the encampment, and she did not survive. He discovers that Witherspoon and Ruby were also at Base One and are unaccounted for. But in a briefing with Captain Stone, he demands that Nevaeh be brought to the Blockade, and Stone grants his request.

On the way to Mammoth Cave, Shipley proposes to Allison Trudy, and she accepts his proposal to marry him.

Shipley and his new team, including Bassett, Trudy and Foxy, are assaulted on the highway en route to Mammoth Cave by a mass of gorgons. Two soldiers are killed after launching an unprotected DTF, disabling their two tanks. Additionally, a new revelation presents itself: the existence of an even greater threat, that of 'behemoth' gorgons: bigger, smarter, and deadlier mutations of the berserker gorgons.

A platoon is dispatched from Shipley's Blockade, which rescues them on the highway, and they finally reach Mammoth Cave. The Blockade there has a Captain, Vance Cardona, who has gone AWOL, and Shipley has been accompanied by another Captain named Miguel Monzon, sent to replace Cardona.

While at Mammoth Cave, they discover that Cardona has been there all along, and that he is *not* in fact AWOL, but rather has the allegiance of his entire Blockade in defiance of the President's wishes. Most importantly, Cardona is preparing to take a stand against her. It is then revealed that Captain Monzon is also in on the resistance and knew about Cardona the whole time. Monzon could not let the President in on his rebellion, nor the fact that Cardona was still alive and well at Mammoth Cave.

Cardona then walks them back through history, introducing them to grim truths that the President is a power-hungry tyrant who has sent numerous people to their deaths. She is preparing three concurrent nuclear strikes to take out not only the gorgons, but also the leaders of enemy nations whom she deeply distrusts.

The President is not to be trusted, Cardona cautions. She must be stopped before she annihilates most of the remaining human race through nuclear destruction and ensuing radiation fallout due to her quest for preservation of power.

After these revelations, Mammoth Cave is attacked by gorgons that are dispatched there by the President herself, using targeted DTF sweeps. The horrifying attack claims two devastating losses: Joe Bassett and Allison Trudy. Everyone else flees to rendezvous with Cardona at the appointed hour.

A deeply distraught Cameron Shipley loses faith to the point of catatonia. He is grappling with both the loss of his bride-to-be as well as having killed a fellow soldier in cold blood. Shipley is met by Cardona and Monzon, who escort him, Foxy, and the rest of the survivors to their new base.

Dissonance Volume III: Renegade

Cameron Shipley has gone rogue. He is now a renegade under Captains Vance Cardona and Miguel Monzon, along with other members of his team. A resistance has formed in the wake of horrifying revelations that President Graham has sinister intentions that will cause the murder of thousands of humans as well as adversely affect Earth's climate for generations.

After immeasurable loss and against incredible odds, the team of renegades heads to Wright-Patterson Air Force Base in Dayton, Ohio to launch their counterattack, Operation Dewdrop, against two deadly enemies: the queen gorgon, and the President. Upon his arrival, Cameron is promoted to Captain, and he subsequently promotes his friend and comrade Foxy to Lieutenant.

He reunites with Pastor Rosie, who he discovers is an honorary US Air Force Major. She has the respect of the masses, and she is married to Monzon. Monzon was an insider under President Graham, monitoring her stratagems and movements while providing reconnaissance to the resistance, who he joined at Mammoth Cave.

Pastor Rosie confronts Cameron about his murder of the young soldier at Mammoth Cave. She tries desperately to convince him of the difference between justice and revenge, both of which belong to God. Rosie insists that President Graham will eventually face justice, and that all Cameron needs to do is to trust that that process will unfold.

While at Wright-Patterson, a very nervous Colonel Keegan informs the captains of the plan to rendezvous with Admiral Evelyn Lynch aboard the USS Harry S. Truman, stationed at Norfolk, Virginia. The plan is to sail out into the North Atlantic using intel gained from the inside, as well as rally the massive upswell of dissent against Graham for a counterstrike against the gorgon queen and the funnel in which she is laying her eggs. Simultaneously, operations are taking place in the east to sabotage Graham's plans to detonate nuclear explosives in the vicinity of her chief foes, masquerading it as annihilation of the gorgons and prepared to call it "collateral damage."

The resistance is then attacked by both gorgons and Graham's aerial forces after the President detects that the nervous Colonel Keegan has deceived her regarding an important weapon in their possession.

There are many losses, and the Colonel dies. Sacrifices are made, but Shipley, Foxy, Vance and Miguel make it out unscathed, except that Shipley receives a gunshot wound in his leg. Undeterred, he and the team, led by Monzon, immediately dispatch to Norfolk to join up with Lynch and her team aboard the Truman. It's a game of cat and mouse as they maintain their secretive posture in order to fool the President into believing that they are still allies. Cardona and his wife, along with Rosie, retreat to an undisclosed location.

Once aboard the Truman, Lynch and her team successfully link up with hackers in Graham's three target regions of China, North Korea, and Iran. They successfully hack their way into the interfaces that control the nuclear detonation devices and disarm them. They do, however, allow the giant mass of DTF emitters and DTF bombs to detonate, thereby destroying all of the gorgons that have been swept there by the President.

The only gorgons now remaining on the planet are those at the funnel with the queen and sporadic numbers that somehow evaded the sweeps across the planet. Those gorgons will eventually be rooted out.

Seeing she has been betrayed, the President goes ballistic and launches an aerial counteroffensive against the Truman and her carrier strike group. But before that, led by Captain Monzon, Shipley and Foxy are trained as 'wizzos' (Weapons Systems Officers) aboard the F-15 Eagle fighter jet. They and the rest of the Air Force team launch their assault against the queen and the funnel, destroying both, commencing the return of precious ocean water back to the Earth from the mysterious craft suspended in Earth's orbit that has all along been harvesting the planet's water.

There is a joyous celebration, but it is short-lived, as they run out of ammo and encounter an incoming aerial fleet of squadrons obviously dispatched by the President. But all is soon well, as they discover, to their relief, that these squadrons are all defecting to the resistance. It turns out that no one supports President Graham, and everyone is aware of the nuclear annihilation she attempted to commit with her Illuminati. All fighters land aboard the Truman as it sails back home to Norfolk.

Meanwhile, in a fit of rage, Graham has murdered her own VP and been arrested. The planet is free of the gorgon threat, and people begin to breathe the free air again. Graham will be tried and convicted by such persons as can be found in such a short time under a jury of her peers. War crimes and crimes against humanity are just some of the charges. Cameron and Foxy are escorted in F-15s back to Nashville, where they will give sworn depositions and testimonials before retiring back to their Blockade, DN436, in Clarksville.

At Clarksville, Cameron reunites with Captain Stone, "Stoney," and they reconcile. He also reconnects with little Nevaeh, whom he had attempted to rescue, and Ruby and Witherspoon from Harvill Hall; both survived the escape to the Blockade. Tanks, planes and rescue vehicles fan out all across the globe in order to spread the word while providing food and aid. Foxy is also able to connect with Maureen, Joe Bassett's wife, to relay to her his thanks for how Joe saved him in the Mammoth Cave tunnels.

An informal vote is held and ratified by the acting President *pro tem*, Peter Capra, and that vote is comprised of various military personnel who are thought to be able to bring the country together, to rebuild. Based on his long preparation and successful revolt against the President, all fingers point to Captain Vance Brennan Cardona, who, with his military experience as well as political experience as an advisor to the Secretary of Defense, becomes the front runner. He is elected to be President of the United States in the first vote held since 2026.

Cameron and Foxy begin an important journey together, back up to Harvill Hall, to celebrate Christmas Day by the little tree that Cameron and Rutty had sat by prior to their ill-fated lojack mission. He says goodbye to Rutty's grave, and then both of them head back to Wright-Patterson in order for Foxy to see his love, Janine, the daughter of Vance & Andi Cardona.

On the way there, Foxy leads Cameron to Ally's highway gravesite, as he was one of the only people who knew where it was, in order for Cameron to pay his respects.

The story now continues in the year 2045 in…

Dissonance Volume IV: Relentless

1 1 REBUILDING

Saturday, March 4th 2045 · 10:33am

It had been a long time.

As I strolled across the White House lawn with Andi, my beautiful bride by my side, I stared up at the crisp blue sky. Trace amounts of clouds dotted the cerulean ceiling above us, but they were white, not black. Large. Not small. Floating by; not hovering ominously. I remembered, fleetingly, where I was when they came in 2026.

And then, just as fleetingly, I remembered where I was when they were gone.

My bride was beside me then as well, up at that commercial park off Highway 70 in Enon, Ohio, after we left

Wright-Patterson Air Force Base. What a ride that was, watching everything go down remotely. Lynch did a fantastic job quarterbacking the raids. I owe her a huge debt of thanks to this day. We all do. She's out there, somewhere, in the Atlantic. Like *they* once were…

• • • • •

"Hey, Sleepyhead," Andi said. "You can't doze off; you've got a country to run, remember?"

My eyes fluttered open, and I felt my lungs involuntarily expand to take in new air. Clean air. Free air. I had to admit, the grass on the White House lawn hadn't been this green in decades. It had felt like a decade just getting back here from Nashville.

"You were thinking about *her* again, weren't you?"

"Mmm, yeah. You know me, baby-cakes. I just love me some disgraced, convicted, house-arrested, near-octogenarian former president chicks."

She scowled. Rightly so. I stroked her hair in defiance of her disapproval, sinking deeply into those glowing brown orbs of hers, framed in the softest face set against the backdrop of the sky.

"See? I knew it. She gets to live rent-free in your head while I have to suffer here with your head in my lap. I carry the weight of your head *and* her. Such is my burden," she said, melodramatically.

"Nah, she's a featherweight now, hon. You know that. You're my heavyweight."

"Did you just call me heavy?"

"What are you gonna do about it? Can't hit the President, you know."

"Oh, yes I can," she glared at me, but then she tossed a quick look around to monitor for the Secret Service.

"First Lady Leandra Dempsey Cardona, are you jealous?"

"No!" she abruptly protested. "Of *Jean Graham*? No way. Of how much time everyone *else* on the planet needs from you, leaving us this little bitty time on the grass? *Yes!*"

I chuckled, stroking her hair again. "Andi, honey, there's still only fifteen percent of us left. That's one point two billion people. If that. Imagine if you had to deal with eight billion of us."

"So I should be thankful?"

A smile stretched out my lips. "All I know is I'm thankful for the fifteen percent of my day I get to lay here with only *one* of those one point two billion."

"Well, *two,* if you count Jean Graham."

"I'm not counting Jean Graham. I'm counting only Andi Cardona, the most beautiful First Lady this world has ever seen."

"You're just saying that because it's true."

"Ha! It is true. I love you, sweetheart," I said, scampering up and wrapping my arms tightly around her.

She tilted her head and watched me suspiciously as a knowing smile crept across her face. "Okay. I accept. I'll take that fifteen percent of your day, mister. I'll suck up every last second, at least until you have to do your umpteenth press conference." She rolled her eyes.

I rolled mine in unison. I hated doing them, and she hated watching them. The only one who seemed to enjoy my press conferences was Mrs. Janine Mayfield. Our little *Neener.* In one of Earth's very first post-liberation weddings, Janine married her sweetheart, Liam 'Foxy' Mayfield in August of 2043. He was a tried and true, battle-hardened soldier, and a good man. It was obvious to all that he loved her, though, in my humble opinion, no one was quite good enough for my little girl. She herself had proven to be quite the warrior. It was good to talk to her every few days on Zoom and see how she was faring up at Wright-Pat. She liked it there, and didn't really see any necessity to leave. Liam had taken a few trips to his hometown of Blue Spring, Kentucky with Cameron Shipley, but he had always itched to return home there as well. Andi and I were so happy for the two of them.

I kissed my First Lady, and poured myself back over her shoulder, melting into her and wrapping her up, consumed in my thoughts.

Thinking was all we could do. We had to do a lot of thinking to undo all the lack of thinking that got us here in the first place.

I wrapped my arms around her as we sat in silence, consumed in memories that spanned nineteen years.

•   •   •   •   •

We were making progress, but it would take a long time, certainly. And there was a *lot* to make progress on.

It began with the detonation of that craft in April of 2044. After the war, it took a year and a half for us to get enough good people space-ready to go up there and load that ship up with nukes. They had to wear masks over masks, in case there were any more of them floating out there. But the craft had been emptied, thank God; it seemed their entire force had been dispatched to Earth from that thing. Now, none remained, we deemed.

Satellite telemetry reported the craft to be four point seven by two point three miles wide. A parabola was at its front, and it was sleek and shiny, but organic, and encrusted with these strange obelisks every few hundred feet. What they were for, we didn't know.

We could never get inside it. The thing appeared to have thrusters at the stern that implied forward momentum. Obviously, it had some kind of sub-light engine. The thing was, all of the sudden, right on top of us in the invasion of 2026. It was different with the gorgons themselves: they had no thrusters, and nothing to imply propulsion. But they were *fast.* We know now that the craft was concealed behind our moon. As such, blips on our scopes registered merely a drifting rock in space. Had we known then what we know now, we would have taken more caution. Hindsight is always twenty-twenty.

The images we got back strained credulity. There were crystalline fragments all around it: remnants of the water that had not quite fallen back to Earth when they took out that funnel in the winter of 2042. They captured some of the ship's materials and brought them back for analysis.

We planted the detonators and oversaw the ensuing explosion. We hit the trigger, and every eye on this side of the sun saw it. A ball of light ate up the sky and gave us a meteor shower for months, raining debris back down on earth that glittered and sparked, burning out noisily over hundreds of miles in our canopy above.

Every nation was advised to wear some form of ear protection. That blast – *fuggedaboudit!* Loud as thunder from a lightning storm in hell. That boom lasted a good twenty-seven seconds, cascading over this ball like a sonic steamroller. If DTFs didn't kill off any straggling gorgons, that blast surely did.

The Funnel in the north Atlantic had been destroyed by subs, and the eggs harvested and then burned. None remained. The decrepit remainder of the Funnel snaked down to the ocean floor and disintegrated. The nest had been destroyed, and was now withering away, to be calcified and covered over by algae blooms.

We hadn't seen or found any more of them out in space, but astronomers and researchers at International Cloud Atlas – and others – had resumed their usual scanning. They had found various hydrometeors, lithometeors, photometeors and electrometeors out there.

Curiously, however, techs at various agencies had discovered a few anomalies. They weren't quite certain what they were; these anomalies hadn't appeared on any of our previous charts. And then, at 0900 Coordinated Universal Time on February 27th, the Hong Kong Observatory for International Cloud Atlas called me on behalf of the WMO. The World Meteorological Organization was alarmed. One 'anomaly' in particular traced an unknown origin from deep space, probably from the TRAPPIST-1 system which housed a red dwarf star and seven exoplanets. Any time they checked on it, the anomaly's trajectory had slightly shifted. Any object with a non-standard orbit, deviation in trajectory, or any unusual mass was to be reported immediately, I said. Especially that one. They opted to refer to it as a comet for now, labeling it, simply, 'Francine 45.' They promised to keep me posted, but that was constantly nagging at the back of my brain like a woodpecker. I couldn't tell Andi yet until I knew definitively, but I quickly sent a message to Commander Sinclair at NORAD. He confirmed they were already tracking the unidentified object. I gave him the run down. He assured me he'd keep on it.

That was in outer space.

Down here on Earth, the tragic truth was that the gorgons had leveled our world. Earth was a graveyard only slowly re-emerging from its forced subterranean escape, crawling back to life above.

The scouring operations all went as planned. All Blockades and remaining military were commissioned to hunt down the gorgs and root them out of any holes they may have still been hiding in. I had good people on good teams all over. I know their names and will never forget them. The military was very much alive and well, and all remaining Blockades – there were five-hundred-seventy still in operation – were emptying. But not just that; they were being restocked with fresh supplies and prepared just in case the gorgs ever returned. We couldn't take the chance of being caught at unawares a second time. Andi questioned why I gave the order to restock them; I can't remember what excuse I gave her. My intuition told me that it was not an option; we *had* to keep them operational.

For now, however, we had reclaimed our planet and were rebuilding. But that process wasn't without its complications: so many people were used to keeping quiet and speaking in sign language from their lives in the shadows. It was strange. We could talk freely now, at normal volume, but so many everywhere were reticent to do so. Conditioned from living silently, trying to stay alive. Communication was slow, and trust between members of our own race required some work. All things in due time.

One thing that was of paramount concern to everyone was reproduction. It was an inescapable ache: eighty-five percent of us had been killed off, and that included most animal life. Thank God we had various centers, repositories and vaults that contained seed, fauna and DNA in order to repopulate the earth and begin our own genesis anew. In a unanimous resolution, the UN called upon various agencies: The Frozen Ark Project out of the University of Nottingham in the UK. The Svalbard Global Seed Vault in Norway. The Millenium Seed Back in Wakehurst, Sussex. The S.A.F.E: Global Fauna DNA Vault and Museum in Egypt. All of them were called upon to begin replenishing the earth and pull their precious cargo out of cold storage. To begin gene splicing. To begin researching potential host candidates and ova to allow the cellular DNA to take form and begin its cellular mitosis so that animals could roam the ground once more. All of that was over my head, but we had good, competent scientists who had thankfully survived our apocalypse, and they were working on it.

Speaking of scientists, we decided to classify the gorgons, much to everyone's loathing, but it was a job that needed to be done for our own edification and education. *Praedatum polypus astronomicis telepathia.* Essentially, *Predatory Telepathic Space Octopus.* Amusing, but not really.

The short, impromptu December election went off without a hitch right after the war. It seemed people didn't want to waste any more time. There were no other candidates they wanted, and I was humbled to be so honored.

It was unanimous. I was sworn in on January 20th, 2043 with this pretty lady by my side. I had free reign to choose anyone I wanted by my side for VP. Miguel didn't want it; he felt it was an office far beyond his capacity. Evelyn Lynch didn't want it: she was at home on a carrier, and commanding the Truman was her calling, she said. And Rosie would never even consider it; she was satisfied with her honorary title.

So, I went with Major Veronica Bayless from Blockade DN282. It felt right to have a woman in the office with me, representing both genders that, working together, bring life. Andi didn't mind the euphemism. Additionally, Bayless' Blockade had overseen two major developments in the war. One, the development of the mask technology by Allison Trudy, the woman Sergeant Cameron Shipley had been briefly engaged to. Two, the wrangling and comprehensive study of a live gorgon: the only Blockade to do it beyond the team at BNA. Those were monumental achievements that elevated her status and fame.

As honored as I was to be President, I felt, admittedly, out of place, and often confided in Miguel. Something within always called out to me from the recesses of my mind: memories of being out there on the battlefield. Remembering what a thrill it was to be living on the edge, every day, that close to the brink of going out forever. I was in my element. In here, I was insulated and flanked by Secret Service. I appreciated the trust America had placed in me, but sometimes I found myself wondering if this was who I was really cut out to be.

Since our deliverance, the threat of another invasion had loomed like a specter over everything we did. They say that in the years leading up to the arrival in 2026, people were developing cellphone neck. Scoliosis was definitely a thing; people stooped over their phones. We had made good progress reversing that phenomenon. Now, however, people were repeatedly staring up at the sky: watching…always watching.

Included in that demographic was the military, of course. I ensured that a great and relatively unchecked distribution of military defenses were distributed all over the nation, and, as strategically as we could, throughout the world. Many of the top brass felt we were living on borrowed time. We needed to have some measures in place to protect ourselves should more of them ever again set their sights on this tiny blue ball in space. After all, no one was truly convinced that they were all gone. It would take sixteen years – and maybe more – of being left alone, to undo the brutal sixteen years we had been under siege.

It was surreal. Cars were out in droves. The slow, cautionary beeps of large construction machinery became a revered sound: it could be heard a mile away with so little din to interfere. Granted, four-fifths of us were gone, but there was a growing hustle and bustle.

Every state had its own rural Broadway and Rodeo Drive as their stragglers, now free of their underground prisons, emerged to breathe the free air again.

The first airplanes were heard overhead, proudly ferrying passengers from one side of the country to the other. I had ordered another full ground stop of all air traffic in case of any electromagnetic interference when their alien ship was destroyed, but now we were back up in the skies once more.

We were living and breathing again, but it was not without its share of sadness, certainly. The carnage wreaked by the gorgons brought Earth's nations to their collective knees.

The damage was overwhelming, and the repair and construction would be long and hard-fought.

The land had taken a beating. Weeds grew up and took on a life of their own, choking all the big cities. Tree roots eroded the road systems, turning cities into forests and plunging streets into disrepair. Wildfires had burnt unabated in the near two decades of catastrophe, and smoked out whole towns. Natural disasters had expanded unhindered, demolishing landmarks and reshaping the land. Floods, tornados, hurricanes, eruptions, earthquakes: all of it took its toll. Forest fires scorched the earth. Earthquakes split us in two. Tornadoes dangerously reshaped our horizons. Hurricanes hurled trees over our Blockades. Floodwaters washed away survivors. It would be some time before we all returned to some semblance of normalcy.

Buildings had crumbled. Cellular service was gone. Power needed to be restored to large swaths of the earth. Construction crews were working night and day toiling endlessly to reclaim our terrains with buildings and industries that could once again attest to our survival and will to persevere in the face of annihilation.

And the remnant? Well…it had been a long, long time of hiding underground. Consequently, we were all deficiently low on Vitamin D. Supplements had to be distributed, but the potency of vitamins diminished over time. So, high fat foods needed to be made available. Thus, re-establishing livestock and supplementing the food chain from our DNA and feed vaults. The FDA said that it takes about six to eight weeks to recover levels once supplementation was restarted. But for the first few months of re-emergence, everyone was pretty pale. On top of that, so many of us needed dental work. Cavities abounded. Teeth needed to be extracted. People were in pain.

Without human oversight, glitches in nuclear and oil plants led to nuclear explosions, fires, and radiation fallout. Hydroelectric plants shut down due to flooding, and the loss of electricity shut down nuclear power plants as well, causing meltdowns. Cities crumbled, bridges fell, and fields were overgrown. Dams and levees built on rivers and streams had eroded.

Termites destroyed houses and creepers grew through the cracks, causing the wood to rot and eventually collapse. Concrete structures deteriorated due to extreme weather conditions, leading to their eventual collapse. In colder areas, pipes froze and burst, and basements filled with soil and water.

The pumps that kept water out of underground services failed, and the subway tunnels filled with water. Then, the rats came out of hiding and roamed around. They became easy targets for the gorgons, further decreasing their population. The water creeping under the cities caused corrosion and the destruction of major steel structures all over the world such as the Empire State Building, London Bridge, Golden Gate Bridge and many more. Roads turned into rivers, and iconic monuments like the Taj Mahal, Sydney Opera House, and the Leaning Tower of Pisa became susceptible to corrosion. The Eiffel Tower had actually collapsed entirely.

We lost over two billion cows, a billion pigs, and twenty billion chickens to the gorgons. The zoo animals that escaped from their cages were consumed.

Without humans producing trash, there was a sharp drop in the population of cockroaches. The only net positives were that head lice went extinct, and the oceans were now teeming with fish, except in the area of the North Atlantic where the funnel was located.

The earth itself groaned under the weight of our sixteen-year oppression. We had only just been liberated and our whole country, indeed the whole world yawned, stretched and tried valiantly to throw off the heavy blanket of grief. All around was incremental progress: some animals reemerged from their holes – we protected them like there was no tomorrow – and humanity ventured out once again from their Blockades. It would take time to recover a feeling of security and normalcy however.

We lost seven point two billion people overall, a number impossible to fully comprehend. Incentive programs were put in place to encourage reproduction. We had to rebuild the human race. I was advised to extend massive tax breaks and stimulus payments to couples who procreated. Extoling the value of human life became top priority. But just when we were celebrating human life, we were mourning it as well.

We lost Rosie last month.

That beautiful lady. She was eighty-one. Died peacefully in her sleep. It brought me so much joy to know that she saw the end of the conflict she had guided so many of us through. I don't think the good Lord up above was gladder to see another human, because that woman was something else, truly. Losing her was tough on Miguel, but he's holding up well. The dude's a tank anyway. I'm just glad they got to get formally married before he lost her.

We held a formal memorial, and I announced her death on our single national TV channel, which was slowly coming back. All those in the war effort knew and remembered her, and especially those from the Blockade in Clarksville. Beyond that, the rest of the hiding world hadn't known her. I think she would have preferred it that way. She was tough, but she was also humble, and sweet as pie.

We all held our hands out palms up in honor of her life, remembering her for a good eighty-one seconds. I was by Miguel's side at her memorial: he was somber, stoic, and speechless. He took the worst wound of his life at that parting. To have finally reconnected with her…only to lose her so soon after our deliverance.

It all seemed so ironic. So unfortunate.

So cruel.

However, Miguel was a survivor, like we all were. I appointed him Chief of Staff of the Air Force, and my overall Chief of Staff, *period*. We were all pulling double duty anyway. Besides, that man would be just fine: after all, he and I had been through a lot together.

Hell, we had *all* been through a lot together.

•   •   •   •   •

Saturday, March 4th 2045 · 11:49am

Almost go time. The press corps was waiting outside. They did my face, my beard, and made sure I was prettied up for the cameras. *Whatever.* I just hoped no one else had been scanning the bands independently and picked up on those anomalies that any of the agencies had discovered. We didn't need any rogues sowing fear among the populace with rumors and hearsay. I actually found myself repeatedly praying that it was just a harmless meteor. Civilization was only just crawling back up from being on its knees, and we were all on shaky ground with weak knees.

For now, I just had to keep my chin up and continue imparting hope. Sometimes in the mess, you can't see the clean. I had to impart vision for them to see that clean wanting to shine through the ashes. But as to actually seeing the clean?

Well, it had been a long time.

2 | DUTY

Saturday, March 4th 2045 · 5:03pm

Sometimes I hated this job.

Former President Jean Theodora Graham had been arraigned and sentenced in a military tribunal in Nashville in December of 2042. She was convicted on all counts, and by all rights should have been executed by firing squad in 2043. *Or something less gentle,* I had wished. But then I winced, remembering something Rosie had told me about revenge. She had drilled that so hard into Cameron Shipley, she wasn't about to let me off the hook either. Nonetheless, Graham faced justice.

She wasn't let off easy, and she wasn't let off the hook either. She should have been executed. But there was tremendous pushback when it came time to execute her. It seemed all of mankind had something to say about Graham. There were countless arguments for clemency because of her role in getting the DTF emitters and mask technology mass-distributed. My head spun. It was a contentious dilemma. Vice President Cooper's family – what remained of it – wanted her dead. *Eye for eye, tooth for tooth.* They deserved justice, truly. Graham was also found guilty of the murder of Colonel Lance Cartwright. Unfortunately for her, some of his family survived as well, and they chimed in too. The courts had to weigh that desire and those victim statements with the fact that the planet was partly liberated, like it or not, as a direct result of the leadership actions taken by President Jean Graham. So, as much as people loved to hate her and wanted blood, we owed her a begrudging gratitude.

True, she was responsible for the mobilization of the DTF technology and the masks that drove the gorgs out of here and helped us defend ourselves. But more to the point, however, *no one* wanted to restart our world on a foundation of blood. Pastor Rosie was the strongest voice in that choir.

So, all in all, her life was spared, and she was confined to a lonely rambler near Washington DC, under constant guard, ankle bracelet, GPS-monitored, the whole thing, not far from the White House. She was far too dangerous and sinister to be allowed to escape. She was cut off from news sources, and any TV channels were only reruns. She was not allowed to be informed about current events until a parole hearing in ten years. Keeping her in the dark seemed to be fitting for all.

The woman was seventy-seven now, a shell of her former self. And today, I would be meeting that shell, for a very important reason. As she was allowed no Internet communication, no phones, no radios, that meant only one thing.

I would have to go visit her in person.

•   •   •   •   •

Saturday, March 4th 2045 · 5:46pm

"Thank you, Branson," I said. The driver nodded to me and held the door as I stepped out. Young kid. Good kid. A transplant from Nashville, serving under Graham: one of her former drivers, and now my lead Secret Service agent on my detail. He was the one who brought Shipley and Mayfield to the Embassy Suites from the airport as I recall.

The other five suits jumped out and flanked me as I approached the house.

We walked up to the tiny rambler. Branson went to the front door and greeted the guards. Some of them were patrolling the perimeter, their rifles slung across their backs. This house was guarded for a reason.

Branson opened the door. That *reason* greeted me instantly, with derision. An elderly woman, sitting in the shadows, her gray hair dimly illuminated from the late afternoon light faintly passing through her rear window blinds. The smoke of her cigarette wafted upwards in lazy spirals. She tossed a Time magazine swiftly at my feet. I started, and Branson's hand went to his holster.

On the magazine at my feet was a familiar face belonging to another woman. She was Canadian, in her late fifties, with dark hair and a stern jaw. Framed behind the word *Time*: the first time, in fact, that that magazine cover had been issued in nearly two decades. I knew her well. She was a well-respected five-star Fleet Admiral now, even though the U.S. hadn't used that title on an Admiral since 1946. But she was deserving of the cover, which was in as much circulation as they could find, and distributed freely. As much information as could be assimilated into one periodical daring to cover nearly two decades of alien oppression, they stuffed it in there.

"Lynch got the cover instead of you. Hmm. That must have miffed you," the husky voice greeted me sardonically. I could tell she was smiling grimly behind that smoke.

I stared at her without the slightest trace of reverence. "Evening, Jean. And no, actually, not in the slightest," I said, walking in and touching Branson on the shoulder, nodding. He released his grip on his pistol. "She is worthy of the honor, and now everyone knows who she is. Next year, Miguel Monzon will be on the cover, who I believe you knew well. And after that, Rosie Campion, followed by Cameron Shipley, Liam Mayfield, Allison Trudy, Joseph Bassett, and many others. All deserving of praise."

Her eyes glinted in the darkness, and I could tell she was wearing a nightgown. Made sense. The former President wasn't allowed to go anywhere or do anything except for sit outside in her tiny backyard. I could clearly discern her disdain through the darkness of her room. She switched on a lamp on a tiny oak coffee table next to an aged couch. There she was, wrinkled, powerless and equally aged, fusing seamlessly with what she was sitting on.

"*Monzon*," she sneered. "Yes, I knew the traitor well. All those years he pretended to be allegiant, hiding under my very nose talking to *you*. And yet here you are, all high and mighty, with your crown and scepter. I suppose you've come to gloat? Or can it be that you're seeking new counsel now that you've lost your precious pastor?"

I shook my head. The audacity at mentioning Rosie with such flippancy. I shook it off. I needed something from this wicked witch, and the sooner I got it and was out of here, the better. "Oh, believe me, Jean, I wouldn't trouble your repose here only to seek your counsel on matters of operation."

She tilted her head and looked at me under her brows. "Operation?"

I nodded, walking around through her tiny house. I could feel her eyes on me, though her head didn't turn. "Yes, Jean, *operation*. It seems that while you were in office you kept some files on your desktop that you must have had Cartwright – you remember him – or someone else encrypt. We've got new technology in the works that requires information from your files, and we're going to need the decryption key please." I was surveying her tidy kitchen with my hands in my pockets, my back to her, but now I did a one-eighty and turned to face her.

The former president was facing me with a hardened, teasing smile, her head shaking ever so slightly, while she blew out a long trail of carbon monoxide straight at me. "And you came here because you thought you could just ask me nicely, and I would nicely give. Is that it? I suppose now we come to the point where you offer me some irresistible deal to lessen my sentence and ease my suffering so that one day I might dig my toes into the sand once more, with the sun on my face, yes?"

"If that's what you'd like."

Her condescending smile slowly faded into a concrete chin and a sullen stare. "Go to hell, Vance. You and I both know that I'm never getting out of here. You'll get what you want and throw me right back in this hellhole when you're done. Or worse, you'll use me, discard me, and have me bumped off and then make it look like an accident."

"I'm afraid you have my behavior confused with that of a previous president," I said quickly, looking at her squarely.

Moment of silence as we eyed one another. "Unless of course you prefer to stay in your tiny rambler, to live out your days watching sitcom reruns from a world you nearly destroyed, wallowing in your confinement and stewing in bitterness. Shall I name the terms?"

She eyed me curiously. "What exactly is it you're wanting, Vance?" I didn't mind that she didn't address me as *Mister President*. Such platitudes from despots were unnecessary and insincere.

"Just what I mentioned. Decryption keys. For certain files on your drive labeled 'Tailback.' We don't have enough guys ready and available to crack that. All your stuff was confiscated, as you know, but only recently have they stumbled upon this certain drive. As it's government property, we'd like to get inside it please."

She smirked. "And what of your *pro cyber* team?" she scoffed. "Lynch's crack squad. The ones you had aboard the Truman that disarmed my nukes. They can't just

brute force their way in anymore? Lost their touch, *eh?*"
Another smirk while poking fun at Lynch's Canadian jargon.

"They're on the other side of the world right now,
and as you can probably guess, your server was a silo, off the
grid, for security purposes. It's not like we could just FedEx
it to them," I answered.

"Indeed. We need more planes, do we not?"

"Yes. We're still busy removing certain pesky
AN/ALQ99 DTF sweepers from all of them first," I jabbed,
though the opposite was actually the truth. We were
ensuring that every single military plane was equipped with
them.

Graham looked at me, taking a long drag on her
cigarette. If she was trying to feign ignorance at all the
knowledge we had amassed on her, she wasn't succeeding.
The corner of her lip twisted upward in a wicked, knowing
smile.

For a brief moment I thought she might be enjoying
this banter. I was losing patience. "Think about it," I said,
"but don't think too long. I know you have all the time in
the world, Jean, but we don't. We'd like to continue our
operations, and we need your decryption key. You know
where to find me."

She squinted at me as I turned away, stopping me as I
walked out. "What do you mean you 'don't have time?'" I
could feel her eyes narrowing on me.

I stopped, and slowly turned. She had risen. I had
forgotten how tall she was. In the underlighting of that lamp,
she looked writhen and strained, unkempt and stretched far
beyond her years, but nonetheless menacing. However, her
face was now pulled taut, and she donned a worried look.

"You've found something. Haven't you? Is that it?" she asked me nervously, as a strange quiet settled upon her.

It was time to make a final plea. "Work with us, Jean. I think you'll find it in your best interest. In all of ours."

And with that, I think I had communicated enough. *Yes, we found something* were words I was not going to say outright, but she had been a president once as well, and, working her way through the system, knew how to read people. She had certainly done that with Colonel Keegan. For now, the subject of *Francine 45* was on a need-to-know basis only. With Graham, it was on a *deserve*-to-know, and the truth was that she deserved *nothing*…except perhaps punishment and isolation.

Graham stared at me. Her shoulders shrugged, and her chin tilted up as her jaw shifted to the side. She heaved a great and steady sigh. "It's a simple Caesar Shift cipher. Four spaces to the left," she said, and then she sighed. *Here it comes,* I thought. "Shift them back the other way and you'll get it. *FQOPEJ.*"

For a moment, she looked taxed, and I wondered how precious the information was that she was being pushed to divulge. I stared at her and nodded somberly. 'Why four, Jean?"

The ex-President regarded me with hollow eyes. "I was in my fourth term, which was stolen from me. Why not?"

"FQOPEJ?" I asked once more.

"FQOPEJ," she confirmed, slowly, breathing it out in a drawn and tired murmur.

I thanked her without considering the matter any further and walked out. My agents closed the door behind me, leaving Jean Graham alone with her thoughts. "Goodbye, Mr. Franklin. Mr. Branson," she saluted the few Secret Service guys that were once in her employ.

"Ma'am," they answered, and closed the door. The patrol swiftly returned as we walked down her dilapidated steps back to the Suburban.

I had Branson work the letters, each one of them, four spaces to the right. My men opened the Suburban door for me and I climbed in. Branson entered into the front seat, turned to me and showed me a notepad with his decoding, wearing a confused face.

I wasn't confused. The notepad said it all. *FQOPEJ* was the cipher key. Easy to remember for her. Shift each letter four spaces back to the right, and you come up with a name. One very memorable name.

I sighed.

JUSTIN. The name of her only son, whom she had lost to the gorgons in early 2034. This decrepit and horrendously sinister woman had only one piece of her sullen heart left for one person. She had chosen to memorialize his name in a cipher key she would always remember.

I sighed again and shook my head. "Get that decryption key to the guys as soon as you can, Branson. Back to the mansion please."

"Yes, sir."

It's dealing with the past that hamstrings the future. Now I was actually feeling sorry for Graham. Perhaps she intended it that way, to evoke mercy and grace from me. All I could do was stare out the window and wonder what it was like for her to lose her only son out there in the field so very long ago.

All the while I loathed having to wonder *anything at all* about her.

Sometimes I truly hate this job.

3 | FRANCINE 45

Saturday, March 4ᵗʰ 2045 · 8:29pm

Here it came. There was no mistaking it now.

"Confirmed," said the SETI tech over the call. "Hubble's got it. Object has deviated course point four-five degrees, approaching at a parabolic course in a geometric trajectory heading toward Saturn's orbit past the outer planets. Too fast for a meteor, too large for a comet or other celestial body. Origin confirmed as well." I held my breath. "TRAPPIST system, likely TRAPPIST-1D or 1E. Goddard Space Flight Center tracking it, and they verified too."

He was watching his screen intently, his face brightly illuminated as he spoke. "We thought it might be some wayward rock pushed along by solar winds, but it's not, sir."

"*Shhhhit,*" I angrily cursed loud and long through my teeth.

The Chief of Staff of the Air Force did the same, in his husky Mexican voice. "*Mierda!*"

This news meant only one thing.

I turned to Miguel, and he flashed me a nervous look as I returned my eyes to the tech. "And you're confident this is Francine 45, the one you've been monitoring? There's no reason to believe that it's some other stray?"

"All intel points to it being a vessel of some type, sir," the tech answered. "Tracking intercept course via remaining satellites. Should rendezvous with our orbit within the next week if it holds its present speed and bearing.

"We're also picking up a faint audio signal on an encoded frequency, Mr. President," he continued. "It's almost like sonar pings, at regular intervals. We confirmed ascension and declination, put it through system diagnostics, checked the reference points. We went off-axis, set manual target frequency, and were scanning all bands in case we happened to lose the signal. Definitely a partially-polarized set of moving pulses, amplitude modulated 3.82, 25 gigahertz, hydrogen times pi," he rattled off. I hadn't a clue what he was talking about.

"Right ascension twenty-three hours six minutes 29 seconds. Declination negative five degrees, two minutes, 29 seconds. Puts it at TRAPPIST-1 system. F.U.D.D. was reading it too. Interferometry checked and verified," he said. "The VLAs at NRAO in New Mexico all verify. Redundant peak intensity read one-hundred-sixty-eight janskys, which is huge, Mr. President. And the spectrum analysis had harmonics in the signal with an offset audio carrier, which we confirmed on the negative sideband.

"Also, source has now been confirmed: it's coming directly from Francine. It's alien in origin, Mr. President. We ran it through audio de-scramblers and the computers don't place it anywhere in the catalogues. The signal is mathematical, sir; it's not random. It's like somebody out there is dialing a phone number repeatedly, and no one around us is picking up."

I took his words in. This was not good. Not good at all. My lungs filled with angry air that I huffed out. "Yeah, that's because we blew up their phone on this end," I grunted in frustration. "Alright, thanks for the tech-speak. Keep me informed. Call Commander Sinclair at NORAD and let him know please. Thank you, Mountain View. I'm going to give you my personal cell number. What's your name?"

"Greene, sir. You have working cell service?" He couldn't hide his excitement that maybe soon everyone would have coverage.

"Long story. Limited, but it works. You're in charge, Greene. You text me with any updates yourself please. And get in touch with our techs here, Romero and Jens. They're through the main switchboard. Yes?"

"Aye, aye, sir," the tech answered. SETI switched off. There was no ambiguity, no emotion, no whining; just a monotone acknowledgment that something was approaching our planet, and approaching it fast. Francine 45 was no comet. No meteor. It was changing speed and bearing at will, and that could only mean one thing.

Somebody's coming over for dinner.

"Here we go again, Miguel," I said.

"Here we go again," he echoed, somberly, and his teeth ground together so loud I swore white powder was going to pour out of his mouth. "Now we would need *mi flor preciosa* the most. How I miss her, Vance," he groaned.

"I miss her too, my friend," I said. "Let's just pray she's got the ear of the Big Man, because whoever's in that craft is coming straight at us, and they're going to be here in a week."

"And they're going to be pissed," Miguel said.

"And they're going to be pissed," I echoed. "Better get in gear, my friend. Mobilize. We thought this day might come. Time to show them we won't go quietly into the night."

"I can't believe we're back here. I *cannot* believe this, my friend," he said, shaking his head. There was gritty anger in his tone, certainly, but there was more reason here than the possible return of the gorgs. I turned to face him.

"Hey," I said, "I know losing Rosie is hard. But we gotta do what we gotta do, right? It might *not* be them. We don't know that yet. Can I count on you to ready the briefing?"

He winced, but it was more of an intentional one, as if snapping himself out of a fog. I felt him stiffen as he looked up at me. "Yes, Mr. President. Absolutely. For Rosalita."

I smiled at my old friend. "For Rosalita. And you don't need to call me that. I'll always be Vance to you."

Miguel smiled back and clapped my arm on his shoulder. "Esta bien. Let's go get ready, Vance."

"Time for our special plan."

Miguel nodded and saluted, and then he walked out to make some very important calls.

I grabbed my cell phone, one of only a few working on T-Mobile, which was the only service actually running in such a short time. I dialed Andi.

"Hey, Mr. President!"

"Hon, I need you here. I need to talk with you."

"Is everything okay? Is Neener okay?"

"Just fine. I just need you here."

"I'm on my way."

My head drooped and my shoulders sank. *Shit*. We only got less than three years into our rebuilding. And now they were coming at us again.

We were fools to think they wouldn't return. I blew out hot air as I suddenly had a trillion phone calls to make, dialing VP Bayless, and then Peter Capra, my SecDef, right away.

•   •   •   •   •

Saturday, March 4^(th) 2045 · 8:56pm

I was sitting at my desk when Andi arrived. My assistant, Cora, welcomed her and showed her in. She noticed my expression and slowed her pace.

By that time, I had received confirmation. Long range scans revealed it to be neither a comet, meteor, wayward meteor shower nor black hole, but a *ship*: some kind of vessel, akin in shape, as much as they could tell this far away, to what had first visited us in 2026. The first one had remained just out of sight up there in the mesosphere. Now, a *second* one was on its way, and would be here in a week. SETI confirmed it, and I was sent scans. The DSN, our Deep Space Network, confirmed it through radar and radio astronomy observations compiled and sent to SETI, and then Greene texted me confirmation.

Andi walked toward me in the Oval Office. I sat motionless at the Resolute Desk, leaning to the side. I just looked at her under my eyebrows.

They say married couples can know what the other is thinking. Andi had mastered this gift, and she proved it once again, tilting her head as her jaw dropped. She stopped in her tracks. "No. No way. *No.*"

I nodded, and didn't say anything else. Just sat there. Andi's face went white. Her purse fell to the floor, and she reached out to steady herself on the couch. I got up to help her. "Hon, now, we don't know exactly yet…it *is* something, but we don't know for sure *what* yet. It's too far out, hon, and-"

She put her hand up, waving me off and crossing around the couch to sit down. "No," was all she could breathe. If I didn't know better, she looked to be bordering on hyperventilation.

"Yes," I said, momentarily. "Unfortunately, yes."

She turned to look back at me. "Y-you just said you don't know."

"We know enough to know that it's alien. That it's not a meteor. And that it's been sending out calls on a beacon in our direction - calls that are going unanswered. Put two and two together, that only means one thing."

"It's them."

I nodded. "We have to assume that. We'd be remiss if we didn't assume that." I sat down next to her. "I already called Wright-Pat. Janine and Liam are on their way here now. There are enough pilots and jets up there now. We're going to retreat to the PEOC below." She started breathing harder despite my assurances. "Hon, we've got equipment. Miguel's on it. The deterrents are in place. If it *is* them, we'll know well before they get here."

"How long do we have?"

"A week. Maybe less."

"A *week?*" she shrieked. "Vance! You're telling me that we have a *week* before they come? Holy shit! You've got to be kidding me. Guess I better get all my shopping done now, huh?" she joked in anger, and then buried her face in her hands.

"I know, hon. It's traveling fast. We only just found out. We're not fully back online yet. They caught it as quickly as they could."

"They're coming because we killed their queen. We killed their queen! That's got to be it," she said frantically. "So what is this, their *king?* Hon, we can't deal with another attack, we've only just begun to dig our way out of the last one. We'll never make it!"

"I know it's poor timing," I said, stoically, regarding her gravely. "I know, hon. We can only do the very best we can. But since December 2042 we've put measures in place."

"Yeah but will they be *enough?* Look what they did the first time around! We can't take another sixteen years of living underground, it'll kill us all!" She buried the sockets of her eyes in her fists.

"Hon, think. *Think.* The first time we didn't have DTF emitters by the hundreds of thousands. The first time we didn't have DTF devices on a nuclear scale. We're going to plan a preemptive strike. I've already got Monzon and

Capra working on it. A plan has always been in place for this, just like it was at Mammoth Cave, hon. We've prepared for this contingency.

"We survived there, and God willing, we'll survive here. The Blockades will be reactivated. We'll get people to shelter once more. The military will provide defenses, and we've got more powerful weapons now. They won't get us without clenched butt cheeks this time around. There was a reason I never closed the Blockades."

I sat down beside her on the couch. She needed to rail at me, someone, *anyone*. The mammoth unfairness of it all was incalculable. Janine and Liam had only just married. Rosie had just died and Miguel was still grieving. Construction crews were all so busy trying to give us a livable, habitable world again. This felt too much like a cruel boy stepping on a just-built anthill.

Andi grew quiet and she shut her eyes. My wife took a deep breath, and then shook her head once more. "I'm with you, hon. I'm with you. I just-" here she looked up at me, eyes red and strained. The First Lady started to weep. "Neener…our grandchild…our *world*," she sobbed.

I scooped her into my arms and held her close to me. And then I was sobbing too. As would our world be, once they found out what was coming at us yet again. They were out there, all along. What incredible hubris we had operated in thinking that perhaps we had been delivered. Rosie would have a thing or two to say. *They're coming.* Two ominous, foreboding and excruciating words that bounced around inside my cranium.

The door to the Oval Office opened once more, and Cora stepped in. "Is everything alright, sir?"

I turned to her. "We're alright, Cora. Thank you. I'll be out momentarily."

Cora dismissed herself and closed the door again.

"We're not alright. We're not going to be alright," Andi moaned through her tears.

Everything in me felt that she was absolutely right.

·   ·   ·   ·   ·

Saturday, March 4th 2045 · 9:37pm

Andi had left for our room. I warned her not to tell anyone. *It may be something else,* I said, and she scoffed. I told her we don't know anything concretely, so just please keep it to herself for now.

She promised, shrugged, and left, beside herself from a mixture of wrath and dejection.

As for me, I went back to my phone. Miguel called and said that he had setup meetings with the rest of the Joint Chiefs in eight minutes. He had also made some important calls on what we were calling our 'special plan.' I knew what that meant.

I confirmed I would meet the Joint Chiefs. The tech at SETI sent me a message. Another course deviation, and definite acceleration. Pings continuing, unanswered, growing in intensity. I texted confirmation to the VP and the SecDef. My Secretary of Defense was a good man. Peter Capra was much relieved that he wasn't helming the planet since his name was in the hat for President. He had lost his entire family in the years following the attacks. However, he had come to terms with it and was still a good, decent and loyal public servant.

I called Admiral Lynch on Zoom, and told her the news. She handled it well. Always no-nonsense, that woman. She was still aboard the Harry S. Truman aircraft carrier, and the rest of the entire naval fleet was either being retrofit with DTFs, or underway out there somewhere. I told her to bring the fleet to a state of readiness and that we could potentially have incoming in a week.

"Their previous ship was positioned middle of the north Atlantic," I said. "My hunch is that's the trajectory for our new incoming. Keep your eyes peeled. I'll be in touch."

"Aye, aye, sir," she said. "We'll be ready, eh?"

"Eh," I echoed in true Canadian fashion, and switched off Zoom.

Time to head to the meeting with the Joint Chiefs. I took a deep breath, and fired off a quick message to Commander Sinclair of NORAD, and then an even more important one: the Secretary-General, Maddox Leone. It was time to inform the United Nations of our discovery. They would be key to an international response.

• • • • •

Saturday, March 4th 2045 · 9:45pm

I shook Bayless' hand, and she took a seat next to me at the end of a long oak table in the Cabinet Room.

"Ladies, gentlemen, thank you for joining us," began Miguel. "I apologize for this late hour. We have an important meeting tonight, and no time to waste, so let me bring you up to speed as quickly as possible, and then the President will have the floor. Thank you Mr. President," he said, nodding to me. I nodded back.

Miguel began by clearing his throat roughly.

"A few of you have heard the news, and rumors are spreading, so let us deal plainly with the facts. Many of you might remember that in June of 2024 – two years before the initial invasion - the Office of the Director of National Intelligence released a report concerning unidentified aerial phenomena, or UAP." Here Miguel handed out papers around the room that appeared to be a report. "Two researchers created a data set using information from the Gaia Mission, which was a spacecraft launched by the European Space Agency in 2013. Its purpose was to monitor over a billion stars throughout the Milky Way galaxy. Their distance-measuring technique, parallax, allowed a baseline to measure distances and motion. Some of the kinetics of these uber-distant objects require time to decipher.

"They revealed that there is a sort of 'Earth transit zone,' around three hundred light-years around our sun. The question that they pursued was, in effect, 'what other visitors would be able to see us?' Seven of the stars mapped by the two researchers were found to possibly host exoplanets that were considered to be potential candidates possessing natural liquid water, and, concordantly, the ability to sustain life. One of these planets, Ross 128b, apparently was in Earth's transit zone for about two thousand years. It effectively could have 'seen' Earth somewhere between the tenth century BC and the tenth century AD, during which time we saw the rule of Alexander the Great, the fall of Rome, as well as the apex of the Mayans. The best known view is yet to come, and is geolocated around another star named TRAPPIST-1, a red dwarf in the Aquarius constellation. This star has a radius slightly larger than Jupiter, about nine percent of our sun. It contains in its orbit seven exoplanets that are approximately the size of Earth. Four of them are at the right distance from TRAPPIST-1 to conceivably support life. We believe that one of these seven planets may potentially be where the *gorgos* – excuse me, the gorgons, sorry, that's how we say it in Spanish – hail from." Upon hearing that dreaded name again, people visibly shifted in their seats. "We initially suspected either TRAPPIST-1G or 1H. They would have an equilibrium temperature of roughly negative one-hundred fifty-five degrees Fahrenheit, similar to that of Earth's south pole. These exoplanets fall near their star's frost line, though they could harbor liquid water under a hydrogen-rich atmosphere, either primordial, or resulting from continuous outgassing combined with internal heating. Existence of such an atmosphere has been strongly disfavored by observations in the years 2021 and 2022 in the Astronomy and Astrophysics international journal. If ice-covered, it could also potentially harbor a subsurface ocean by way of tidal heating, which could lead to cryovolcanism in the form of erupting geysers. The inner planets would still contain water, at a less threatening orbit.

"However, in long range scans, SETI and the DSN have now reported what they believe to be confirmation of the volatility of these more hospitable planets, namely TRAPPIST-1D and TRAPPIST-1E. They have no magnetic field, similar to Venus and Mars here, and thus, the star's solar wind strips away the more volatile components of these two exoplanets' atmosphere – including water – leaving them hydrogen-poor. Satellite images," -here he turned to his laptop tech to pull up new images to display- "note the coloration differential here, display significantly different hues from when the system was first catalogued, and now. Something has happened. There is far less water now on both of the planets on these inner orbits."

"Excuse me, Mr. Monzon, but just what does this all mean?" the Commerce Secretary interjected. He was growing weary.

"It means, Mr. Alberts, that the system is dying, and the planets are being robbed of hydrogen. No hydrogen, no water. No water, no habitable environment. No habitable environment, the gorgons seek out another planet to inhabit. This is precisely why they did what they did in 2026.

"Many of you are aware that when the gorgons were here, they did not prefer the summer, and would generally diminish in number, and when they were found, they were somewhat submerged in waterways. Clearly, they have an affinity for water, and the queen herself, as everyone here knows, setup base camp in the North Atlantic at the foundation of the funnel which we destroyed. And then, we destroyed their craft, which appears now to have been little more than a reservoir for transporting our water back to their planet, or wherever else they intended."

"Okay, so goes the history lesson," Alberts sighed in exasperation. "We now know where they most likely came from. What does that have to do with now?"

"It means that we can track a line from there to here, sir, and we wouldn't be sitting here if there was no new activity."

"'New activity?'" he asked confusedly, and then the color drained from his face. "Wait…you're not…dear God…"

Miguel continued right away. "At 0900 Coordinated Universal Time on February 27th, the President received a call from the ICA, citing an object of potentially unknown origin displaying deviations in trajectory. They have since identified both the target and the origin, and all major installations such as the VLAs in New Mexico have confirmed it." Miguel motioned to an assistant who punched a few keys on his laptop, and the monitor at the end of the room sprang to life.

Before our eyes we could clearly see a small object, framed against the constellations and the thick ink of space. The tech panned through subsequent images as a moving object bloomed into view. It was clearly not stationary. Sequential images definitely revealed movement, inching its way through the cosmos.

It was growing in size, inching closer to earth.

"There it is, folks. Straight out of TRAPPIST-1. Unless we're absolutely off our collective rockers, what we've been referring to as 'Francine 45' has now been confirmed to be an alien spacecraft closing in on our sun's orbit. They'll be here within a week, maybe slightly sooner."

The collective deflation in the room was palpable. Everyone received the equivalent of a gut punch which hammered its way straight into their sense of stability and peace. There was dead silence as the meaning of what Miguel had just said settled heavily upon us.

Nichols, the Education Secretary, suddenly burst out with agonizing intensity, swearing profusely.

Profanity aside, he had said pretty much what we were all thinking. Everyone gasped. If expelled carbon monoxide could form visible letters, everyone's respirations would spell out *Not Again!* in hot clouds throughout the room.

"That's correct," said Miguel, finally. "And now, I will turn it over to the President. Sir?" he beckoned to me. I felt the heat of every eye on me, except for those few who had buried their faces in their hands to hem in their sobbing and desperation.

"So, there it is, people," I said, rising out of my seat and pacing around the room. "Something is on its way to us. We don't know yet if it's the gorgs, folks. We're awaiting confirmation of that. But, it behooves us to plan for the worst, and assume malignant intent. All the Area 51'ers out there will say we've been visited by extra-terrestrials before. Fine. To many of us, that's pure conjecture or supposition. But the annals of Earth's history will forever maintain the certainty of visitation when they invaded in 2026. I would ask you to suspend disbelief with me as we prepare for what could be, unfortunately, yet another imminent invasion." I looked around at them. With the exception of Bayless, Miguel, Capra and Homeland Security Secretary Stephan Roe, none of them expected to hear such awful news.

"I know this is not what any of us wanted to hear tonight. We've only just begun to rebuild. Nonetheless, that thing is out there, and it's on its way. And I'll be darned if I'm gonna let a second gorg invasion take another crack at us. We're stronger than that. We beat them once, and we can beat them again. They won't be catching us with our pants down this time. With that, let me take a few moments to assure you of what we have in place should it prove, in fact, to be what we most fear."

I went back to my place, and Bayless handed me my notes.

"Five hundred seventy fully-functional and restocked Blockades to house the general populace. DTF emitters distributed to all corners of the globe at various intensities. DTF bombs and superbombs armed and ready. Aerial reconnaissance and fighter planes equipped with DTF sweeps. All military bases and fleets on high alert. All branches readied and equipped with deflector mask technology and supersonic weapons. Commanders in place, some of whose names you've heard. I have a meeting with them tomorrow morning, combination in-person and remote. We've set DEFCON 3.

"But that's not all, folks," I added, holding up a finger. "That's just ground forces. You're all well-aware of the defenses we've been arranging. All submarines have had SLBMs retrofit with DTF bombs. But we have some additional toys to play with. The *Tsar Bombas.* Ring a bell, anyone?"

Darrell Austin, the Secretary of Agriculture, my acting Vice Chairman of the Joint Chiefs of Staff, and the eldest in my cabinet, spoke up. "Uh, I do, sir," he said. He was eighty-eight now, and the last surviving member of the previous cabinet. He would have been a toddler when the *Tsar Bomba* was detonated in 1961. "If memory serves, sir, the *Tsar Bomba* was the culmination of a series of high-yield thermonuclear weapons designed by the Soviet Union and the United States during the 1950s, for example, the Mark 17 and B41 nuclear bombs. It was scaled back, but could yield a hundred-megaton drop. They tested that sucker when I was three."

"You have a good memory, Mr. Austin," I said.

"Thank you, sir. Yessir, they scaled it back by fifty percent. Dropped it on Sukhoy Nos of Severny Island, fifteen kilometers from Mityushikha Bay, north of the Matochkin Strait. The flare was observed in Norway, Greenland and Alaska. Mushroom cloud rose to forty-two miles. The blast wave circled the globe three times, sir."

"Right again, Mr. Austin," I smiled at him. His memory was solid. "But there's another issue here. The Russians never stopped working on it. They've got a large *Tsar Bomba* factory at Dombarovsky. When the gorgs were destroyed and we began to rebuild, the Russians started rounding up and mass-producing these again. They have *twenty-two* of them at one-hundred megaton rating. *One-hundred megatons each, folks.* Mr. Austin here will tell you that's a big boom, and we've got the Russians' help.

"They've mounted the *Tsar Bombas* on Russian RS-28 Sarmats. These are NATO codename: SS-X-29. They're an apex engine of atomic annihilation. Each ICBM can shower up to fourteen independently targetable nuclear warheads on targets thousands of miles away."

"I remember those," Austin replied, "but didn't the Russians have a series of negative incidents at the Plesetsk Cosmodrome, the Yubileynaya test launch silo that they built for the Topol-M ICBM? Those Sarmats were thirty-five meters long and two-hundred twenty-nine tons. Our Minuteman IIIs were only sixteen meters and forty tons. Are the Sarmats reliable? I remember satellite images showing massive damage after the Russians' failed tests."

"The Russians assure me they're good now, Darrell," I said. "Their confidence is high. So those will be for the ceiling attack. For our subs and silos, every one of them has been affixed with the highest yield we can safely provide just this side of nuclear. You remember Israel's Iron Dome?

Think of this on a planetary scale. We're going to launch a preemptive strike against their ship before it reaches us."

Homeland Security Secretary Roe cleared his throat. "Now, that's a heckuva blast going off, and that raises a lot of red flags, sir. If even a single nuclear bomb detonated in space, you're talking the release of an epic amount of radiation through gamma rays and x-rays. Electromagnetic pulse would fry unshielded electronics and disrupt vital systems on board all spacecraft and the ISS, even though it was decommissioned in 2042 after abandonment. If we ever want to go back to it, it'll be a nonfunctional shell. Then you have space debris we'll have to navigate around. That's just for a single sub-two-megaton nominal yield. You're talking *twenty-two* warheads with *hundred*-megaton yield, sir. That will surely have bearings on our ozone layer, to say the least, but even worse, it could potentially knock Earth off of its axis, affect the tidal patterns, rotation, everything. The EMP shockwave could crumple our moon, Mr. President, and destroy all satellites in the blast radius. EMP would hit us down here too. To say nothing of the fact that the explosion would create a ring of charged particles looping around the Earth. It'd be another Van Allen belt. You'd have to shut down everything just prior to detonation. And I mean *everything*."

"The concerns are documented, legitimate, and understood, Mr. Roe. Thank you for bringing them up. We have techs analyzing the effects now, as well as the optimum detonation point to protect Earth as much as possible."

"Anyway," voiced Capra, "at this point it's certainly the lesser of two evils: protection of the ozone layer and axis versus potential annihilation of the human race."

"Exactly," I agreed. "The gorgons won't be back to steal our water. They'll be here for revenge."

Roe rolled his eyes and sighed. The nuclear option was certainly unappealing, but it was all we had for a defense away from our planet itself. "And just exactly how do you know that, Mr. President?"

"C'mon, Stephan, we killed their queen," I barked, not in the mood to indulge his sour attitude. "What happens when you smack a beehive with a baseball bat?"

"I don't know, sir," he shot back, "it's been nineteen years since I've seen a beehive."

"Fine. Just know this: should our nukes not deter or destroy them, we've got hundreds of SPAAGs out there. These self-propelled anti-aircraft guns have been rolled out ever since we drove them off, and at least twenty of them are positioned at strategic locations in every major metropolitan city. The defenses of our planet have never been more ideal. I've spoken to the Secretary-General. We have Leone's full support of course, and all nations will be informed tomorrow morning."

Capra chimed in. "Mr. President, if I may," -here he turned his attention back to the Cabinet- "the subject of high-yield nukes is a nervous topic for many. There was much dissent to the use of nukes ever since the gorgons invaded us. It's a dangerous topic to even broach. The Doomsday Clock has been reset to 11:59 and 45 seconds PM. That's the closest we've *ever* been. I know you're scared, people. I am too. I'm sure the President is as well. You all know what I myself went through. A few of you are in the same boat. But I can assure you, as nervous and afraid as this makes me to my very core, I've never felt more prepared for this, and we have a President to lead us through it this time who is not his predecessor. President Cardona brought us through our last crisis. He'll do so again." Capra turned back to me.

I nodded to Peter. "Thank you, Mr. Capra, I appreciate it. Speaking of the former President, I recently paid her a visit and we've now gained access to some much needed information. I expect word back on what she had kept encrypted, and will relay that to you as soon as I am able. Ms. Bayless," I said, turning to Veronica, "you've been charged with communicating with the remaining Blockades. How ready are the soldiers who remain enlisted there?"

Bayless cleared her throat. "Yes, Mr. President. Coming from Alpharetta myself, I know it well, and I can say with assurance that, in the teleconferences and video calls we've had to date, I don't have any concerns over their readiness. All have remained online since the victory in December 2042, and have been working diligently during this reprieve to bring their Blockades to a state of readiness. We've only just found out about Francine 45 of course, so none of them have been informed as to this new threat or its confirmation, but we're ready to relay that at your command, sir."

"Thank you, Madame Vice President," I replied.

"This is ridiculous," Nichols protested again, and all eyes turned to him. Realizing his own outburst, he backpedaled. "I'm sorry, okay? I'm sorry. But dangit, this can't be happening! We'll never survive this!"

"No we won't," I shot back. "Not with that thinking."

"Vance-" Alberts started.

"*Mister President*, if you please," jabbed Miguel.

The tension in the room was growing.

Alberts shot a defiant look at Miguel. "Fine, excuse me. *Mister President,* I appreciate the comfort you're trying to convey, but don't you think this is more at the stage of consolation than comfort? Too little, too late? I mean, when did the WMO first spot this sucker? How long have they been dragging their feet on this?"

"Mr. Nichols," I replied, "I understand your concern. There'll be no pointing fingers here. There was certainly no need to raise alarm until we knew what it was. There are millions of wayward celestial bodies out there, and everyone needed to be sure. They were only just sure of it as of 2125 hours this evening, Jeff. That's hardly dragging their feet."

He grunted dismissively and put his swollen and angry red face in his hands again.

I read the room. "I think it's plain that we're all feeling what the Education Secretary is feeling. Not a single one of us wants or deserves this. But we have to face the music, or it *will* be the end of us."

"Mr. President," said Capra, "you mentioned Jean Graham earlier. Have we made any inroads with the three countries she targeted? Iran…China…North Korea…all are nuclear powers. All have resources that we will need should this prove to be the gorgons yet again, sir."

"That's a good question, Peter. I have spoken with them, and, as usual, North Korea remains the holdout. Most resistant to play ball, even despite the news. But when the truth came out, and everyone and their mother found out what Jean Graham had done, can you really blame them? They don't want anything to do with us. I mean – Bill, uh, Secretary of State Curtiss will have more to say on this, perhaps?" I motioned to Bill Curtiss.

"Thank you, Mr. President," said Curtiss. "Well, it's not good news…yet. It seems that our extensions of goodwill, and visits with the respective ambassadors, have done little to yield a return on our investment of said goodwill. So, for now, I wouldn't count on them, no. But we'll hear more once the United Nations reconvenes in a video link tomorrow. Everyone is required to be there: all member states and those wanting democracy and forward momentum."

"That witch," breathed Alberts in disgust. "We need everyone in this! We can't afford rogue or hostile nations not pulling their weight against a *planetary* foe," he grunted again, and no one opposed his thought. "We need to work together on this!" Bill simply nodded, since he was now just stating the obvious.

There was silence in the room for a moment. Everyone seemed to be lost in thought.

"Folks, listen to me. Please," I implored them. "They got us good before. No one is denying that. They have the potential to wreak immeasurable damage yet again. No one is denying that either. But lest we forget, a young warrior-scientist in Alpharetta" -here I looked over at Bayless, who Allison Trudy had served under- "developed mask deflection technology, and those boys at BNA developed our DTF tech in less than five years' time. Since their development, they've each been mass-produced and improved upon exponentially. Our Blockades are glorified bunkers, sure, and no one wants to live like a mole. But we've all survived. And now they're being reinforced and restocked. Since the war of 2042, we've seen several million enlistees across the globe, wanting to serve and give back.

"What does all that add up to? Relentless spirit. Relentless heart. *Relentless* commitment. If those are in fact the gorgs coming at us for round two out there, then they're relentless as well, certainly. But they've not met a more relentless foe than us, and we showed them that once already. It's incumbent upon us to show them that again. Standing here in this room, knowing what we have going for us out there, I don't have any doubts who will emerge the victor. We know them too well now. They're just flesh and bone, and we have the tech to stop them cold. A whole planet of relentlessly pissed-off warriors is the only thing they're going to find here. They're messing with the wrong species. And this time, we have the upper hand of advance warning."

Each one of them slowly nodded, sighing and resigning themselves to an inevitable fight that none of them wanted, but were silently resolving to win. I could see the desire for revenge brewing in many of their eyes, especially Austin's. He spoke up.

"Mr. President, if I may, why didn't we 'notice' them before?"

"A fair question. All of the agencies involved – SETI, the ICA, the WMO, International Cloud Atlas, all of them – didn't know precisely what to look for then. Our planetary defenses have always been more geared toward meteorological phenomena, not slow-moving crafts or alien invasions of any kind. They were more calibrated for ELE events by collision, not invasion. Only since the war, getting back in the saddle of these monitoring stations, did we know what to look for."

"ELE?" asked Nichols.

"Extinction Level Events," I clarified. "Asteroids. Meteors. Those kinds of collisions. But not invasions. We now know that the craft achieved sub-light speeds and came in behind our own moon. When they invaded in June of 2026, it all just happened too fast, and there was no time to properly scramble. But that's neither here nor there now. The point is, we know this one is alien, we know it's coming, and we have to get in gear now. Agreed?"

Simultaneous nods, *aye sir's* and yesses echoed all around the room.

"Alright. You all know Chief of Staff Monzon, and how critical he was to our victory. I'd like to relinquish the floor to him, as the defense will most likely be *heavily* aerially coordinated, and this is his purview. Mr. Monzon?"

Miguel stood back up. "Thank you, Mr. President. Thank you for all you have done, and thank you for all you are now doing for the American people." I nodded to him in gratitude. "Ladies and gentlemen, much of our armament has already been described to you as far as the capabilities we are prepared to employ. I have been in touch with every major air force chief around the world. We are now drawing up plans for aerial strikes. We will meet them in the air and the ground, gentlemen. International inventory is still being conducted, but we have, at present, roughly thirteen thousand fighters all told. Coordination is underway, callsigns are being issued, and all cooperating nations have pledged to flex international boundaries to allow crossover when and if we engage. Of course, all civilian air traffic will once again be grounded well before we anticipate the point of contact.

"As before, all fighters will be equipped with standard ordnance, ammunition, radar-guided or IRST system-based AMRAAMs and infrared tracking AIM-9s.

Since before the war of 2042, American fighters localized to BNA Nashville, amassed by President Cardona's predecessor, were all retrofit with DTF emitters and DTF bombs. We've had nearly three years, and in that time, priority one has been to ramp up mass-production and distribute our technology to all the States, and then, to the world. NATO reports that all member states have a fighting contingent equipped and ready to go.

"Beyond our atmosphere, NORAD will continue to monitor the approaching craft and relay intel to all stations. Many of you know that central headquarters at Peterson Space Force Base in Colorado was nearly destroyed in the September '26 attacks. Nonetheless, the offices in Alaska and Manitoba report full readiness to report and engage. On the ground, we have prepared for this event, with special forces and commanders in place. They're on their way now."

"Mr. Capra, what's your status?" I asked Peter.

"Thank you again, Mr. President. Folks, once President Cardona holds his address to the nation tomorrow, we'll get people where they need to go and then implement the ground stop. Our plan is to address it as a precautionary measure only; none of us wish to stoke fear or create a panic. Citizens will be instructed to maintain calm and order and gather only the barest of essentials and make for the nearest Blockade. That order will be given tomorrow, and they'll have two days to get there. Any such active local broadcasting networks as we can find will be issued an emergency memorandum immediately following the President's address tomorrow.

"Then? We close the Launch doors at each Blockade and wait. All gun towers at all Blockades are locked and loaded, and all now have central DTB units at the epicenter of each Blockade halo."

"DTB units?" asked Roe.

"Dissonant Tidal Bombs," Capra clarified. "They're the next evolution in the DTF technology developed at BNA. We can only use them barely up into the mesosphere; after that, there aren't enough molecules to carry sound waves in either the thermosphere or the exosphere. We've got to hit them in layers, and a sound attack will be Priority One if they make it past the *Tsar Bombas*. The anacoustic zone, roughly ninety-nine miles up, well, the air density is too low for sound, so we actually have to let them come in through the front door a bit before we hit them."

"Good Lord," Roe said.

"Exactly. Anyway, that's it, Mr. President."

"Thank you, Mr. Capra. Mr. Monzon. I appreciate it. Now, I know it's late, everybody, but there's one more thing I feel compelled to address." I leaned forward into the table to connect with them. "I appreciate you bearing with us through all of this regrettable news and preparing to do what's needed. But we wouldn't be here today without the prayer, affirmation, and direction of Rosalita Campion. Many of you knew her. Her spirit is still with us, folks. And in the interest of all those present, as well as for the survival of mankind, I can think of no better way to begin our defense than by invoking the wisdom that Rosie was known for. Everyone who knew Rosie knows what that is, and I invite you now to do it as we begin."

One by one, moved by honor and an inner compulsion to see it through, they stood, raising their hands palm upwards in token of receiving.

Receiving whatever might come our way, gorgons or otherwise. Receiving our survival – or our demise. Receiving the duty and responsibility now thrust upon all of us.

Receiving.

"That's it. That's all," I said. "Please inform your teams of the necessity of absolute silence until I brief the nation tomorrow. Mum's the word. We can't afford an overnight leak or a panic on our hands. It will be absolute hysteria, and we don't need that. Prepare yourselves and get a good night's sleep. I'm proud of all of you," I said, casting my gaze all around the room. You could read the anxiety in all of their faces. "We'll get through this. Dismissed. Good luck. God speed."

They nodded, and began to disperse.

•　　•　　•　　•　　•

Sunday, March 5th 2045 · 0700 hours

I don't remember even going to sleep. It was well after 1am when I had exchanged the last messages and calls with the Secretary-General and a few other world leaders, SETI, NORAD, Capra, Bayless, and finally, Monzon. I didn't feel I needed sleep, but they all insisted.

I relented, finally laying my head down next to the First Lady, who had reluctantly managed to fall asleep. A frown traveled the length of her face. Her eyes fluttered opened, and she whispered *I love you* through the quiet of the room, and then said no more.

Finally, fitful sleep took me.

I awoke hours later in distress, meeting an even more fitful morning. An address to the nation was imminent, followed by dreadful information that would be disseminated all around our country and the world.

I showered, pounding the walls around me and shaking my head. The cleansing water brought no semblance of fresh morning revival. Instead, it felt like a scalding.

This address to the nation would only be my tenth. It was going to be the most difficult. I didn't want to employ any theatrics to evoke fragile trust in false promises. I needed to be honest with the American people. I felt, perhaps foolishly so – we would soon see – that they could take it. After all, we had been through so much together already.

Time would tell.

•   •   •   •   •

Sunday, March 5th 2045 · 0756 hours

The address was in four minutes. Monzon and I met, had a quick breakfast, and went over the speech together. Concise, encouraging, hiding no crucial details, and trusting that the American people would be able to receive the truths we had to convey.

It was time.

The First Lady met me outside the office. Even through her valiant attempt at a warm hug and kiss, I could feel her trembling. I shared the knot in her stomach. She took a deep breath and nodded to me. I took her by the hand, released it, and then walked past Bayless and Capra, who were standing next to my assistant Cora.

There I was now in the Oval Office. I sat down at the Resolute Desk. Time slowed. The cameras were ready; a cameraman asked me if I was. I filled my lungs with slow, steady air, held it there for a moment, and then exhaled, willing myself to be calm. The teleprompter beside them held words of dread that they couldn't see. I knew that these cameramen had no clue what I was about to announce, and it was up to me to keep calm, cool and collected, and not let their reactions, live and right in front of me, disturb my train of thought. Just like the Americans tuning in via satellite phones, HAM radio, US VHF Radio, online message boards, text, FRS/GMRS, landlines, working radio broadcasts, and gathering places, they wouldn't know. How could they? Every single one of them, here and scattered abroad, was about to have a bomb dropped on them.

I composed myself, and then nodded to the cameraman and the director. They gave me the finger count.

Here we go.

"Citizens of planet Earth, NATO member states, world leaders, international partners, Secretary-General Leone, my fellow Americans," I began. "I'm coming to you today with some unsettling news that needs to be addressed."

I inhaled deeply, but an inadvertent pause held me back. I had to swallow, and shake it off. *C'mon, Vance. You're the President of the United States of America. You can do this.* I glanced over at Andi, and she nodded affirmingly to me. Miguel did the same. I continued.

"Since December 2042, we have all been passionately committed to rebuilding our world following the invasion and attacks that took place in 2026. We have made great strides. Our world is improving. Homes and buildings are being rebuilt. Societies are in positive reform. Mankind is growing in population again. We've all done our level best to rise again, victorious, following the siege of our world."

Time to pivot and give them the truth, I thought.

"Unfortunately, however, it falls upon me today to tell you that, sadly, things may not remain that way. On February 27th, at 0900 Coordinated Universal Time, I was informed by the World Meteorological Organization, a UN agency, that they had spotted an object of unknown origin approaching earth, and displaying signs of intelligent life. It was not a comet or an asteroid or any other meteorological body, they assured me. I asked them to keep me posted on its status and location.

"Yesterday at 8:29pm, I received confirmation that the object in question is in fact an alien spacecraft, and that it has been regularly deviating from its course. It is now approaching Earth at a parabolic course. The scientists and technicians at the WMO, in partnership with SETI, which is the Search for Extraterrestrial Intelligence, and International Cloud Atlas, have confirmed that the object most likely hails from the TRAPPIST-1 system, which is roughly forty light-years away. Along with its projected route to rendezvous with Earth, the technicians have monitored a faint geometric audio signal, a 'call,' if you will, being sent out by the craft in our direction. We do not have the technology or linguists to know what the call is saying, but it is a foregone conclusion that the call was – or is – intended for the previous craft that was suspended in our atmosphere, from which the gorgons first came."

One of the cameramen gasped.

I paused, allowing it to sink in with him and others, and to release myself from his distraction. "Yes. You heard me correctly. *Gorgons*. Based on the incoming craft's apparent course heading, makeup, attributes and apparent velocity, that makes it highly suspect, and it all but confirms that we have inbound attackers once again.

"Now, I and everyone else around me know full well this is *not* what we anticipated, desired, or hoped for. It is an entirely unfair and cruel twist of fate. But I want to take this opportunity to assure all of you, we have the very best people working on it even as I speak to you now.

"We have weapons. We have communications. We have more powerful technology than we've ever had, in order to quash this threat once and for all. We are prepared to exercise a formidable deterrent well before the craft even reaches Earth's orbit. Beyond that, should they intrude, we have ground artillery and anti-aircraft guns, along with powerful audio-based weapons designed not just to ward off, but to annihilate."

I leaned in. "I want you to know, as your President, that I am committed to your safety. We outlasted and survived them once. If needed, we will do it again. We've had a few years of sunshine. If we are called to live in the storm once more, so be it. There is high confidence that this craft is in fact the same alien invaders. Therefore, to that end, we are reactivating the Blockades."

A tangible deflation spun throughout the room. No one wanted this. Gorgons reappearing was one thing, but having to go back underground was a prison sentence for many. I could feel the resentment and frustration coming from those directly in front of me. I could only imagine the collective groans rising toward the heavens as an outcry all over the planet. One of the cameramen released the grip on his tripod and buried his face in his hands.

"Beginning now, I am implementing martial law. Effective tomorrow morning, all United States citizens and residents are to return to the Blockade they resided at, or to the nearest one they can find, as a precautionary measure. Tomorrow night, the skies will begin to close, as we initiate another full ground stop of all air traffic. We'll all need to get undercover, and away from the skies.

"To that end, the Blockades have been improved, retrofit to more modern standards, and stocked with fresh equipment, computers, weapons, ammunition, supplies, food, water, and medicine. We've had a lot of babies in the past few years, understandably so. Soundproof nurseries have been implemented, which I'm sure parents will appreciate. If you're an American citizen living abroad, I urge you to return home. Accommodations are being made as best as possible for those citizens living abroad, but we cannot guarantee the same shelter or community in foreign countries, as those are not our jurisdictions, and we must honor their sovereign policies and protocols. We have five-hundred-seventy Blockades still in operation around the world. We do not have the time to construct more, so for those of you who are unable to get to one, I highly advise you to contact your local consulate or US Embassy to find the best place to shelter.

"You've all either been previously issued, or will be issued, the most up-to-date deflection technology masks to protect you from these creatures. They are still being mass-produced, so, out of courtesy to everyone else, please bring the ones that you've already been issued."

Moment of truth. This is what was going to affect them the most. I sat back and took a short quick breath to steady myself. "Now, there's one more thing. A terrible truth is upon us. I'm asking you to brace yourself, because this is surely the most unpleasant news of all. The best guess for arrival of the craft appears to be" -here I paused, as I strove to just get the truth out no matter the panic that might ensue- "in five days, eight hours and twenty-three minutes. That puts the alien craft to us this Friday, March 10th at 4:35pm."

Someone squealed in fright. Something heavy dropped in the corridor. I heard footsteps running. It was jarring, and, I admit, sent a tremor through me. I blinked and sighed. "Ladies and gentlemen, we must remain calm. I too wish we had more time. We don't." I gripped my desk and cracked my knuckles. "We must do what we need to do and not waste time, because we don't have much of it. I am encouraging each and every one of you to make final preparations *now*, and get yourself to a Blockade or place of shelter right away.

"The respective branches of all partnering international militaries will be operational, and we have plans in place. We're going to show these aliens that once was once too many, and twice demands their obliteration. We have survived, and we'll continue to do so. I'm counting on you, and you can count on me – on all of our military and the militaries around the world – to protect you as best as we can. We will inform the respective Blockade leaders when the nuclear strikes will be made in outer space, as the craft approaches. Until that time, get to safety.

"Thank you. God bless you, and God bless the world."

That was where I deviated from the script. It said *America*, to be sure, but this was an international issue.

The cameras switched off, and I rose…but my knees buckled a bit, and I was just as nervous as the rest of us.

•　　•　　•　　•　　•

Sunday, March 5th 2045 · 0937 hours

"And where are they now?" Andi asked. We were heading down the elevator to the PEOC, the presidential bunker under the East Wing. "Are they almost here?"

"Yes, Ma'am," said Andi's aide. "Mr. and Mrs. Mayfield should be arriving in under an hour."

I breathed a sigh of relief. "Thank God." I hugged Andi to me as we walked. Martial law was in place, and even with the reduced population, there was sure to be looting and ransacking of stores, potentially even rioting.

"How is the PEOC now, Miguel? Readied for a few more occupants?"

"Yessir," he affirmed. "All is in place, my friend."

The bunker was not comfortable by any stretch, but it was large enough to handle several dozen staffers with sleeping quarters, showers, food, drink, communications, ammunition, and supplies. It could survive all but a direct nuclear strike, and was highly secure.

A sentry buzzed us in, and I had a flash of a memory of being at Mammoth Cave, with the Sentries at the Launch.

All over the world, starting tomorrow, Sentries would be back at their posts. Gunners would be back in their gun towers in a protective halo over their Blockades. Civilians and military personnel would be back in close quarters once more. For all intents and purposes, this PEOC was our Blockade, and this was our Sentry.

Surreal. I walked into the bunker. I had only been here once, upon first moving into the mansion, on a guided tour by the previous Chief of Staff to Jean Graham's predecessor, who had managed to survive. The bunker had been cleaned and restored. Gorgons had gotten down here and killed the previous VP, and then Graham had chosen Eric Cooper as her new VP. She eventually murdered him, of course, but not before the gorgs had done their damage and killed everyone off in the White House and bunker before finding their way back to the surface. One of them didn't make it out of here. Apparently, it was unable to find its way out, and they found a grotesque skeleton while on a recon patrol of the bunker prior to our tenancy.

I just couldn't shake the thought in my head: *I can't believe we're back here.*

"Miguel," I said, turning to him, "as much as it pains me to say it, some difficult arrangements need to be made. We need to transport our 'special citizen' here. As reviled as she is, she's still a former President. She needs to be here within the bunker, as much for her protection as for ours. We'll keep her in solitary confinement under guard."

"Yessir, you got it, Mr. President," said Miguel.

"Vance," I corrected. He just held his hands up helplessly. Andi looked at me. I held my hands up helplessly to her as well.

•   •   •   •   •

Sunday, March 5th 2045 · 1022 hours

"Daddy!" she exclaimed, and I ran to her. My little girl was here. Janine threw her arms around me, but I realized something was in the way. I looked down.

I couldn't find the words. My jaw dropped as I met her eyes again. "Yes?" I asked with joy.

She nodded amidst tears, and then hugged me. Her bump was tangible as I felt it. I hugged her tight. Andi squealed for joy and started to cry as she embraced our daughter. Janine giggled and nodded, somberly, switching to Andi to be swallowed up in her embrace.

My wife kissed her hair and cried. Caught in a tempest of joy and fear, they both trembled with expectation of not one, but now *two* arrivals: both life-altering: one welcomed and one dreaded.

I turned to Liam, standing proudly beside her. He saluted me right away and stood to attention. I turned to him and embraced him. "At ease, First Son-in-law," I said. I saluted back and rubbed his shaven head. "This is a different look for you," I said in surprise. He still sported a pink scar along his forehead that he had acquired during the war.

"Well, I'm formally in the service now, sir. *Want the drill sergeant sane? Give up the mane.* That was the rule."

"A good rule." I laughed heartily. "Welcome, *Corporal* Foxy, you previous member of the mop-top club."

"Thank you, sir," he laughed, as I hugged him.

"Congrats on the promotion, kid." I play-punched him in the chin, and then looked at Janine, whose face was being cradled by Andi as they smiled and talked. My eyes went back to Liam. He was beaming. "Congratulations on the new addition, too. You guys didn't waste any time!"

"Well, ya know, there's that incentive check and all."

"Yes, I'm sure that's the reason."

"Seriously, not at all, sir. We wanted it to be a surprise, sir…she's only sixteen weeks along, but obviously we're in a place where none of us need any more surprises thrust upon us. Right?"

"I appreciate that. And stop calling me sir or I'll make you name your baby Vance."

He laughed. "Thank you, sir. I mean Vance, sir. I'm here to serve, and you can count on me." He smiled a wicked smile. "Sir." Liam had grown up since we had seen them last year. He was now twenty-two. I still remembered the scrawny kid with the bushy blonde locks and the baseball caps, playing talisman to Captain Cameron Shipley. I was proud to have him as my son-in-law.

This was a moment of levity and heart warmth that we all needed, especially right now. "Come on, you two. I have *so* missed you. Come here, baby girl."

Janine melted under my right arm as I held her close with Andi beside her. I wrapped my arm around Liam's shoulders to my left.

My family was here, and they were safe. That was a good start amidst the threat of a bad end.

•　　•　　•　　•　　•

Sunday, March 5th 2045 · 1235 hours

The craft was getting closer, and there was no stopping it. We were all readying. From what I was told, there was very little opposition to martial law or the Blockade mandate. International leaders proceeded along similar protocols, preparing their own countries.

Miguel was running to and fro, taking and making back-to-back phone calls, while I remained in the Situation Room with Bayless, Capra and Roe.

A security detail was dispatched to bring Jean Graham here under lock and key. She would be here shortly, after gathering whatever necessities she felt she couldn't live without, including, no doubt, her cigarettes. It was then that I remembered the cipher key.

"Mr. Capra?"

"Yes, Mr. President?"

"Anything on the decryption of Graham's drive yet?"

He shook his head. "I'm sorry, sir, but in light of everything that has happened with the approaching craft, that's taken a back burner."

"It's fine," I said, dismissing it with a wave of my hand. "She'll be here soon anyway, and it might benefit us to let her know what's transpired. I think we'll find her more cooperative when she knows we have guests coming for dinner."

"Horrible analogy, sir, if I'm being honest."

He was right, actually. I didn't think about that phrase carefully enough. "Yes, forgive me."

"Do you really think she'll cooperate, sir?"

"Well, Peter, I don't know. I hope to God she will. I saw her just yesterday, and for an instant there, I thought I actually saw some heart. A sort of," I paused, "I don't know, a willingness to be vulnerable for a moment, sensing something big was happening. We left shortly after that."

Capra nodded and turned back to his notes. "Speaking of, I've got to make a few calls to our friends in the East. Word travels fast despite limited communication, and once they know that we're essentially harboring what they're still referring to as an international fugitive from justice, there are going to be angry questions."

"You got this, Mister. Good luck," I encouraged him, and he returned to his office.

"Madame Vice President, do you have an update on the Blockades?" I asked my VP.

Veronica brightened up. "Yes, Mr. President, it's all good news so far. All of them have received the directives and are making final preparations to receive incoming residents. Some of the Blockades have already begun their intake of tenants."

"Have you heard anything from Clarksville? How about Alpharetta?"

She smiled. "Alpharetta is my hometown, sir. They're doing just fine. Good man in charge there, Captain St. James. He's brought it up to snuff. For Clarksville, well, he had retired, but he's back in business. Captain Maurice Stone. I believe you knew him well?"

"I did, indeed. A very good man. What about enlistment?"

"Yessir, record turnout. People are pissed, to put it mildly. A second invasion never crossed their minds. Your address galvanized support, and residents are exchanging driver's licenses for dog tags in high numbers, sir. Gunners are in good supply at each Blockade, we have medical staff and plenty of infantry. All five-hundred seventy of the Blockades around the world are in operation. All two-hundred forty-one in the states are reporting near-full readiness. They'll take in as many as they can reasonably house and then close the Launch doors well before we send our birds up."

"Mm-hmm, and what about the ones in DC?" I asked.

"All at maximum readiness, sir." She flipped to a few pages in her cluster of notes. "DN002 in The Ellipse of President's Park is all stocked, reinforced, capacity three-hundred, ready to go. DN005 on the Capitol Building lawn can house one-hundred-seventy-five including military personnel, fully stocked. And DN004 by East Potomac Park is seeing a slow but steady influx. We've got ferries coming up the Potomac bringing people up from Ronald Reagan Airport to alleviate the traffic congestion over the 14th Street and Williams Memorial bridges as well as the Yellow Line and Long bridges, so that's helping. 004 is the biggie, and it can house four-hundred fifty. Then there's us, DN001, and all you see around here, sir. All units in the Defense Network of Blockades are reporting in with citizens inbound and filling up."

"Good. Mr. Roe?" The Homeland Security Secretary was texting a message and then stopped, looking at me over the rim of his glasses. Reminded me of Rosie for a moment.

"Yes, Mr. President."

"National Guard in place, as many as we could rouse, curfews, martial law, all of that going okay? How widespread was the address? Enough coverage?"

"I think so, sir, I do. We were sparing of the details regarding the nuclear option, as that would have really sent people flying off the rails, I think. Gorgons *and* nukes would be too much to bear. They already suspect we're going to exercise a nuclear option, but I think you were very wise to spare them the enormity of the details concerning what we're about to attempt. All municipalities are reporting that there were large gatherings in town halls and public spaces such as they could rig up with short notice for the address. The fortunate thing is that since most cellular networks are still down and large swaths of the country are still without internet access, power, or both, the town halls are how they've been getting their news anyway. We were using forums familiar to them. I'd say we reached ninety-two percent of the population, except for those who intentionally live off the grid."

"Ninety-two. Good Lord," I muttered. "That's just not enough. It is what it is." I rubbed my eyes and yawned, sticking knuckles into both eyes. Despite running on minimal sleep, I knew I had to ask the next question. "Best estimate for casualties?"

Roe looked back down at his phone. "That's just what I was talking with regional commanders about. Vice President Bayless and SecDef Capra are on the same thread. Considering all the manpower we're going to need, and the necessity of aerial engagement, internationally the figures predict another two percent of the population gone if their force is anywhere near as savage as it was before."

Two percent. Making it eighty-*seven* percent of humanity killed off by these savages, over nineteen years. They had initially killed off eighty-five percent of us, but apparently that wasn't satisfactory enough for them.

"*Eighty…seven…percent,*" I muttered, slowly enunciating the foreboding words as I let them settle into my conscience. I shook my head and sighed, rubbing my eyes again. "Capra, what's the latest on the craft?"

"Parabolic course still, should be to Saturn by Wednesday," Peter replied. "From there, it's a slight course alteration and we'll be swinging around the sun, dead ahead. Still pinging."

Still pinging. Whoever was in that ship was calling for their precious queen, and there would be no answer.

Miguel suddenly opened the door. His eyebrows were up. "Mr. President, we have a visitor." I read his expression, and I knew who he was talking about.

"Ladies and gentlemen, will you excuse me for a moment?" They nodded as I walked out with Miguel to the blast doors leading to the elevator. Janine and Liam were out in the main area talking with a few of the enlisted officers down here who Liam apparently knew.

The blast doors opened. The hallway behind them was dim, but I could make out a figure.

The individual walked in, unaccompanied, hat in hand and dressed in army fatigues from head to boot, gazing around in wonder. Miguel and I looked at each other.

Liam nearly exclaimed in recognition and moved toward the man with his mouth agape.

We all knew who it was. Miguel's and my 'special plan' had arrived.

In walked a man, twenty-six years old, with a stern face and a beard, but it was him. The same smoldering eyes, the same look of dedication about him, the same readiness.

Lieutenant Cameron Shipley had arrived.

Here he came, and there was no mistaking it.

4 | TOGETHER

Sunday, March 5th 2045 · 1303 hours

Here we all were again.

"Reporting for duty," said Lieutenant Cameron 'Jet' Shipley.

His new little brother, Corporal Liam 'Foxy' Mayfield, strode up to him and gave him a high shake. "Jet! Good to see you, man!" he exclaimed, laughing.

"Who are you, and what have you done with Corporal Foxy?" he asked him, rubbing his now shaven head.

"Yeah, yeah, yeah," Foxy replied, laughing. "How are Christine and the kiddo?"

"Fine. They're safe now," Jet replied. "Wyatt's almost one," he smiled. "They're heading to DN436. Home sweet home," he laughed, and looked Foxy up and down. "Been a while. Good to see you too, little bro." Foxy didn't reply; he just smiled heartily at Jet. And then, the two of them snickered, remembering all they had been through together. The male size-up crumbled as they embraced. Jet pulled away, seeing Janine over Foxy's shoulder. "Is this Neener? And…?" He looked at her bump, and then back up at Foxy.

Foxy nodded. "Yep. You can't have those procreation stimulus payments all to yourself, you know."

"Oh, man! Congrats, Janine! Congrats, Foxy!"

"Thank you, Cameron!" Janine exclaimed, and Andi hugged her.

Miguel had suddenly been pulled away by a phone call. But just then he returned, his phone pressed to his ear. His mouth dropped, and he exclaimed, "Oh, my goodness, I've got to call you back." He snapped his phone closed. "Sergeant Lieutenant Captain Lieutenant Sergeant Lieutenant Shipley," he breathed out slowly, enunciating each rank, remembering Jet's promotions and subsequent demotions through the war. Jet laughed. "It's *so* good to see you, mi amigo!" Miguel strode over to him and embraced him, pulling away and taking him by the shoulders. "You're lookin' good, my friend. Everything ok back home?"

"We're fine, Miguel. Good to see you too, Mr. Chief of Staff," he replied somberly, and then clenched his lips. "I'm so sorry about Rosie. My sincerest condolences, brother."

"I appreciate it. She lived a full life. Got a few truth bombs in while she did, right?" He winked at Jet.

Jet laughed through his breath. "She sure did. I'll always carry those with me. How you holdin' up, old man?"

"Good, very good. Still young enough to kick your butt though, especially if you don't shave this cat off your face." He scratched Jet's beard. The look in Jet's eyes showed that he recognized the truth in those words: Miguel still had a hulking physique from all those years of weightlifting.

And then he looked at me. "Wish we could be here under different circumstances, Mr. President."

I nodded. "I do as well. But they're not different, so let's get started, folks. There's obviously a lot going on. I'm gonna give you guys a few minutes to catch up, find your rooms and settle in. Corporal Radloff here will show you all to your quarters. Meet me in the Situation Room at 1415 hours. We've got some important calls to make."

"Captain Camjet is here to serve once more," Jet said to me, winking.

That brought a smile to my face. "If my math checks out, you were demoted twicely and promoted thricely, Lieutenant. We'll see if my math holds and you get restored to Captain this go-round."

•   •   •   •   •

Sunday, March 5th 2045 · 1415 hours

Our team strode into the Situation Room. Joining me were Miguel, VP Bayless, SecDef Peter Capra, HS Secretary

Roe, Jet, and Foxy. Janine was off with Andi catching up on baby stuff.

"OK, everyone, here are your briefs. Shipley, Mayfield, you guys are new, so these should bring you up to speed beyond what I told you on the phone. Shipley and Mayfield here will coordinate ground assault in the DC Metro area. We'll want to protect the White House and everything else. Lotta history, heritage and legacy here. America can't afford to have us weakened yet again, and we won't have our nation's capital brought to its knees, and its leaders driven out like rabble. Not again. The American people will want to know that we're on top of things."

I looked at Jet, Foxy, and Miguel seated side by side, and a smile crept across my face, brought on by old memories. If these three performed as admirably now as they had in the war of 2042, our world would be just fine. We were lucky to have them.

"Here are our roles. I'll be in the bunker with Bayless and Capra. Miguel is coordinating the air defenses from the cockpit. I bet it'll be good to be back in the saddle again, eh amigo?"

"Yes *sir*," he growled. "Put me in front of forty-three thousands pounds of thrust and I'll be a *niño* again."

"Alright. Shipley and Mayfield, you'll work in tandem with Miguel to coordinate echoing firepower from down here. Gonna be a shooting match at first. But if these are gorgs, and they do get through, you're gonna have to scramble and coordinate tactical for the men on the ground. You both have plenty of close-quarters combat experience. CQC leadership is what we need. Everyone will be issued masks, but there's just no guarantee. Gorgons are smart, strong, and adaptive. They proved that the first time, and there's no reason to suspect that their abilities are any different than the ones before. It's gonna be short-duration, high-intensity confrontations between combatants at close range, just like you guys are used to."

Foxy looked at Jet and raised his eyebrows. Jet put out a fist, and Foxy fist-bumped him.

"General Everett Carson is commanding ground forces. Shipley, you'll report to him. He's scheduled to get here late tonight, flying back here from home in Baton Rouge. We've got twenty-thousand troops coming in to protect the Capitol, and they're going to post up in the city at strategic locations. We'll see him tomorrow morning."

"I've heard of him. His reputation precedes him," Jet exclaimed. "They say he defended DC singlehandedly."

"Something like that. Shipley, we're gonna need snipers. All of them need to stay hidden and form a perimeter. There's a CQC slash sniper team that's heading in. Be here tonight. You'll work directly with them. Corporal Mayfield, you'll report to Lieutenant Shipley, as long as you're okay with that."

"There was a time where he was below me in rank, sir," said Foxy, "and I gotta say I enjoyed those five precious minutes. But I'll deal with it," he jabbed, looking sidelong at Jet. Jet chuckled.

"Good. Fall in with each other. Once you've got your plan together, I wanna hear it. You'll present it to General Carson tomorrow. As far as I'm concerned, having worked with the two of you, formalities aside, you're equals. All three of you," I said, motioning to Monzon. "Proud to have all of you guys here. Please be careful. Especially those of you who happen to be the father of my first grandchild."

They nodded, and Foxy smiled proudly.

"I've got an appointment for a group call with the Secretary-General, NORAD and the NATO commanders around 1500. But before that," -here I looked them over in turn- "I have some other news. The last time you fellas fought together, we were fighting two enemies. Well, both of them happen to now be inbound."

Jet tilted his head in confusion.

"Jean Graham is on her way here."

There was almost a palpable sound of air movement as their jaws opened simultaneously. Miguel just laughed, of course, as he had been in the know.

"J-Jean…Graham…?" Jet blurted out.

"The one and only."

"She's coming here for federal protection?"

I nodded. "And maybe more. She was president for four terms, kid. She's got intel that might help, sure, but that's not primarily why she's coming. She deserves the same protection that any other previous president would have. She was on house arrest up there, and she'll be on a tight leash down here. Don't worry. There's some information we've been trying to get from her, and having her close under a watchful eye will help."

Jet rolled his eyes and sighed. "Wow. Yessir."

"None of us like it, that's for certain," Miguel cut in. "But she may be able to help, and we've got to see how. If those are *gorgos* on their way here, we need as much help as we can get."

"Yeah but sir," Jet spoke up, "she was never on our side. She was only ever in it for herself. That much was always clear. How can she possibly help or unite any of us in this? She's a lightning rod of hate, and she'd throw any of us at a gorg if it meant she could get away. We all know that beyond a shadow of a doubt."

"That may be. Time will tell. Until such time as she tries – and even if she doesn't – we'll keep her in solitary down here. Got it?"

Jet and Foxy looked at each other. "Yessir."

"Good. Now, let's get to it."

•   •   •   •   •

Sunday, March 5th 2045 · 1627 hours

The joint call took longer than expected. Nations were reporting their states of readiness to the Secretary-General, and Leone expressed that some of them were loath to 'fall in' behind the military leadership of the United States, given our sullied reputation under Graham. They had incurred heavy losses in their own defenses. In particular, the DTF barges that Graham had erected in the nations of Iran, China and North Korea had become a blight on their geography. The cleanup persisted to this day, and it was hard, disgusting work. She had had those barges and jetties built, they said, without their approval. She had deceived all the rest of us, all while maintaining that she had the full support of every involved nation.

There was also infighting. The DTF barges were technically the property of the United States military, but, when the celebrations subsided, and each nation turned inward to begin the rebuilding process, mercenaries and illicit capitalists swooped in, seizing the equipment and selling off pieces of it at exorbitant prices. And then, to add insult to injury, the countries in question all claimed eminent domain, asserting that what was on their land now belonged to them.

However, Graham had prepared for that, and all units were designed to work wirelessly together, as a cohesive unit. They couldn't be split up and farmed out to buyers all over the world, as they would be outside of signal range. That was why she had the physical detonators onsite at each location, each unit tied into the next: they were useless as self-contained units. They were designed to work together.

As a result, angry buyers now had useless equipment eating up inventory space. Negotiators and brokers were attacked and beaten, some of them killed. Thankfully, all of it was eventually returned and refunded. Even mercenaries understood how valuable this equipment was in destroying the gorgons, and how valuable it would be again. They were compelled to act honorably in at least this.

"I sympathize with them," I had said, but I was forced to consult with the Secretary of State for diplomatic arrangements to be made, and I had a gut feeling that I would be forced to make certain concessions to allow the countries in question to either buy them from us, or, if that failed, to simply keep them.

The cumulative cost of washing America's hands of the kill zone equipment would result in a net loss of ninety-one billion dollars. In a frail economy that had only just begun rebuilding, we needed that capital.

However, simply relinquishing it to them *would* result in goodwill. It would just take some training on how to use them. I had a feeling that we would find those answers on Graham's drive.

In the end, I had to stall the Secretary-General, informing him, simply, "I will have an answer soon."

·　　·　　·　　·　　·

It was nearing dinnertime when Graham herself was led in. All eyes were on her. Every bit of motion came to a stop, and the room fell to a palpable hush as her heels clicked along the floor.

Jean Graham was still tall, dwarfing the guards who led her inside in shackles. I met her at the entrance to the bunker at the base of the elevator, arms folded across my chest. A trace of a smirk was on her lips as the doors opened. Upon seeing me, though, all that bravado dissipated, replaced by cold regard. All she had been told was that she needed to be relocated for the time being, under guard, with us down here. The click of her heels on the stone floor reverberated throughout the bunker as all eyes followed her to her guarded quarters.

I turned around and looked back at Miguel. He took a deep breath and shook his head. That's exactly what I felt like doing. However, the truth stared me in the face.

Jean Graham is not the enemy.

Once she was, perhaps. But now, along with everyone else, the former president would have to surrender her pride, and work with all of us to survive.

Whatever her role might yet be in this, I couldn't foresee. But she had one, nonetheless.

We would all have to work together to survive.

Here we all go again.

5 | PREPARATIONS

Sunday, March 5th 2045 · 1901 hours

It was not good news, any of it.

The craft had either sped up, or was slung toward us by gravitational forces, deliberately traveling further out in the elliptical orbit. If it had traveled around a supernova, it could have been accelerated. Romero didn't know. All I knew was that, suddenly, its ETA was now updated to early Friday morning. As if some urgency had seized it, the alien vessel had accelerated, and it was now punching across the stars at an inexplicable clip.

On top of that, down here there had been looting and minor rioting in a few of the metropolitan cities. The sentiment was the same everywhere: people were loath to return to life in the Blockades, no matter how much they had been souped up, no matter the protection it would afford them, no matter the edict. This was an inconvenience of epic proportions for them. Mostly, it was the rich who had returned to a life of quasi-luxury, reclaiming their mansions and land, and they were not willing to relinquish that for a life of 'subterranean bondage,' as they called it.

I almost didn't blame them. We had it good here.

The uprisings were small and short-lived, but a few people had to be taken into custody and forcibly transferred to the Blockades at gunpoint, and two people were even shot: not at all what I or anyone else in authority had wanted.

The only sliver of potentially good news was when the IT department reported that they *might* have found something on Graham's drive. I headed that way to see what it was.

*   *   *   *   *

Sunday, March 5th 2045 · 1906 hours

"I don't know, sir," said Jens. "There are all kinds of scattered files on here, but you'd need to have her sit here and explain it to us. It's kind of Greek to me. There are thousands of these little files, and we'd need to analyze each one, or come up with some kind of decryption program in a hurry in order to hopefully make sense of it in time. There's the one main file that is an index of agendas and directives she's given, most of which the world already knows. And we already know about all her associates."

Her Illuminati. Those national leaders who were in league with her, willing to take out China, North Korea and Iran. They had already been tried and either executed, or were on their own form of house arrest.

"No, Jens, she's a crafty woman. She had a cipher for the drive; she's certainly got a cipher for the contents as well. I'm not surprised she gave us only a portion of what we needed. Keep looking."

"Aye sir," he replied.

Time for another little chat with Jean Graham, but first, I'd need to get a sit rep from everyone else on the status of preparations. All the while, I felt the pressure of the Secretary-General who was waiting for my response regarding the kill zone equipment. The Treasury Secretary would have a thing or two to say about that.

•　　•　　•　　•　　•

Sunday, March 5th 2045 · 1910 hours

Treasury Secretary Barrett Roth didn't just have a thing or two to say. His complaints numbered in the dozens.

"Absolutely no way, Mr. President. I do not endorse taking this hit. It would be an unprecedented and fiscally irresponsible move in this dangerous economy. We've only just begun to start climbing out of the trillion-dollar repair hole those monsters left for us!" He was shouting.

"I understand, Barrett," I said to him, one hand on my hip, the other trying to calm him. Thankfully, we were in a closed off conference room with just Roth, myself, and

Bayless. "I didn't say this would be an easy decision. However, the three countries in question are playing hardball with us right now. They're the *only* ones in a standoff. They have the equipment, but they won't put it together OR let it be operated unless we make some sort of concession. We *need* their cooperation if we're going to fight off a second wave of these things."

"Yes, Mr. President, I understand that of course, but washing our hands of ninety-one billion dollars just so they will point their guns at the sky with the rest of us? Screw 'em! Let 'em be invaded while we're safe over here. Why should we take the hit?"

"Oh, come on, Barrett, that's enough of that," I fired back. "That can't honestly be how you feel. This kind of stuff eventually evens out in the end. *Another* end, however, might be coming for us this Friday, and we have a decision to make right now to ensure the survival of Planet Earth, not just America. It's that kind of thinking that made our counterstrike take far longer than it should have."

Roth rolled his eyes and sighed heavily, leaning forward with his head in his hands. "Mr. President," he said, shooting back up, "with all due respect, sir, this is asinine. Surely, they can come up with *some* purchase price and meet us halfway. The fact that it's on their soil doesn't mean they own it. It's got *Made in the USA* stamped all over it, for crying out loud! It's ours!"

"Yes, of course it's ours, but you're leaving out a huge diplomatic piece here. We're *going* to take a loss on this, Barrett, that's the only way that they'll play ball with us against the gorgs."

Bayless spoke up. "The President is right, Mr. Roth."

"Oh, Veronica agrees with the President! This is new!" he complained sarcastically.

"Mr. Roth!" I raised my voice. "You'll address Ms. Bayless as Madame Vice President, is that clear?"

Roth rolled his eyes. "Fine. I'm sorry, Mr. President. My apologies, Madame Vice President."

"Listen to me," Bayless pleaded. "I know this doesn't make fiscal sense – it doesn't make sense to me either! We need *every…single…nation* to rise to the defense of our planet, Mr. Roth. Surely you see that a compromise is in everyone's best interests."

"A compromise, yes," Roth shot back. "A gouging, no!"

Bayless threw her arms up. "I give up," she said. "Your turn, Mr. President."

Barrett Roth crossed his arms in a huff.

I looked at him under my eyebrows. His complaint wasn't devoid of merit. Surely, taking a ninety-one-billion-dollar bath was out of the question. However, there had to be a middle ground.

"Barrett, I understand your position. This looks terrible on the bottom line, and we need all the capital we can get to climb out of this hole. I hear you on that. Talk with Curtiss and see where we can go from here. I'm sure we can reach a deal with the countries in question. We'll need their firepower, and they'll need ours. They must respect the fact that we provided that equipment in the first place. We should have the tools to enable them to use it for their defense – for *all* our defense – with the stipulation that we get it back afterward *or* we'll agree on a reasonable and fair sale price."

Barrett looked at me hard and long, and, finally uncrossed his arms. "Fine."

"Thank you. I'll leave you to it," I said, looking at Bayless. She shrugged her shoulders. "Thank you, Mr. Roth. Please keep me posted."

"Will do. Thank you, Mr. President," he said glumly, and got up and left, apparently as exhausted with us as we were with him.

I glanced sidelong over at Bayless. She shook her head. "You wanna create a schism and prevent people from working together? Best way to do that is with a fight over money," I said.

She shook her head again and flicked her eyebrows up. She knew I was right.

•　　•　　•　　•　　•

Sunday, March 5th 2045 · 1938 hours

The sniper team had arrived.

"Welcome, folks. Delta Six?"

Their leader nodded and saluted me. "Nice to meet you, Mr. President. Thank you for trusting us."

"My pleasure," I answered. "This is Lieutenant Cameron 'Jet' Shipley, he'll be overseeing the ground forces around DC. And that is Corporal Liam Mayfield, my son-in-law. You can call him 'Foxy.' I'm sure you've heard of them."

"Yes *sir*," the lead sniper replied. "Whoa – what an honor. Meaning no disrespect to you, Mr. President," he said, looking back at me. I waved him away and wasn't offended at all. These guys had a boots on the ground kinship. I was a behind-the-scenes mover-and-shaker who hadn't really fired a gun in the December 2042 war. No worries there. "We've heard all about you guys. Aren't you the two that were in the F-15 Eagles at the funnel over the Atlantic?"

"The very ones," Jet said. "Under the qualified leadership of our trusty Latino boss, Chief of Staff Monzon here," he said, gesturing to Miguel.

"No *way*," said the sniper. "I'm Nate Pease. You're Monzon, who flew the XA103? You took down that queen, right, sir?"

"I sure did," said Miguel proudly. "But we all did it together. These two guys dropped the-"

"The Venom-10s, I know, I know!" Pease exclaimed. "*Whoa.* I'm practically rubbing shoulders with royalty. You guys have no idea how many times you've come up in our conversations," he said, laughing. The others behind him jostled in starstruck wonder, looking Monzon, Shipley and Mayfield up and down. "Wow, man. Just…wow," he said, beaming at the three of them.

My guys looked back gratefully, appreciating this modicum of hero worship.

"Yeah, well, just remember, I was the one that got in the final shot that took down the funnel, so…ya know," Foxy put in. He looked around self-approvingly, gawking.

"That's worth something!" Pease said. "Sweet. This is my team," -here he whirled around and introduced his six-member team, left to right- "Reynolds, Mitchell, Lefebvre, Grant, and Toole. Our guns are yours."

Jet nodded.

"Pleased to have you all. Lieutenant Shipley, the situation room is yours," I said to Jet, and motioned all of them that way. "Take all the time you need."

We started walking that way.

"I'll be in my office," I said. "Monzon and I will be getting an update on the craft: ETA, trajectory, point of orbit, all that. I know it's late. Just let any staffer know if you need anything to eat or drink. Your families all accounted for and safe?"

"Yessir," said Pease.

"Alright then. Get to it. I'll check back in at 2030 hours."

•　　•　　•　　•　　•

Sunday, March 5th 2045 · 1942 hours

"Neither trajectory nor velocity has changed," said my contact at SETI. We had Greene patched in via teleconference with Mike Romero, who was assigned to follow updates on the craft. Mike was a bit of a surfer holdout, and sometimes struck me as a bit too casual for his paygrade, but he was nonetheless a great tech. "Course heading remains on the flip side of the orbits, ETA Friday morning 8am-ish," said Greene.

"Unless it presses its turbo boost," Romero joked.

"What's the best guess on orbit position?" I asked.

"Hard to tell now, sir," said Greene. "I mean, considering the Earth's rotation and orbit five days from now, it could be somewhere over south America, or over

Greenland. But it's possible they'll alter course to rendezvous with the exact coordinates of the previous craft's location."

Romero nodded in agreement. "Those were my thoughts, sir. They might try to just hit the same spot again. Kinda like a dog wants to piss on other dog's piss spots."

"Okay. Crude, but okay," I said.

"You know what I think, Greene?" Romero asked. "See, look here, you can see the parabola. These projections should see them lining up with us somewhere around Mexico. Still, catching any kind of gravitational flux or solar winds could speed up their intersection with our rotation slightly, and the angle might be on the antipodes."

"The what?" I asked.

"The flip side."

"Got it. So, the point is, basically, we don't know where exactly they'll hit us, and we'll need to dispatch teams to the correct areas."

"Bingo," Romero said.

I looked at the screen and the projections displayed upon it. "What happens when they enter our atmosphere? Last time they sent in the gorgs in clusters, smaller, able to enter slowly and without burning up. They didn't bring their craft down, evidently, until we were all in hiding or being killed off, once their drones were all activated. But if they try to bring that big mother down through the mesosphere, lower this time, what happens then?"

Greene shook his head and exhaled. "Big problems. I mean, unless it's specifically constructed to be atmospheric-capable, it's going to have its own problems, so I don't think they'd try. If they did, they'd have to make some kind of creepingly slow entry under thruster power the whole way down, which would take hours to descend. Displacement of air is a huge problem."

"Right, I get that, but what about effects on the Earth? What about down here?" I posited. Greene could definitely err on the geeky side and was fairly verbose.

"Oh! Got it," Greene said. "All that air needs to go somewhere, and that could create hurricane-force winds and devastation tens of kilometers around the landing area, sending tidal waves and swells for miles out. And higher speed in the lower atmosphere will make the devastation exponentially greater. This is if they even try it. Why do you ask?"

"Well," I answered. "They surprised us before, sneaking around from behind our own moon. If they aren't getting the answers they need from the previous craft, they may suspect something and just decide to go balls-to-the-wall down to us. They didn't care about us before; there's no reason to think they care about us now. And all of that speed and wind rushing outward is going to create problems for our birds in the air."

"You think they're that smart, sir?" Romero asked.

"I don't know, Romero. They were smart enough to find our planet, devise a craft to steal our water, fan out all over the planet and wait there for ninety days until our suspicion slept, and then spring their attack. And our guys on the ground – Shipley and Monzon here – saw them exhibit plenty of intelligence on the way to Mammoth Cave in the war. From their reports of the behemoth gorgons, as well as the attack structure by the mass of gorgs that hit them, they were exhibiting intelligence far and away beyond anything we had seen in the previous fifteen years.

"All of that to say nothing of the gorg queen herself, and that birthing chamber below the surface of the ocean that she had. Oh yeah, they're smart. How smart? I don't know. But smart enough to kill off five-sixths of us."

I stared at his screen for a moment, considering their plan of attack. "Relay this to NORAD please, as soon as you can, guys."

"I have, sir. They're already patched in on the same info stream. Updated every five minutes at least, barring a manual refresh," Greene said.

"Okay, good. Thanks, Romero. Thanks, Greene. I'll leave you to it."

Miguel and I walked out.

"Miguel," I said to him, "I have a problem. I want you to keep tabs on Roth, if you can. I know you're up to your eyeballs with everything else, but we're going to have to make some kind of deal with the three countries Graham targeted. I'll need to pay her a little visit here soon as well."

"What do you think we'll need to do?" Miguel asked.

"Well, we're going to have to figure out what's going to pacify them. All that equipment sitting over there useless does our planet zero good if they're just going to stall and browbeat us."

"Understood, sir. *No problemo,*" he replied.

I nodded to him. "Time to have another chat with Jean Graham. Care to tag along before you spy on Roth?"

He nodded.

"No Spanish profanity, you got it?"

"No promises, señor," he quickly replied.

I smiled.

•   •   •   •   •

Sunday, March 5th 2045 · 1947 hours

Jean Graham had comfortable quarters, and she had already lit up another smoke. She eyed me carefully as I walked in, offering me one.

"No thanks," I said. "Gave it up last year. Just doesn't taste the same as clean air."

She smirked. "I understand. And yet here we are, underground again, with manufactured air."

I wasn't about to BS with her. "Graham, please sit. We need to have a conversation, you and I." Her eyebrows went up, and she studied me for a moment, then slowly sat on her couch. "I assume you know my Chief of Staff, Miguel Monzon," I said, motioning toward him.

She didn't say anything, just looked sidelong at Miguel and blew smoke his way. Long had he served right under her nose, feeding me intel. Long had he tolerated her while I revealed the dangerous truth to him about her, insisting that he remain on the inside at his post, though he desperately wanted to leave and be with Rosie. There was certainly no love lost between them.

Miguel said nothing as she sat down.

"Alright, Jean. Here's the truth. An alien craft is on its way here, likely from the TRAPPIST-1 system, forty light-years away. It's set to hit Earth Friday morning. We're anticipating a second wave of gorgons." I didn't see the point of stalling, much less mincing words.

Graham's face was a study of emotions. While plotting her own nefarious course, she certainly equipped the planet with tools and stratagems that eventually rid us of them. Consequently, there was anger there. Frustrated anger boiling over under the surface, masked by a cold, calculating apathy, trying to play it cool before us.

"*Tragic,*" she said cooly, taking a drag on her smoke. The smell of it was tempting. I should have instructed the guards to forbid it. "You're certain of this?"

"NORAD is tracking it, SETI, the DSN, the ICA, the WMO, International Cloud Atlas, everybody. Parabolic course, inbound from the TRAPPIST-1 system. Same make and model as the previous one. Sending out regular pings like a phone call to the previous ship we blew. No answer of course. They will be understandably pissed, if they're not already. So, NATO member states, the Secretary-General, all of them, are aware, and we're preparing with a global defense plan."

She blinked, taking it all in. She didn't seem to be breathing, and those eyes were smoldering behind that wrinkled face.

At last, she snuffed out her cigarette and leaned forward, her elbows on her knees, hands clasped. "I'm amazed," she said. "Incredulous might be more apt. I never believed they were truly all gone. They had to have come from somewhere," she sneered, shrugging her shoulders.

"We need your help, Jean."

"The cipher didn't work?" she asked in a gravelly voice, and then coughed amidst her smoke.

"No, it worked. But you have some kind of firewall still in place, and a bunch of files that they're combing through. It would help if you could just lay out for us anything that you have on those drives that would aid us in our defense."

A look of blank confusion rolled down her face. "I don't have anything on there other than what was going on at the three strike zones. 'Operation Shake N Bake,' remember? That was it."

"There's nothing else?"

"No. What do you *think* is on there?"

"Jean, let's not play games. All of those systems work in conjunction with each other. All of the DTF bombs were controlled by detonators, and they're linked together. You know as well as I do that they're programmed as a unit. So, it's pretty clear that we need to control the unit. Each unit, in fact."

Now, understanding enveloped her face. She had figured it out. "Ah, so the other nations are not cooperating with you. Aren't they? Now I get it. They want the equipment for themselves, especially since it's already over there and I already tried to use it against them. Who's going to be footing that bill, I wonder?"

"Maybe the US, if we can't provide some sort of collateral. It would be a fiscally catastrophic loss. I think you know that."

"Mm, yes, I do. Somewhere just shy of one hundred billion dollars, if memory serves. We had a lot invested in those units."

"Well, *you* did. *We* do now."

"Who is putting up the most opposition?"

"Who else? North Korea, as usual. Kim Jong Un is gone, but your friend, their new Supreme Leader is still there. And he's got the allegiance of the SPA. That's hundreds of members in a single chamber. A lot of voices to appeal to, Jean, most of whom don't want any kind of deal made. 'It's on our turf,' they say, 'therefore we own it.'

Diplomacy has reached an impasse, and they want us to buy it back from them. They all do. Secretary of State Curtiss hasn't been able to make any further inroads."

"Iran and China are at an impasse as well?"

"Yes, but the consensus is that the other two are going to dovetail with whatever North Korea says. They formed a bit of a hivemind in the wake of your little operation, and they all feel a little recompense would go a long way, especially in light of these new revelations about the second wave of gorgs heading our way. Aerial and ground forces will only go so far." I could feel Miguel shifting to my right, wanting to rise to the defense of the Air Force, but he stowed it. He knew what I meant. Nothing was going to compete with the power of these new DTB units.

"I see." I watched her. She was thinking. "Let me talk to them."

My eyes widened. "Out of the question, Jean. No way."

"Vance, see reason for a moment." She leaned toward me in an eerie sort of way, speaking slowly. Reminded me, frankly, of stories of the serpent in the Garden of Eden. "They want an apology. I've never given them one. That will only go so far, but it's a start, of course. Let me appeal to their better nature and see what they want from me. You know I'm right in this."

I had to admit, her suggestion had merit. Respect and decency were paramount in China. In North Korea, their people worshiped their leader as a god. And in Iran, a formal apology from the President of the United States? That was sure to appeal to their pride. I wondered.

"What would you even say that all of us haven't already tried?" I asked her.

"Exactly, Ms. Graham," Miguel piped up. "What makes you think you would fare any better than our own Secretary of State and our own diplomatic negotiations to date?"

A smile teased at Graham's lips. "I think you already know the answer to that, Mr. Monzon. You once called me a *silver tongue.* I doubt you remember it, but it was after my speech to the pilots in the attack of 2027, when we sent in the SR-72 from Patrick Space Force Base and those forty-one jets against the funnel."

"Is that so?"

"Yes. And I suppose it's true. I do have a silver tongue. I've needed to have one ever since I took office, to reassure the American people – and the world – that we would make it out of our crisis. And we did."

"It wasn't your silver tongue that got us out of that crisis, Ms. Graham, as much as you'd no doubt like to take credit for it. You used your silver tongue against me as well, luring me into your graces and acquiring information from me in my naïveté that almost cost hundreds of thousands of lives, possibly millions of lives. You didn't do *anything.* It was the heroics of people like my sweet Rosalita, and Lieutenant Shipley, and Corporal Mayfield, and President Cardona here! You're nothing but a lowlife bottom-dwelling treacherous bi-"

"Miguel!" I said, cutting him off. "That'll be all." I whirled back at Monzon, and his face was red.

I turned back to Graham. She was squinting her eyes at Monzon, grinning deviously. He did not look away from her. It was Graham who first broke the connection and retreated from his gaze, moving her eyes back to me. But her contempt for him was obvious. He was her mole, right under her nose, all along.

"Mr. President, I'll say it again," she breathed. "You know I'm right. They don't know you. They did know me, and they did have international dealings with me all throughout the invasion and subsequent attacks. They may not like me. Hell, they may want me dead. I'm fine with that." She heaved a big sigh. "Universal disapproval has a way of making one worry far less. My load is lessened. But I can appeal to them in ways that you cannot."

I stared at her. If anything, it was worth a shot, and we were running out of time.

I glanced up at Miguel. He didn't look at me. His eyes were still narrowed on Graham.

"I'll have to talk with the Secretary of State and Vice President Bayless first, of course. I'll let you know my answer in the morning."

She nodded, with a look that I couldn't decide was empathetic or sinister.

"Let's go, Chief."

I got up and walked out past Monzon. He stood his ground, hands behind his back, staring daggers at the former president. She looked at him over her nose, her head thrown back and tilted, trying to deflect his hatred.

It wasn't working.

"Mr. Monzon," I said. "Time to go."

Miguel relented this time, slowly, and turned to follow me. We walked out together, and once more, Jean Graham was alone. The door closed behind us.

"I hate that woman, Vance. I hate her with my life."

I nodded. "So do I, Miguel. I hear you. But we may just have to place our lives in her hands."

He shook his head. "The very notion is abominable."

"I hear you, my friend," I said. "I hear you."

Abominable. That's what all of this was. I felt like no one was getting anywhere. People were at my throats and at each other's. The Treasury Secretary would want a fair deal. The Secretary-General was expecting my answer. The Iranians would want placation. The Chinese would want a respectful apology. The North Koreans would want the humbling of a former president.

The gorgons would want all of us.

I was going to have to deliver some news to all of them, and I had one shrinking feeling coursing through me.

It would not be good news. Any of it.

6 | GUERILLAS

Sunday, March 5th 2045 · 2030 hours

Time for the commander to meet his soldiers.

Jet Shipley and Foxy Mayfield were in the situation room with their CQC and sniper leaders when Miguel and I walked in. Pease flinched and greeted me, almost in a PTSD response. "Whoa! Mr. President. Good to see you, sir." He saluted me.

I saluted back. "At ease. How's it coming, guys?"

"Good, very good, sir," Jet replied, rising and saluting. "Any new developments?"

"Well," I sighed, "not really. We have some diplomatic issues that need massaging, and they involve President Graham, but we're working on them."

"President Graham!" Lefebvre blurted out. "That woman, man. Boy if I sighted her in my scope, I wouldn't think twice about pulling the trigger. Ever. Why, if she were here, I'd-"

"You stow that, soldier," Miguel ordered. "You're talking about assassinating a former president."

Lefebvre stopped, gobsmacked, apparently unaware of the line of thought he was proceeding down, and probably surprised that we didn't sound off in unbridled support. He tried to fumble his way out of it. "Oh, Mr. Monzon…uh M-Mr. President, I wasn't- I-I mean I didn't mean to-"

"Stop. It's fine," I said, holding up my hand. "There'll be no talk of that kind around me. And the former President is down here in the bunker with us, soldier." His eyes went wide. "She's entitled to equal protections, same as any other human, and more because of the presidency."

"President Graham is down *here* with us?" he asked.

I narrowed my eyes and began to walk toward him. "Do you have a problem with that, soldier?"

He paused and said nothing, which basically said everything. "N-no, sir," he said, grimly, and his jaw clenched. I glanced down at his hands; they were balled into fists.

I stared at him. Pease moved toward him to my left. "Mr. President, sir, allow me to talk to Lefebvre here, sir."

I looked over toward him. "Thank you, Pease. Please assure your colleague that we have rules and decorum down here, same as we do on the surface, and no matter how much a human being is reviled, we're all we have left. It's time we all started working together, or we may find ourselves excused back up to the surface." I directed my last sentence to Lefebvre, and I could tell he acknowledged the threat.

Pease took Lefebvre aside into a corner of the situation room. Lefebvre had his hands on his hips while Pease gave him a quiet butt-chewing.

I looked over at Miguel. He flicked his eyebrows up and looked irritated. "There. Now that that's established," I said, "what do you guys got? Jet? Foxy?"

Jet pulled his eyes away from Pease and Lefebvre and acknowledged me. "Yessir," he began. "We're going over schematics of the DC Metro area. We've got various points of elevation we'll be able to hide out in. Of course, the gun towers over each of the three metropolitan DC Blockades are going to provide the second best deterrent next to the new DTBs we've heard of" -here he shook his head and widened his eyes- "– those sound heavy, sir, *whoa* – but we'll take up positions here, here, here, and here." He pointed to various points of elevation throughout DC Metro. "The Basilica, the Old Post Office Building, Washington Union Station, and the Capitol Building Itself. That's where we'll be, and we'll form a perimeter of four square miles, protecting the White House, Congress, Capitol Mall, Smithsonian, all of it. The last two we'll have at the southeast corner atop the Lincoln Memorial, and Healy Hall at Georgetown.

"That's the six snipers. Foxy and I'll be serving on the ground with Carson, wherever he wants us, but probably in the thick of things. We've got communications in line for all of us, and all the rifles have the new DTF bump stocks. When we root 'em out again they'll be hurting before they're even in our sights, sir."

"*Muy bien,*" said Miguel.

"Sounds like they won't stand a chance. Let's pray they never make it that far, boys," I said. "You'll be the guerillas on the ground of course. The goal – and Miguel here will be heading that up overhead, of course – is to never let them descend to lower altitude. The SPAAGs and the Vulcans will help with that as well, should they make it past the *Tsar Bombas*. Miguel will head up our aerial guerillas. How are you coming along with the aerial defense plan, Miguel?"

"Yes, Mr. President, it's coming along well so far. Commander Sinclair has all of our fighters – thirteen thousand in all – readied. All are equipped with heavy ordnance loads, tactical weapons and mobile DTF emitters. Pilot helmets all have the new reflective mask tech. On the note of the masks, Bayless has been overseeing that and all Blockades should have more than enough for each civilian and military occupant there, Mr. President. I'm sure she'll confirm that later. I think we're in good shape, sir."

I looked them all over. "Alright. We'll confirm everything with the General once he arrives, and then it's his game. We'll be running point on ops directly from in here, and we'll all have frequencies assigned. Should you meet any stragglers, you'll each carry a few extra masks to hand out and equip any who couldn't get to a Blockade. Take note, however: your mission is not recon-related. That may come later. Hopefully, it won't come to that. For now, it's strictly defense, and hopefully we'll win the day."

I paused, taking a deep breath. "If worse comes to worst, however, or should you find yourself cutoff, or lose your men, you get your butt to these three Blockades double-quick. Priority One is to ensure the survival of our species, and that comes from keeping yourself safe, not taking out the enemy. You all remember what happened when we fired at them before. You kill one, you draw three others to you.

Don't make that mistake. We've learned too much since '26 to make the same mistakes twice. So, don't. Keep your wits about you. Stay alive."

The room grew calm and quiet. Moment of truth. I leaned into them.

"It's guys like you that kept all of us alive all these years. We wouldn't have survived without soldiers performing all those recons scavenging for food, ammo, and supplies, and survivors. We owe you. There's a high probability that those creatures will get through. If they do, it's down to ground assault and close quarters combat. We have to be prepared. You are our most valuable assets out there, so I repeat: think smart. *Stay alive.* Copy?"

"Copy," they all echoed.

"Alright. Keep working. I've got to make some more calls and check in on the craft. Then we all need to get to sleep."

Tomorrow was coming.

Time for the soldiers to meet their General.

7 | CARSON

Monday, March 6th 2045 · 0600 hours

He marched in as if he had already been victorious.

General Everett Carson. The man was a legend unto himself. He had headed up a massive defense in the DC area in 2026, holding the gorgs at bay, and preventing invasion of the metro area for several weeks before the gorgons finally infiltrated the White House. Carson's direction enabled thousands of civilians and government personnel to flee. Many owed their lives to him. Then, like so many of us, he went dark.

That was in 2026. Running down through the years like a phantom pushback, Carson ran the three Blockades nearly singlehandedly, shuttling back and forth between

them as a ghost. He was reportedly always on the move.
When the directive was given by Graham to resume
tunneling, he fired up the Big Berthas and began burrowing
between them. Long tunnels still existed between the three
Blockades, allowing transit and passage of goods and
supplies. And, as for Carson, he settled down in DN005,
right there on the lawn in front of the Capitol Building,
commanding there all these years as many others had done at
their own Blockades. The previous President had been
airborne, landing at BNA, Nashville, of course. The
previous VP had been at the White House. After Trump &
Vance had been killed, she and Cooper took over from
Nashville, governing from afar. But the White House and
the Capitol Building grounds were never assaulted again, not
under the formidable presence of Carson. We owed him a
lot in protecting the heritage, the history, the memory of our
nation's capital.

It was a confidential and well-kept secret that we
used a Big Bertha drill to tunnel between DN001 under the
White House, and DN002 under the northwestern end of The
Ellipse of President's Park, across from the National
Christmas Tree. The tunnel from the Capitol Building to
DN002 was public knowledge, however. DN002 was a
straight shot south of the White House and allowed for
passage between it and the PEOC bunker, should there be
any further attacks. It was even further underground than the
bunker, if that were even possible. There was a smaller,
much more narrow passage between DN002 and DN005 at
the Capitol Building.

If the gorgs attacked one location, we would be able
to flee from the one to the other. Homeland Secretary
Stephan Roe and Secret Service worked in tandem to

maintain security between the two Blockades. But survivors, it was said, always felt safest here in DN001 under the White House. It was treated as the first Defense Network Blockade.

And now, here came the bastion of preservation, the commander of upkeep, the general in charge of history, prompt and punctual as ever, General Everett Forrest Carson. He had his M107A1 slung over his back. Apparently, he and that rifle never parted. The man slept with it, if he indeed slept. The thing had a reputation for being loud. If his bullets didn't pierce his gorgon targets, the sound of the M107A1 certainly did.

The PEOC was quiet and dark, with only a few staffers awake and at their posts. VP Bayless was already awake and off with Miguel, Roe, Roth and the others in a side conference room, reserving the Situation Room for myself and the General.

I had retired at 2330 hours after a flurry of calls, texts and reports last night, arising at 0430 hours this morning. I didn't want to waste any time; I had a big day ahead of me. I kissed Andi as she snored fitfully, mumbling something about babies in her sleep. Morning briefing aside, I checked in with my staffers and went to the gate to meet the General.

"Mr. President," he greeted me, gruffly. That gritty growl of his could make a cat think a quake was coming and run for cover. Reminded me of Staff Sergeant Joe Bassett from Alpharetta, just without the drawl.

"Thank you for inviting me here. Shame we have to deal with this crap again, sir." He saluted me, sticking his thick chest out with decorum and class. The man had a burly figure, layered and hardened by years of survival underground. His face was etched with stress and preoccupation for the survival of the human race. A gargantuan scar ran from just under his left ear to the top of his forehead, tracing the arc of his face. Many said it was directly from a brawl with a gorg, which he, of course, had bested. He was missing his left eye and donned an eye patch overall. Legend held that he was actually face-to-face with that gorg – maskless – and that the gorg simply couldn't get through his indomitable spirit. They say it managed to freeze his left eye, but that's all it got. As a result, the loss of his eye just made him that more focused as a monocular.

He was sixty-three now, so that would have happened when he was just forty-four, during the occupation. The man was an iron horse, but he was also highly intelligent: a palpable threat to the gorgons.

I was once that threat, too, while at Mammoth Cave. Rallying troops wherever I went, and presenting a formidable offense to those accursed beasts, living in grit from the bowels of a cave. Surviving. Now, I was a far cry from those days. The General was who the boots-on-the-ground troops looked up to.

"A shame, indeed, but people like yourself make it more bearable. Glad to have you here, General. We've got a team ready to go as your seconds-in-command."

"What's the status of the craft now, sir?"

"Not much change, but they'll be passing into Neptune's orbit soon, according to my briefing this morning. I'll get a fuller look at it after your meeting."

We reached the Situation Room, and there were Jet and Foxy, along with SecDef Capra, rising to attention and saluting. Jet was now clean-shaven. "At ease, soldiers, Mr. Capra," I said, and then I noted their steaming mugs sitting before them on the table. "Nice shave, Camjet. How you like that joe, huh? Nothin' beats a good solid cup of coffee that does *not* originate from a Blockade, right, fellas?"

Shipley laughed. "That was always one of my primary complaints, sir. This does just fine. Sure wouldn't mind some of that macadamia nut coffee from Mammoth Cave. Remember that, Foxy?"

"Yeah, man, I sure do." Foxy looked very sleepy and sipped at his mug.

I smiled. "I remember that well, Jet. I have some here, so you're in luck. *After* the briefing, however."

"I'll look forward to that, sir," Jet replied.

"Sorry for the early reveille. Gentlemen, this is General Everett Carson. The room we're standing in still exists because of him. Washington DC still exists because of him. We're lucky to have him around," I said.

Jet and Foxy both saluted.

"Yessir! Thank you, sir."

Capra shook the General's hand and thanked him.

"Corporal Liam Mayfield here, callsign 'Foxy,' is my son-in-law. Valiant soldier and one heckuva trusty fighter in a pinch. And Lieutenant Cameron Shipley, callsign 'Jet,' has been through a heckuva lot by virtue of my delightful predecessor. He and Foxy here were instrumental in the war of '42. Took down the funnel. Both of them."

"Gentlemen," Carson growled, and he reached out to shake their hands. "That's one thing I can't do: fly. These boots are too heavy to go shootin' around at ten-thousand feet up. Glad we had you guys in the saddle. Nice work. Looks like you might get a second shot at a giant here, if these dang things are what we think they are."

Jet and Foxy nodded.

"We're not sure about that just yet," I said. "But it's plausible. Let's sit, please. Have you received the briefing we sent over?"

"Yessir," he said, sitting down and releasing a metal clipboard from under his arm, flipping it open. "Last night after I got back from Baton Rouge. It's all here."

"Well, probably not all of it. Graham is with us."

"Jean Graham? Here? That's news. Where are you hiding our despicable turncoat?"

I smiled. "I understand how you feel. She's got quarters down the hall. She's entitled to protection, though I might add 'unfortunately' to the end of that. She may come in handy, however."

He scoffed. "I can't see how that's possible."

"We might have some international advantage in her still," interjected Capra, "but not certain just yet. There are some diplomacy issues we're working on with the three nations she betrayed."

"Yes, well, good luck with that." He scoffed again, tilting his head and lifting an eyebrow.

"Thank you, General." I turned to Jet. "Shipley, why don't you bring the General up to speed on what you and your CQC sniper team have come up with. It's a foregone conclusion that ground assault will be inevitable, General. We must be prepared."

Carson nodded, and then looked at Jet.

"Thank you, sir," Jet said. "There may be hundreds of thousands of gorgs as before, worst-case scenario. The President has briefed us on the DTBs and nuclear deterrent to try to thwart their entry into the atmosphere. Should that fail, we've got men positioning Vulcans and SPAAGs throughout the metro area and beyond. They'll all be centrally-located, sir, and you'll have that from wherever you want to post up. We have twenty-thousand troops reporting in, and that represents only a marginal enlistment from the local Blockades. These are free enlistees, reserving plenty of infantry for each of the three here in DC. All ground force commanders have been sent defense specs and plans of action for the protection of the city. Sniper teams will be posted up at The Basilica, the Old Post, Washington Cathedral, the Capitol Building, Lincoln Memorial, and Healy Hall at Georgetown. That's four square miles of coverage, sir."

"Excellent. Not sure you need me. I'll just be going now. Good luck, men," he offered in jest. Jet smiled in vindication, as did Foxy. Carson smiled at them.

"I guess that leaves only one thing," I said in return. The General turned back to me. "Let's talk the nuclear option. We need to have a discussion and figure out nominal yields, the deterrent factor, proximity, all of it."

"Alright, Mr. President." His smile faded.

"You're aware of the new big boys we have?"

"The *Tsar Bombas*."

"Correct. General, we have twenty-two ICBMs. Intercontinental Ballistic Missile, for the laymen here," I clarified. "One hundred megatons each. I just checked my math," -here I fired a sidelong comical glance at Jet- "and that's a combined twenty-two-hundred megaton yield. This will be no joke. We're going to coordinate with strategic command and NORAD to intercept the craft when it hits eight-thousand miles of our orbit. Max distance for an ICBM is ninety-three hundred miles. If it comes behind our moon again, that's two-hundred thirty-nine thousand miles away, and the moon's currently closer to apogee than perigee. But it may accelerate rapidly and spring its trap. We need to be ready. We can't launch too early, or our birds may run out of fuel on intercept course and just float blindly like drunks. We launch, and then we shut down right before detonation to avoid EMP damage."

"That's a massive blast, Mr. President, Mr. Capra. The *Tsar Bomba* was originally cut in half to fifty megatons only. You get a single one-hundred megaton yield anywhere close to the Earth, you vaporize eight million people and injure four million others. You'd have an inhospitable zone of roughly thirty-five miles diameter. Anyone within, say, forty-five miles of the blast will receive third-degree radiation burns. Again, that's just one nuke. The eight-thousand mile factor will mitigate that, of course, but someone correctly observed in the briefing that many nukes detonating cumulatively might create a shockwave that could, in fact, reach us, shift Earth slightly off its axis. Affect the ozone, tidal patterns, rotation, the Van Allen ring, all of it. Are you sure you're willing to take that chance?"

I nodded, and then looked at Capra, who nodded as well. "We all are, General. Every single NATO member state has adopted the plan, and we're launching jointly."

"It's our only option at this point," Capra echoed.

"I see. Given the details of the briefing, the craft appears to be the same make and model as the previous one we blew. Should take their ship only a few hours to get here from the moon. As far as the counterstrike, an ICBM's boost phase is only a few minutes, but midcourse phase ascent would put them at around fifteen-thousand miles per hour. There wouldn't be a terminal phase, of course, since the birds are staying aloft. All that to say that we'd need to be prepared to launch in the earlier morning hours on Friday if the craft's ETA hasn't changed. That sound about right to you?"

"That sounds about right for intercept. Of course, the earlier we shoot, the more advance notice the enemy has to take evasive action. Therefore, NORAD has proposed a staggered launch. We may lose some birds in the process if this thing *does* take evasive. Hopefully, though, the next few rounds would have more success. After all, we don't need a direct hit; we just need proximal strikes to inflict shockwave damage and crumple the ship on its approach. So, we hit them with the *Tsar Bombas* nukes first, and then the DTBs and all other DTF variants if they aren't deterred. Then it's down to dogfighting and ground assault."

"Are you prepared for protestors?"

I narrowed my eyes at him. "Meaning?"

"Well, suppose it is the gorgs. Everything we've been doing here, all this strategizing, it's all on the money. But if it's *not,*" he said, and he held up both his finger and his eyebrows, "then we potentially just blew a friendly alien species out of the sky."

"*The enemy of my enemy is my friend,* you mean." He nodded. This line of questioning, frankly, irritated me. I looked over at Jet and Foxy, briefly, and they appeared confused. They were watching Carson. "General," I said, "I wish I could believe that were even a possibility. But we don't have that luxury. This isn't E.T. on his way home to us. There's no time to assume that it might be friendly, and prudence would counsel that we treat any inbound visitations as potentially hostile."

"Guilty until proven innocent," he shot back. "You and I know that. That's our *de facto* response and should be the one we take, no doubt, out of caution. I'm just advising you to be prepared. That isn't going to be well-received by the masses."

I thought I heard a conversation coming from the hallway across the bunker, muffled yet growing in volume, and I looked over that way, squinting my eyes. "Good thing we don't have many masses anymore," I said curtly.

He scoffed once more, rolling his eyes. "That's the God-awful truth, Mr. President. Just be prepared. Not everyone will agree with what you're about to do."

I heaved a sigh and cleared the stress out of my lungs, looking back to them. "Indeed, it is. Listen, gentlemen, I have a call scheduled at 0700 hours with Secretary-General Leone. We've got some diplomatic avenues we need to explore, and he wants answers. I've got to give them to him. Before that I need to check in with the techs on the craft. Would you mind-"

Gunshot. The unfamiliar and virgin-to-these-halls sound of ammunition ringing off metal filled the floor with a thunderous *crack-crack-crack.* We all jerked out of our seats, tense. The General drew his sidearm. Jet and Foxy did the same.

"What the hell?" the General uttered, standing erect.

Capra moved toward the door.

I tore out of the Situation Room. An alarm sounded and the walls began flashing red. More cracks of gunfire. A security guard ran out from the far hallway clutching his side. He was bleeding, and his chest was red. He collapsed thirty feet from us as another guard ran to his side and began to administer aid. Someone was screaming from beyond, in the corridor opposite us. Gunshots continued to echo, and someone was shouting at the top of their lungs: epithets, profane rants, and slurs. I sped toward them.

"Mr. President, wait! No!" came Miguel's cry, and just as he did so, Foxy caught up to me and held me back. "Sir. No. Please wait here." Foxy put a hand on my chest and stopped me, as he and Jet raced down the hall, posting up at the corner. More gunshots. The hall flashed red all around us as a claxon sounded. People were filtering out of their quarters, and then some of them retreated back into them as they noticed the din from the corridor.

"Freeze, Lefebvre!" Jet shouted. "Put the gun down!"

Lefebvre? I thought. *The sniper who made threats against Graham? Oh no. He was trying to kill her…*

Jet hadn't even finished the word *down* when bullets whizzed past him and struck the end of the corridor. Jet whirled back around the corner.

More security raced into the adjoining corridor with Jet and Foxy. More bolted up beside Miguel, who sprinted up to the other end and stopped at the opposing corner. "Lefebvre! Put it down, *now*!" More shots. More screams from within a room in the hall. Miguel grunted and spun back around, dropping to the floor.

"Monzon!" I cried, jerking toward him, but General Carson and Peter Capra held me back. "Miguel!" Miguel looked at me with wild eyes.

Just then, Jet fired repeatedly. The security officers at Miguel's corner spun around and fired as well. A salvo of ammunition went careening through the hall, and lightning lit up the hallway. The screams of horrified citizens were amplified. My thoughts suddenly went to Janine and my wife. *Where is my daughter? Where is Andi? Dear God…*

A sudden thump in the hallway, and then time froze. All was quiet for a moment, and then, abruptly, frenzied screaming broke out anew. I knew that voice. It was a deeper woman's voice, filled with terror and pleading, whereas it used to hold the power of command.

President Jean Graham.

"Clear!" yelled Jet.

"Clear!" echoed a guard at the other end. Jet and Foxy filtered into the hallway to Graham's door.

"Medic! Get a medic in here!" I yelled, tearing myself away from Carson and Capra, and bolting to Miguel's side. I got there and looked him over. He was breathing hard. He had been hit in the left shoulder.

"It's not bad, amigo," I said, thankfully. "You're gonna be okay."

"I've taken worse hits from Rosie," he joked, but I knew he was all talk. Looked like it smashed into his clavicle; his shoulder had exploded in blood and bone.

"Get a medic over here!" I screamed. Soon, one came running with a trauma kit.

I peered around the corner. There lay Lefebvre, a pin cushion of bullets: bleeding, expressionless, and still. A pool of blood spread outward underneath his motionless form. He had tried to assassinate the former president right under our noses. Brought in at my request to wage war against the gorgons, he revealed his true colors last night as having a grievance against Graham. Where was Pease, the sniper leader? Surely, he would be able to expound on this.

General Carson strode up, leaning tall over us. He squatted down and put pressure on Monzon's wound while the medic worked feverishly.

Jean Graham was screaming her head off. Security unlocked her door, and prepared to transport her to different quarters, and all the while she wailed, spouting complaints and terrorized indictments, denouncing our intentions. They led her down the hall until we could only hear muffled shrieking. "Keep her under guard! And make sure she's not hit," I yelled after them. I shook my head and sighed.

Jet and Foxy were standing over Lefebvre. Jet looked at Foxy and shook his head, and then turned, clapped Foxy's shoulder, and walked out. More medics brought a stretcher to take Lefebvre to medical. He was already dead. They would be back with another stretcher for Miguel once they had preliminarily tended to his shoulder.

I looked down at Monzon. "Hang in there, buddy. You got this," I encouraged him. But he was shaking. Granted, he was still one ripped hombre, full of muscle, but the sad fact was that he was seventy-four now. He wasn't as limber as he used to be.

They picked him up, and he gave me a weakened smile. Sucked the air out of me. He took a hit. He needed to live. Especially now that Rosie was gone. I watched him limp down the hall until the medics met him halfway with a stretcher.

He hobbled toward them as if he had been mortally wounded.

8 | VOTE

Monday, March 6th 2045 · 0653 hours

Everyone was okay, down to the last human.

I checked in on Andi and Janine, who awoke to the sound of gunfire. Thankfully, they were in the Presidential Suite, and Andi was already yawning. She had tensed and shot up, shielding Janine, escorting her to a safe room in the back of the suite. They were a little shaken, but otherwise unharmed.

The medic working on Miguel said that he'll be bruised up and pissed off for a while, but should be able to splint up and be back on the floor with me late tomorrow. Miguel would have to have a procedure to extract the bullet. They were now prepping him for surgery. I breathed a sigh of relief; he was much-needed as both Chief of Staff *and* Chief of the Air Force.

Jens approached me with a printout. He didn't say anything, just handed it to me. It was a dossier on Lefebvre. "What am I looking for here, Jens?"

"Look at the family tree, sir."

I scanned the sheet, and then I found it. Lefebvre was the nephew of VP Cooper, whom Graham had murdered. This was personal. I swallowed hard and looked up at Jens, handing the printout back to him. "Thank you, Jens. Dismissed."

"Yes, sir."

Pease and the rest of his team awoke and returned to the bunker early for their 0700 briefing with the General. Jet filled him in on Lefebvre before they arrived. He was consumed by regret, ashamed, apologizing repeatedly to me until I had to put my hand up. "Thank you, soldier – that'll be all. I appreciate the sentiment. Better to sift the chaff now rather than later," I said, although I think that comment stung him a bit. Jet and Foxy consoled him; apparently, Pease had been longtime survivors with Lefebvre and had forgotten his connection to VP Cooper, and, thus, the animosity that consumed him. The whole family wanted Graham's head; he just happened to be afforded a stone's-throw opportunity. He threw his stone.

"Looks like HR needs to pay more attention to our sniper resumés," I faintly heard Jet mutter in a vain attempt at humor as I walked out of there.

After making the rounds, I checked in with Romero about the craft, quickly, before my 0700 call with the Secretary-General. "Good morning, Mr. Romero. Sit rep please. What's going on now?"

He saluted me, and then sat back down. "Good morning, Mr. President. Yessir, four days to go, and she's still tracking. On course and pinging like there's no tomorrow. The pings have grown in intensity. Listen." He handed me his headphones.

It was a strange, warbling sound, akin to a groan played in reverse. Each pulse shifted downward in pitch, almost like pleading. From forty light-years away, it had broadcast this pathetic, whimpering beacon to its queen, nevermore to be answered.

"Somebody's horny, Mr. President," he jested, gawking at me.

"Alright, alright, Mike, just give me the 4-1-1."

"Right. You can see here it's really close to Neptune, sir. This is Neptune," -here he pointed to a faint blip on his screen- "and that's our visitor, right there. You can see the course plot here," he said, toggling to another screen. "It's sped up a bit, but nothing major. It's gonna hit a few meteor showers on the way if its trajectory holds. There's the Perseids right there, and over here is the Taurids, and then this one is the Geminids. That should give it a bit of pause, at least, but not by much."

"What's its mass, you got a reading on that, yet?"

"Oh, yeah," he said, as if that was something he meant to bring up. "Identical to the first one."

"Let me guess," I interrupted. "Four point seven by two point three miles, yeah? A few hundred protrusions, kinda like a giant space cucumber, yeah?"

"Yep, that's right, sir. Space cucumber," he said, shunting a giggle. "More like a dill pickle. You can see it slowly making its way across the screen if you stare at it long enough."

"I don't have that kind of time, Romero. You send this to Greene yet?"

"Yessir, if you recall he's on the same feed."

"Oh, that's right. Okay, please send it to Commander Sinclair again as well."

"Also on the same feed, Mr. President," he said, smiling and turning to me.

I smiled back at him. "Thanks for staying on top of it, Mike. Let me know if that cucumber turns into a pickle."

He let out an obnoxious snort. "Roger that, sir."

I walked out of there, back to my office. Bayless caught me on the way. "Would you like me in there, Mr. President?"

"That would be great, Veronica, good morning. Thanks."

"Good morning, sir. All Blockades still report full readiness, sir," she said, pivoting and walking with me briskly. "Just got an update from NATO on the three-hundred twenty-nine Blockades outside the US. They're having some trouble getting the word out to people, but we still have time. They've taken to the streets with megaphones. The usual areas are seeing some difficulty in bringing in folks on the fringes of the broadcast signal or in inclement weather, but they're working on it."

"Alright, good. Thanks for the update. Let's get Maddox on the line."

I sat down behind my desk and Bayless closed the door behind me. "How's Miguel, sir?"

I looked at her and shook my head, sighing. "The guy's a tank, but even a tank can take a hit in the right spot. I'm just surprised it didn't bounce off his muscles."

Bayless smiled. Miguel's Schwarzenegger-like physique preceded him. "Yessir."

I dialed Secretary-General Maddox Leone on speaker, looking at my watch. "0700 here; it's got to be 1600 there."

The phone rang a few times, and Leone's assistant, Valeria Ronchi, picked up. "Pronto, Ufficio del Segretario Generale. Comé posso aiutarti?"

"Uh, buon giorno, Ms. Ronchi, this is President Vance Cardona of the U.S."

"Ah! Good morning President Cardona. Mr. Leone is expecting your call. Momento."

I looked at Bayless and cleared my throat.

"Buon giorno, President Cardona!" Leone greeted me happily. He was a diminutive man with a thin, whispery voice. He was elderly, and had survived the gorgon onslaught while in Venice, visiting with other dignitaries for an international leadership conference. Most of those leaders had been slain by the gorgons. The majority of his large family had also lost their lives. Yet, he somehow retained his jovial spirit.

"Good morning to you, sir, or should I say good afternoon? Nice to hear your voice again, Maddox."

"And yours as well, Vance. I trust everything is being prepared handsomely and that we're ready to face this new, unwanted threat."

"Well, as much as we'll ever be, Mr. Secretary-General. How are things over there?"

Leone paused. "I must say they've taken longer than expected. We have fringe elements, unfortunately, that are insisting that this is a hoax, that there's no governmental proof, that this is some new forced mandate such as those who made a mess out of the Covid pandemic. Consciensous objectors everywhere you go, sir. They are rioting and looting out there in places."

"I know what you mean. In case you hadn't heard, we had an attempt on President Graham's life early this morning."

"*Mio Dio!*" he hissed. "Are you serious?"

"I am, sir. She's fine, and we neutralized the shooter, but she's not a popular woman, Maddox: reviled and despised everwhere she goes. The shooter was her VP's nephew. We just found out."

"Oh, Vance, I am terribly sorry to hear that. Was she injured?"

"Nothing except frayed nerves."

He paused, and it sounded like disappointment. He was to be excused; pretty much everyone on Earth felt she deserved far more pain and suffering than what she had been sentenced to. "Well," he said, clearing the air. "That's good. I am scheduled to fly back to New York City tomorrow to be at the UN Secretariat. I had thought about Geneva, but felt it would be good to be at actual headquarters. It did not matter where we were the first time they came; I don't believe it will matter the second time, and I need to show strength and resilience so that the world knows its leaders are still alive."

"Exactly why I'm still at the White House, sir. Good call, Mr. Secretary-General."

"Let's get down to business, shall we?"

"Yes, sir."

"I have some news for you."

"Oh? What's that?" I asked, curious.

"I've spoken with the Triumvirate of Dissent – that's what they're calling themselves, the TOD – and China has been apointed spokesman of their coalition. North Korea, Iran and China have all expressed their continued displeasure with the negotiations concerning the equipment on their sovereign land. They have managed to rally nearly every remaining piece of the dispersed equipment, and are reassembling it to the original specifications given the present crises. They report it has been painstaking."

"I'm sorry for their inconvenience," I said, dryly, rolling my eyes at Bayless.

"Indeed," he replied. "They are willing to relinquish the equipment to you, Mr. President," he said, and my eyes widened in disbelief, looking up at Bayless. "But of course, they do have some stipulations."

"That's good news, Mr. Secretary. All of them are in agreement?"

"So says China."

"Amazing. Alright, let's hear the conditions, and we'll see if we can't make them happy campers."

Leone cleared his throat. Apparently, he was reading from a list of conditions provided to him by China. "Condition Number One, all equipment to remain in the existing locations for the defense of each country for the time being, until such a time as can be deemed that the crisis has passed."

"Noted. That shouldn't be a problem."

"Good. Condition Number Two, they are to be provided precise instructions for linking and running the detonators to ensure maximum effectiveness."

"Understandable and no worries. Next?"

The Secretary-General paused. I thought for a moment we had been disconnected. "Maddox, are you still there?" I asked, leaning in toward the speakerphone at the rear center of my desk.

"Yes, Mr. President. My apologies." I listened. "Condition Number Three, they demand the immediate transfer of custody and extradition of President Jean Graham to China."

I looked up at Bayless in horror, and she did the same to me. I was speechless. Flummoxed. Incredulous.

"Mr. President? Now, I believe it is my turn to ask if you are still there?"

"Y-yes, Maddox, I'm here. I'm-I'm frankly shocked at the request, sir. This is clearly preposterous. Regardless of the near-universal negative sentiment toward Jean Graham, if this is indeed a stipulation of theirs, surely they must have considered what this would do to world stability, to say nothing of the fact that we do not have any extradition treaty in place with any of the countries represented by the, the-"

"TOD. Triumvirate of Dissent," he clarified.

I rested my face in my right hand and covered my mouth, exasperated. "Mr. Secretary-General," I continued, "extradition is governed by the US Constitution. However, no such treaty exists with China. Such a measure would need to be ratified by Congress, and there's no time. That craft out there arrives to us in only four days' time, and that time is shrinking with each minute that passes."

"I understand, Mr. President. I am simply the messenger. I have dictated their terms. Please rest assured that prior to this, I communicated your State Department's proposals from Mr. Curtiss regarding an offer to sell. They have flatly rejected it."

"So instead of hard capital, they want Jean Graham's head on a plate, is that it?" I could feel my face reddening, and Bayless tilted her head. She knew that what I said was somewhat out of line.

"Mr. President," said Leone, "I am not here to be a moralist, and it is not my role to affirm or denounce such requests, so let us compose ourselves. I do not think a case can be made concerning potential threats to Ms. Graham's life, especially since she just survived an attempt on American soil and in your custody. Now, don't mistake me, as I mean no offense by that! The fact remains that the former President's crimes do fit the bill of Dual Criminality: the alleged acts were crimes in both countries. That satisfies that part of the exchange.

"While the absence of a treaty can make extradition unlikely, you are the President and do have the power to draft up an agreement signed by your Attorney General, Jody Willingham. I urge you to consider this. The mass of DTF equipment located on the three jetties is still there, and there is plenty of it at each location.

"While the nuclear deterrent has been eliminated, these DTF emitters served to successfully annihilate ninety-eight percent of the remaining gorgon infestation in 2042. They need to be used again.

"You cannot enter a sovereign nation and reclaim equipment which you say belongs to you without a formal international edict anyway. The TOD has pledged to use said equipment in the defense of the planet, and we all need those devices to work. It is in the best interest of the United

States, the TOD, and the world, to negotiate, which, in this case, includes the extradition of Ms. Graham."

I was watching Bayless from under my eyes, my fist to my mouth. Leone was right, however much I wanted to disagree.

"What are their intentions with Ms. Graham if we did extradite?" I asked.

"Mr. President, to that, I do not know the answer. I can assure you that I have not received any hint from them that they wish to do her harm. However, as an international fugitive from justice – that is what they are calling her – she is answerable to each of the member states of the TOD for her crimes, and a tribunal would take place. Whether that results in capital punishment is beyond me. But the fact remains that it *is* something the TOD is entitled to."

I pulled my fist away. This was too much for now. "Mr. Secretary-General, thank you. I don't mean to delay this any further, but, of course, I must consult with my cabinet on this quandary. This would be a move simply without precedent in the two-hundred-sixty-nine years our nation has been in existence."

"Understood, sir. As a matter of precedent – and not to belabor the point – the door swings both ways. You have had two instances where presidents of other countries were extradited to you: the former president of Honduras and the former Peruvian president. The extradition of Graham would be a show of goodwill that the US does not stand on rogue policies and is willing to flex rather than remain an island unto itself. This is not an upstanding citizen we are discussing here, anyway. This is a loathed infidel who operated as a renegade and attempted to brazenly assassinate three world leaders. There would be nothing to apologize for. You would have more support than dissent."

"And if she is unwilling to provide the detonator link codes?" I asked him.

"Then, I imagine you'll have to find some way to *compel* her."

Torture. That's what he meant. I let that sink in for a moment, as the gravity of what he just said settled upon us. "Alright, thank you. It's food for thought, sir, and I appreciate you bringing it to my attention, Maddox. Thank you."

"Thank you, Mr. President. When can the TOD expect your answer?"

I didn't like being rushed. "I'm not sure at this point, sir. Hopefully by EOD today."

"Haha, very good. By EOD for the TOD." He hung up. I rolled my eyes at the joke, as did Bayless.

I stared angrily at my VP, and she stared angrily at me. Her slow intake of breath sounded loudly in my little office, matched only in volume by my own.

•　　•　　•　　•　　•

Sunday, March 5ᵗʰ 2045 · 0751 hours

The rest of the CQC sniper team were ready to go, as was the General. We were now all in the Situation Room, and it was time to bring everyone up to speed on this insidious new proposal. I looked around the room. Capra, Bayless, Roth, Curtiss, Roe, Austin, General Carson, Jet,

Foxy, Romero, and the five remaining snipers. It was packed. I collected myself for the announcement that I was sure would drop their jaws in stunned silence.

"Ladies and gentlemen, thank you for joining us at this early hour. I want to let you know that I checked in on Chief of Staff Monzon, and he is recovering nicely. He's scheduled for surgery at 0900 hours. Our thoughts and prayers are with him, and he should be just fine. I have some other news, however. There's not a lot of time, and every hour brings that thing closer to our atmosphere, so let me get right to it." I cleared my throat.

"You all know now what happened here this morning. An attempt was made on Jean Graham's life by a member of our new senior ground assault sniper force. I want to stress that this was conducted alone, and was in no way connected to General Carson, Lieutenant Shipley, Corporal Mayfield, or any of the rest of the team here," I said, motioning to Carson and the others. "The assailant was neutralized. He was, as it turns out, the nephew of Vice President Cooper, who Graham murdered."

Astonishment buzzed through the room. *Okay, at least that part was news.*

"As it would seem, more than one person wants to get their hands on President Graham. At 0700 hours this morning I had a scheduled call with Secretary General Leone. Secretary Curtiss, SecDef Capra and VP Bayless here are all well aware of the domestic inroads we've tried to make to secure our DTF technology from the three countries that Graham betrayed. They have a coalition now, per Maddox Leone. They're addressing themselves as the TOD. The Triumvirate of Dissent. Any of you can guess what that means, and the bearing it will have on our massive stockpile of audio weapons in the Middle East and Asia.

"It's not good, folks," I said, taking a large breath to come up for air. "They won't play ball with us unless we give them one thing. Now, before I get to that, they have stipulated two other conditions. One, all our DTF equipment remains where it is, so that each country can use it for their own defense in the coming confrontation. And, two, that they are given the precise instructions for linking up the detonators and running them properly.

"I was endeavoring to dialogue with Ms. Graham prior to the attempt on her life. She had previously provided us with a cipher, a decrypt code, in order to obtain access to one of her drives. We believe the drive contains instructions to link up and resurrect the detonation equipment so that they're all working in tandem again. Before I could talk with her, we had the incident with the assailant.

"Nonetheless, there's a new wrinkle. Maddox Leone called me representing the TOD, and he presents me with an impossible choice. They have specifically requested that we extradite Jean Graham to China, for prosecution by military tribunal, or perhaps other purposes more nefarious."

I gave it a minute to let it sink in as they gasped. More astonishment. The faces around me were studies in incredulity, except for the ones already in the know.

"That's right. All of the effort that Mr. Capra here, Mr. Curtiss here, and VP Bayless and I have tried to make since the end of the war hinges on this one trade. Dissent has grown, and we're fractured. If the nuclear deterrent fails, then we need that equipment up and running properly to ensure the survival of the human race, even if it's just in those three countries. They will not let us have it, and they won't buy it from us at a reduced price."

"Mr. President, I suggest a simple answer to this dilemma, if I may," Bayless said. "We're a democracy. In this room are staffers appointed by Congress to head up the nation. We should simply call for a vote."

"I don't know that it is that simple, Ms. Bayless," I countered. "The moral issue at stake here is that, if they receive the codes to run the DTF equipment and defend their own capitols, sure, they might survive in that concentrated defense zone with our dissonant tidal bombs, but the rest of us would be dead. Unless we give them Jean Graham so that they will use our DTFs in the invasion and not sometime after the rest of the world is annihilated. That's a considerably unfair trade staked to the life of one person. It's just not that simple."

"Nothing is anymore, sir. The gorgons leveled our world, and now they're coming back. I think some tough decisions have to be made in light of that, as you've done so far, sir, in an exemplary way, might I add?" She looked around the room, nodding. Folks were nodding with her. "In my mind this is a non-issue. Jean Graham does not amount to several billion dollars' worth of audio deterrent that was successful in killing off the gorgons last time. Respectfully speaking, Mr. President."

"But how can we devalue one life just like that?" I asked her. "Isn't that what Graham herself did? Isn't that what her assailant just did? Dare we stoop to that level?"

"It's not stooping, sir. Not in this case," the General cut in. "You're making a trade to ensure the survival of the human race. If I may be so bold as to interject some faith, that's exactly what Jesus Christ did, long ago. He traded himself to ensure our spiritual survival. And so did every single soul who has served in every single war on every single continent through every single century down through time, sir."

"Thank you, General Carson. I appreciate the reality check, however they all went willingly. We would be trading one life, no matter how despicable, and, to use your faith example, Jesus died for the *ungodly*. No one here would dispute that Jean Graham is 'ungodly.' So, how can we, therefore, determine who goes unwillingly to their possible death?"

The General cocked his head at me. "Sir, no one disputes it's a moral quandary. But as Commander in Chief, sir, well, you make that choice every single day. This soldier, right here, and this one as well," -here he put his hands on Jet's and Foxy's shoulders- "they served under the command of those who report to you, discharging their oath and fulfilling their duty, knowing that's what was asked of them. Their commander put these soldiers in harm's way, because that's what they had to do. VP Bayless here, Major at DN282, sir, she put soldiers in harm's way, doing what must be done. That's all you're doing now, doing what must be done. We don't have time to debate over the moral implications of a prisoner swap for a trove of equipment that we *know* will be effective against the second wave, sir."

I glanced back at the General. His face was red and heated so much that his scar looked like it was pulsating. I locked eyes with Jet, who was squinting at me, nodding. Then on to Foxy. Liam. My son-in-law. One heckuva fighter, and someone I had come to know and respect as no-nonsense in tactical warfare. His jaw was clenched, and he, too, nodded. If I could read his face, it said, *Sir, your choice is clear.*

I scanned the rest of them: no one appeared to offer any kind of recalcitrant opinion, and it wasn't because Jean Graham stunk to high heaven. It wasn't an easy throwaway for them. She was, after all, a human life, and she was part of the sanctity that we were all needing to protect.

It was simply doing what must be done.

"Alright," I relented. "Yea or nay. All those in favor of the exchange, vote yea now." I went around the room.

Sixteen yeas, and zero nays. It was unanimous. Mine was the final yea. I took a deep breath.

"Folks, it seems we're all in one accord on this, and we don't have any time to waste. Bayless, please contact Attorney General Willingham and have her draft up an agreement and send it over. Thank you, everyone. Please return to your assigned stations, and I'll pay a visit to Graham and get the last cipher for the detonation links. After that, I'll break the news to her and call the Secretary General."

I watched them filter out. We had probably just signed Graham's death warrant. But how would that have been any different than if a judge had done it at her 2042 tribunal? I wondered.

We were down to one human, and she would not be okay.

9 | THE TRADE

Sunday, March 5th 2045 · 0833 hours

It was time for an exchange of information.

Graham was in her cell. I was on my way to see her. My first stop, however, was to see my Chief of Staff, who was about to go into surgery for the next two hours.

Medical was in top shape, and they had everything they needed. He was in good hands. There he was, on a gurney, hooked up to a bunch of equipment I'll never pretend to understand. The PEOC had plenty of medical personnel who were more than equipped to handle health concerns. Nurse Sorenson had sedated him slightly, and his IV drip of saline, vitamins and antioxidants, electrolytes, Toradol – and of course morphine – was doing its work, coursing through his body and bringing much-needed comfort to his shoulder. He turned over and looked at me sleepily.

"Hey, Chief Amigo, how you holdin' up, my friend?"

"Mr. President," he said, attempting to bring his arm to his hand up in a salute.

"Hey, cut it out, man. I'm *Vance*, and I believe we've met."

"Okay, okay, Captain Presi…Vance…sir."

I shook my head and chuckled. "What's the Spanish word for knucklehead?"

"*Cabeza hueca*," he informed me tiredly. "Or, if it's any easier, *knucklehead-o*. You add an 'a' to it if it's female, Mr. President Vancedona, sir." He grinned crazily.

"Somebody's loopy."

"Yeah," he chuckled, "I think I am, just a little bit. They gave me morphine."

"I can tell."

"It got pretty painful. Looking forward to that surgery to get this stupid thing outta me."

"I bet. Listen, Miguel," I said, leaning over the rails of his gurney, "are you lucid enough for some news?" He nodded. "Maddox Leone said that the three countries want Jean Graham extradited. They are unyielding. We put it up for a formal vote. Everyone sounded off. Unanimous. They want her in exchange for us allowing them to use the DTF strike zones against the second wave. Tactical detonator codes as well. Then we get it all back after we've defeated them."

His eyes opened wide. "Lemme get this straight, señor. They get the equipment, the codes, *and* Graham? Would they like fries with that? Perhaps a nice bottle of chilled Bordeaux and some *corrido* music while we massage their feet?"

I smiled. "They asked for that. I told them you'd be the one singing. I hope that was okay."

Miguel laughed.

I stared at him as he winced from his guffaw, reaching for the nurse page button. "Listen, Miguel. I want to tell you before you go in there. I'm-" I faltered. Was I really getting punchy? *C'mon, Vance. Tell him how you feel.* "Well, I just wanted you to know that I'm glad you're okay, brother. We go back a while."

He turned back to me and looked at me as alertly as he could despite the drugs.

"This is a tough job, amigo," I said. "I need you by my side. You're my best friend. You took a bullet today. You didn't take a bullet in all the years I've known you, and we've been in more perilous places. I just wanted you to know that my thoughts are on you, and I'm praying for you, buddy. Come out of the surgery okay."

He smiled at me blearily. "I will, *Capitan* Vance. I promise. I can't let you run this country alone, you know," he voiced in a sleepy murmur. And then his eyes closed.

I gazed down upon my friend, my partner-in-arms, my confidant, the one who had served so faithfully under the President's very nose, feeding me conspiratorial intel and bravely staying at his post when he wanted to abandon it with every fiber of his being. He was a hero of the people. A respected soldier. And, though older and frailer now, he had a long way to go. I *prayed* he had a long way to go.

The nurse headed my way along with another medic, preparing to wheel him into surgery.

"Hey, brother. Look at me," I said. Miguel's eyes fluttered open again, looking at me groggily. I held out my arms, palms up. *Receiving.* "Just like Rosalita Campion taught us to do." I saw a faint twinkle of recognition in his eyes.

"Rosalita…*Monzon*," he breathed out a correction.

I nodded. The nurse took the gurney from me and said they were ready for him. I stepped aside.

"Take good care of him, guys," I said. "That's my Chief of Staff right there, and, more than that, my best friend. Take care of him," I repeated.

They nodded. "Yes, Mr. President," they said in unison, and they were gone. How they were able to wheel that heavy gurney, much less with Miguel's hulking physique weighing it down, was beyond me.

Bayless texted me. The agreement had just been sent over by Attorney General Willingham. Jean Graham was to be extradited to China. I printed it out and headed over to break the news to a certain former president.

•   •   •   •   •

Sunday, March 5th 2045 · 0849 hours

"Yes, of course," she said, inviting me to a seat across from her. Graham was nervous but composed; jarred but lucid, relying wholly on the glowing cigarette between her gnarled fingers to assuage her anxiety.

She grabbed a remote and turned the volume down on a small TV on a stand next to her loveseat. I didn't recognize the program playing on it. Obviously a rerun: neither any live nor prerecorded entertainment had been produced since the war had ended, and she still wasn't allowed news down here.

"Thank you," I said, sitting down and assessing her. I leaned forward with my elbows on my knees, my hands clasped. "I'm glad to see you're okay. I truly mean that, Jean. I'm sorry about that incident. I don't know if you've been briefed yet, but the assailant was the nephew of Eric Cooper."

Her face became a slate, and her eyes slowly drifted away from me. In the hollow recesses of her pathological mind, I wondered if a young, healthy face of her former VP presented her with memories she was capable of holding with any degree of warmth. She had murdered him in a fit of rage toward the end of the war, slitting his throat. The weight of full comprehension fell upon her now.

"Well, that does make sense, now, doesn't it," she muttered lamely.

No response was needed from me. I'm sure she could appreciate that my sympathy would last for only a finite amount of time before we would have to get down to brass tacks. I was right. She looked up at me and asked, "Why are you *really* here, Vance? Surely it's not because you genuinely feel sorry for me in this?"

I laughed grimly, and unclasped my hands, putting them on my knees. "Yes, we do have an agenda, don't we?"

"Always," she said, rolling her eyes, and for a moment I sympathized with her. She too had held this office, and for far longer than me, though most – if not all – of those terms were undeserved. This elderly, knobby woman understood the pressures of the presidency in ways that I had not yet been required to face. Hiding from gorgons, commissioning new initiatives, overseeing Blockades, supervising the mass-production of the DTF technology, losing her son on a recon patrol, disseminating the reflection masks, and having to quarterback wickedly difficult plays.

'Wicked' being the operative word here, I thought. Sympathy gone. The truth came back to me, and I had no illusions about who I was dealing with: a cold-blooded, diabolical, narcissistic tyrant who was rightfully deposed and prosecuted.

"I have some news for you, Jean. We've made a deal with the three countries you targeted."

"Oh? Last I heard I was going to perhaps talk some sense into them for you," she said, snuffing out her cigarette and reaching with a trembling hand for another. A moment of yearning passed through me, harkening back to my smoking days. I was never a chain-smoker like she had become. Still, a smoke sounded nice right about now.

"Yes, well, there's been a change with that," I said matter-of-factly. This was either going to go over surprisingly well or incite her to fly off the handle. "The three countries have coalesced into a new faction called the TOD. Triumvirate of Dissent."

She rolled her eyes. "Gawd," she moaned. "How pathetically original." She smirked.

"That's not all. They're preserving eminent domain, but have agreed to let us have the DTF equipment back, the detonators, even the jetties, all of it…after the invasion. They want to use them in the coming conflict, and they've requested the codes to link up the detonators once more."

Pause. She studied me. "Well, that's not a problem," she declared. "No harm in that. But you act as if there's something weightier still to come."

"And," I said, struggling to assess the caliber of her coming response, "they want *you*. They've demanded your extradition, Jean. We've voted, and it's been decided. We're going to meet their demands. I wanted to let you know first before I called Maddox Leone. China is heading this up, and that's where you'll be extradited."

She stared at me blankly. And then, in her little suite, with only the two of us there save the guard outside her door, Jean Graham began to laugh. Her belly expanded before it burst up and out of her. Something welling up deep inside, whether out of incredulity or unbridled satisfaction at this turn of events, simply could not be contained. A giggle escaped her, morphing easily into an irrepressible cackle that made me tilt my head in confusion, smiling along with her. However, age and lungs caught up with her, and she paused mid-chortle and let out a bellicose, ashen, tar-filled cough, wheezing oxygen back into her blackened lungs.

Jean Graham leaned back, staring up at the ceiling, panting. "Oh my stars, but I've waited for this day, Vance."

"Oh? How is that? I rather imagined a different response," I answered her.

She tilted her head back down at me with a suddenness that surprised me, and her face was eerily underlit again by the glow of the TV beside her. "You rather imagined a different response? I rather *imagine* you would have rather imagined!" she cackled, breaking out anew in ashen laughter. "You think you all know me so well." She laughed again.

I sat back and sighed, tiring of her antics and awaiting an explanation. She shook her head and took a long, hearty tug on her cigarette, with the occasional chuckle.

"Oh, Mr. *President*," she said, and I noted her theatrical use of my title, "how I have longed for this day. The day I would get to see one of my ne'er-do-wells face to face and be able to curse them head-on." Her smile faded. "All three of these nations reviled me. All three of them filibustered and hamstrung me. So? I filibustered and hamstrung them back. It's eye-for-an-eye, Vance. I was tired of them. No one will ever see that or be able to understand that I did what I had to do to ensure that there was harmony amongst the leadership of our planet by getting those wretched beasts out. No one gets that. I don't expect you to. But someday, Vance," -here she leaned in toward me, crossing her arms over her knee and brandishing her cigarette at me- "someday you'll have to make the exceedingly hard choices as well, and you'll have to do something you don't want to in order to ensure that life goes on. You'll have to do the hard thing."

"Well, Madame *President*," I echoed back to her, exhausted with her bullshit, "I believe I just did. You see, agreeing to extradite you *is* a hard choice. No one person should ever have to pay so that millions, even billions, can go free. This morning, I did something I didn't want to in order to ensure that life goes on. I did the hard thing this morning. We all did. No one likes you very much, Jean, but you're still a human being, and I still believe in your worth as a human being. The gorgons may not, but I do."

She just eyed me, squinting, taking another hard drag on her cigarette. Finally, she flicked her head to the side, looking at a picture of herself in her younger years in presidential garb, encased in a cheap, cracked frame on the credenza. "When do I depart?"

"As soon as I get the clearance from the Secretary-General," I said.

"And I suppose that there is to be yet another military tribunal that I shall have the joy of being part of?"

"Most likely."

She studied me, but only briefly, shaking her head.

"Let's not pull any punches, Vance. We both know that I'm never coming back from China. I'll die over there, or they'll kill me: a foreigner in a foreign land, abandoned."

"Ms. Graham, if we don't take several steps over the next few days, we'll all die everywhere, killed by foreigners in our own lands."

She eyed me curiously. "Will I have protection? I don't just mean armed guards from whatever wonderful assailants await me in my Chinese gulag. I mean from the gorgons."

"I'm sure you will. They have Blockades as well. I imagine that's where you'll go."

She shook her head. "Fine. And I suppose you'll just be needing one final thing before I go, and that's the detonator link codes."

"Yes, please."

Graham bowed her head, and shook it, pondering this turn of events, no doubt. Momentarily, she looked up at me under her slim eyebrows in a chilling regard. "None of us are going to get out of this alive, Vance. The gorgons aren't coming to steal our water this time. They're coming to steal our lives. It's futile to even try to defend ourselves."

"Then there's no reason not to share the codes with me," I offered plainly.

Another long drag on her cigarette, watching me under those thinning eyebrows. Another big exhale of smoke. Decision time. At last, she spoke.

"I like you, Vance. I hope you make it out of this."

"I hope you do as well."

"Sure," she said, sitting up and snuffing out yet another cigarette. "The files on my drive are separated by subfolders. You'll find one entitled Karma. There are several documents in that subfolder. One is entitled 'Civilians,' one is entitled 'Inventory,' and one is entitled 'Not Known.' Civilians, C, for China. Inventory, I, for Iran. Not Known, NK, for North Korea. In each subfolder are twelve random .txt files. Take the first letter or number from each paragraph in each subfolder document, and you have the respective firing detonator codes. Take care, Vance," she finished blandly, staring at me.

"I'll relay that to my techs. As someone who worked in IT, I commend you. You really thought all of those out. Thank you, Jean. And," I offered hesitantly, "good luck."

"We'll see," she said, getting up and heading toward her bedroom. "Now if you'll excuse me, I have to pretty myself up for the Chinese."

She disappeared into the bathroom and locked the door behind her.

I guess that concludes our negotiations, I thought, and headed out without a word. I reassigned the guard outside to be stationed inside and placed her on suicide watch. What Graham said and what she did were often two different things. She could off herself and curtail justice. The TOD would call it a cover-up and never forgive us.

I instructed the guard not to leave her suite, no matter what

•   •   •   •   •

Sunday, March 5th 2045 · 0916 hours

Leone's assistant Valeria Ronchi answered the phone once more with "Buon giorno, Ufficio del Segretario Generale. Comé posso aiutarti?" like clockwork.

"Ms. Ronchi, this is President Vance Cardona once more."

"Ah! One moment, sir. Please hold for Secretary-General Leone."

Momentarily, Maddox Leone was on the line.

"Maddox? Vance. We're a go. Graham is all yours."

"That is wonderful to hear, Mr. President. I'm sure that wasn't easy."

"Doing the hard thing never is," I said. "But sometimes the easy thing can become harder. This was actually easier than I thought. Let's pray it doesn't become harder as we go through the process. Let's pray that the TOD keeps their end of the bargain."

"I see no reason why they wouldn't, Mr. President. That equipment is meant to save human lives, and we have gorgons knocking on our doorstep for another attack. They'll comply. They're humans too, of course."

"I hope you're right. For the sake of *humanity*, I hope you're right."

We concluded the call, with Leone pledging to call the TOD and confirm their readiness to receive Jean Graham as expediently as possible.

I had done the hard thing.

It was time for the exchange.

10 | SPLIT

Monday, March 6th 2045 · 1022 hours

It was splitting.

Bayless quickly informed me that Miguel would be out of surgery in an hour, and then she retreated. I was now with Romero watching the craft. Greene had texted me with the report, and now Romero and I were watching it on a split-screen with him.

"Are you sure? How can you tell?" I asked him.

"I'm sure, sir – all three complexes around the world are tracking two distinct signatures now. They're all one-hundred-twenty degrees apart in longitude for redundancy's sake, sir, to prevent discrepancy. It's passed Neptune, coming through Uranus's outer orbit now. Right ascension and declination now pinpoint two distinct signatures. Cartesian and galactic coordinates mirroring. I'll zoom in, here you go," he said, enlarging the picture. "Uh, let me just augment this part here," he said, leaning in toward his screen. "See that? That hairline fracture, right there, with slight course deviation on the left. It could be that it encountered a collision on the way, but DSN doesn't have any close-orbit meteor showers in that sector, just the ones I reported before. No acoustical signature detected, no disruption in pings, sir. It's like it just detached."

"Approach vectors changed at all?" I asked him.

"Nah, they're the same minus a marginal percentage of a single degree. Greene, you pulling up the same info?"

Greene nodded. "Yep. Five by five, deviation confirmed," he groaned theatrically.

"The orbits are much slower in the outer rings. They've got a few more orbits to trek through. Thankfully, projections have us on the far side of the sun from them on Friday, but solar winds should speed up their acceleration if they're smart enough to ride them. Otherwise, they're set to cut straight across and around the sun in a parabola here," he said, gesturing to the screen again, "which gives us our Friday morning arrival. Both pieces of the original appear to be moving in tandem, sir."

I stood slowly back up as the two of them studied their data. Two different signatures meant the craft could approach Earth, and thus attack us, from two different vectors. This was not good news at all, in a continuing string of not good news. I gritted my teeth and dialed Commander Sinclair to let him know. I needed to connect with VP Bayless, Peter Capra and Bill Curtiss as well. Jet, Foxy and the CQC team were off with the General.

"Send that to my screen, please, Romero," I instructed him. "Thanks."

"Yes, Mr. President."

Miguel would be out of surgery shortly and he would need to know once he was lucid, though he wouldn't resume his post until tomorrow at the earliest. In the meanwhile, I had appointed Capra as my Deputy Chief of Staff. He was pulling double-duty, but then again, so was everyone else. I quickly fired off texts to them to meet me in my office.

They all arrived shortly. "Folks, bad news. Look at this. Latest intel on the craft has it splitting into two distinct objects, separating somewhere out by Uranus. It'll be coming up on Saturn Wednesday morning. Only a few more planets to pass before they both hit us. They're still scheduled for a Friday morning arrival, but now there's two of them."

"Good Lord," breathed Bill. "Mr. President, we need to contact NORAD right away."

"Already done," I said. "Commander Sinclair is on it. He's communicating with all EDC members to helm nuclear launch protocols and spearhead that effort." Bill nodded.

"Mr. President," Bayless breathed, "suppose they attack from multiple vectors – and God forbid that craft splits yet again – will we be able to properly coordinate a planetary defense? Assuming we don't know their precise approach vectors and it doesn't go straight where it did before over the North Atlantic, we're going to have to scramble military and civilian personnel quickly to get to where they are."

"Sinclair knows this, Bayless," I said, rubbing my eyes and shaking off some fatigue. For some reason I was feeling extra irritable. "He's working up a plan for vectors as we speak. We'll need to have Capra or Curtiss take the General's plans and relay those tactics to the other nations. That way they can replicate our plans in additional international jurisdictions as best they can."

Suddenly, headrush took me, and I steadied myself on the desk, quickly sitting down. A swath of black swam before my eyes and my ears rang.

"Mr. President, are you alright?" Bayless said, rushing to my side.

"Fine, Veronica, fine. Thanks. Just a bit of headrush."

"You should take a break, Mr. President. Get some rest. Go see your wife."

I looked up at her. "That sounds like a delightful idea, actually. I'm operating on four hours' sleep and cheap coffee, running back and forth in here without my COS. No offense, Capra, you make a terrific deputy."

"Thank you, sir," he chirped merrily. "But Madame Vice President is right. You should take a break. Perhaps even a nap. At least until Mr. Monzon returns."

"Well," I said, tilting my head and rubbing my face, "I'd like to be here for when he comes out of surgery, but they may be taking a bit longer with him anyway as I haven't heard anything. I think you're right though; I think I'll do that." I stood up slowly, steadying myself again. "Wake me if there are any problems. Say the craft runs into Saturn and explodes. Or if we find that it's loaded with unicorns. Either would be just fine," I said, staggering up and out of the office.

"Yes, Mr. President," giggled my VP. I could feel all their eyes on me as I ambled over to the Presidential Suite to find Andi and Janine.

•　　•　　•　　•　　•

"Where's my First Lady?" I asked in a sing-song voice, entering the suite.

"Hon! How's it going out there?" Andi squealed in excitement, jumping up to come embrace me. Janine followed her, though a bit more cautiously and slowly.

"As good as can be expected, I guess." I kissed her. "And who is this, my little First Daughter?"

"No daughter in this room is getting any littler," she snorted, feeling her bump.

"That's right," I said, grinning at her with pride. "Let it be so. I'm so excited for you, sweetheart. And for Foxy."

"*Liam*," she corrected me.

My daughter hugged me. "You're right. Liam. I think he likes his callsign, though, honey," I said, kissing her head.

"Well, he is kinda foxy," she yawned, raising an eyebrow in the process.

"Are you taking a break, sweetheart? Can you do that?" Andi asked.

"I've practically been ordered to. Almost passed out in the Situation Room. I only got four hours of sleep. Been dealing with sniper fire, alien crafts, Secretary-General, Graham, our guys, the General, the computer geeks, Miguel, and everything else."

"Crafts? Did you say *crafts,* plural?"

I stopped and looked at my wife, free-falling onto our bed.

"You've got to be kidding."

"I'm not. It's the same one; it split into two. They're reading two separate objects, still on the same trajectory, same ETA."

Andi shook her head and rolled her eyes, piling into the bed beside me. Janine sat down in a side chair next to my end-table. "What does that mean?"

"It means," I yawned, "that we need to consider multiple approach vectors. Sorry. Tech speak. They could be coming in from different points, which complicates our defensive postures."

"But we have enough DTF equipment to fight them off, still, right?"

"That's the hope," I said sleepily. "We're extraditing Graham to the countries she betrayed."

"I heard that."

My eyes squinted. "Who did you hear it from? That's supposed to be classified information, lady. I might have to report you."

"Report it all you want. There's a nice, bald, tired man somewhere around here who I think is in charge. But you might have your work cut out for you; I hear he likes me."

I smiled at her.

"Capra told me. I asked. Anyway, I think that was the right move. We need our equipment working, the ones that the three countries have."

Janine was listening to all of this while staring off into space.

"You okay, punkin'?" I asked her.

"Hmm? Oh, yeah, sorry," she said, taking a deep breath. "Just not sure how this is all going to end up. I worry for Liam, of course. He's going to be out there fighting those *things* again. He shouldn't have to. None of us should have to. They had their chance."

I nodded. "Yes they did. But apparently they're not satisfied. Nor will I be unless I get a nap so that I myself have a chance of fighting them off."

Andi smiled warmly at me, running her fingernails gently down my cranium, sending a wash of tingles rippling over my skin. She propped herself up on an elbow beside me, looking down endearingly. "Well," she said, "we're safe for now. You sleep, hon. You protect all of us out there. We'll protect you in here."

"Thank you, hon. Thanks sweetheart," I said to my daughter, and that's all I remember hearing or saying.

•   •   •   •   •

Monday, March 6th 2045 · 1315 hours

"Hon…hon, wake up." Andi shook me gently. "Hey, sleepyhead. You're needed out there. VP Bayless just asked if you were awake yet."

I looked at the clock. 1:15pm. *Is that all?*

I turned to her and opened my eyes wide, inhaling a deep breath and galvanizing my lungs for action. "Okay. I'm up. I'm ready. Let me splash some water on my face."

Andi moved aside and rubbed my back as I passed by her. I looked past my wife and noticed Janine was asleep on the bed. She had lain down next to me during my repose, undoubtedly snuggling up to her daddy. That warmed my heart. Pregnant women needed naps more than Presidents, and this little woman had been forced to be a warrior for too long. I remembered back to the days of Mammoth Cave where everyone knew that you didn't flip my daughter any crap. A tough cookie, indeed.

I threw some water on my face and pulled back, sputtering. My hands gripped the countertop as I stared into the mirror. My eyes were bloodshot. Were those bags under them as well? Here we were, yet again, strained by dissonance, struggling with each other, juggling political nonsense, trying to put ourselves forward, having to handle international messes, when all the while a violent threat drew nearer to our planet with every intention of wiping us out. A perfectly good sniper was killed because of his own blindness and hatred, the former president was almost assassinated, staffers were stressed and oppositional, foreign countries wanted Jean Graham's head on a plate, there were riots and protests in the street, and we were forced to retreat once more to subterranean prisons in order to outlast this second scourge.

I took a slow, measured breath, and held it, closing my eyes. I released it quickly, three times, puffing in and out, and shook my head to wake myself back up, shaking off the sleep. I was the President of the United States of America, and the leader of the free world. I needed to be at my best. People were counting on me through all the stress and nonsense.

And then I heard it, as if from beyond. A calling, a responsibility, or some kind of assurance. A dim and removed voice, but one that I knew all too well. I heard her: communicating gently but with authority, quietly but with urgency, from the wells of my soul.

Know whom you trust, Vance. Know who is worthy of trust. If it has ever been about anything, it has always been about trust. Trust is inevitable if you let it be so.

I knew that voice. I knew that style of speech. To my mind came the ethereal and posthumous image of a beloved friend, fighter, pastor, parent, grandmother, cohort, and fellow warrior, smiling with warmth and encouragement.

Pastor Rosie.

My heart warmed at the sight as I listened.

"You okay, hon?" Andi called quietly from the adjoining suite.

I smiled, knowing full well who had the ear of the Man Upstairs. "Yeah, baby. I'm fine."

Time to go trust.

I kissed Andi and held her tightly, looking deeply into her eyes. I knew my first stop was Miguel, to see how he was doing, and to let him know that I just heard his sweet wife's voice in my spirit. That would encourage him greatly.

•　　•　　•　　•　　•

Monday, March 6th 2045 · 1357 hours

The kitchen called out to me first. Miguel could wait a few more minutes. I realized that I had entirely skipped breakfast except for coffee, which was probably why I was dehydrated with headrush. I devoured some food by myself, amazed by the silence. Everyone else was out there working. Allowed me some peace and quiet to think. Next stop, Chief of Staff Monzon.

There he was, lying in his gurney, still asleep. He would be that way for probably another hour while the Propofol wore off. He was still hooked up to an IV, and his heart monitor beeped a steady rhythm: signs of life. His shoulder dressing had been changed, and he was glowing in white.

He deserved to sleep. I got my nap; this was his. I checked in with Nurse Sorenson, who assured me everything went well, and he would make a full recovery, save for a small, permanent scar. I laughed at that; Miguel was scarred up plenty from all the conflict he had been in throughout his life. Scarred and battled-hardened. He'd be just fine.

I returned to visit Romero once more. "Only been a few hours, Mike, I know. But…any change?"

"No change yet, Mr. President." He stood and saluted me. "Still inbound and pinging steady like a smoke alarm with a bad battery," he whined.

I looked over at Jens. "Jens, did you receive the new decryption information for those subfolders on Graham's drive?"

"I did, Mr. President," he said, giving me a thumbs up. "Everything checks out."

"Alright. Please relay that to Secretary of State Curtiss to provide to our friends in the east, so they can link up the DTF equipment, yeah?"

"You got it, sir," he said, and saluted.

"Alright, thanks, boys."

•   •   •   •   •

Monday, March 6th 2045 · 1502 hours

I was back in my office with Jet and Foxy. General Carson had run off to grab a late lunch. I wished, briefly, that we had a full Joint Chiefs regiment here, but we wouldn't be at that stage for a while. We were still digging out of a nineteen-year hole. Most of them had died before the war, and the others were either out serving or still too young. I was just grateful we had someone as seasoned and tested as General Carson around. His presence imbued confidence in our defense, and the Joint Chiefs that we *did* have would be here for the Launch. We'd take all we could get.

"Well, Camjet," I said to Shipley, "how are you coming with our defense plans?"

"I think we're fine, Mr. President-"

"Please, please, buddy," I said, opening and imbibing some bottled water. "You know better than that. Call me Vance."

Jet smiled genially. "*Vance.* Ya know, I still remember seeing you in the dim light of that cave, sir, looking out at me from under your hood, taking a drag on that smoke. You were mysterious then, and you're mysterious still. But ever since I met you in the forest up above the cave mouth, I knew you were a force to be reckoned with. It's been a while since we've been under the same roof. Glad to be serving in close proximity to you again, sir."

"Me too," echoed Foxy. "Of course, I've been under your roof for the past three Christmases, so, ya know. I'm kinda used to you by now, like an old shoe."

I smirked. "Old shoe, huh? Well, you're a leg up on Jet then, my dear son-in-law. Just count yourself fortunate that you haven't gotten me a fruitcake yet. You'd be right out the door," I said, thumbing behind me. "Speaking of the past, Jet, where are you and Christine now? I've only heard snippets. And," I said, "congratulations on little Wyatt. I had heard from Foxy that you two were pregnant, and I think you've chosen the finest name possible," I said, holding up my water bottle in salute.

He grinned. "Thank you, sir. Yeah, it was kind of a no-brainer. For some reason, Christine had her heart set on 'Myron,' but that always sounded so 'old' to me. When I told her the full story of my brother, she caved instantly. She was on board with *Wyatt* after that."

"And where are you living now?"

"Same place," he said. "Moved back home."

"Back home? To your original home before the Blockades?"

"Yessir. Christine's from Virginia, so, kind of close. Southeast at least. She likes it down there. No sense moving anywhere else regionally that would take us out of what we know. I took her up there in '43 to show her where I grew up, and there it was. Same old house. A little bit of disrepair and a horrible mowing headache, but we applied a little spackle and some napalm, and *bam,* we had a house again. It's taken some time to fix it up, but I've taken up carpentry, and there's some nice folks down the road that knew my mom and dad. He remembered me. I felt bad that I didn't remember him, but I was only six, or even less. Anyway, old guy knows a thing or two about electrical, so he's helped me rewire some stuff. It's not there yet, but it's coming along."

That brought joy to my heart. "Ya know, that's just the kind of testimony we need. 'Someone moved back to their home from before the war, and rebuilt.' I'm glad to hear that, Camjet. And Wyatt's almost one?"

"Yep," he said, nodding proudly. "We didn't wanna wait. Born April 15th last year. Tax Day," he said, laughing and grinning at us. "Not that there's a tax day right now, thank God. Hope you're not in any rush to bring back the IRS, sir."

"Not a chance in hell. Carry on, my wayward son."

"What?" He tilted his head.

"Before your time. Tell ya later. Liam, how 'bout you? Janine is very proud of you, young man. Comin' all the way from obscurity at Harvill Hall to rock the gorgs off the planet and then sweep my daughter off her feet. Whodathunkit?"

Whodathunkit? he said in unison, knowingly. Jet looked back and forth between us questioningly, sensing some exchange that he wasn't privy to: our family catchphrase.

"Yeah, we're still up at Wright-Pat. I enjoy repairing the place, and Janine is loving serving in medical. It's where she belongs, sir. She's actually overhauled the hospital there and made it a lot more efficient. Other nurses look up to her."

"I know, she got Chief Resident pretty quickly. I know it's more an honorary title for now, since no one's had the proper schooling, but…" -here I looked at both Foxy and Jet in earnest- "you guys know all about honorary titles, don't you?"

Foxy winked at Jet and chuckled. "Yes, we do. I outrank him, he outranks me, I outrank him, he outranks me," he jested, elevating one hand above the other alternatingly, squinting his eyes in mock-disapproval. "I don't really know who to salute anymore, sir."

"Me."

"Right," he finished, giving me finger-guns.

We paused, reflecting over old memories from an aging war that was about to be resurrected. "We've been through a lot together, that's for sure. We've gained and lost," I said. And then I thought of Allison Trudy and Joe Bassett. One look from Jet said he was thinking about Ally, and one from Foxy said he was thinking about Joe. Two valiant soldiers, formative to our victories and critical in the war effort from the very beginning. They were heavy losses, those two.

"Well," I said, clearing the air, "the command remains the same. Stay alive out there, fellas."

"How's Miguel, dad?" Foxy put in.

"Gonna be just fine," I said, waving him down. "Yeah, nurse says he'll be out of it soon. I'll check in with him and then prepare to send our special cargo off east."

Jet snorted. "*Special cargo.* To think that she was shipping special cargo over there just a few years ago, since she was hellbent on destruction. Now we're shipping *her* over there, since we're hellbent on survival. My, how times change."

"Indeed, they do," I agreed.

•   •   •   •   •

Monday, March 6ᵗʰ 2045 · 1543 hours

"How you holding up, soldier?" I asked him, sitting down on the side of his gurney.

Miguel scratched his head and yawned, sitting up. He winced and swiveled his shoulder.

"Yeah, that's gonna hurt for a while, señor," I warned him. "You're not twenty anymore." I gave him a smirk.

He gave me a stern look of disapproval. "I'm fine, I'm fine. Take a lot more than that to keep me down," he protested proudly. "Besides, seventy-four is just twenty…rounded up," he said, chortling out a pained laugh as he clutched his shoulder, still trying to sit up.

He blew out hard and then took a deep breath, looking over at me and smiling heartily.

"Good as new," I said.

"Almost. What's new? Fill me in."

As slowly and as painstakingly as I could, I filled him in on all that had transpired since he lost consciousness. My conversation with Graham. The plans for her upcoming extradition. The craft splitting in two. Rosie.

"Rosie?" he asked, lifting an eyebrow. "My Rosie?"

I nodded. "I *heard* her, Miguel. Wanna know what she said to me?"

"Please," he said, quickly.

"She said, 'Know whom you trust, Vance. Know who is worthy of trust. If it has ever been about anything, it has always been about trust. Trust is inevitable if you let it be so.' I know it was her. It was too long not to be her."

"Si," he laughed, "she was long-winded sometimes, wasn't she?" he joked, breaking into uncontrollable laughter. "That definitely sounds like *mi flor preciosa,*" he said, and then his face contorted in pain. Not from his shoulder, but from the aching and untreatable pang of grief and loss.

"You've always called her that."

"I have," he muttered, drying his eyes. "I miss her, my friend. I sure wish she was here now."

"I do too, Miguel. I do too."

I looked at him. He would need some more time to recuperate, but I did need him back on the job. As he lay there, lost in thought over the memory of his dear wife, I smiled upon him and placed my hand on his arm.

"That thing split in two, did it?"

"Yes, it did, my friend. Now we have two problems."

"Hmm. Seems like we'll have more than that."

"You're right," I said.

"Of all the times for Rosie to leave us," he breathed.

To that, I had no answer. Sometimes words just get in the way.

•　　•　　•　　•　　•

Monday, March 6th 2045 · 1803 hours

It was Maddox Leone. The Secretary-General was calling me to confirm readiness for Jean Graham's extradition.

I took it in my office, and we exchanged minor pleasantries. He had spoken to each TOD ambassador.

Graham would fly out from Dulles tomorrow morning on the first westbound flight. It would take her twenty-two hours and thirty-three minutes. Two stops via private US governmental charter under fighter escort. A long, grueling trip, only to be seized upon arrival and escorted to an inescapable prison to await a tribunal.

Such was her fate. But the woman made her bed; now she had to sleep in it.

Leone was cordial, but I sensed that he was excited by this arrangement, which made for awkward conversation. If there was a phantom fourth member of the TOD, I couldn't shake the irritating thought that it would be him. I sensed that he had some greater part to play in the extradition arrangement than I knew.

Nonetheless, we concluded the call amicably with a summary of the craft's location, the news that it had split, the confirmation of Blockade readiness throughout our nation, and his instructions to await further confirmation of the flight plan and manifest.

I didn't want to go see her and relay the news. I sent the message with a staffer that she needed to be ready to go by 0500 tomorrow morning. She would be taken via Marine One to Dulles, and then sent off via a private charter that would take her to Los Angeles and then out over the Pacific. To her final destination. To China.

My head was splitting.

11 | SETBACK

Monday, March 6th 2045 · 2019 hours

An inescapable conflict was coming, and we all felt it in our hearts and souls.

Some of the senior staffers had peeled off for the night, wanting rest from the long day that had begun with Graham's assassination attempt. The techs, however – God bless them – kept at it, and were monitoring everything steadily. They had at least taken naps in shifts.

I had just checked in with Miguel to see if he needed anything else. Nurse Sorenson was wonderful, he said, and she had taken care of everything he had needed. He was reading through the latest intelligence briefings as I walked out.

That's when the alarm went off. "PEOC, PEOC, lockdown, lockdown, time 60 seconds!" came the overhead announcement. The blast doors were slowly dropping down to the floor across the various sectors of the PEOC. Once again, bookending the day, the walls flashed crimson, and a claxon sounded. I jumped out of Medical and ran to the center of the PEOC, looking around wildly. A security guard ran past me and toward the elevator doors to take up his post.

"What's going on?" I cried out to him.

He didn't answer me except to say, "Please retreat to your suite, Mr. President!"

I saw Bayless walking briskly toward me, along with Jet and Foxy. They were flanked by Secret Service. "Mr. President, get to your suite please, we're coming with you!" The agents were escorting her toward me, and two more agents passed them and began to escort us all together.

"What in God's name is going on?" I shouted at them, puffing. We certainly didn't need another 'incident.'

"Perimeter breach, Mr. President. Please come with us," one of them announced robotically. He held his free hand up to his ear and was listening, acknowledging someone speaking up on the surface. "Roger. Broadway is being secured, over."

Broadway. *My code name,* I thought. Heck, Reagan was *Rawhide,* Bush was *Timberwolf,* Clinton was *Eagle*, W. Bush was *Trailblazer,* Obama was *Renegade*, Trump was *Mogul*, Biden was *Celtic*, and Graham was *Iron Maiden.* Only fitting that mine was something from New York.

They rushed all of us into our suite. Andi jumped and Janine yelped. They had been talking when the alarms went off. Where my cabinet and staffers were, I didn't know.

Foxy ran toward his wife, and Janine melted into his embrace. Jet drew his sidearm and stood next to me in cover formation. One Secret Service agent entered with us, while the other three remained outside the door. I recognized this one as Agent Jesse Garrison.

"Garrison, what is it? What's going on?" I asked him.

"Security threat above, Mr. President. Rioters have infiltrated the White House by the dozens. We just didn't have the security forces to defend it. They're at the top of the elevator shaft. They don't have the codes, sir, but they could get them soon."

"This is madness! What do they want?"

"I don't know, sir. I wasn't told. But it might have something to do with the forced mandate."

"Forced mandate?" Janine asked. Foxy was cradling her head in his hands. She pulled away from him and looked at Garrison. "Forced mandate for what?"

These weren't the protests the General had alluded to. His concern was for nature-lovers and tree-huggers who thought we would be nuking a potentially friendly alien species out there. One the gorgons might fear, if these new ones were in fact benign. No. These were what Maddox had referred to.

"The order to return to the Blockades," I said. "Secretary-General Leone mentioned that they were experiencing similar outcries in Italy and in other places of the world. People saying it's a hoax. We saw a little bit of this Sunday night. Forced escorts to the Blockades of those who were resistant to the mandate. Guess there's more up above that feel strongly enough about this," I said, wadding up my notes and throwing them across the room. I felt my face hot. Andi walked over to me. "This is not what any of us need right now."

Andi shook her head and rubbed my back while I stood there, my hands on my hips.

"What can we do, Garrison?"

"I'm instructed to keep you here and protect you, sir, that's all I know."

I looked over at Bayless. "How did they even get inside the perimeter? Are the roof shooters all at a *picnic*, for crying out loud?"

And then, the thought occurred to me that someone might be coming to free Graham. She had limited communication in here, different from her house arrest, and may have found a way to communicate with someone on the outside. Far-fetched as it might be, we couldn't take any chances.

"Garrison, do you still have men posted up outside the former president's door?" He nodded. "Radio them right away, please. Have them go inside and check on her. And double the men outside her door, right away."

"Yessir." He turned away from us and spoke into his cuff mic. "Remain here, please, Mr. President, Madame Vice President. We've got men right outside the door for your protection." Garrison walked out and another agent closed the door behind him.

"What is it?" Bayless asked me.

"I don't know. Might be Graham trying to make a run for it. Can't be certain, but we can't take any chances with her causing any diplomatic standoffs with this *TOD* business," I said, waving my hands in mockery at the coalition of countries. I shook my head and exhaled. "If this is in *any* way her doing…" I trailed off.

"I doubt it, Mr. President. She only has closed-circuit communication in here. Meals, medical, that sort of thing."

"We'll find out soon enough."

At that moment, a dim blast sounded out in the open area of the PEOC. And then another. And another. The floor shuddered. I could hear the agents outside yammering. Our door was locked, but they were clearly taking up positions and coordinating with one another. Altogether, we had only eight Secret Service agents down here, and it was up to them to fend off any threat. Everyone else was most likely armed. Jet and Foxy drew their weapons and posted up.

"Mr. President, Mrs. Cardona, Madame Vice President, Janine, could you please wait in here," Jet asked us while herding us back into the safe room. He and Foxy took up positions behind obstacles in the room. The safe room was a tight fit even for two people. It felt like an elevator with the four of us. Five if you counted Janine's bump.

Even with the safe room door closed, I could dimly make out yelling outside in the corridor. I closed my eyes and listened. Shots fired. Janine covered her ears. I held her and rubbed her back. Bayless pulled out a sidearm she had holstered in her blazer. I was unarmed.

I looked out the tiny peephole on the safe room door. I could dimly make out Jet and Foxy brandishing their weapons and training them on the door, away from us.

More shouting.

Whoever they were, they were inside the bunker. *How the* heck *did they get inside the bunker??* This was supposed to be the most secure place in America!

If they were coming for Graham, they certainly were going about it the right way. Shock and awe. They were using grenades and weapons. I could make out Jet and Foxy both spasming in reflexes when the shots sounded close to us. If the infiltrators had any idea we were in this suite, the only things that prevented them from getting to us after those agents were the two soldiers.

Suddenly, I felt Rosie's words coming back to me. *Trust.* Was this part of it? Was I supposed to trust in this instance as well? If I knew Rosie – and I had – it was supposed to be in every single friggin' instance out there. That's what Rosie stood for. Complete trust.

Reflexively, I raised my palms up and took a deep breath. I felt Andi look at me. She put her hand around me and drew close. My heart was pounding. There were more concussion blasts and reports of gunfire. I just hoped the rioters were far from Medical and would leave Miguel alone.

Suddenly, a lot more screaming. The door to our suite never once opened, but we could hear a wild commotion outside. The rush and thump of feet across the floor traveled into our suite and into the safe room. People were running. No: *fleeing.*

It was pandemonium out there. Jet and Foxy held steady as all our hearts thudded. A sound like helicopter blades rhythmically drubbing, hammering outside our suite, in a motion heading away from the elevator shaft.

A full minute passed, and then another. And then, eventually, the noise faded to dull sounds, and the dull sounds faded to silence. I heard an agent shout "Clear!" Foxy and Jet echoed it. We didn't have Garrison inside with us, so we couldn't know what the Secret Service were saying to each other – if any were even still alive. Whoever was responsible for this was going to pay dearly. *Graham had better be still secured in her suite,* I thought.

Someone knocked on the door to the Presidential Suite, and Jet shouted "Identify!" Another voice, dull from the hallway through the door, answered, "Branson! All clear!" We could hear it. Jet rose instantly, motioning a hand to us to have us wait in the safe room. He cautiously approached the door, peering through the peephole. He signaled to Foxy that all was well and opened the door. Immediately, Branson entered the suite along with another agent whose name I didn't know.

Branson, Jet and Foxy greeted each other.

"Mr. President! PEOC secure. I repeat, PEOC secure!" Branson shouted our way.

Foxy echoed it. "Dad! Janine! Mr. President, sir, Andi, Madame VP, it's ok to come out," he said, walking backward to take up his next post close to us as we exited.

What the heck had happened?

"Branson, what happened? Gimme a sit rep please," I demanded, angrily. Smoke was filtering into our room. I could hear the dull chatter of various voices meandering through the open area of the PEOC, waving away the smoke as they coughed.

"They breached the White House, sir. I was up top; there were too many of them and we had to fall back. I don't know how they got the codes, sir, but they got in. I'm so sorry, Mr. President."

Heads were going to roll for this. "How many down?"

"All senior staffers were protected, sir. They got four of our agents."

"*Four?*" I screamed. "No! This is impossible. How could we let this happen?"

I ground my teeth together and began to head out to survey the damage. Branson stopped me.

"Not yet, Mr. President, it's not safe yet, sir. We're clear, but we need to secure the bunker first."

"Who took them out? What was that thunder?"

Just then, a figure strode through the door, tall and proud. Stocky, hulking, and breathing hard, he emerged defiant, angry, and resigned. A cavernous scar up the side of his face glistened with sweat.

General Carson. He was holding his M107A1, and that thing was a loud sucker. It was a twenty-inch fluted beauty with a fully chrome-lined chamber and bore for the barrel: a recoil operated semi-automatic fifty-caliber destroyer. Each magazine held only ten rounds, but you don't carry that gun unless you're the stuff of legend. *He was.* Carson had fired his weapon while pinned down in a corner of the PEOC when the rioters infiltrated. The living legend took them out almost singlehandedly, cycling through ammunition magazines.

I couldn't believe it.

The scar on his face shimmered as he spoke. "We need to go, sir," said the General. "Through the blast corridor and down to zero zero two. *Now.*"

DN002. The next Blockade in the Ellipse. Had it really come to that? Had we really been evicted from the White House to the bunker, only to be evicted once more to the next Blockade under President's Park?

I was incredulous, shaking my head. Janine and Andi were near tears. Bayless was tense. If anything, Carson knew these parts, and knew that Blockade. We'd be safe with him, but all this was sheer nonsense. We were *still* fighting with each other, even as two alien crafts full of bloodthirsty gorgons barreled toward Earth, only three-and-a-half days out. Yet, look at this. *Look at us!*

Who were these *guys trusting in, Rosie?* I wondered. This was pathetic. I was angry, more so than I had been in a long time. Here we all were trying to keep everyone alive, and all the while these idiots were working to keep only *themselves* alive. It was as if someone had copied the formula for Graham and pasted it into the programming of so many undesirable souls. We would not survive with malefactors such as these drifting freely among us. The gorgons would pick us off while we fought each other.

Eventually the smoke cleared. The blast doors went up. Miguel was wheeled out from Medical. Graham was found and confronted by our own Secret Service agents. They believed her when she said she knew nothing of the attack. Curtiss, Roth, Capra, Austin, Roe, Romero, Jens, everyone else was fine. The blast doors had gone down in time.

Pease and his team had joined the outer defenses up top, ensuring that no other intruders would make it into the White House. The five of them were posted up around the perimeter. I had a passing wish that they had been there all along to prevent the rioters in the first place.

But if the rioters weren't coming for Graham, then that meant only one thing: they were coming for *me.* They were storming the White House to get to me.

Anger at the mandate was the most likely culprit, doubtless inflamed by a desire to strike back at *two* Presidents out of loathing for being inconvenienced. Somehow, they had discovered that Graham was down here with us, and that gave them all the impetus they needed. Kill two birds with one stone. Or, at the very least, take us hostage to demand that they be released from the Blockade mandate. I didn't know and I didn't care.

Now, all of us were gathering our things and preparing to make the six-hundred-foot trek through the underground tunnel down to Blockade DN002. Like so many others, it was comfortless and cold, and we might be trapped there for a while. It would be a long night moving equipment, computers, communications, medical, supplies, and more.

A preventable conflict had transpired, and I resented all of it with my heart and soul.

12 | EXTRADITION

Tuesday, March 7th 2045 · 0400 hours

I awoke fatigued and pissed off.

Three days until that awful thing was here, and we were now militarily handicapped because of the actions of a few fringe elements.

It had taken everyone a few hours to move everything over and down to the other Blockade. Being forcibly displaced put most everyone in a sour mood. It was a long trek, as DN002 was so much deeper underground than the PEOC. Stairs had been carved into the passageway, but there were only three motorized carts to use, and they were primarily reserved for shuttling equipment, not personnel. It took everyone working together in multiple trips to ensure that we got everyone and everything we needed to the other side, safely and expediently.

DN002 was as fine a Blockade as we could hope for. But it was not the PEOC in so many ways, and we had to make sacrifices in comfort, especially. I found myself empathizing with all those who were being forced to return to life underground because of the gorgon threat, but that only made me angrier. Why couldn't everyone just do what was required of them and not make trouble for others? Seems like no matter what we've been through as a civilization, we never learn. Thick skulls, the lot of us.

After multiple sighs and complaints, we were all moved. Janine was one of the first to go, as that dust and smoke wasn't good for her, not that it was good for anyone else. In the process of being relocated we discovered that another staffer was pregnant. She wasn't ready to tell anyone yet as she was under twelve weeks, but the raid and subsequent move had forced her hand. Nonetheless, it gave my daughter someone to talk to and share hopes and fears with: an unexpected friend through adversity.

The infirmary in our Blockade had ample medical provisions, and Miguel had been wheeled to our new location with everything he needed for his recovery.

And with that, the blast doors were closed between DN001 and DN002 with a reverberating thud and sound of whistling air. It locked tight, sealing us off from the PEOC in our new home. At the far end of this Blockade was the other passage, much smaller, leading all the way east to Blockade DN005 under the Capitol Building lawn. That would be a much longer trek, if it came to it.

The guard had been reinforced up above to prevent any further entry or ransacking of the bunker, but sooner or later those men would need to join us down here from the main above-ground entrance on the park. At that entrance, eight imposing gun towers stood, same as every other Blockade: tall, formidable and incredibly daunting. People would think twice about taking a ground-level run at Blockade DN002. Priority One was to get gunners in their gun towers before the rest of us moved in. All of that was coordinated by the Secret Service.

My only frame of reference for the inner bowels of a Blockade had been Mammoth Cave, and my short stay at DN436 after the war. DN002 was far different from the PEOC at DN001 under the White House. It was an actual Blockade, much closer in form and function to all the other Blockades across the nation. It was cold and cheerless as a rule, but fortified and sturdy.

All recon patrols set out from The Launch, of course. Last night I found Jet ambling around, eyeing every corner with a strong sense of familiarity, with an almost giddy stroll down memory lane. It must have reminded him of his home base in Clarksville, awakening memories of his youth and long service there. I wondered if the soldier in him was happy to be back underground, preparing for war. I wondered when – or if – he would get to see his wife and son again.

For now, he had Foxy with him, surveying every nook and cranny under the General's direction. Carson made for an imposing tour guide, brandishing that M107A1 and snapping into action. DN005 at the Capitol building was home to Carson, but he had spent plenty of time here as well.

Speaking of the General, after the rioting, he installed himself at the top of the protection chain, spearheading our relocation.

Graham had been asleep last night when the raid happened, trying to prepare for her extradition today. She was jolted out of sleep by the attack, had to move to DN002 like the rest of us, and then tried her best to return to sleep. But she slept only fitfully.

And now, here she was with me, looking disheveled and none too pleased, probably just as pissed off as I was. We had three days until the craft entered our atmosphere, and, for her, the whole of one of those would be spent cooped up on a private flight to China.

She looked even older now, if that were possible: dressed in a thin denim coat and slacks, with some oddly-colored shawl completing the ensemble. It was a far cry from the decorum-laden and emboldened figure proudly attired in presidential fatigues just a few years prior. She was carrying a small paisley purse.

She regarded me coldly as she exited her new room in DN002, escorted by Secret Service. Marine One had landed at President's Park and was whirring above us on the Ellipse. It would take her to Dulles, where she would catch her charter and begin the long journey westward to her new confinement.

I motioned to the Secret Service agent to give us a moment. It was Garrison once again. Thankfully, he had made it through last night's raid. He withdrew a few paces away from us.

"Good luck, Jean," I said to her as I walked her up to the Launch and stood across from her. For now, the doors of the Launch remained closed as we spoke together. Graham was a foot and change taller than me, and, though wrinkled by age and diminished by public humiliation and scorn, she nonetheless still loomed over people. She was still as imposing as a Blockade gun tower.

"Save it, Vance," she snapped matter-of-factly. "We both know this isn't going to end up well for me. It gives me some comfort to know that the frustration of my own eviction is mirrored by your own. In three days, I'll have moved three times. All everyone seems to want to do is shuttle me around to wherever they want me. Fine. I'm looking forward to staring my captors in the eye before I spit in their faces. I doubt you'll get to do the same with yours."

The gorgons. That's who she meant.

"We'll see," I said. "Wherever you end up, I've been told that you'll have as much protection as anyone else when the craft arrives."

Graham didn't say anything. She just stared into my eyes, and then slowly, eerily, moved closer to me, gazing down at me with steely eyes in that gnarled face.

"All that time, all those long years of survival and preparing, you and Monzon were right under my very nose," she said, shifting her jaw and regarding me coldly. "You were both hatching your little plans, forming your little alliances. And then you had the gall to brazenly infiltrate my Embassy with your partner to meet your little spy, Miguel. I should never have relocated you. I should have kept you in my sights. I should have had you eliminated instead of reassigned. We'd be better off."

"No one knows," I countered quickly, unphased by her expected parting shots. "What's plain to everyone now is that, because of the Resistance, we have far more people to fight back against a tyrant because their lives were spared."

"Oh, I'm a tyrant now, am I?"

"I was talking about the gorgons, Madame President. But if the shoe fits," I said, holding my hands up. "The point being, all tyrants eventually face the music. The gorgs did; they will a second time. I wish you luck with your own symphony."

She stared back at me, perhaps in the throes of some scathing response. Our eyes locked, us presidents, and for a moment we felt oddly like contemporaries. But the cold truth found its way into my heart. I was not a tyrant, but rather an honorable servant of the people. Jean Graham was a power-hungry, narcissistic, self-absorbed dictator.

"You have always misperceived me. I am *not* the enemy. I was only trying to safeguard the United States of America as its President, and I did what I thought was best according to what I had to work with at the time." Her speech was quickening, and her voice was rising in pitch and volume. "Those people were standing in my way of delivering us from the gorgons! I just wanted to help us all reclaim our planet. No one understands! They all have only *ever* assumed the worst of me. *Each person is more than the worst thing they've ever done,"* she practically pleaded with me. "A line by Bryan Stevenson."

I recognized the quote, but I had one of my own.

"You can justify your actions all you want, Jean. But, *the greatest enemy to human souls is the self-righteous spirit which makes men look to themselves for salvation.* Charles Spurgeon." And then I stepped back and slowly saluted her, standing at attention.

She eyed me curiously, perhaps affronted by my respectful sendoff, unaccustomed to receiving an honorable salute. Graham shook her head wearily, and then slowly clicked her loafers together, standing at attention herself.

She brought her hand to her brow and mirrored my salute. But she did it with a smirk, and I read it in her eyes.

I relaxed my posture, and then did something that she did not mirror, nor would she ever. Slowly, with reverence, I extended my hands and brought my palms up toward the sky, receiving this moment, this justice, this deliverance from evil. And somewhere, I felt, a sweet, diminutive Mexican woman was smiling down on me as she danced upon the grass of Heaven.

Graham clicked her tongue in disgust, looking away. "That palms-up nonsense again. Good riddance."

"Goodbye, Jean," I said, and then strode confidently back into the Blockade.

I could feel her eyes burning holes into me as I retreated. No matter what she told herself, she had plotted the demise of an already destitute and downtrodden civilization.

She had commiserated nefariously with her soothsayers. She had planned a nuclear attack on the soil of the TOD. She had attempted to assassinate three world leaders.

She had framed me for the death of her Colonel.

Destroyed my Blockade.

Caused the death of three soldiers dear to my compatriots.

Wyatt Shipley.

Allison Trudy.

Joe Bassett.

I said their names to myself, quietly, honoring them as I turned my back on Graham. The agents stepped back toward her and led her up and out to the waiting helicopter.

Whatever Jean Graham wanted to think about herself, she was gravely mistaken. The list of charges against her was long and irrefutable. She would answer for her crimes yet again, in a military tribunal far from home: comfortless, isolated, disconnected, *alone*.

I took one look back as I proceeded down the hall. I don't know why I did. I half expected her to have remained standing there, staring at me with contempt and elderly ire, wrapped up in a desire to curse me and everyone else in a parting shot that she felt might perhaps assuage her own irritation.

Instead, I saw a tall yet fragile woman slowly ascending the Launch, mindful of every step on her way up, gripping the cold railing in tense exhaustion. What once had been so proud and self-assured, bent on securing her own power, was now reduced to nothing. She was wasted away, a shell of herself, removed from power, and devoid of power herself. Impotent and venomless.

Despite her twist of fate, I had no pity. Her extradition would mean that the DTF jetties would be in operation, and perhaps more lives would be saved.

She would sleep fitfully on that flight, if at all.

I would sleep deeply, with a clear conscience and satisfied.

13 | INEVITABLE

Tuesday, March 7ᵗʰ 2045 · 1630 hours

The rest of the day passed uneventfully.

Much of our first day in DN002 was spent sorting everything out and putting it into place. For myself, I needed to check with Jens and ensure that he got the proper ciphers for the DTF linking codes and that they had all been verified. He confirmed that they were. Jean Graham was on her way. That was only one of the conditions the TOD had stipulated. The others were related to the equipment, and all of it needed to be accessible and operational, or there would be no deal, and we would have relinquished her for nothing.

Everyone was coping with our new accommodations as best they could, but some people, like Treasury Secretary

Barrett Roth, were ever the whiner. Constant complaints about lack of space and provisions. For someone accustomed to fiscal conservatism, he sure wanted to be afforded much.

I could hardly blame him, however. After all, we were now underground, yet again, living like moles, and it made it all the harder that we had, ever so briefly, tasted the free air. The memory of that short-lived, tantalizing freedom could not be erased.

Nonetheless, for some people, despite the terror of the night before, the mood was actually lighter – jovial even – except for Roth, that is. It was as if a heavy blanket had been lifted from most of us, and the removal of Graham played no small part in our revitalization.

People were going about their tasks with a sense of purpose, getting settled in for what might become a long stay. My thoughts turned briefly to my daughter and the other pregnant woman having to give birth down here – as I know many had done in the days of occupation – and how that would be for her, for the baby, and for all of us.

ETA two and a half days for both crafts. Not enough time. Just not enough time! I needed to touch base with Romero and Greene and check for any new reports on its movements. I met Miguel in the corridor. He looked a bit hunched over from age and injury, but still alert and foreboding. Jet was beside him, steadying him. Foxy was off with Janine, somewhere.

"Amigo! You're up! How are you feeling?"

"Exhausted," he said. "It's amazing how tiring lying around is." He shook his head. "I needed to get moving."

"Well, careful now…Doc's orders, I'm sure," I reminded him, and then went in for a gentle, cautious hug, being careful of his left shoulder, still in a splint. His left arm rested over his stomach. "You believe this guy, Camjet?"

Jet shook his head. "He's a tank. Always has been. But you couldn't ask for a better Chief of Staff." Monzon looked over at him gratefully. "Seriously. I'll never forget when you took out that queen, Miguel. I said to myself I'd follow you into battle any day. I meant it."

"Well, maybe you're about to again, *muchacho.* We'll see. And speaking of *queen*," -here he turned back to me- "I missed what was probably a pathetic show this morning, yes? You sent away our prima donna?"

"I did. She landed in LA around 11am. I'm sure she's aloft once more. There was no love lost between us. She'll never change. I just hope the TOD honors their agreement."

"TOD?" Jet asked me.

"Triumvirate of Dissent," I enunciated slowly. "It's the coalition formed between China, Iran and North Korea in the wake of Graham's betrayals."

He nodded. "Well, I'm for one glad that I didn't run into her. I've seen and know all I need to about that woman. The further away from me she is, the better."

I studied him for a moment. "You could have been a Lefebvre once."

"Exactly. I *wanted* to become a Lefebvre once. The woman got my baby brother killed. Just when I thought I had moved on, they brought her in here. You think you're strong enough for some things, ya know? That you've moved on. When I saw her, my stomach and my nerves said otherwise. I'll never forget it."

"Nor will I," I said, clapping his shoulder. "Ever. And now, guys, I'll leave you to it. I need to check in with the techs for an update on the crafts. You heading to dinner?"

"Yep."

Miguel nodded and heaved a sigh.

"Take care of him, Jet. I'll see you both in the mess hall soon."

·　　·　　·　　·　　·

Tuesday, March 7ᵗʰ 2045 · 1636 hours

A point of no return was approaching swiftly. We were coming up on a decision to launch, and we needed to commit. "Punch this up right here, please, Romero," I said to him, pointing out a section of the grid. "Is this roughly eight thousand?"

"Yessir."

"Just beyond the exosphere. That's where we plan to hit it."

"That's right, sir. *Blammo* - like *Space Invaders.*"

"Sure. And their present course bears them about here and here?" I said, pointing to two potential arcs passing our moon. Each arc placed one of the crafts at equidistant locations from the other, on opposite sides of the Earth.

"Yeah, Mr. President, that's correct. It just depends on when they split. You can see they're going in a straight line. So, here's their projected course. If we hit them at that planned strike zone of eight-thousand miles out before they diverge, it might work."

"It might. But there's three distinct possibilities. One, we hit them and take them both out. Two, we hit one of them while the other diverges and goes around our birds. Three, they both diverge, and our birds sail right through and hit nothing."

"That sounds about right. I'm hoping for possibility number one, sir," said Romero.

"I'm hoping for that too, kid," I said, clapping him on the shoulder. "And where are they now? They're still pinging?"

"Like a son of a gun, sir. The pings are getting louder as they're drawing nearer. No change in frequency or signal harmonics. They're right here on the orbital plane. See? Passing Saturn here, both of them, eight-hundred fifteen-million miles away," he said, moving his mouse in a circle over the two adjoining dots on the graph, traveling parallel to each other. "After that, its Jupiter and the main asteroid belt. Nearly all those asteroids don't have very elongated orbits, ya know? There are maybe one point five million asteroids in there, about one kilometer in diameter. Millions and millions of smaller ones. Maybe we'll get lucky and one of the biggies will break free and cause a little traffic accident. *Oooops! Sorry,*" he joked, and stifled a snort.

"That would be nice, wouldn't it," I said, not meaning it as a question. "The most plausible scenario, however, is that it will continue on this trajectory and rendezvous with us *here*, right?" I pointed to a location on the bottom orbit around the sun where they would, presumably, approach from. "We're still projected to be on the far side of the sun."

"That's correct, Mr. President. Our orbit takes a whole year. We're only talking four days here. We're already on the far side of the sun. Without any massive solar wind changes, they'll continue at their current pace unless they have some kind of massive propulsion system. Archival reports did have the first one moving at an unconstrained velocity as it approached our moon."

"This one won't be hiding behind our moon."

"No way, sir."

Greene suddenly switched on and patched into our feed from SETI. "Evening, Mike. Evening, Mr. President. Sorry I'm late."

"Good evening, Mr. Greene," I greeted him. Romero did the same. "No problem. I assume nothing's changed on SETI's end?"

"No, sir," he said. "Hubble's still tracking, and the shape of the craft – before the split, that is – can now be more clearly seen proximally. It's definitely got the same shape and attributes as the first one."

"Yeah, I read the same here," Romero said.

"Just for final confirmation, is there *any* reason to assume that it might possibly be something else? Have we ruled that out? We must be absolutely certain that it's the gorgs before we fire on it," I said with a clenched lip. "We've already had a security breach around here from protesters and rioters. If that thing turns out *not* to be gorgons, and we shoot it down, we're never going to be able to mitigate the civil unrest that will ensue."

"Understood, Mr. President," Greene replied. "Telemetry, trajectory, right ascension and declination origin points, mass and DSN scans match it up almost exactly to the previous craft. Hubble's images match it to the T, even with the split. And they looked at the old Hubble images as well. Same."

I drew a long, slow, steady intake of breath into my lungs. "Alright, guys. Thanks again. Keep me in the loop," I said.

"Yes, Mr. President," they echoed.

I texted Bayless, Miguel, Capra, General Carson, Curtiss…

I texted everyone.

· · · · ·

Tuesday, March 7th 2045 · 1705 hours

I found my VP in the mess hall.

"Bayless, what's the situation with the Blockades? How are we doing on residency?"

"Almost there, sir," she reported, finishing off a bite. I sat down beside her with my tray. "Most are reporting around eighty-percent capacity and climbing. Still have some holdouts. Some of them are already maxed and preparing to close."

"What are they doing with the stragglers?"

"Protocol is to refer them to the nearest Blockade of course, but word on the street is that they're taking them in anyway. The mandate was for them to return to their previous Blockade, so population should have, technically, remained the same. We haven't had a lot of babies reported in the latest census," she finished sadly.

"Yeah, well, there'll be one more in here in twenty-four weeks," I said, meaning Janine. "It'll be like having a newborn again, for all of us," I said, waving my fork around the room at everyone in here. And then it hit me, just watching them eat, silently talking amongst themselves.

"Look at us. Look at all of us," I said, gazing around the room at all our Blockade members. "We're one and the same. No hierarchy. Staffers, interns, a general, soldiers, cabinet members, the Joint Chiefs: we're all the same. This is exactly how it was at Mammoth Cave. One big happy family. This how it was for you in Alpharetta?"

She smiled. "Almost identical, sir. The Blockades were all mapped out from the same schematic, so this is really close to what we had at DN282, minus a few attributes and some extra floor space and top-brass accommodations, given its proximity to the White House, of course." She winked at me and then continued to eat. "And it's a *lot* lower down. Warmer in here."

"Do you miss those days?"

She turned to me, lost in thought for a moment. "Sometimes. Sometimes I have dreams, Mr. President, of being back at 282 and commanding. I remember when we first started making the masks. I remember when they caught that gorg. I remember the teams we had and the environment we lived in. It wasn't exactly family, you know: those of us in Command had a bit of forced separation as we had so much on our plates. But, in particular, I do think back to the two we lost while you were at Mammoth Cave."

"Allison Trudy and Joseph Bassett."

She nodded. "Those two were especially formative in our war. What they did, sir…" she trailed off, shaking her head.

I watched her, waiting. "What?"

"Well," she continued, "I mean, look at the masks, Mr. President. What Allison Trudy and Chance Masterson did was give us all a fighting chance. You take away the masks and, even though we still have the DTFs, we're still fighting blind, unable to see what we're aiming at." I nodded, looking around to make sure that Jet Shipley was out of earshot. I could see him, sitting a few tables over in the mess hall, talking with Miguel, as well as Secretaries Roth and Austin. Janine and Andi were sitting with their backs to me, and my daughter was nestled up close to Foxy.

"I remember her," I said. I thought back to meeting her in the cave with Shipley, following our initial encounter up top when my soldiers – including my daughter – surprised Jet and Foxy with the truth about who I was.

"And Joe Bassett, sir. He was a tremendous soldier. Really inspired confidence. One in a million. On the team that wrangled a gorgon, brought it back to the Blockade, losing his sister in the process, and another soldier as well. He studied that thing for a long time. Went 'under the mask,' as we called it, getting up close and seeing how they work. Heckuva soldier."

"He was. You know that he died saving Foxy?"

Bayless' eyes narrowed. "Foxy?"

"Corporal Liam Fox Mayfield, my son-in-law. Jet calls him Foxy. It stuck."

"I did not know that. How did he die?"

"Going out with a blaze of glory," I said, sipping my water. "He helped Lieutenant Shipley and Allison Trudy escape. He helped Foxy escape. Drew the gorgs off of them intentionally. Took his mask off."

She swallowed hard. "I…hadn't heard that. I did spend a considerable time consoling his wife, Maureen, however. Very fine woman." And then she paused, glancing over at Jet and Foxy. "They're close, aren't they?"

"Like brothers," I answered. "Brothers born out of adversity. Foxy is a surrogate, you know."

"For Shipley's little brother. Yes, I've heard the story."

"That story is what started everything, Veronica. Graham's calling those suicide missions. Jet, Rutty – that was his little brother's nickname – and then Trudy and Bassett. All of them lost him at Harvill Hall in December of 2042. Set Jet on a path of no return, wanting justice. We eventually got it. Rosie sure was formative in that."

She smiled warmly. "Rosie Campion. She was amazing, sir. Just amazing."

"More than anyone here will ever fully grasp, except Miguel of course." I glanced at Miguel and saw him laughing heartily over some exchange with Jet and the staffers. That made my heart glad. He was recovering both from the loss of Rosie, and the injury to his shoulder.

"Speaking of Graham, I should get a status report from Maddox Leone on where she's at. He should be calling again soon to update me on what they're doing with her, if not *to* her."

Bayless shook her head.

"It was all inevitable," I mumbled.

"What did you say, sir?"

"Huh? Oh, I was just saying that it was all inevitable. All of it. The gorgs. Graham's rise, her fall. Wyatt Shipley.

The downfall of both the gorgs and Graham. And," I said, turning to her, "their return. All of it, inevitable."

"What makes you say that, Mr. President?"

I smiled. "Just something Rosie said to me." I stared out into space, reflecting on her words.

"What did she say to you?" Bayless pressed.

I turned to her. *"Trust is inevitable if you let it be so.* All of this has been about trusting God to bring us through. She was big on that. Life takes you on a journey whether you like it or not. That part is inevitable. But trust is inevitable as well, if you let it be so. Trust has to be intentional, of course. We just need to let ourselves be taken there. It's all too common to doubt and fear. Rosie was very big on trust. I think she meant that God's already got you; you just have to choose to surrender."

"I wish I could have known her better," said my VP. "She sounds like she was critical to our victory in the war."

I looked over at Miguel. "She was. She, and her wisdom, will be critical again. This enemy is relentless. So must we be."

Bayless looked at me hard. "So must we be. Aye, sir." And then she raised her bottled water to me. Without hesitation, I tapped mine against hers and nodded.

The rest of our lives would not pass uneventfully.

14 | ADAPTING

Wednesday, March 8th 2045 · 2310 hours

We were coming down to the wire, and things were getting tense.

Tension breeds stress, and stress breeds hunger. I was hungry again. I went to the mess hall to see what I could grab for myself, and there was Jet, sitting close to the entrance, alone. He seemed pensive, lost in thought.

"Hey, Camjet," I said, walking up and clapping him on the shoulder. He rose and saluted immediately.

"Mr. President."

I waved him off. "Stop that. Decorum between friends is like Oreos on a pizza. Call me Vance, or I'll throw you in the brig."

"We don't have a brig here, Vance," he said, sitting back down. "I explored the whole place."

"Yeah, I know. I'll have them make one," I said, winking at him. I sat across from him, momentarily forgetting why I had come. My stomach reminded me in a growl of protest, but conversation between friends was good food.

"You talk to Christine?"

His eyes shone. "Yessir, just got off a chat with her. Baby's so cute. I miss 'em," he said, with a heavy sigh. "Wyatt's gonna be taking his first steps any day now. *Any day,*" he said, shaking his head, and the lament was clearly there: he wanted to be there for that moment.

"I'm sorry, Shipley," I said, clenching my lips. "Those are hard moments to miss. They got cameras there though, right? She's got a cellphone so she can record it if he does?"

He nodded.

"Hey, listen," I said, attempting to brighten the mood, "we won't be down here long enough for you to miss it. Right?"

"I'll drink to that," he said, taking a swig of his bottled water. "Anyway, they're safe. Confirmed it with Stone. Really good to talk to both of them."

"Both of them?" I asked him.

"Yeah. Christine and Stone. Had to catch up with the wifey, definitely, but it was good to do a little reminiscing with Stoney as well. He's a good man. He'll take care of everyone there. He always has."

"Maurice Stone. He's kind of like a second father to you, yeah?"

Jet nodded quickly. "Absolutely. We got to DN436 and I was only six, going on seven. Met him at our first orientation. Same day I met Rosie."

"What a power-packed Blockade that was. You guys had you, your brother, Rosie, Ally, Joe, and then Miguel in-house for a spell as well. Even the President at one point."

"*The gang's all here,*" he joked. "We had 'em all. I sure miss Señora Rosie, man. You don't know what you have 'til it's gone, right? I'm just sorry that Christine never got to meet her, and vice versa. She kept me afloat."

"She kept all of us afloat," I concurred.

Jet and I paused. A torrent of memories flowed through our minds, all stemming from the occupation, but especially from December 2042, no doubt.

"Anyway, what's up?" he asked. "Are you down here to scrounge up some food? You must be hungry."

I nodded. "Yeah. Famished, actually. Been a long day."

"Tell me about it. I'm ready, though. Foxy is too. You're a lucky father-in-law, Vance. Bet you never saw that coming, huh?"

I couldn't help but smile and shake my head. "I think Andi saw it first. The way Foxy kept watching her at Wright-Pat ever since you guys got there. And, moreover," I corrected myself, "I think it was the way *she* was watching *him*. That mop-top of his," I finished, and Jet laughed. "That kid always had a mop-top under some kinda backward hat, remember that?"

"I sure do. Ever since I met him. I think it helps him shoot straight. He and Rutty, man, I don't know what it is with the younger guys but both of 'em always loved their RPGs."

"Yes they did," I said, laughing. "He got some good hits out at the base. And *both* of you got some great hits out over the Atlantic. Thanks again, shooter."

He raised his bottled water to me, swallowing through a smile. As he did so, I caught the glint of a necklace shining through from under his fatigues. It was his amulet necklace, with a cracked piece of gorgon technology inscribed with strange glyphs. A gift from Pastor Rosie. She once had it set in silver and inscribed with the words *Deliver Us From Evil.* Jet had worn that all through the war. Rosie had told me all about it. It kept his little brother, Rutty, and his fiancé, Ally, alive in his memories. It had empowered him to go on.

"Ya know," I offered, "I never did thank you properly for Ally."

Jet stopped mid-swallow, looking at me hard. The name seemed to spring out at him from the past, catching him off-guard. It had been three years, but it was a ghostly name that sounded a clear bell of awakening. "Oh?"

"For all she did. That woman set our feet a-dancin.' She gave us a fighting chance. Allison Trudy was a pioneer of science. She gave us the breakthrough we needed, man."

Jet nodded. "She sure did, didn't she?"

"She sure did."

"We got a good one-two punch back then, both from Ally and whoever came up with the DTFs. Both saved our asses," Jet said.

"They sure did. I don't even know who thought up the DTFs, but it's been credited to some tech at BNA. One of the soldiers, it had been said, nonchalantly suggested audio weaponry, and they just ran with it. He's a phantom hero now, whomever he is."

"He deserves credit too, for sure," Jet answered.

"Yes he does. Someday we all will."

•   •   •   •   •

Wednesday, March 8th 2045 · 2337 hours

It was late. Time to hit the hay. I was showering first, however, washing the stress of the day off of me, and reflecting on all that had transpired.

Sunday seemed so long ago, over the slow and steady, stress-filled march of the past few days. We had been through so much already, and would still have much to go through in prep for our defense.

Over the last day, the weight of what Romero and Greene had shared made my shoulders droop. It was a heavy blanket that brought no consolation whatsoever. We thought the gorgons were gone for good. But no: it was definitely them. They were in fact returning, and we were in fact going to have to defend ourselves once more. It was wishful thinking to imagine a second extraterrestrial encounter as possibly benign. No. In the early, youthful, optimistic phase of only just beginning to rebuild, we would be assailed once more. At least this time we would be more prepared with formidable weapons. Nonetheless, it was a cruel twist of fate that would require *all* of us to trust that God had our backs. We would make it through.

Nonetheless, it forced me to ask some serious questions of our civilization in the privacy of my mind.

Had we failed to learn from the first experience? Would we always be living in dissonance with each other? Would we make it through as one, or still be just as fragmented and splintered as we had always been?

My thoughts went to the middle East and Asia. Sure, there was a ceasefire imposed after we won the war with the gorgons. For three years now we had had peace. But the Israelis and the Palestinians were still at odds domestically and politically. The Russians never forgave the Ukrainians, and the Ukrainians never forgave the Russians. Ukraine had been admitted into NATO, finally, but Russian had not. That also drove a wedge.

And then, suddenly, my thoughts were pulled all over the world, thinking back to all of the messy conflicts we were embroiled in, all the natural disasters we had undergone, all the devastation we had lived through from just before the invasion up until now.

In Haiti, gang violence had been reduced, mostly because nearly all the gangs, quite simply, had been eaten by the gorgons. Political instability and gang violence was still an issue, however. Armed gangs seizing control of distribution routes and preventing passage of goods and fuel hurt everyone. Cholera outbreaks were everywhere, straining health and sanitation.

Burkina Faso still had armed groups on the fringes, waiting to strike and seize land once again. Factions abounded. Instability reigned.

Civil war in South Sudan had ravaged the country prior to the invasion, but localized fighting left them weakened and primed for gorgon slaughter. They are still incredibly fragile, and floods and droughts have continued to harm them.

Syria. A decade of war brought the country to its knees prior to September 2026. Humanitarian aid diminished and then stopped altogether, then the healthcare system collapsed, followed by the economic system. They were only just now beginning to crawl out from under the ground.

Armed groups and government forces in Yemen still strove for dominance. Ninety percent of what remained of the Yemeni population floundered in malnourishment and poverty.

The entire population of Afghanistan was still poor, and getting poorer. Economic collapse had already happened, and each winter since the war had claimed even more lives as those who had mercifully survived the gorgons were left to die from exposure. Ironic and altogether tragic.

In Ethiopia, a few hundred thousand were still in need of humanitarian aid despite the November 2022 peace deal so long ago. Aid just couldn't deliver enough.

In Somalia, drought and hunger killed off more than the gorgons had. Climate change, caused by us, leveled their society through endless severe droughts.

Even after sixteen years of alien occupation, people were still throwing each other under the bus, putting themselves forward, and eager for self-preservation regardless of the cost to others. As we emerged from the shadows, we found a world ravaged by destructive forces more powerful than gorgons. *Us.* We did it to ourselves. We were *still* devastating each other's lives. The raid on the PEOC just a few nights ago was just more proof of that.

Jean Graham was the poster child for that, of course. I spoke with the Secretary-General and received my update. She had landed and been taken into custody. China promised that the tribunal would be televised over the Internet, so we would at least see that she was still alive and facing judgment, not stuffed in a dark dungeon and waterboarded.

It was some recompense that the Chinese held up their end of the bargain and provided Attorney General Willingham a signed agreement that they would be releasing custody of the DTF equipment and barges, detonators, triggers, jetties, cables, all of it, back to us following the impending conflict. There was no date provided for when that would be, not even an 'on or before.' *Why would there be?* I thought. *Will we even be alive then?*

C'mon, Vance, I told myself. *You can't think like that. Trust. Just like Rosie. Trust.*

I had returned to my bunk, and was now in the shower, ready to retire for the night. Janine was with Foxy in his bunk. Everyone else had retired. No one liked their new lodgings, and Andi and I – and I daresay Janine, due to being the First Daughter – felt guilty about ours. They were arguably nicer and more spacious. There was a safe room in the back, as there had been at the PEOC, which of course no one else enjoyed in their own bunks. This Blockade had definitely been constructed with the Presidency in mind given its proximity to the White House.

I washed up, brushed my teeth, and emerged from the bathroom to find my wife lying on the bed looking my way. *I knew that look.*

"Oh, hon, are you serious? It's so late."

She smiled at me. "Well…I mean…kind of. But I understand if you're not up to it," she offered in a conciliatory manner. "It's been a long day."

"It has. And this isn't exactly our suite at the PEOC. Just look at that door," I said, pointing to the plywood cover with the swinging lock. "Not exactly soundproof, hon." Oddly, I thought then of all the places we *could* make love secretly in this Blockade. There weren't many.

"You're right. I know. It's okay!" she said as I lay down beside her. She put her hand on my chest and rubbed it, tousling my chest hair playfully. I narrowed my eyes at her and couldn't help but smile.

"You're horny."

"Kinda. But it's okay!" she insisted.

"Is this where you use the line *this could be one of our last nights on earth* and I realize the error of my ways and make passionate love to you?"

"No!" she said, clicking her tongue. "Really, it's fine. I know it's late."

"Yet you continue to tousle my chest hair." Andi giggled. I just stared at my beautiful bride. "Something the matter? Janine okay?"

"No! Nothing's wrong. And yep she's fine. Just thinking about stuff. It's so crazy that we're here."

"I know," I said, rubbing my forehead. "Far cry from the PEOC. Which, in and of itself, is a far cry from the mansion."

"Do you miss it?"

I thought to myself. "Oddly, not really. It's okay. 'It is what it is,' right? Roll with the punches. *Fuggedaboudit* is the easiest thing to do. Adapt and overcome."

"Do you think we'll do that?"

"What?"

"Adapt and overcome?"

"Well, I sure hope so. We kind of have to, my love."

"Yeah."

She looked away and sighed. My heart sighed with her, knowing what was to come. I studied her emotions as she pondered. There was only one thing to say.

"This could be one of our last nights on earth, ya know," I teased.

She turned to me sidelong, flicked up her eyebrows and smiled, burying her lips into mine.

•   •   •   •   •

Thursday, March 9th 2045 · 0500 hours

The alarm woke me up. Andi rolled over on her side and moaned briefly, but that was all she managed.

Once more, I found myself just staring at my beautiful bride as she lay there asleep. I stroked her hair in the darkness of our bunk, and she purred softly. No one was calling for me, so I just sank back down and wrapped my arms around my bride.

The present wasn't calling yet. I just lay there and let the memories consume me.

We had gotten married in 2017 in Katonah. We had both grown up in moderately wealthy New York homes. She was an art major at Columbia, and I was majoring in Information Technology. Funny how that prepared me for sniffing out Graham's dubious intentions. Nonetheless, I ultimately abandoned IT and instead enlisted in the Air Force.

I knew Andi was the one for me.

Beauty is only skin deep, but she wasn't just attractive; she had depth and insight the likes of which I'd never known. We were two peas in a pod: a natural fit. She was completing my sentences by our fourth date. I loved her with all my heart. This woman had me at *hello.*

We always had wanted a boy, but that wasn't fated for us. Nonetheless, we were both overjoyed the day I came home from my IT firm to see Andi standing in our apartment holding the test. There they were: two solid lines. Our lives were about to change forever.

Janine was born on August 3rd 2022. She was underweight and had, at one point early on, approached 'failure to thrive.' She just wasn't nursing properly, couldn't latch. Andi muscled through like a champ. And our little Neener eventually started bottle-feeding and thriving. That's what we called her: Neener. Even as a young preschooler, she would get anyone back who messed with or teased her. She romped and cavorted with a sing-songy, triumphant *Neener! Neener! Neener!* People knew she was full of spunk and ready for action.

Action was what Andi sprang into in the fall of 2026 when the gorgs attacked. She was in Dayton, Ohio visiting family with little Neener, and they fled to Wright-Pat.

Six months prior, I had become an advisor to the Secretary of Defense after serving terms in the Air Force, a Seal Team and covert ops in Afghanistan. However, a back injury relegated me to desk work, and that's when I shifted to politics. I figured a focus on internet security and service in the armed forces made me a valuable asset to the government. And the woman lying beside me had been my backbone all along, supporting me, standing with me as I was sworn in as an advisor to the SecDef. That was a monumental achievement and a huge step-up in profile.

Then the gorgs activated in 2026. I was onboard Air Force One, with Trump and his staff – and House Speaker Jean Graham – set to land at Nashville airport. Andi and Janine were frantic back home, and I told them to put their phone on vibrate and just text me. And, above all else, *hide!* They scrambled. *Boy* did they scramble, just like the jets that day in our counteroffensives. I hate to say it, but thinking back to the invasion, the jets scrambling in the air is probably what saved Andi, Janine, and so many others. The gorgs pursued the jets instead, mostly.

My family was safe – for now. But it killed me to be away from them for so long, communicating only electronically. In that, I related to Miguel being apart from Rosie for so long.

Then I found out about Graham's nefarious plans, and was reassigned after trying to approach Vice President Cooper about my concerns. Cooper himself told me to hit the road, and that I was to be reassigned to Mammoth Cave. Couldn't believe it. That was a hard ninety-three mile walk. They sent me with some peon, Private Kendall Forrester, who wouldn't stop yammering the whole way. I practically almost shot him myself.

At long last, however, the Blockade yawned up over the hill, and down I went into the dark of the cave, and Armstrong went with me. I didn't trust him. Seemed kinda sneaky, and I trusted my own intuition more than him.

All this time I had kept in contact with Miguel and informed him of our progress. I knew what Graham was doing, and what she was capable of. He confirmed my suspicions, as had so many others. When we found out about the large DTF and other shipments of equipment heading east – including nukes – I knew in my heart that she needed to go. I began in earnest to build the Resistance. Admiral Evelyn Lynch was one of the hardest to win over. People who are no bullshit are always the hardest to win over. It's always the dramatic ones that sign up right away.

Maybe that's why Armstrong signed up with Graham to be her little Mammoth Cave plant and spy on us.

All the while, Janine had become a survivor and a soldier. Saved Andi's life a time or two out of her own intuition. *She got that from me,* Andi and I would joke. Janine trekked two-hundred thirteen miles. I'd never felt more afraid in my life. She came with twenty soldiers from Wright-Patterson, journeying over nine days with multiple stops. They lost three on the way to gorgs while the rest of them hid. Never did I hug my daughter tighter than when she came down those steps at Mammoth Cave. I thought I was going to lose her. We radioed Andi together, and from that point forward, my wife slept soundly.

I was already proud of our Neener. And then when she went and married Liam Fox Mayfield, I knew she had chosen well, though, in my humble opinion, no one was really good enough for her. However, Mayfield would suffice, I knew he had been battled-tested and his heart was true. He has proven me right time and time again over the years.

And now, she was carrying his child, and we were going to be grandparents, God willing, if we survived the gorgs.

Friggin' gorgs. That just made me mad, lying here with Andi, thinking about all I, all *we,* had done to try and reclaim our world.

I quickly scanned my intelligence briefing sent over my iPad. I needed coffee. I needed to get up and clear my head. Needed to get myself un-pissed-off and get back in gear.

After all, we had only a single day until the gorgs arrived, and life would change forever yet again.

We had come down to the wire, and things were about to get tenser than ever.

15 | COUNTDOWN

Thursday, March 9ʰ 2045
T-Minus 15 hours and 29 minutes

The warheads were preparing to launch.

Fifteen short hours from now we would need to launch our *Tsar Bombas*. If they proved ineffective against the gorgs, we'd need to use the DTBs at the cloud ceiling and time those as well. If that didn't deter them, by Friday midday, we would be engaged in all-out aerial and ground assault against the dang things.

I checked in with Romero. Two crafts were still approaching, and were now between the orbits of Jupiter and Mars, having just passed the big planet. There was a slight deviation in course between the two of them. Romero confirmed that they were shifting to a new parabolic course to intercept us as we swung around the sun in our own orbit, pinging away mournfully. One had slowed slightly behind the other. I opted not to listen to the ping this time. The signal strength had increased, and they were broadcasting across multiple frequencies and wavelengths. 3.82, 25 up to 28 gigahertz, F.U.D.D. and interferometry still checking out. Signal strength had risen to one-hundred-ninety-two janskys, and Greene suggested it may climb even higher.

"Alright, boys, let me know if there's any deviation. Thanks again," I said, and walked off briskly to the Command Center meeting for which I was already late.

This time, it was a meeting with the Joint Chiefs and General Carson. Connecting remotely were NATO Commanders and NORAD Commander Sinclair. I walked in, and everyone was already seated. They rose and saluted. Another tech who I hadn't worked closely with was dialing in the controls. She smiled up at me, standing and saluting as I entered. Miguel, Jet and Foxy were here as well. Miguel was still in his splint but was doing much better. He was sore, and needed to temper his movements, but he had improved.

"All set, Mr. President," said the tech.

"Thank you. What's your name?"

"Shanna, sir."

"Nice to meet you, Shanna. Thank you."

I turned my attention to the large, wall-mounted screen at the far end of the command center, the nucleus of this Blockade. On the far wall, dozens and dozens of tiny squares stared back at me, perforated here and there by black dots of those who didn't have webcams but were patched into audio. All had been issued secure access and a temporary pin for this all-important briefing. Thankfully, there was a split-screen in Zoom where whoever was speaking would be magnified, so I didn't need to resort to scanning the grid.

There she was, a third of the way down on my screen, in a tiny square: Fleet Admiral Evelyn Lynch. She was readying her fleet. All submarines and ships would be under her tactical command. The bulk of the tiny squares were occupied by international sub commanders, aircraft carrier captains, brigade pilots, ground assault force directors, and other military personnel of all kinds.

By this time, the twenty-two *Tsar Bombas* ICBMs had been inspected and primed. Every fleet had DTB-ready Submarine-launched Ballistic Missiles, SLBMs. The Russians also had two Akula-class submarines, the *Zashchitnik*, and the *Molotok*, partnering with Lynch's fleet to perform close monitoring and communication with Moscow for the *Tsar Bombas.* Should the vessels persist after detonation, Lynch's fleet would try to take them out with the SLBM-mounted DTBs, of which there were thousands. Every militarily apt nation had been, by now, equipped with *Dissonant Tidal Flood* and *Dissonant Tidal Bomb* technologies, both of which had been mass-manufactured in case the gorgons ever returned. For a brief moment I paused to thank God that, despite all the interpersonal disputes, big and small, between nations, every country was now united against the gorgon threat. No government was so cavalier as to cease production of defenses. We were all as ready as we would ever be.

It was past time to sign on. I looked over at Andi and exhaled. She gave me a thumbs up and mouthed *you got this.* I winked at her and then turned back to Shanna. She motioned to me to proceed.

I turned to the monitors.

"Welcome, everyone, United States President Vance Cardona. Thank you all for joining me. We're down to the wire, so I'll make this plain. You've all received the briefings that we'd held here, and they all contain the news that we most feared: alien crafts – plural – are heading our way, and they are undoubtedly gorgons, hailing from the TRAPPIST-1 system. We don't have any infrared scans yet and have no idea how many gorgons are inside each one, whether it's the same numbers from the original attack or not, but even if there's just one of those things inside, I'm not willing to let those suckers back down here." I gritted my teeth. "We *must* hold them. We have a plan, and now we just need to execute." Suddenly my eye caught the word 'China' at the bottom of one of the grid tiles. The Chinese were watching. And then I saw 'DPRK' below another, and 'Iran' below another. I didn't know the current state of Jean Graham, but I didn't care. It was some consolation that the TOD was here and paying attention.

"So, with that, I'll relinquish the floor to NORAD Commander Gabriel Sinclair, and then we'll have Fleet Admiral Evelyn Lynch, Chief of the Air Force Miguel Monzon, and finally General Everett Carson take point. Again, thank you all."

Sinclair's tile lit up on its periphery. "Thank you, President Cardona. Folks, the intelligence briefings we sent you have our launch plans. I will oversee a staggered launch at 0300 hours tomorrow morning to intersect with the crafts' apparent trajectories. That's 1000 hours Coordinated Universal Time. We all know there's debris still up there from the detonation of the previous craft, and though its supposition on our part, it is now safe to assume that the gorgons won't be heading for the same coordinates. At this point, judging by the rotation of the earth and their current angle of approach, we now put one craft targeting entry off the coast of Virginia. We'll refer to that as *Hostile 1*. The other craft is now trailing slightly behind and has shifted by a few degrees. *Hostile 2* is now projected to appear in the skies above Osaka, Japan if current projections hold true.

"Our staggered approach will take precedent. Our 0300 hours launch may have zero effect. We don't know yet. Or the crafts may take evasive. We don't know, of course, because no one speaks gorgon." His statement unintentionally elicited some nervous laughter from a few of the grid tiles. "All we can do is our very best, and hope in turn for the best. Nonetheless, the launch will go forward as planned, and we only have a short time left. I advise everyone to remain at the highest level of alert. NORAD has lowered DEFCON to level 2. That's DEFCON 2, folks. Last time we were here was fifty-four years ago during the 1991 Gulf War. Before that, the Cuban Missile Crisis in 1962. Tomorrow," he said, pausing presumably to ensure that everyone could hear him properly, "we'll be setting DEFCON 1. That's World War III, everyone. Only, contrary to whatever pundits may have expressed down through the decades, our world war is not against each other. It's against enemies that want a second chance. I say we don't give it to them. We must…think…rationally. We must…act…efficiently," he said, enunciating every word. "The survival of the human race depends on the success of each nation acting strategically for the whole. If those murderous things do get through the dome, we'll be launching both DTB-mounted SLBMs and tactical air defenses to take them out. And should *that* fail, I have full confidence in each nation's military to engage in a successful ground assault. God help us if it comes to that. Let's give 'em hell. Right. Fleet Admiral Lynch?"

Lynch unmuted herself and took the floor, clearing her throat. Her tile lit up. "Thank you, one and all. Thank you, Mr. President. Thank you, Commander Sinclair. Ladies and gentlemen, I'm United States Fleet Admiral Evelyn Lynch commanding aboard the USS Harry S Truman from Norfolk Virginia, currently out over the north Atlantic off the eastern seaboard.

"The instructions in-hand are for the Russians to launch the *Tsar Bombas* at 0300 tomorrow morning for a preemptive strike. That's T-Minus 14 hours. All twenty-two warheads will track the targets and detonate in close proximity, or a direct hit if we get a lock while in the exosphere. ICBM maximum is nine-thousand three-hundred miles. The *Tsar Bombas* will be split evenly between targets, yielding eleven-hundred megatons per craft group. All perimeter subs and vessels are on high alert across fleets and will communicate across open channels encompassing UHF, VHF, HF and VLF as needed. Tactical IP and SATCOM are also in play. Universal protocol for launch phase includes codes distributed five minutes prior to launch, and manual firing triggers will be engaged per captains' discretions in the event of any malfunction or other incident. Agreed?"

Various nods showed up across the scattered tiles. Apparently, this last directive was to prevent any false starts.

"Please brief your people, including Blockade commanders and all civilians. These weapons have an explosive yield many, many times that of Hiroshima and Nagasaki. The sky will be illuminated in a white flash that will light up the sky at both impact zones and across the hemisphere as if it were day. Anyone caught looking directly at the sky upon detonation will – not could, *will* – experience dangerous retinopathy. Please ensure that your people are protected. We will maintain a T-Minus countdown to safeguard that the strikes are timed. These will most definitely be *felt.* I'll be quarterbacking the DTB sub launches and naval defenses immediately following. I can be reached on the open channel or hailing frequency. That's all. Good luck. Chief Monzon?"

Lynch muted herself.

Miguel stepped up. "Thank you, ladies and gentlemen. I'm afraid it falls to all of us, yet again, to give each other rousing speeches. I will do my best," he said. "By now many of you will know that there was an attempt on the life of former President Jean Graham." I glanced quickly at the three members of the TOD. No response from them. "In thwarting the assailant, I was wounded but am recovering. I will be just fine by tomorrow morning, let me assure you, and nothing will stop me from joining my friends in the skies all over the world.

"Following the SLBM bombardment on the influx of invaders, we're going to be joining them in the skies. All battalions have their callsigns, so remember them please. All aerial squadrons by now have had RF shielding implemented to mitigate the effects of a DTF burst. Those of you who do not, I caution you to sit this one out. We are the last line of defense before the *gorgos* get through to ground level. Keep on those VHFs, boys. Cut the chatter to essential communications only. Know your wingman's location.

Stay in formation as much as possible. You gotta turn and burn, you announce it using the universal signals in the briefing. Remember: the *gorgos* are cold-blooded. Heat-seekers won't help you. Use your AMRAAMs and your guns. Defend your airspace. Pursue and destroy. Watch your scopes and don't run into each other. It could get very messy up there. Relay coordinates constantly. NORAD will track all of us as they are able. E-8 Joint Surveillance Target Attack Radar Systems and E-3 Sentries will monitor us as well unless they're taken out by the enemy, or we wander off grid. Speak to your teams and coordinate strikes *only* after the last DTBs have gone off. Otherwise, hold back at the designated outer markers until permission to engage has been granted. We launch at the rising of the sun, ladies and gentlemen. Get a good night's sleep. That's all."

I felt General Carson step up to my left. "Thank you, Admiral Lynch, and thank you once again for all you did in the war. Many of you might not know this, but the Fleet Admiral here was not only responsible for spearheading the destruction of the alien funnel, but also the disarming of the nuclear threat in the East, perpetrated by President Cardona's predecessor. We owe Ms. Lynch dearly."

I glanced toward the TOD again. No change of expression. I wished briefly that he hadn't said that. No one needed the reminder that a United States President had had such a despicably savage part to play in world history.

"Alright," Carson said. "Let us talk ground offensives. The Earth is too broad, the curvature too great, the distances too vast to coordinate a unified ground offensive. And that's what we're calling it: an *offensive*. This is not defense, folks. We must stick it to these monsters if we're to survive. I have no idea if they've ever encountered a species as relentless as us, but we beat them before, and it's incumbent upon us to uphold our reputation. I didn't get this scar for nothing," he said, pointing to his face. "On the ground will be our last stand."

I scanned the grid. He had their attention.

"Never before have we been so equipped with so much military technology," he said. "These things are alien, but they're flesh and blood. We've seen it before. They're fragile and can be destroyed. So, I say we take advantage of their fragility and destroy them."

I looked over at Jet, who was smiling approvingly. *Ever the warrior,* I thought. If I didn't know any better, I would say that he couldn't wait to get his boots and M5 back out there on the battlefield.

"It's full battle rattle for each of you. Every one of our ground forces should have gear and masks…*always*. You step out for a smoke or a crap without your mask, we can't help you. My advice is quit smoking now and stop eating beef." Pervasive laughter across the screen as there was no beef left to eat. "You get stranded or have to bail out, you fight your way out; there is no dustoff, and no evac, until those things are destroyed. Stay inside your tanks as if your life depends on it, because it does. All international militaries around the world have been equipped with deflection technology and DTF repellers. Use DTF units at maximum volume. Get those earplugs in, people. All ground forces have free reign to repel the gorgons as effectively, and as much, as you can. We fight until every last one of them is extinguished. While unrestricted DTF tech is permitted everywhere, all DTB use" -here he took great care to emphasize the *B* for 'bomb'- "needs to be authorized prior to deployment. Remember that. Coordinate with the teams around you to ensure your own blasts aren't going to knock out your own defenses. If you've got improved RF shielding, make sure and use it. Same goes for tanks. Mobile SPAAG units, Abrams, assault vehicles, all of that has been assigned. They'll all be equipped with DTF emitters, as before.

"Here in DC, we'll be ready with snipers and CQC teams. Multiple offensives and ops. Frontal attacks. Flank. Envelopment. Pincers. Bull horns. We'll use everything we've got, and I've been working in tandem with Lieutenant Cameron Shipley and Corporal Liam Mayfield," -here he motioned off screen to them- "whose names you most likely already know. We've been working together over the last few days combing over logistics. We'll be ready on this end. Those of you in Osaka – and *everywhere*, if they break through – keep your teams informed. Communication reigns. You go black on guns or fuel, you report it. If we have to root out these animals like we did before, so be it. If those things make it past our sky dome, it's open season and they're fair game. We'll give them scars like these and tell them Earth is off limits. That's it. Good luck and give 'em hell," he said, waving them on with his fiery charisma.

I stood back up and approached the camera until I could see myself in the screen again.

"Well, that's it, everyone," I said, with what I'm sure must have appeared to be a beleaguered sigh. I truly was tired. But now was the time to pull up my socks and meet the moment. They were counting on me. "I've never been a great orator or someone who inspires the masses with fancy speech. My role has been to move chess pieces into position to defend against an aggressor, and utilize such means as were available to me to that end. This meeting is squarely for that purpose. *You* are that purpose," I said, trying to meet the tiny eyes of each person on that grid.

"We were nearly wiped out before. But the gorgons failed. They failed because of our ingenuity. Our resiliency. Our determination. They failed because of our technology and our pioneering spirit. And now, God willing, they'll fail again. But failure isn't a happenstance thing. It doesn't just 'take place.' It is up to *all* of us to *make* them fail. For myself, I don't relish the notion of living underground for another sixteen years. I've tasted the free air and danced unafraid under the night sky. I won't surrender that willingly. I've relished the surface, and basked in peace with the sun on my face. I've lived life and loved well. I've roared in gratitude for freedom up here, and I will not willingly mute myself again, not without a heckuva fight. I've given and received that most precious of exchanges: love." I looked over at my bride, who was beaming. "I don't like to lose, folks. We lost once. Never again. *Never again.*"

Maybe I was a fine orator after all, because every one of them held their hands up and applauded, silently. I stared at them with grim determination. If I could have found a way to imbue some kind of fortitude, solidarity, resiliency and potency into each one of them, I would have. For now, passionate words would have to do it. "And now," I concluded, "join me as we invoke the power and trust of a dear friend, one whose name you all know and remember." Miguel lifted his head high. "She trusted in our Creator, God Almighty, to the end of her days, and I daresay beyond. It's time we do the same, together, as Rosie did."

I stood and backed away from the camera, lifting my hands up and raising my palms in hopeful trust for our deliverance. As I did so, I glanced over at Jet. Tears were running down his cheeks.

It was unanimous. Every single little cell on that grid had a talking head in it before. But now, the figures grew smaller, stepped away from their webcams, and raised their hands, some all the way to the sky, reaching out to *The Father*, as Rosie called Him.

"Know whom you trust, fellow souls. Know who is worthy of trust. If it has ever been about anything, it has always been about trust. Trust is inevitable if you let it be so. So let it be so," I concluded, and I saluted all of them, regardless of rank. Each one of the members of our Cabinet and this Blockade stood and saluted everyone else in this solemn assembly.

"Go with God." I nodded to the Joint Chiefs and everyone else on the screen. One by one their cells went dark as they prepared for the final defense of our planet.

"Vaya con Dios," Miguel echoed.

As I was walking out of the meeting, the General approached me and asked if he could speak to me in private.

Bayless stopped us on the way to give a quick report on Blockade readiness. They were all closing their doors, all around the world – for good – until the threat had passed. "The census hasn't been taken yet, but numbers show that it's at or just under the original population. There's nothing we can do for the holdouts, sir."

"Understood. Thank you, Veronica," I said, and she scurried off back to the Command Center.

The General and I went a few paces forward, away from the noise, the staffers, the cabinet members and the soldiers. "What is it, General Carson?" I asked him.

He looked around skittishly. "Sir," he said, "we all know what those critters can do. We've been through this before and we've survived it, but some of us haven't. We know their names, and we know how they died. We never speak of it, of course, to honor them and preserve their memory."

"What do you mean, General?"

"I'm saying that, should some of our guys fear the worst, we need to provide them a viable way out, sir."

"Viable way out?"

And then he looked directly into my eyes, and he didn't have to say anything further. "Give them to me," I said. "Give all of them to me, please, Carson."

General Carson sensed my disapproval and heaved a sigh. He opened his mouth to speak, but then, perhaps, thought better of it, and reached into his pockets. He handed me several small silver cylinders. I knew what they contained. "Thank you, General, that'll be all."

Carson saluted and then retreated.

I stared down at the tiny cylinders. I prayed that it would not come to that. I needed to get back. An inevitable moment was approaching, and we were on a countdown.

Our warheads were about to launch.

16 | LAUNCHING

Thursday, March 9ᵗʰ 2045
T-Minus 4 hours and 2 minutes

God help us. The *Tsar Bombas* were going to launch. It was now 10:58pm.

Miguel was off, along with other qualified pilots, to Bolling Air Force Base in southeastern DC. They took them over in a chopper. He was going up. I knew in my heart that he would be glad for that, but I worried about him with that wound. Briefly, I remember when Jet Shipley was shot in the leg, and he was about to go up in an F-15. That weaselly doctor at Wright-Patterson had legitimate concerns about Jet's health in such a scenario, as did the doctor here at our Blockade for Miguel's.

I wished him well and saw him off. All any of us could do was hope for the best. Squadrons all over the world would take to the air at approximately 0600 hours in anticipation of the entry of the two crafts. God help us.

I had given one more address to the nation, arranging for it to be played in every Blockade in America, and every public screen that would carry it. They had it patched into local radio stations and broadcast in public meeting centers and across public address systems. Newly-rebuilt phone systems were tied into and landlines relayed it to all those still blessed with connections.

That's when the interference kicked in.

I stopped one more time by Romero's station for an update on the craft, and his screen was glitchy. Greene was barely coming in on his secure internet feed. His signal was glitchy too.

They were coming. Romero still had the craft in his crosshairs, now four hours and two minutes from earth, currently in Mars' orbit, closing in on the moon. The crafts were now a mere two-hundred eighty-nine thousand miles away.

Mike looked at me lackadaisically as I approached. It was almost like he didn't understand the gravity of what was happening, nor the intent of what was coming. I admit I was tiring of his laissez-faire, slapstick attitude. "Fill 'er up unleaded?" he joked.

"Just give me the positioning, please, Mike," I said, leaning over the back of his chair. He was trying to discern through the occasional static blips.

"Sorry, Mr. President," he said sleepily. "I can't tell for certain, sir. Lotsa interference. Greene, you there? Somebody pulled the curtains down, sir. Hang on. The second one appears to have drifted somewhat more astern of the first one, but I can't be certain. Telemetry still has them inbound at the projected coordinates. DC's will be off the Eastern seaboard at approximately Latitude 37.857799, Longitude -74.757918. Osaka's trajectory looks dead center over the city. Neither one appears to be slowing. But they have to upon entering our atmosphere, when it begins to affect their gravity; all that kinetic energy needs to dissipate. If they got heat shields, neither craft is showing that yet, sir."

"What about armament? Can you detect any?"

"What, like alien ray guns, plasma cannons, something like that?"

"Not funny, Mike."

"Sorry, sir. I don't see any. Never have. That's a big sucker, Mr. President. The last one didn't have any weapons on it. Hopefully, this doesn't hold any surprises either. Hello, Greene, can you confirm?"

Greene didn't answer. We looked over and his screen was frozen; he had disconnected.

"It's definitely magnetic, like the first one. Resonance imaging is affecting the satellites, sir," continued Romero.

"That's okay. We know it's coming. Thank you, Mr. Romero." I started walking back to check in on Andi and Janine.

"Aye aye, Captain," Romero said.

I stopped and turned back around to stare at him once more. He didn't even see me. I wanted to say something but thought better of it. It was almost as if it escaped his intellect that the things in those crafts wanted him for a meal. He was simply regurgitating data points and spitting out updates without truly understanding our peril. I hoped to

God that we would all truly grasp our peril, and not take it lightly. We could *not* afford to take this lightly. Earth, and all of us, would not survive if we ignored or protested the inconvenience of this imminent threat. I felt for Romero, but I had greater things on my mind.

I needed to make sure Andi and Janine were safe.

In a few short hours, we strike.

•   •   •   •   •

Thursday, March 9th 2045
T-Minus 3 hours and 41 minutes

"No matter what happens, you stay in here. Understand?"

"I will, daddy," Janine said. "Be careful," she urged, throwing her arms around me and pulling me close. I could feel her shaking. "And take care of Liam. *Please* take care of Liam."

"I will, hon. He's a seasoned warrior. He's going to be just fine. He and Jet." My baby girl released me and looked up into my eyes. I took her face in my hands. "The plan is to keep them from even getting through, honey. And he's serving under a tried and tested General. Carson will take care of both of them. I promise."

I turned to Andi. "I love you so much, hon. I've gotta go hop in the saddle. We've gotta quarterback this from the Command Center. And I've gotta get the guys sent off. Please promise me you'll stay in here and keep these masks on."

She nodded quickly. "I understand. I love you, Mr. President," she whispered in my ear, wrapping her arms around me in turn. "I love you so much. Please be careful, hon."

My thoughts went back to last night, and the love we exchanged. She was still so warm in my embrace, and the smell of her hair was intoxicating. "I love you too, sweetheart. Always. Stay in here. Please. I'll be right down the corridor. You'll have security posted up outside. Just stay in here and you'll be fine. We'll know what kind of shape we're in by tomorrow night."

I pulled away from her and looked them both over, up and down. "It may get crazy out there. You may hear sounds that you don't want to. Just stay in here. Stay away from the door. Block it from the inside if it makes you feel safer. And keep this radio on Channel 3. Don't scan the bands; it'll just be noise and more to worry about. I love you," I said, as I took both of their hands. "I love you both so much."

They both clenched their lips at me. This was the moment we knew was coming, where I would have to separate from them and go back out there. The fact that we knew it was coming didn't make it any easier.

And then Andi pulled her hand gradually out of mine, and saluted me, slowly, with all the decorum of a fellow soldier. We had been through a lot together in New York, Wright-Pat, Mammoth Cave, Dayton, DC. She was my lovely bride until my dying breath.

Janine watched her mother salute her father, and she followed suit. I stood at attention and saluted them back, slowly.

And then, turning away and not looking back, I walked out. I could not look back. I *would* not look back. If I did, I'd never leave them.

•   •   •   •   •

Friday, March 10th 2045
T-Minus 2 hours and 57 minutes

As I walked up the stairs toward the Launch, I could hear muffled voices ahead. Jet and Foxy were by the main Launch doors with Pease and his team. They saluted me as I approached. All had their masks up over their helmets, cameras mounted, which allowed us to supervise their progress through an array of monitors down in the Command Center.

"Grant, Mitchell, Toole, and Reynolds," I greeted them. They looked grateful that I remembered their names. "Pease. Shipley. Mayfield. All of you. You're our last line of defense.

"But that doesn't mean you have to go and be heroes. You find yourself in a hole, you take care of you. Got that?" They nodded. "Stay on Channel 8 at all times. Whatever you do, don't switch away. We'll need you. Where is the rest of your team assembling, Shipley?"

"The troops are massing on the Ellipse above," Jet answered. "From there, we'll fan out and take up defensive positions. We'll be ready in the event of penetration, Mr. President. Snipers will take up their posts in the aforementioned spots. Troops are already taking up positions. We've got more jeeps ready to take the rest, with loads of ammo."

"Where will you two be?" I asked him and Foxy.

"We're going to take cover in the Hoover Federal Building to the east, sir. Punch out windows, shoot through those, and fan across. We've got some low-volume DTF units set up above on the Ellipse to act as lures. We'll place them at the southeastern end, away from the gun towers of DN002. That should irritate them but not hurt them. It'll summon them in to attack, and then we can take 'em out right there. Snipers will be focused on the sky from bell towers and other elevations. SPAAGs and Vulcans will be all over at various positions, and we've got 'em manned with qualified guys. Oh, and the General will be with us, sir. He didn't want to be pinned down here. Said he'd feel caged."

This was the first I'd heard of this. "What? That was not approved. Where is the General now?"

"Back in the Pavilion," Foxy said. "Or, whatever you guys call it here. The meeting place."

"Thanks," I said. I looked them over, and clenched my jaw. Maybe Carson was right. I took a deep breath. "Guys, there's one more thing. I don't like it one bit, and I wasn't going to give them to you, but the General is right. There's no getting around it. I don't sanction it, nor do I hope it comes to this, but should you lose your mask…should you find that…well," I stuttered, "I mean…should it come to it that you have no way out…"

Words failed me, and my mouth stopped working.

"Sir," interrupted Jet. "We understand what's required of us. We know what the gorgs can do. It's okay, sir. Carson already told us," he finished.

I looked at him and studied him.

How had he and the others become so battle-hardened that they couldn't regard a cyanide pill as anything other than another emotionless protocol in their vast array of operations?

I cleared my lungs vigorously and then reached into my pocket, handing them one each of the small silver cylinders that General Carson had surrendered. *Sippies,* as we all had called them out in the field during the war. Slang for *CP,* cyanide pill. I held them out in my hands, knowing that what I was offering had the power to end their lives, dispensing them with no words, and ending with Foxy. My eyes looked up to meet my son-in-law's, and his were shining. Here before me was a young kid grown into a man, his rocket launcher slung over his back next to his pack, his military cap tight on his shaven head, his eyes glinting proudly in the dim light of the Launch. It was hot up here with all the soldiers gathered. He was sweating. I hoped it wasn't from nervousness.

"Don't you *dare* take this, son," I said with anxious resolve, handing him the sippy. "You're coming back. My daughter needs you," I breathed. "And so do I," I finished, swallowing hard.

He spoke no reply, just nodded his head, jaw clenched firmly. "Thank you, sir," he finally muttered as I placed the cylinder in his hand, sealed his hand over the pill, and brought his fist up to his own heart.

"So do I," I said, and then I could feel the tear run down my cheek. "Stay alive, Foxy. You too, Camjet."

I turned to the rest of them. "Stay alive, *all* of you. And keep hidden when the blasts go off. Use your shielding. You don't want to be looking up when those nukes blow."

I couldn't hold it back. My tears came in torrents as I was overcome by emotion. I sent them all on their way. But as Jet and Foxy advanced out, I reached forward and grabbed them both by the arms, spinning them slowly back around to look at me. I stared at Jet and Foxy and leaned in close. "You two, and *only* you two. You're family. I'm not losing you. Anything goes desperately wrong, switch to Channel 10. This is just between you and me," I said, between sniffs. "I love you guys. Be safe out there."

They both nodded. Foxy echoed, "Love you too, Dad." I embraced them both, and then I pulled away. I needed to talk to the General. I shook their hands and stepped back as the three of us saluted each other.

•   •   •   •   •

Friday, March 10th 2045
T-Minus 2 hours and 40 minutes

"General, I do not approve of this," I said. "Not one bit. You're needed *here*, Carson."

"To do *what*, exactly, sir?" he growled coldly, his one eye staring grimly into my eyes. He was holding his M107A1 rifle proudly to his chest, slung over his shoulder by a weatherbeaten and faded strap. "Sit behind a desk, sir, sending other men to their deaths?"

"Don't you say that, General. Not another word like that."

"I don't have another word like that, Mr. President, because I don't send men to their deaths. I march out with them to *life.* It's what you said earlier, sir. About trust. *Trust is inevitable if you let it be so.* This is inevitable, and I'm part of it. I'm a soldier, and I'm needed out there on the battlefield, Mr. President."

I stared into his eye, wondering what those years must have been like here, nearly alone, hardened, traveling back and forth between these Blockades, surviving on adrenaline and primal instinct, fueled by the constant threat of death by gorgon. He had become a coarse combatant, a legionnaire, a diehard, tried by fire. Who was I to refuse him? We would be relatively safe down here. He would need to ensure safety up there. And maybe, just maybe, he could protect Liam. If Janine were standing here, she would have pleaded for it.

I was once a soldier out in the field. *Look at me now,* I thought. Dress shirt, tie, and slacks. Looking ever the diplomat and world ruler, grim yet political. Is that who I really was? Didn't I belong out there on the battlefield too?

I relented. "Stay alive, Everett," I told him, and then offered my hand to him.

He flinched, tilted his head, and stared at me for what seemed like time immemorial. "It's been a long time since anyone has called me by my first name, Mr. President."

I extended my hand further toward him. "Well then, perhaps now is the time to consider us friends. You're a friend, Everett."

He looked down and grabbed my hand, shaking it slowly. "Thank you, Mr.-," he fumbled. "Thank you, *Vance.*" Everett shook my hand tightly.

I smiled at him, grateful. If anyone was tried and true and was going to survive up there, I figured it would be General Everett Forrest Carson.

•   •   •   •   •

Friday, March 10th 2045
T-Minus 1 hours and 27 minutes

It was now 1:33 AM on Friday, March 10th. The fatigue was creeping through my skin, and I needed rest, if even a little. But I just couldn't.

No one could.

We were scrambling around in the Blockade. Everyone was experiencing some interference in either landline communications or cellular – for those who had it – and the monitors were glitchy with static. The things were drawing closer.

I couldn't be bouncing back and forth between the Command Center, Romero and Jens. I asked them to feed us a broadcast screen to the monitors suspended throughout the Blockade. I needed a T-Minus count and the crafts' locations, as close to us as possible.

Now, glancing up at the one nearest me, I could see it clearly. Less than an hour and a half to go. Both crafts had passed our moon at apogee and were closing fast. Gravity was now working to their advantage. They would be here sooner than expected, closer to 6:30 AM. The only saving grace here was that it would still be a few minutes past sunrise. At least we could see them and know with more precision what we were all shooting at.

Before I knew it, it was T-Minus 1 hour, and we were getting close to the ICBM launch. Confirmation came through to the Command Center that the Russians were arming and preparing for launch as scheduled. Twenty-two silos were opened, and twenty-two Russian RS-28 Sarmats, codename SS-X-29s, raised up and aimed toward the sky.

Jet and his team had departed, and were now preparing the Hoover Federal Building for a ground offensive with two thousand men positioned throughout.

The General had taken another five thousand men and stationed them all throughout the Ronald Reagan Building and International Trade Center, the Postal Service, the John Wilson Building, the Mellon Gala, the Andrew Mellon Auditorium, and the US EPA to the east of the Hoover building. Every soldier stood ready at their posts. All of them were on Channel 8 as ordered.

The rest of the troops were dispersed throughout the city, some at greater distances than others, but all taking up concealed positions and waiting.

Our hope was that the gorgons would be unfamiliar with our gun towers over the Blockades. These would be new invaders, and, hopefully, they didn't have any means of interstellar communication other than their response ping. The intent was for the troops to squeeze the gorgons between them, lure them out over the southeastern end of the Ellipse, and hammer them hard.

Now, it was just a waiting game. I bowed my head and said a quick prayer. This was it.

I headed up to the top. I was going to have myself a look at the approaching crafts. I caught Bayless on the way up. "Let's have a look at our visitors, shall we?" I asked her.

My heart was pounding in my chest, frankly. We were down to the wire, and they were coming; there was no escaping that for any of us.

Bayless and I quickly ascended the stairs of the Launch.

We headed out onto the grass. The Ellipse was a flurry of activity all around us.

To our east, the National Christmas Tree was still up. America collectively never felt the desire to take it down. I stared at it, solemnly waving there in the wind from the choppers, its tiny multicolored ornaments swaying and clinking together. Some of them had fallen off the branches and tumbled to the ground.

The tree itself maintained its winter beauty, and the lights were still on. It was a testament to the Christmas gift we had received only three short years prior: deliverance from the gorgons and Graham. And, as Rosie would often say, a testament to the greatest Christmas gift mankind had ever received: Christ himself. The baby Jesus, from which Christmas derived its name, where God entered mankind's story as a little child. My throat caught watching that resilient tree. Energy swirled around me, and noise enveloped us as we stepped out. Yet I could not pull my eyes away from that tree. My eyes began to well up.

Would we ever celebrate it out here again?

I felt a soft touch on my right arm and looked over. My VP, Major Veronica Bayless, smiled at me. "Mr. President? We'll be okay, sir," she said.

And then my radio sounded. "Vance?"

I grabbed it and lifted it to my ear. "Cardona. Go ahead."

"Lieutenant Shipley. We're in position, sir. It's, uh, it's beautiful, isn't it?"

"Yes, it is. I take it you can see me?"

"Yessir. I see you. And Rosie sees us. And God in Heaven sees all of us. And, frankly, sir, the same thing caught my eye on the way out, as well."

"What did I just see, Shipley?"

He paused. "Days gone by, sir. Cherished memories. Rutty and I gazed down upon a tiny little tree in Harvill Hall not too many years ago, the day before he was killed, sir. It's the sweetest memory I have of him, Mr. President. He's up there with Rosie now, somewhere, and I'm sure they're pleading our case. We'll be okay, sir," he finished.

Bayless smiled. "See?"

I glanced back at her sidelong and smiled, heaving a labored sigh. "I see," I said to her. "Thank you, Camjet," I said.

"You're welcome, Mr. President, Vance, sir."

"Good luck, my friend. Rub that shaven mop-top's head for me, will you?" I knew Foxy was somewhere close by. His voice popped over the radio, chirping in his signature cheeriness.

"He can't, sir, I've got my hat on, Mr. President."

"You always did love your hats."

"Yeah, well, I'm proud to wear this one, Dad."

I searched along the outer windows of the Hoover building and could just make out two figures waving at us through the searchlights and chopper wind. I waved back and sported the 'victory' sign with my fingers.

Soldiers meandered all around us, some scurrying by at different paces. Masked people whose names I would never know except, perhaps, in silent memoriam when all was said and done. *Nameless.* I hoped that would not be the case. There were thousands upon thousands of men and women gathered right here in this little elliptical stretch of grass, all ready to fan out, dustoff and take up positions.

"Look, sir," Bayless said, pointing. "There they are."

I craned my neck and squinted out past the construction lights and rigging, peering through the wind.

Framed against the night sky, to the right of our moon, two pale dots were shining. Miniscule against the vast expanse of outer space, yet they were ominous: objects of menace and dread, filled with a predatory species that was out for revenge and coming straight for us. Romero would have given me that right ascension and declination mumbo-jumbo if he were here.

Occasionally they would flash dully, as if they had glinted off some primal stray beam of sunlight shooting through the cosmos. Sunlight, which usually communicated hope. But not for this visitor. There was no hope to be found here.

They were coming.

•   •   •   •   •

Friday, March 10th 2045
T-Minus 13 minutes

The suspended monitors read thirteen minutes to go. It was 0247 hours. No one slept in our Blockade, and I daresay in any Blockade or shelter anywhere in the world. Mankind knew what was upon us, and we were all now preparing for the worst.

The crowd above had dispersed shortly after Bayless and I had retreated from the Ellipse. I caught one last soul-stirring sight of the Christmas tree swaying gently in the wind, shaking nervously silhouetted against the backdrop of helicopter lights and the shouting from patrols and infantry as they fanned out. The Launch doors shut with a loud clang. The Ellipse was quiet now, and the lures had been set. The teams were all on Channel 8, with occasional soundings of readiness and reporting in. All branches in this sector reported to General Carson. *Everett.*

I prayed for my friend. I prayed for Miguel. I prayed most of all for Jet and Foxy, in extreme danger up there.

Bayless and I returned to the Command Center. They all stood or saluted quickly as I entered. All civilians, Andi and Janine included, and all non-cabinet members and senior staff were ordered to their bunks. Everyone was provided with masks and some form of weapon or another, though all paled in comparison to what Carson wielded. I didn't see what Foxy had beside his rocket launcher. I assumed he had a sidearm as well. Jet had an M5 and a sidearm, I thought, plus a few grenades for both of them. At least, that's how I remember them being armed at Mammoth Cave.

Mammoth Cave. Was that really so long ago? I had been reassigned in 2038 and had spent six years of my life there, moving up by Wright-Pat with Andi during the last part of the war. Yet here we were again. *At war.*

Jens approached me and quickly handed me a mask, which I fitted over my sweaty, bald head. I held it in my hand for a moment before donning it, staring at it in angry incredulity.

They were not going to win again, I resolved.

I glanced around the Command Center. Everyone was here. The two Joint Chiefs we had – the *only* ones who remained with us – were both patched into their own channels and regions to command their own sectors and report status. These were David Grady, who was Chief of Staff of the Army, and Vice Chairman of the Joint Chiefs of Staff, Darrell Austin. I relieved Capra back to SecDef once Miguel was better. Now, he was somewhere out there in the skies, preparing for battle.

Everyone in here had masks either on them, over their heads, or lying next to them at their stations. On a side table, there were multiple guns, rifles, and sidearms together, along with various grenades and flashbangs, masks, and vests, in case we needed to arm ourselves and retreat. Our Command Center doubled as our armory.

Miguel was airborne. Evelyn was waiting off the eastern seaboard. I could see them piped into our grid once again. Miguel's camera revealed the cockpit of some plane I didn't recognize, but gave us a thumbs up. "Vaya con Dios," I breathed silently to my best friend.

Time to straighten up, get into gear, and do this. I stood quickly, rolled my sleeves up to my elbows, and shook out my arms, cracking my knuckles, rubbing my hands together fiercely as I worked out the kinks.

"Alright, tactical on screen, please," I said, and Shanna, Jens and Romero were at the controls. They popped up another monitor and let us see a glowing illuminated tactical view of the metro DC area. Smaller grids on the screen included Osaka on one, and a map of the whole continental United States in another.

"What's the situation on Osaka? Readiness report?"

"All in place, Mr. President," Jens reported. "Prime Minister reports full battle stations."

"Projected arrival coordinates still the same?"

"Yessir."

"Alright. Give me a report on the three DTB jetties: Iran, North Korea, China." As I requested this, I briefly wondered where Jean Graham was and the security status of her prison. She was on her own now.

Three additional grids popped up on the left screen displaying working video feeds of the three regions of the TOD. As promised, the equipment was readied and technicians were scrambling in each zone for final preparations.

"All systems in place, sir," said Romero. "North Korea reported some difficulty in linking, but that was," - here he paused, pulling up an earlier report- "two hours ago. Sounds like they got it ironed out."

"Confirm that, please, Romero," I said.

"Yessir."

I glanced at the clock. T-Minus 4 minutes. 2:56 AM.

"Capra, you're up," I said.

Peter stood and took position next to me. "Thank you, Mr. President." He turned to face the grid. "All branches, this is SecDef, Peter Capra. Report in, please. Army?"

Chief of Staff of the Army, David Grady was sitting in the Command Center. "Aye-aye. Carson, report please?"

General Carson's growl sounded through the com. "Ready, sir." He was in his element now.

"Navy?"

"Yessir, standing by," Fleet Admiral Evelyn Lynch replied. "Ready to go, sir. SEAL Teams integrated with Marines in the major cities, sir, as ordered." I smiled. I was a Navy SEAL. Memories surged through me.

"Air Force?"

I watched Miguel lean forward in his cockpit and acknowledge with a thumbs up. The silly man had a smile on his face. *This* guy was in his element. Miguel belonged in the sky. I wondered if I had held him back by appointing him my Chief of Staff. He was Chief of Staff of the United States Air Force, and he belonged in the air.

"Marines?"

"Roger. Ready, sir," echoed Commandant Orlando Miles, who was stationed in Los Angeles. He had several thousand men scattered throughout LA, New York, Clearwater, Daytona Beach, Friday Harbor, Santa Barbara, Cannon Beach, Boston, Key West, Seattle, San Diego, and other coastal cities. The thought was, if the gorgs tried to finish what they first came to do and try to steal our water again, they'd try to head us off at the coastlines. The Marines would deny them that. Miles himself wanted to be with his men rather than with Command in DC. I applauded him. These people – Miguel, Carson, Lynch, Miles – these leaders, they were diehard. They wanted to be with their charges.

"Commander Sinclair, are you reading all of us?" I asked him. He turned toward the camera and nodded. "Yes, Mr. President, I'm here. We are a go. I'm patched in with Russia. On with Chief of the General Staff, Aleksandr Vasilyev now. We are a go in T-Minus 4 minutes 30 seconds."

One conspicuous absence was the presence of the Coast Guard, which had, for simplicity's sake, been integrated into the Navy. It was common knowledge that they would report to Lynch.

"Thank you, ladies and gentlemen. Be ready. Avert your eyes from the sky, please, and keep us informed. The Russians are online and are preparing to launch," Capra said.

T-Minus 3 minutes.

One of the grids enlarged, seemingly by itself, and took center stage on the right monitor. The two pale dots Bayless and I had seen up in the sky were magnified.

There they were.

Two crafts, with a widening cavity between them, steaming full-tilt toward Earth. They were hazy images, and, once again, our transmission was showing some breakup due to their magnetic interference, but there they were.

"Craft on speaker, Mr. President."

They fed the painful, mourning pulse into the PA system. We all heard it in the Command Center, and no one heard anything *but* it for a moment. It was pathetic, whimpering, almost a dirge of sorts, lamenting its fallen mate, crestfallen and desperate, crying out for an answer.

We have one for you, I thought to myself. *It's called 'one billion pissed off humans telling you to do a one-eighty and get the heck out or we'll hammer you hard.'*

"Jens, get me Vasilyev here as well, please."

The clock continued to wind down. *T-Minus 2 minutes.* Vasilyev appeared on screen and turned to the camera. "President Cardona," he said in Russian, "good evening, or, good *morning* to you. We're ready, sir."

The translation appeared as captions at the bottom of our screen here. "Thank you, sir. God speed, Vasilyev. Good luck."

He thanked me and switched off. No time for pleasantries.

I pulled up my radio. "Jens, patch me back in to the Joint Chiefs, please." My heart pounded. *T-minus 1 minute* was suddenly upon us. Sixty seconds to launch the *Tsar Bombas* and twenty-two hundred megatons of fiery vengeance. "All troops, listen to me. We've got sixty seconds. Cover your eyes. Those nukes are going to be in the air and should impact somewhere between twenty-five and forty minutes. Best guess is thirty. Be safe, gentlemen! As soon as we have a report, we'll get it to you."

T-Minus 30 seconds. A hush fell over the room.

"Pull up the silos, please."

T-Minus 25 seconds.

Seven images enveloped the screen, yet the two dots remained, hurtling toward our atmosphere, leaving the moon behind them as they prepared to ransack Earth.

From gantries raised high, the seven images showed steam emerging from silos. Beneath the large, steel barn doors raised toward the heavens, twenty-two threatening projectiles were warming up.

T-Minus 10 seconds.

Vasilyev switched back on, watching his screen patiently. Beneath him was a bank of monitors and controls, and he was flanked by personnel all in blue jumpsuits, their silhouettes clarified by endless control panel lights revealing an unearthly glow from a bunker somewhere. He had a key inserted into a lock switch and was mirroring someone in his command that had another identical redundancy switch, both of which needed to be turned in unison.

T-Minus 4 seconds.

I gulped hard. I closed my eyes and prayed. *God help us. Rosie, I trust God. I hope you're right.*

"Chetyre...tri...dva...odin," Vasilyev counted down.

T-Minus 1 second.

Vasilyev looked at his partner. His fingers were perched over a large, red button encased in a plastic security housing.

"And...go for launch," read the screen after Vasilyev said it in Russian.

Out of the silos, slowly at first, emerged twenty-two conical masses in jet black. They rimmed the cylinders of tubes, the length of which were impossible to behold, rising toward the heavens with threatening speed, all of them pouring incendiary thrust and smoke, steam and thunder in their wake. The smoke trails curved upward, and the screens lost them from view. We all watched in silence, and I prayed against any kind of malfunction. God forbid one of them failed or fell back to earth and created yet another Chernobyl. Disaster on top of more disaster.

"Tactical overlay, Romero," I said quietly, my fist in front of my mouth over my crossed arms.

Romero punched up a graphic acknowledging the presence of nuclear missiles in the air as tiny dots. I counted twenty-two of them. Our own national defense systems sounded a warning which could not be deactivated. Nuclear missiles from another superpower had just been launched. In a reflex, our own defense network sprang into action, and alerts buried other windows beneath them.

"ICBM launch confirmed," Romero verified numbly.

Those on the ground would have seen the warheads ascending toward the sky at incredible speeds, leaving billowing signature smoke trails as they screamed heavenward.

On our tactical, we saw tiny red dots increasing in altitude, rising, rising toward the heavens, punching through the troposphere. The stratosphere. Up. Up. Into the mesosphere. Rising through the thermosphere. And finally, into the exosphere, carrying not just twenty-two hundred megatons of nuclear destruction, but twenty-two hundred megatons of hope and dread.

Had we just destroyed our moon? Would we destroy ourselves in the process, ruin our tidal patterns, destroy our ozone layer, fry every electronic-based system known to man? Were we now going to be destroyed ourselves?

Only time would tell.

The missiles had launched. It was now 0300 hours. God help us all.

17 | ADVENT

Friday, March 10th 2045 · 0319 hours

The gorgons were coming.

The *Tsar Bombas* were on their way, and we were all praying, holding our collective breath as each precious second sounded like a thudding war drum through the uncertainty of our hearts.

The tiny spears were carving their way through the exosphere, targeted for eight thousand miles at best-guess coordinates in line with projected travel paths for each incoming craft. My cabinet members, myself, our techs, and everyone on that grid was watching some monitor or another, some tactical readout providing intel on our missiles versus their ships. No one knew if we would be successful.

I glanced over at Bayless, who was chewing her nails. I reached over and gently pulled her hand away from her mouth. "Easy, Veronica."

She shook her head and widened her eyes, exhaling.

"Range five-zero-zero-zero. All *Tsar Bombas* at midcourse phase ascent. Approximate time to intercept: eight minutes," muttered Jens slowly, watching his screen. "Both crafts inbound on current trajectories, velocity thirty-three-thousand five hundred miles per hour and slowing."

"Slowing? What, Jens?" I asked him, moving to his side.

"Expected, sir. Probably anticipating gravitational pull and not wanting to smash into the planet, sir," Jens answered. I watched his screen with him. Both crafts were running in parallel trajectories, but the gap between them was growing wider. They were starting to branch off slightly, and, with the rotation of the earth and their slowing, they would reach their projected latitude-longitude points if they held their course. "Range five-five-zero-zero." A minute later, "Range six-one-five-zero."

I looked up. The tiny red dots on our tactical overlay were rising ever higher, following their programmed courses without bias or sentiment, about to collide with the crafts' apparent trajectories.

"Range six-six-two-five. *Tsar Bombas* are beginning on course divergence...*now,*" he said, and tactical mirrored that. "Range six-nine-eight-zero. Seven-one-five-five, Mr. President."

Right now, the nukes were being armed, programmed to explode at eight thousand miles up, creating two masses of shockwaves that would, hopefully, create enough blast to crumple their ships. Earth held its breath.

As predicted, the gap between the crafts began to diverge even wider. A yawning chasm of space opened up between them, and, as if they were two doors bending outward, they swerved dramatically and broke off.

"Tell me you're seeing that, Jens."

"I am sir; it's what we thought they were going to do, but it doesn't look like an evasive. Shanna, Romero, you got the same readouts? The split is approaching five point five miles wide and growing."

I looked over at Shanna. "Confirmed, I have the same, sir."

Romero nodded quietly. Maybe he was finally understanding the gravity of it all. "Range seven-three-five-zero," he said. "Nearing detonation coordinates at eight-triple-zero." Indeed, as he said that my eyes went to tactical. Our tiny red flickers of light, our twenty-two tiny missiles, were nearly over the outlines of each approaching craft.

"Range seven-six-eight-five," Jens reported. "Craft velocity still decreasing. ICBM midcourse ascents nearly complete. Detonation in roughly thirty seconds, sir."

I looked at my watch and spoke into my radio. "Everyone! Engage RF shielding. Send the command to reboot all satellites...*now*. Prepare for ground shutdown!" Jens and Shanna acted swiftly. That included all cameras, except for a CCTV ground-mounted camera they had set up a few hours ago, running off a portable Jackery battery and piped directly into the Command Center. Jens now pulled that one up on a separate monitor. Our timing had to be right.

I signaled to Peter Capra. He whipped his radio to his face. "All troops, all troops, SecDef. Prepare for detonation; repeat, prepare for detonation. Eye shields up. Go dark. See you on the other side."

"Range seven-nine-two-five. Here we go," said Jens, and he hit a final key on his keyboard.

In seconds, the room went black. Emergency lighting kicked on. The only thing showing was the smaller screen piping in the feed of the outside camera.

The Command Center was utterly silent. We waited.

Suddenly, from a point out in space, white-hot light ballooned outward at far beyond the speed of light. It tore up the sky and swallowed up the black of the early morning. Unbearable lightning raced across the sky in a violent flash with searing radiance as from the wrath of a thousand supernovas. The wisps of lingering clouds were thrust away, and then the external camera went dark.

•　　•　　•　　•　　•

We heard a few scattered reports and yelps from outside the Command Center. Within the Blockade, various pops and crackles sounded from small equipment that had no RF shielding and was unprepared for the blast.

"Romero, get a safety team to check the perimeter, please." He raced out of the room. "How soon until we're back online, Jens? Give me a sit rep, please," I urged.

"Need about two minutes, sir." Jens was checking his equipment, up and down, to ensure everything was still functional. He scrambled, and Shanna helped him.

The lights in the room returned, and other monitors sprang to life. Whirs and clicks of servers and towers sounded, and fans started spinning once more. The towers rebooted, one by one, and the images slowly came back to life on the screens. The crafts – if they hadn't been destroyed – were still much too far from Earth. However, complicating matters, there would now be auroral phenomena waving across the sky, from south of the south magnetic conjugate area to far north of the north conjugate area. There would also be resonant light blips from lithium debris scattered across the northern and southern hemispheres, high up in the exosphere. All of it would obscure our view up through our own skies.

"C'mon, Jens, get our satellites back up. What did the *Tsar Bombas* do?"

Jens pulled up everything as feverishly as he could. Romero came racing back in to retake his post. "What's the situation, Jens? Shanna? We back up?"

I snapped my fingers at Capra. "Check with the troops."

Capra switched his radio back on and hailed the Joint Chiefs and Carson, since he was close outside. All reported a state of readiness. "Sir," Capra leaned toward me. "I forgot to tell you in the frenzy of preparation; I'm sorry, sir. I commissioned one of our Blockade scientists – Leslie Trejo is her name – out there with the troops. She had goggles on, and she's got a radio, sir. She may be our best look at the view before the eyes in the sky kick back in."

"Patch her in, please, Peter."

"Trejo, Trejo, SecDef Capra, come in, over?"

"Trejo, sir," she answered nearly instantaneously. "Thought you'd be calling. Reading you five by five, sir. Wanna hear the weather report?"

"Let's hear it, soldier," he said. Capra motioned to Shanna to start recording.

"Brilliant white flash, sir. Changed to an expanding irradiance. Greenish hue," she recalled. "Spread out, more or less, in fingers like cirro-stratus clouds forty-five degrees above the horizon. They arced downward toward the North and South poles. Uh, now it's more like, uh," she paused, and it sounded like she was looking through something to get a clearer image, "concentric rings expanding from the blast in a slowing velocity. All told, took about sixty-five seconds. Now the impact zone – it was purple before – is more of a fading magenta at the zenith. The footprint of this sucker is about fifty degrees north of east and south of east, kind of like a pale red semicircle. White rainbows. It's actually quite spectacular, sir."

Jens snapped his fingers. "Back online. Phew! Everything's up, sir." He and Shanna sat back down.

"Give me thermal. Infrared. Anything," I said. "Something to see through the colors and strata. Anybody else seeing anything? Everyone else back online?"

The tiny squares in our split screen began to repopulate, morphing from lifeless black to talking heads, nervously looking back and forth from whatever console was in front of them, darting to speak to someone, and returning to their view. Some would occasionally give a quick thumbs up.

"Anything?" I pleaded. "Where is it?"

"Just a minute, just a minute," said a voice. "I think we have something here, sir. Different vantage point from lower elevation." The voice was that of Commandant Orlando Miles in Los Angeles. "Standby."

An anxious ten or so seconds elapsed. "We're getting the visuals now. It looks li-" We waited for him to continue, but he didn't. His screen froze, and the audio cut out.

"Commandant Miles?" Peter said. "Commandant Miles, can you hear us?"

"Why can't we hear him?" I said to Peter. He shrugged, waiting for a reply. "Jens why can't we hear-"

I had turned to Jens, who was staring at his screen. His face was a deathly sheet of white. "Jens? What is it?" I said. He didn't respond. His eyes were glued to his screen. "Jens?"

Peter heard me and turned his attention to Jens. "Technician, reply to the President," he ordered.

Jens managed to pull his eyes away from the computer, centimeter by centimeter, slowly moving them up, with a visible labor, to meet mine. I watched him intently. Slowly his gaze reached my eyes, and his eyes welled up with tears. I furrowed my brow. And then I knew, with utter horror. *I knew.*

"I'm sorry, Mr. President. I'm s-so-" he faltered, with his lips quivering. Shanna heard him and quickly sat back down at her desk, mirroring his station. Her jaw dropped.

"No…way…," Romero muttered. "You gotta be kidding me."

I raced around the side of the station and monitored Jens' screen. His head bowed. And then I saw what he saw.

The crafts had not diminished in size. They had not been obliterated, they had not been impacted, they had not been fragmented in any way, and they had not been knocked off course. There wasn't a single visual dent. Whatever shielding those accursed things had around them, they just sailed through twenty-two hundred megatons of raw nuclear destructive force, dispassionately, coolly, with zero regard for our strategy or nuclear power. Both were still moving straight for us, heading right down toward our planet.

Our *Tsar Bombas* had done absolutely nothing! Just like that, they were all wasted. Romero, Greene and I had discussed only three possibilities. How foolish we were to think that the gorgons hadn't thought of a fourth. Our missiles had done absolutely *nothing*.

Pandemonium enveloped the Command Center. People were yelling to their contacts to take cover. Others were asking desperately about the status of the moon. Still others were yelling at their computers for a check on the ozone layer, answerable by someone just as frenzied as them on the other end of their com.

Shanna was patched into NORAD and trying to hail Commander Sinclair, who was scrambling, barking orders to whomever was on the receiving end of his fear-filled rant. No one was listening to anyone.

I need telemetry now!!

Can you confirm negative impact!? What's the status of the lunar surface!?

I need radio soundings!! What's the UV level!?

Any deviation in course!? Can you confirm target variance!?

Confirm polar axis, I say again, confirm polar axis!!

In the mayhem, one voice rose above all of them.

Mine.

I wrenched my radio up to my lips and yelled with every fiber of my being and the fire of a thousand suns. "Fleet Admiral Evelyn Lynch, prepare to fire! Prepare the fleet! Prepare the *entire* fleet to fire on those things now!" I screamed.

A few of the Joint Chiefs and many others in that tiny room began to weep. Something roiled in my gut, and a wave of vicious, fearful nausea washed over me.

Secretary of Defense Peter Capra slumped down into his chair and put his face in his hands.

•   •   •   •   •

Friday, March 10th 2045 · 0403 hours

All wings had reported in angrily. Every one of them was shouting. No one could believe it. A fierce determination had seized all of our men, seething and brimming over with unbridled rage and thirst for vengeance.

"Give me Bolling, now. *Now!*" I said to Jens, who suddenly, as if by a seizure, snapped himself back into gear when I barked. "Jens, I need Miguel. Chief Monzon, Chief Monzon, what's your status?"

Miguel's face showed in the camera, and he was speaking, but his lips were moving noiselessly.

"Jens, I need *audio!*" I screamed at him. "Settle down, everyone! *Quiet!!*" The din in the room was still quite high, but everyone simmered down and regained their composure. "Miguel, do you read? Peter, get on those VLA array reports and verify telemetry with Romero or Shanna, please. Miguel?"

His voice came in suddenly, mid-word, "-firmed, Mr. President, ready to go. All wings have reported in, and some have already launched. We're up for the goat rope and holding at the outer marker until the SLBMs are blown."

A messed up situation. He had told me once what *goat rope* meant. *Messed up, indeed,* I thought to myself.

"Very good. Look alive, boys. Be careful. Keep those masks on!" I barked. "Capra, make sure ground troops are ready. They're going to punch through! Fleet Admiral Lynch, do you read? Come in!"

"Roger. Preparing for launch."

"Get ready to give them everything you've got!"

"Yes, Mr. President," she said coolly.

"Craft slowing to suborbital approach, closing in on the thermosphere," said Shanna. "One hundred seventeen miles and closing, sir."

I glanced at the clock. 4:05 AM. *Too soon, too soon!* I thought. *Our fighters won't have visual once the nuclear blast auroras fade.* "Chief Monzon, they're almost in. It's too dark! Keep those pilots using all their eyes *and* their scopes!"

"Roger!" he confirmed, slapping his visor down.

•　　•　　•　　•　　•

Friday, March 10th 2045 · 0419 hours

Our jets were up. Thirteen thousand of them all told, spanning the world, armed with guns, AMRAAMs, and heat-seekers. The numbers were split between the two crafts, six thousand five hundred each. All fighters were either aloft or climbing to monitoring altitude, steering clear of the designated entry zones. The crafts were about to push through our clouds, targeting off the eastern seaboard as well as over Osaka.

Capra spoke. "VLAs tracking two large inbounds," he said, staring with horror at his screen. "Sixty two miles up, each. Oh, no, no! Look at the size of those things! Destinations confirmed, Mr. President. *Hostile 2* has swerved and is now heading west toward Japan. They'll be entering the mesosphere in five minutes, sir. No, no, no, no, no," he pleaded.

Capra was falling apart.

"Relax, Peter; this is what we prepared for. Carson, come in, over?" I had patched my radio into a headset and signaled the General.

"Carson here."

"Everett. Nukes failed. Crafts are still inbound."

"Yes, Mr. President, I heard. I'm sorry, Vance."

"Me too, Everett. Get your men ready. God speed, my friend."

"God speed to you, sir."

Carson clicked off. My eyes quickly flashed to a separate screen in the bank of them that had the helmet camera views of Jet, Foxy, the snipers at their various locations, and a few others. The General's helmet cam was included in there as well.

"Miguel?" I said.

His voice came back muffled. "*Si, amigo.* I mean, excuse me, yes, Mr. President," he said, returning to decorum.

"Those things are inbound. Tell everyone to watch out. We're gonna have some deafening sonic booms as they enter. Make sure as many of you are at as low an altitude as possible. That thing is gonna be carrying radiation. Turn and burn! Time to scrape the building tops."

"Mr. President, there's going to be intense heat and air compression, maybe some loud crackling sounds. Earplugs might be good," Shanna offered.

"Got it. Carson, did you hear that?"

"Roger," echoed the General.

"Miguel, keep your visors down and masks on; it's still bright up there. Keep the fleet back and do *not* engage until called upon. You don't want to be near those DTBs when they go off. Let the craft empty, and then we'll squeeze the gorgs in the middle. Copy?"

"Copy, Mr. President." Miguel relayed all of that to his squadrons. In his cockpit camera, I could see him, clearly. Out through his windows I could see fighters innumerable. I'd never *ever* seen the Air Force so galvanized, nor so many jets in the air. And these fighters and their jets were from every single country in the world. Tactical had them all heading northeast from Bolling AFB, now out over the Atlantic, far from our coastline, clustered together over the Labrador Sea, preparing for a wide circle south once called for. At our signal, they'd turn and burn once recalled to the fight.

"Three minutes until sky dome impact and subsequent entry, Mr. President," Jens said. His voice was drawn and quaky. "I'm pulling up the CIA's ECHELON stream so we can hear it, but it should also be safe to step outside while it enters our atmosphere. It's slowing down, sir. Both of them are," he said, wiping his eyes.

"Alright. I'm gonna step out and see ours. Visibility?"

"Uh, partially overcast with visibility thirty miles, sir, but vertical visibility is unimpeded. You'll be able to see it against the auroras," Jens said, and I was reminded of June 6th, 2026. I think we all were. It was a perfect day: mostly cloudless and blue all over the earth, when the gorgons first drifted down nineteen years ago.

"Anyone else want to come with me, now's the time. Lynch, here it comes. Get those sub rockets ready. Carson, be on the SPAAGs and Vulcans and hit 'em with everything you've got on Sinclair's mark. And watch out for raining debris. The main ships obviously have some kind of invulnerability to compression waves. We're going to have to target the skies once the gorgs are out of the mother ships. Commander Sinclair, is that your assessment too?"

The Commander nodded. "Yes, Mr. President. Admiral Lynch, General Carson, all teams, that is correct. Wait for the go," he said.

"Aye aye, sir," said Lynch. Carson replied with an affirmative.

Peter Capra nervously got up. His legs were shaking, and he had a wet stain in his crotch. He looked cold and clammy. "Peter, take a break. Get some water. This is only the beginning."

"Yes, Mr. President," he replied weakly.

I grabbed a pair of binoculars from a supply near the Command Center. It took less than one minute to get to the Launch. I turned and glanced down the ramp as I ascended to the doors. Bayless had followed me, along with Austin, breathing hard. Behind him were Grady and Roth. Somewhere back further, beyond the Command Center, my wife and daughter were undoubtedly trembling.

The doors opened. The wind hit us immediately. It didn't take long to see what we needed. I lifted my binoculars to my face and beheld it.

An opaque and threatening shadow four point seven miles wide by two point three miles long, stark and ominous, was descending down through the haze of the colorful upper atmosphere, which was still illuminated from the nuclear bursts. A prism of tints relinquished their dominion as the dark mass slowly thrust its way through, its rims glinting with fire and smoke. The cloud cover was being pushed away as it came streaking down through the strata.

And then we heard it.

Rolling toward us, too dangerously near, yet still far off and thirty miles up, a barreling sound made its presence felt. The five of us watched it, breathing hard and panting through the blustery wind. A spine-altering shudder warped the air all around us, and we were thrown to the ground as the boom hit, taking out our knees. And then another one.

Flickers of lightning danced around the edges of the craft. Osaka had to be seeing the same thing.

We got back to our feet and stared open-mouthed at this new threat. It had seemed so innocuous and infinitesimal framed against the dark black of space less than a week ago; just a tiny blip in the endless cosmos of space. Yet here it was, inviolate and intact, having survived twenty-two hundred megatons of nuclear deterrent, proud and unflinching in our face, embodying disdain, invading the sanctity of our planet.

The auroras were fading all around it, its vast expanse gobbling up the view of the stars and thrusting itself forward, pushing through friction and gravity toward our home world once again. It lit up the sky with fire. But this one was different. It was descending lower, faster, more plainly, without reservation, without fear, heeding not our puny little projectiles and caring not for our feeble stratagems.

The gorgon mother ship, half of it at least, settled down into our stratosphere, now twenty-seven miles up, floating and decompressing, white iridescent vapors shooting out around it as it steadied itself to hover.

It was almost beautiful, hovering there, that giant ship: an indescribable and organic fusion of mineral and mechanical alien manufacturing. The sound of crackling could be heard from afar, way up there, as it decompressed and achieved its desired position, just off the coast of Virginia and over the Atlantic Ocean once more. Massive jets of pronounced air jetted out of it in multiple directions from its pale underbelly.

And then, as if to dispel any and all doubt about either its intentions or its occupants, I saw it: a vapor, ethereal and swirling, began enveloping the craft on all sides, misting around and eddying in the early morning air. This wasn't the effect of the fading aurora shining through some opaque colorless haze and projecting its own colors through it. No. It was bluish-green, through and through, and we'd seen that vapor. Felt it. A shudder ran through me as I recognized it. I'd been shivered by it. We all had. I knew, far out over the Atlantic and miles up in the sky, that mist was deadly cold.

My heart thundered in my chest, pounding against my rib cage as I witnessed the inevitable.

Moment of truth. We watched.

As only pinpricks of light from our vantage point so many miles away, tiny hatches suddenly sprung open all over the craft. The mother ship took on the resemblance of a colander lit brightly from within, filled with luminescence that now streamed eagerly out through those pinpricks. Its rays burst outwards as tiny shapes hovered at each of the openings.

Suddenly, those tiny shapes sprang into action.

With a violent speed and screams loaded with malice, they jettisoned from the craft by the hundreds of thousands. We heard them down here. Not silently, drifting down through our clouds as they had done so many years before, seemingly innocuous and benign.

Not tranquilly, as supposed angelic ambassadors of peace before yanking the wool from our eyes with murderous cruelty.

Not with friendly purpose.

Not for harvesting nor replenishing their home world. Not for anything other than pure, cold-blooded, thirsty revenge.

This time, they rent the skies, hissing with their terrible cries and shrieks that could stop the heart. No such malevolent species had ever set their sights on our planet twice.

This time, it was not for self-preservation.

This time, it was for annihilation.

Scourge of the universe.

Cancer of the animal kingdom.

Intergalactic predators full of malice and dripping with vengeance.

The gorgons were upon us.

18 | DEFENSE

Friday, March 10th 2045 · 0438 hours

We all screamed and fled from their wrath.

Back through the vertical doors of the Blockade we ran, yelling as we fled. I hurled myself down the Launch railing and bolted back to the Command Center as the heavy iron doors closed fast, meeting in the middle.

Holdouts emerged from their bunks, staring at us in terror as we passed by.

"Get under cover! Back in your bunks!" I yelled at them. I slammed my radio to my face. "Fire, Lynch! Sinclair, fire! All birds, launch! *Launch!*" I screamed. "Carson, they're coming!"

We reached the Command Center.

I was panting and sweating and so very tired. I hadn't slept. Jitters spasmed over me. Chills and nervous twitches. Watery eyes. Restlessness. I willed myself desperately to move forward, trying to shake off the webs of exhaustion that clung to me. "Lynch, report," I gulped between dry-mouth swallows. We were out of breath and back at the Command Center.

"Mr. President, I read you. SLBMs and DTBs engaged. Staggered launch from all ships. Ours are almost there, sir. Proximity to target forty miles and closing."

Tactical had ballooned into dozens of images segmented out across the screens. Gone were the grids of the world leaders, the administrators, and those charged with our defense. Replacing them were live views of aerial and ground defense engaged in a fiery counter assault. The grid tiles flashed here and there, lit up by weapons fire. In every grid, if you looked closely enough, dark shadows flew by.

Seasoned warriors cried out in terror. Recent enlistees shouted bravely. It was a cacophony of voices hollering over one another. Helmet cameras spun every which way. One camera caught a soldier in the distance shooting at a gorgon, which proceeded to alight upon him in fury, ripping the mask off his head and freezing him on the spot. The soldier watching with the helmet camera turned and fled, wailing.

Whatever communications had gone out unbeknownst to us from the previous queen, it seemed this new wave was familiar with our technology, and some way, somehow, they took it all into consideration and zeroed in on us with a savage offense.

"Stand by for detonation," Lynch said. "Five. Four. Three. Two. One. Go for detonation."

"Plug your ears, gents!" I yelled over the radio.

We heard it inside. Multiple concussion blasts that hummed and pulsated, expanding outward in a visceral wave of energy. The DTBs sent out their audio shockwaves over and over. Like popcorn in the sky, they erupted everywhere, bathing the heavens in a frenetic cavalcade of unrelenting balls of sound and light. Perpetual yellow flashes illuminated the underbelly of the craft and the surrounding strata.

Various reports came in that a few ground forces' communications cut out. Some of them were back online momentarily. Those that remained had RF shielding, and many of the soldiers there were cheering.

"Visual, please! Off the coast, what can we see?" Capra shouted.

"Hold on," said Jens, tapping his keys. His headset hung loosely on his sweat-drenched head, swinging freely. His glasses were fogged up from tears and fears. "Got it. Cape May Lighthouse."

Jens brought up the view off the coast of New Jersey. A much-needed sight brought confidence and joy to our hearts. Dark dots plummeted from the sky and splashed freely into the cold of the Atlantic. More were flailing in the air, careening wildly and hurtling into structures up and down the cityscape, taking other gorgons with them in their path. The screen flickered from interference, but the sight of those sick shapes dropping like flies was exactly what we needed to see.

A cheer went up over the com. Soldiers on the ground rejoiced and cried, beholding the demise of such a great host of the enemy.

"All vessels, fire at will; repeat, fire at will," Lynch ordered.

All at once, more fiery bolts shot up into the sky. From multiple origin points, tiny projectiles sprinted heavenward in disunity, discharging one after another. They were all launched from the decks of the massed fleet headed by Lynch. Thunderous ballooning waves of sound burst in the sky very near the base of the craft. Dark dots scattered, desperate to outrun the violent sound bursts. Many of them did not and thus met their doom, writhing and splintering, crackling and withering in midair, then plunging thousands of feet to their death below. A tremendous ringing sounded throughout the air as DTB met DTB in the skies.

Nonetheless, thousands more gorgons took their place. The wave did not dissipate. *The entire craft must be stuffed to the rafters with gorgs,* I thought.

The SPAAGs moved out like autonomous robots across the horizon, shooting at any and all aerial targets, mounted with machine guns, autocannons, surface-to-air missiles, or a combination. Mindless drones controlled by an operator somewhere, they engaged. Grady had them up on a display with coordinates and ordnance counts. Some of his units were already being attacked viciously.

Soldiers were screaming across various headsets, under siege and pinned down.

It was every bit of the pandemonium we expected.

Lynch's fleet kept launching.

Subs fired off SLBMs with more powerful DTBs in their cones, and our ears popped. Gorgs for miles were assailed, flailing midair and dropping in altitude, but shaking it off and resuming their pursuits, bleeding from their ears.

The ground strafed the sky in proud defense, while soldiers everywhere scattered.

The snipers were at their posts, taking down gorg after gorg, cleverly concealed in their towers and structures. These gorgons were just as fast as their predecessors, but nothing outruns a committed rifle and a sniper with a good working eye and a grudge.

It didn't take long to register dim concussions and thuds overhead. More visuals came in. A swarm of them, darkening the sky, threw themselves at the capitol and the other major cities in close proximity. That meant New York. Philadelphia. Jersey City. Trenton. Wilmington. As they had done before, they fanned out.

Only this time, it was at precipitous speed, slicing across the sky as if for an appointed rendezvous. Lasers shot back up at the sky, tracing their passage, screaming across the horizon in the orange rays of munitions' heat trails in hot pursuit.

But the targets were fast, and many more were heading this way. I could make out the voice of the General commanding his men, preparing to take aim. He instructed one of them to set off the lures. And then he turned and fired. His audio signal blanched and bounced back again and again under the heavy strain of his rifle's thunder, ripping up any enemy he could sight.

"Perimeter warning, Mr. President. Multiple bandits inbound," Romero reported. "Uh," he said, leaning closer toward his screen, "quantity unknown, sir, but it's major."

They were everywhere. It was a veritable shooting gallery. Osaka was reporting the same. Flashes of lightning and percussive thunder echoed above us. Deafening pounds of heavy fire sounded around the perimeter, lighting up the sky over Washington, DC.

And then, much closer to us, a dull reverberation could be felt. Not powerful enough to destroy gorgons, but an irritant nonetheless.

The lures had been activated.

Audio was patched in between our warriors up above. My eyes darted back and forth between every screen, trying to take in all the data and video streams being presented. *Where is Miguel? Where is my son-in-law?* I thought. *Where is Shipley in all of this? And Everett?* My mind raced. Soldier helmet cams caught black waves of gorgons soaring overhead, screeching with irrepressibly threatening rage and blotting out the sky, a darker spot against the blackness of fading night.

We had killed their queen, and her hive had come to avenge. We watched helplessly. Here they came!

The gun towers overhead, encircling DN002 as a crown, began sounding vicious blasts in defense. We could hear them whirring and rotating frantically, shooting at anything and everything. The halo of eight guns above us fired salvo after salvo into the sky. The competing clinks of hundreds of rounds of ammunition being fed upward into the guns sounded loudly from the Launch bay.

"They're coming!" sounded our gunners. Jens jumped and started to get up.

"Technician, back at your post, now!" Capra snapped briskly. "Do not leave your post!" Jens sat back down feebly.

Multiple collisions sounded down the hall from the Launch. They were too low to shoot, and hundreds of them must be barreling into the ground to smash the irritating DTF emitter lures there. They had passed the sightline of the gunners, and now they couldn't do anything to repel them.

The sound of glass shattering and a high-pitched wail reverberated down the corridor.

"Peter, how secure are we? Could they breach through the gun towers?"

"It's possible, Mr. President; I don't-" He was cut off by a horrible collision above us that sent soot and dust raining down inside the Command Center. The screens flickered.

"General Carson! Shipley, Mayfield, whatever you're gonna do, you better do it fast!"

"Go, Foxy, go," said a voice. It was Shipley.

"On my mark! Three, two, one!" yelled my son-in-law. I glanced over at the screen grid showing their helmet cams. A long tube projected out over a warrior's shoulder, filling up a corner of his helmet cam screen. The RPG flew out of it and left a white smoke trail, blinding his helmet camera.

We felt a tremor above us and heard the muted shrieks of gorgons as several of them were incinerated. And then, rising upward in tone from a low pulsating growl to a high-pitched reverberating whine, a slew of DTF emitters went off. They had been set up in haste, encircling the perimeter of the Ellipse. The gorgons knew it and they started to flee. Not many made it out of there. The sonic blast wave hit and pulverized them. The Ellipse was littered with decimated gorgon carcasses.

But just like that, more and more came.

"Lynch, keep firing! Hit it with everything you've got! They're still coming!"

"Yessir. We're trying, sir," she assured me.

On a helmet cam, we could see a soldier bolt past the Christmas tree. It was burning, swaying sadly in the wind as flames licked hungrily at its branches. Consumed by smoke and crackling fire, it billowed and disintegrated.

And then, more glass shattering from the Launch. A stifled cry, followed by gunfire.

The tree was too much for me. The glass shattering cemented it in my heart. I grabbed an M5 from the table and pulled my mask down over my face. "Masks on, everyone, masks on! There are too many of them. They're punching through!" I clipped my radio to my belt and kept the earpiece in. I holstered a Beretta on my belt and quickly grabbed magazines. Good for backup once I run out of ammo for the M5.

Darrell Austin jumped up, pretty spry for an old guy, and grabbed the next rifle below mine. "I'm with you, Mr. President," he growled.

Capra mustered his wits and moved past his own urine, thrusting a rifle into the arms of Jens. "Make yourself useful, kid," he barked. "This might be it. Hope you know more than just computers." Jens sighed and cursed, taking the weapon.

We slowly filtered out of the Command Center, heading toward the Launch with guns drawn. It was eerily quiet. All of the towers had been silenced. In the distance we could hear the muted concussion blasts of further DTBs and cannon fire, SPAAGs, and Vulcans booming proudly on the battlefield of our lives. Behind us, the Command Center was nearly emptied except for a few individuals not willing to advance down the hall. They had rifles in their hands, but were holding back out of raw terror.

I switched to Channel 3 briefly. "Hon, Neener, come in."

Pause. Then, suddenly, "Daddy! Are you okay?"

My precious daughter. "For now," I said. "Just making sure you are. Hold tight. I know you're scared. Whatever you do, stay in there."

"Oh, no, Daddy, are they inside? Is Liam okay?"

"Don't know. Stay there. Liam's fine for now. I love you. *Stay...there.*" I switched to Channel 8. "Everett, Jet, Foxy, come in, over?"

A voice whispered back to us. "Sir. Quiet." It was Jet. "They're right over the Blockade lid. They're holding back and waiting for something. Think they might have figured out our location. Do not engage."

I paused, not willing to endanger them with my voice coming over their radio. I looked down the hall. The lights had gone out at the Launch. The smell of something burning filled my nose, wafting down the hall from a chilly morning breeze filtering in through a new crack somewhere. A hanging fluorescent lamp had come loose on one side and was spinning wildly, playing off of the smoke and mist.

I peered cautiously, rifle forward. The others behind me pressed in, and I held my fist up, signaling them to stop. I kept my eyes trained forward. The quiet of the Launch mixed with some static bursts and quick flashes of electrical sparks from the Launch doors. Thankfully, they were still closed. But the smoke remained, and something had knocked that light loose and sent it spinning.

The smoky mist cleared.

The gorgon was on us before we could even think. It launched through its own mist, the color of which we couldn't see in the mysterious disarray of the Launch bay. I threw myself to the ground! It missed me and hurled itself onto Darrell Austin. He never got a shot off. I leapt out of the way and watched in horror as it began to claw and assail him, mask or no mask. Jens reflexively shot it off of him, but he was no marksman or trained soldier. His spastic bullets sprayed the gorgon and then continued to spray into the elderly body of Darrell Austin.

"Jens, stop!" I cried in horror.

Jens howled, clutched his own head, dropped his rifle, and fled back up the passageway to the assumed safety of his own bunk.

Darrell Austin lay there dying. "Mr. President," he gasped, "it was an honor, sir."

"Oh, Darrell, no, no, no," I breathed, taking his hand in mine. I looked at his wounds. There was nothing we could do.

I looked back. Other gorgons could now be plainly seen squeezing through the turrets of two of the gun towers. Lifeless human bodies hung limp out of the gunner cups. One of them had been cavalierly thrown to the ground of the Launch as a gorgon squeezed its way through. Three of them were in here now with us, humming and bobbing their necks in that sickening manner they always did. I tilted my head and opened fire at them. "Capra! Assist!" I cried, and Peter came up, spraying gunfire at the besieged turrets. Dark shadows sprang back and flew around the Launch bay, concealing themselves.

My rifle was soon out of ammo. I scampered behind and retrieved Jens' rifle from the soft ground, whirling around and continuing to spray at whatever I could hit. The Launch bay lit up with flashes of lightning. Between my salvo and Capra's, a few ghastly shapes dropped to the ground.

And then the gorgs just stopped. I could see them, their dim green glowing eyes lingering at the threshold of our Launch, peering through shattered windows on two of the mangled gun towers. They paused, looking up at the sky, back at us, then back at the sky once more. With a hiss and a growl, they took off, every last one of them. The sound of scattered gunfire from the surrounding buildings pursued them as they fled. Some youthful voice yelled, "Yeah, you better run!" over the com.

I looked at my watch. It was 0612 hours. Sunrise was near. It had seemed an eternity that we had all been engaged in this shooting gallery.

Just then, a familiar voice came over Channel 8.

"Permission to engage, Mr. President?" someone asked with a disturbingly out-of-place giddiness.

I laughed a grim laugh, full of optimism, recognizing that accent. I knew full well that all those men in the skies were under the leadership of a very talented pilot who would destroy many more gorgons before they could destroy him. But at the same time, I was filled with trepidation. That very talented pilot was my best friend. I feared for his life.

"Be careful, Miguel," I said between laughs punctuated with relief. "Nick of time, dude. Permission granted, amigo."

"Roger. Light 'em up, *hermanos!*"

We ran back to the Command Center and watched the monitors. Jens was nowhere to be found. Tactical worked just fine without him, and Shanna and Romero were still there. "Squadrons on screen, please," I said, panting.

Tactical aerial overlay scrolled over the terrain map, revealing four thousand five hundred signals inbound from the northeast, screaming at Mach-2 toward the east coast. And, taking point, outrunning the rest of them, was Captain Miguel Monzon, Chief of Staff of the Air Force, my Chief of

Staff, and my best friend, in a jet with the tail ID of 'XA103.' Another two thousand of our fighters were coming in from the southwest to pinch the enemy with a vice grip in the middle.

Every single jet lit up the sky with a deafening roar, screaming toward our adversaries with an unrivaled vitriol.

The sun rose triumphantly behind the main fleet racing across the Atlantic, and an eastward wind was at their backs, gathering across the ocean. They screamed west. The others were burning it east toward them. All were now locked and loaded on their targets with devastating weaponry.

That weaponry included powerfully murderous sonic DTF emitters and bombs.

The gorgons felt the wrath of our squadrons rolling over them like the gathering wind at the onset of a storm. Their numbers had been reduced, but they were still many. There was only one thing left for them to do.

The gorgons all shrieked and fled before the wrath of our coming.

19 | LAST STAND

Friday, March 10th 2045 · 0619 hours

Anticipation coursed through my veins.

Miguel and his squadrons were screaming toward the enemy, many of whom retreated back toward the mother ship. Forty-five hundred American fighter jets from the east met two thousand proud compatriots' jets just off the craft's western rim. Catcalls sounded over the coms.

"Fangs out, *mi gente!* Here comes the Iron Gorilla!" Miguel screamed. "Guns guns guns! Punch through, people!" he signaled to his western squadron members that he was going to fire, and that they should clear out of the way. Miguel was a *niño* again. You could see it in his face and hear it in his voice. He was *alive*.

Constant and sometimes indecipherable chatter lit up the Command Center as tactical revealed thousands of pinpoints of red light intersecting with thousands of pale green 'x's' signifying bandits. My heart pounded as I strained my eyes to listen clearly. The red swath punched through the perimeter of the bandits. Pilots were calling out squadron and missile shots as they barreled through a giant mass of gorgons slowly descending out of the mother ship.

Patriot-14, Fox 3!

Watch your tail, Jonesy! Shake him, baby.

Aaaand…direct hit! He's off your back. Roll, baby, roll!

I'm almost on them. Low to the ground over Baltimore. Get clear, Sanberg! Heavy Driver comin' in. Lightning-10, Fox 2!

Guns guns guns! Watch it, Anthony, move it!

Daisy cutter, comin' through; look out, boys!

Check your six, Fontana, bandit, bandit!

Lightning 20, Manson, Winchester, Winchester!

Romeo-9, Fox 3!

Trandum, you've got three on your tail; firewall it!

Different languages came through on the com, all patched into the same channel. The gorgon diaspora and resulting rebuilding process had, after all, shifted international communities all over the planet.

¡Apártate del camino, Sauve, cuidado!

Bandiet het my gekry, ek slaan uit!

Ashab alywyu ya Alfahzi, laqad hasalt ealayhi!

Jag är slagen, jag är slagen!

Розгорніть свій DTF зараз!

Voices collided with each other over the com as fighters and gorgons did the same in the skies. Green and red lights flashed and then disappeared. Pilots cried out for their wingmen and swore profane rants at the invaders. Some started to speak, until a rush of wind overwhelmed their headsets in static as they were pulled from their cockpits and hurled from the sky. Gorgon hisses echoed through the com; stunted cries from pilots starting to speak when their masks were ripped from their heads. Jets colliding with one another.

Soon, sixty-five hundred jets were sadly reduced to forty-eight hundred, and the numbers kept dropping. But the gorgons' numbers had been cut by two-thirds. An estimated count showed them at just over one hundred thousand still in the air, being pursued by our raiders. Their numbers were dropping rapidly as well as our jets deployed DTF bursts all around them.

Lynch came over the com. "Mr. President, I suggest we clear the fighters out and have them hold back at the perimeter again. We need to deploy more DTBs, sir. We stand ready."

"Roger that, Lynch. Miguel, get your boys out of there; we're going to hit them with more DTBs." No answer. "Miguel?" Still no response. "Shanna, where is the XA103?"

Shanna's fingers flashed over the keyboard. "There he is, sir. He's still aloft."

Suddenly, he answered. "Uh, Mr. President, you're going to want to see this." Miguel swore. "You're going to need more jets, sir."

"Monzon! What are you saying? Shanna, pull up the Cape May Lighthouse view, or whatever can see it best. Has the craft shifted? What's he talking about? Monzon, give me a sit rep!" But Monzon didn't reply again. He was too busy instructing his fleet to take evasive action.

"Pursue and destroy on your way out, but get clear! Repeat, evasive; all craft pull out!" he screamed.

"Monzon!" I cried. His cockpit camera had him repeatedly whipping his head around and looking backward through his helmet as he flew away.

"Shanna, what *is* it?" I said, turning once more to her.

She was gawking at her screen. "Oh, my Go-" she stopped. "M-Mr. President..." she trailed off, pointing to her screen.

"For goodness sake, put it on screen! What is it?!" I screamed at her.

Shanna moved her view up to the main screen.

Off the coast, the craft could be seen hovering there. It hadn't moved or shifted course as far as we could tell. Coordinates were verified. But the craft had opened up, and something else was coming.

Something big.

It ate up the sky as it approached, howling and whipping through the air, its obsidian-like body illuminated by the early morning light and the flashes of lightning around it. It shone and reflected. Its skin looked hard and tempered.

We watched in horror as the alien abomination filtered out from its own ship, dropping from the sky like a manhole cover, gyrating and snaking its way toward us, its belly swaying sickeningly. It was coming right at the White House, and, as it did so, it let out a roar that stopped my heart.

I glanced down at the bottom corner of the tactical display. A superimposed graphic had just erupted on screen, which said, simply, *Threat detected!* Readouts below that listed the beast as seventy-five feet wide by one hundred ninety feet long. *Smaller than the queen*, I noted, which made sense. In many insect and animal colonies, the male was smaller than the female. *Sexual size dimorphism,* I suddenly remembered from high school biology class. I jerked my attention back to tactical.

The thing was swimming its way through the air, alligator style, dripping with slime, tentacles dragging behind it. The venomously cold vapor enveloped it upon approach, and it let out another bloodcurdling roar. The smaller drones echoed it in their obedient worship, supporting and clinging to it like remoras to a shark.

My beautiful wife's words suddenly came back to me. *They're coming because we killed their queen. We killed their queen! That's got to be it. So what is this, their king?*

Was it a king? Whatever its rank, whatever its relation to the gorgon queen that we had annihilated, we knew its purpose: the eradication of all those who had obliterated its mate.

Drone gorgons encircled it by the thousands, racing around it and following in its wake.

"Oh my-," I started, and then called out in a wide-eyed reflex, "Lynch! Fire at will! *Fire at will!!*"

Indeed, Lynch already had, and she gave no response. As we watched the abomination in horror, tiny tracers zipped across the skyline, trailing behind the overlarge filth. They exploded like popcorn in the air, shattering its tinier offspring, its workers, as they mindlessly fell from the sky. But it was watching the missiles on their approach, and it veered off course with horrifying speed, dodging and weaving between the blasts. A few burst in close proximity, which made it do little more than wince. And still, onward it flew.

Lynch's fleet fired another volley, and this time the DTB bursts struck closer to it. A tightly-gathered mass of gorgons clustered just above the mate's dragging tentacles, and a Dissonant Tidal Bomb burst in the center of them, sending lifeless gorgon bodies rocketing out in all directions. The mate let out a thunderous, sorrowful, rending cry as it was propelled forward clumsily, righted itself, growled, hissed, and then resumed its course. But the way it was flying was somehow a bit erratic now.

Just then, I wondered. "Peter, get in touch with Osaka. Do they have one of these things too?"

"Will do, Mr. President."

I glanced at the tactical view. Over forty thousand bandits still remained. "Lynch, the beast is below the skyline; hold off. Monzon, all fighters, defend the capitol!"

"Roger that, Mr. President. Fleet, you heard the President. Balls to the wall!" The scream of all of those fighters' afterburners rocked the skies over Chesapeake Bay, turning back northward to converge with the path of the mate. We could almost hear it down here.

But then we heard something else. It was an unearthly bellow, piercing through iron and sediment, punching into our hearts and stealing our sense of peace. The mate was nearly over Washington, DC. Gorgon drones trailed it, being taken out one by one by snipers. SPAAGs lit it up from underneath, and it winced repeatedly as it settled down on the Ellipse, the park filling with a cloud of that accursed vapor.

The General barked at his men. "Light it up!" Instead, we felt a hammer punch come down upon the ground very near us. Alien fists beat on the ground overhead.

"Gorgon king is at the White House; it's demolishing the White House, sir!" Shanna yelled.

"Stop calling it that; we don't know it's a 'king!' And it ain't no royalty in these parts, not if I have something to say about it. Everett!" I yelled, pressing my headset into my ear.

"Yes, Mr. President!"

"Target that alien trash and fire at will!"

"Yessir! Boots on the ground!" he confirmed, and I hoped to God that that didn't include Foxy and Jet.

Helmet cameras revealed soldiers running and a haunting view of a beast smashing the White House into pieces. Jeeps and military SUVs passed them, carrying heavy-duty DTF emitters.

Simultaneously, the jets re-entered the fray, engaging the gorgons again. Numbers continued to drop. Fighter and Fox calls sounded. Explosions came over the coms. Frantic pilots wailed in desperation.

We were losing.

The numbers kept dropping. Gorgons were now at twenty thousand, and our jets numbered only thirteen hundred. We had lost so many souls! We were making them pay, but it was costing us dearly. And then came a sound that I would rue to the end of my days.

"Mr. President, I'm hit, I'm hit!"

No. My eyes flashed over to Miguel's cockpit. There was fire inside it. He was batting away at it while careening wildly. "Miguel! Report!"

"I'm not going to make it, Vance," he said, and he ripped off his oxygen mask, breathing rapidly. "*Gorgos* just smashed through the starboard engine. Navigation system failing. Patriot-1, going down! Patriot-2, you're in charge. Mayday, mayday, mayday!" Indeed, I could hear warning sounds from inside his cockpit, and his blinking panels reflected off his visor. The skyline behind him was tilting. "Punchin' out!"

"Miguel, no!" I roared, hoping there was another option. If he wasn't able to bring the plane down into the ocean and attempt a crash landing there, he'd plow right into the ground. Ejecting, then, was truly his only option. But we all knew what that meant. A slow-moving target silently descending to earth equaled easy pickings for a gorgon.

Lord, Miguel needs you now, I said, and I lifted my palms up. *I trust you, Lord. Rosie, you got His ear.*

Miguel ejected. Tactical showed his red dot disappearing from the screen somewhere over the Anacostia River and I-695.

My head bowed. I felt a thunderous punch to my gut.

Capra yelled out, "Osaka reports no such beast in their craft. Gorgs by the hundreds of thousands though," he read off his screen. "Aerial bombardment continues. Fleet hunting them down. Surprise in store."

Surprise? What did that mean? I wondered.

The soldiers reached the mate, thundering away at the White House, trying to get inside…or something. Indeed, it had leveled the East Wing structure and was now digging downward through the rubble, feeling through the elevator shaft down to us below. Up the corridor beyond the blast doors, we could hear tremendous commotion as the area was hollowed out and concrete and beams fell down into it.

The jeeps screeched to a halt, careening as they flipped around. They pointed their DTF emitters at the mate. At the same time, soldiers running up carried more of them, and they set them to work. Soon, the incredible sound barrage hit the mate, and it howled in agony and pulled its fists up to its ears and roared. Its back convulsed and buckled, dropping it to the ground. But in a furious frenzy, it was back up. It whipped its head around at them and pulsated its own sounds directly at them.

The soldiers froze. Their helmet cams caught the mate inching toward them, locking eyes with the entire group of them. Not a single helmet cam moved. Every last one of them – there were over a dozen – stood completely still, and there was no sound except for the beast. A ghostly quiet settled over the soldiers. One of them slowly tilted over and then collapsed to the ground, soundlessly, without so much as a grunt.

The mate turned back to the White House.

What the heck was that? All of those soldiers had their masks on! Could it paralyze them right through their masks? Was it that powerful?

The soldiers didn't move.

Carson reported in. "Mr. President! Sir, the beast was hit by the DTF's, Vance, but," he growled, "it appears that its telepathy is strong enough to punch through our masks. We just lost some good soldiers, sir!" And then he yelled for Jet and Foxy. They didn't answer. "Shipley! Lieutenant Shipley? Mayfield? Report!"

There was no reply. "Dangit!" the General yelled, and then signed off. His helmet camera showed him running, brandishing that large rifle of his. He paused at one point and fired his beloved fifty-caliber rifle through the windows of the Hoover Building, firing ten straight shots and emptying his magazine. And then he ducked. The mate whined and convulsed, tasting Everett's fury. It looked around, unable to find him. It growled venomously and resumed destroying.

Snipers continued to fire repeatedly at it. Ground troops hurled grenades at the mate, some of which connected. One of the soldiers complained, "We're hitting it, but we're just not doing enough damage, sir!" Smoke rose from the Ellipse as the beast trembled at every painful blast, its back opening up and splitting off fragments of protective covering. But the damage was slight, and each time it would whip around and freeze its tiny assailants and then continue with its savagery, desperate to get in. It was sniffing hungrily, attempting to locate humans in there. Why would it try to get in there? What did it want? How could it possibly know that this was the very capitol of our country?

My thoughts were cut short by a helmet cam belonging to my son-in-law. My eyes widened. There they were! Jet was loading Foxy's tube. He patted Foxy on the helmet and whispered to him. Foxy lifted up over a ground-floor window and took aim. He fired.

Another RPG – Jet called them *torpedoes* – tore across the Ellipse and nailed the mate on its soft underbelly. The thing actually lifted off the ground and flailed in midair, recoiling and clutching itself. It was knocked over on its back like a helpless beetle. The ground above us shuddered again. A tremendous quake sounded throughout the earthen walls. Smoke and vile ooze poured out from the wound, and it bellowed in agony.

The mate flipped back once more, and smoke from incendiary fire mixed with its terrible vapor. It looked around slowly, growling and hissing angrily, searching for its latest assailant. By that time, Jet and Foxy were far away, running to reposition and take aim once more.

A few minutes later, another jet of white shot out from the northeast, smacking the mate on its hindquarters. Bloodied chunks of alien flesh were peeled off it and thrown. Once more, the mate howled and searched in vain for the torpedo shooting humans who once more had managed to escape.

Go, Jet and Foxy; go! I thought.

Others, not so fortunate nor quick on their feet, continued firing at the mate before losing their own lives.

The beast returned to its demolition while snipers fired at it from afar. But now, dark ooze drained from its wounds, and its movements slowed.

•   •   •   •   •

As the war raged below, the skies were lit up above. There was no report from Miguel. Parachutes don't have a tactical signature. I didn't know where he was or if he had landed safely. Maybe I would never know. My heart ached at the thought of losing my best friend.

Lynch reported heavy bombardment and incoming dive-bombers. Those gorgs were actually *dive-bombing* the USS Harry S Truman, among others. I prayed she would fare well and make it through. The entire fleet was continuing to launch DTBs wherever they could, raining fire into the canopy above.

Tactical continued to show sporadic red and green images. The red signatures were, sadly, almost gone. Our jets had crashed into gorgons, barreled into the mother ship in a vain attempt to inflict any damage, collided with each other, or plummeted to earth, the pilots ripped from their seats and tossed like rag dolls to their deaths far below. There were only eight hundred left to the gorgons' some six thousand. But they battled on! Occasionally, we would hear the muffled concussions from the explosions of downed fighters. They were slamming awkwardly into the ground around DC after a gorgon found its mark, sending them into a fiery cataclysm. The thump of gorgons into the ground reverberated above us.

"Osaka reports heavy bombing by stealth bombers, Mr. President," Capra said. "They're taking the city down with the gorgs, sir."

"*What!?* That's suicide."

"I guess that was their surprise," he said sadly. I blew the stress out of my lungs. Capra continued, "well, it sounds like the city was evacuated, sir; and their country is well-acquainted with rising from the ashes." I knew he meant Hiroshima and Nagasaki.

"Lord in Heaven. Dropping bombs on their own city. What desperation!"

Everett Carson came over the com. "Sir, I've lost Shipley and Mayfield. They're not reporting in."

"They're somewhere in there, Everett. Keep looking. Good work, my friend. Their numbers are dropping."

"Sir, are you seeing the beast over the White House rubble?"

"What about it?"

"Uh, I think you should take a look." He moved for a clearer shot. The mate was positioning itself up over the yawning crater that it had created. It reflexively arched its back as if it had something stuck in its throat, almost in a gag reflex. It lurched and expanded, lurched and expanded. And then, grotesquely, it heaved its mouth into the hole it had created, opening its jaws wide.

Out of its gaping maw there came not one, not two, but several dozen tiny shapes in a sickening flood of spew and vomit: wriggling things that squeaked and undulated as they fell, riding a crest of bile down through the hole leading straight to the PEOC. Even as those around it continued to fire at it, it convulsed and vomited its putrescence into the gaping hole above the PEOC.

"What in the name of-" I started to breathe.

And, just like that, its entrails evacuated, the mate's mission was accomplished. It suddenly leapt into the air and flew off to wreak havoc elsewhere.

Capra and I looked over at each other in disgust and incredulity.

"Mr. President, did you just see that?" the General said. "I would get out of there, sir. Whatever that thing just deposited, it did so for a reason."

I didn't know what to think. There were forty of us still in here, secured behind thin bunker doors, being as quiet as we could. "Patriot-2, Patriot-2, this is President Cardona; do you read?" I cautiously whispered into my radio.

A red blip answered me. "Patriot-2 here, yes, Mr. President. Whoa," he said, dodging a gorg. "Guns, guns, guns, look out, Jentzen! Yessir?"

"Identify yourself, pilot," I answered.

"Lieutenant Asher Collins, Mr. President!" he said. "Goin' for a split-S, standby," he grunted, feeling the g-forces. "Ahh, that's better. Aaaaand, you're done, pow!" he said, taking out another of the enemy.

"Collins? That flew out over the Atlantic with Shipley?"

"Yes, Mr. President!" he yelled.

"Keep it up, kid. I hate to break it to you, but you guys have got quite the nasty visitor headed your way. Watch your six, Collins."

"Yessir!" he said, and his cockpit camera showed him looking around wildly.

Suddenly, a tremendous crack ruptured through the walls of the Blockade, and a thunderous cacophony of howls broke loose up from beyond the blast doors.

"Mr. President…" Capra muttered slowly while nervously rising from his seat.

We turned and stared intently down the corridor leading to the blast doors. Our jaws dropped.

Something was pushing on the doors from the inside. They were slowly expanding outward, swelling from the other side. I lowered my radio and watched in horror. Tiny splits and hairline fractures began to race along the concrete in all directions as it gave way.

I didn't waste any time. I reached out and hit a button on a wall claxon. The Blockade came alive in color and screaming red sirens. "Red alert, red alert, abandon the Blockade, repeat, abandon the Blockade," I said.

Howls of despair and fright sounded from down each dormitory hallway as those taking refuge obediently filed out into the main gathering area with us. There were Andi and Janine! My daughter was clutching her belly and looking most agonized. "Hon! Neener! Over here!"

The ceiling shook. Dust rained down upon us. A giant crack appeared in the wall. People screamed and fled. Everyone bolted for the Launch. "Quick! Up the stairs, hurry!" I shouted. "Capra, lead them on. Get outside, and get under cover, quick! General Carson, do you read me? Everett!"

"Five by five, sir. Still no sign of-"

"Forget it! We're leaving the Blockade. Prepare for bandits from below! Bring up those DTF emitters, whoever can! And prepare to launch a DTB!"

"Say again, sir, a DTB? You want an actual bomb?"

"Just do it, Carson!" I said, forsaking his first name.

We were all scrambling. Fissures opened up at our feet. Cracks ran along the wall. Steam poured out behind us. I took one look back as we scaled the railing up to the Launch doors. Bile and spew splashed into the Blockade behind us as a portion of the blast door gave way. A few unlucky souls herding others out were caught in the sticky, phlegmy ooze, disappearing below the wave and crying out as they submerged. They did not resurface. What was in that slime?

We were almost up. "Everett, the bombs!"

"Yessir, stand by, sir. Are you sure, Mr. President? The entire Blockade'll be wasted, sir!"

"Carson!"

"Roger. Stand by."

Briefly I wondered why we hadn't just raised the blast doors on the other end to flee to DN005 by the Capitol Building. But we had no idea what was happening underground! It was something huge and catastrophic. The earth was groaning and splitting all around us. That would have been a lengthy trek in the dark through that tunnel to DN005. I had lived in Mammoth Cave, and I could certainly manage it. I was uncertain about the others.

We all came streaming out of the DN002 Launch hatch and tore across the Ellipse lawn. Some were running every which way and screaming. Gorgs dive-bombed from the sky and plucked a few of the less fortunate ones. I looked over. Capra was snatched up into the sky just to my left. I gasped and winced, reflexively reaching for him. It was too late: he was gone.

In the skies above us, I witnessed several jets pursuing a massive shape flailing in the air. Collins and his squadrons were taking down the mate with heavy bombardment.

My mask was fogging up. Everyone's was.

The earth rocked beneath our feet. The Blockade ring was lifted off of its position and tilted dangerously. The crust, sediment, rock and dirt underneath it were rupturing and spewing dust into the air with a hissing noise.

And then, out of the ground crawled several ballooning figures, still expanding. I counted at least three, almost the size of a private jet, each of them, slick, slime-coated, and still growing. They were densely packed together, and all of them resembled the mate.

Of course; why not? I thought, glancing back in revulsion and terror. That's how they reproduce. *One mate produces tons of others, all of them impregnating the queen to produce drones.* But these things had some kind of accelerant, some rapid-growth genetic predisposition. The mate must have known it was ready to deposit its spawn. And the mate could either impregnate or be impregnated. Was it also a queen? I didn't care. I just wanted to run.

Sickened, we all fled. *Rosie, what are we supposed to trust in this? Who will save us?*

The abominations crawled up out of the ground, roaring and bellowing, and we felt their cries reverberating through our terror-stricken rib cages as we ran. They were almost out.

"Stand by, everyone. T-minus five…four…three…." The General stopped talking. We were mostly all clear.

"Jump! *Jump!!*" I shouted to Andi and Janine as we crossed over 15th Street into the Hoover building.

Behind us, a flash went off: not a fireball of incendiary detonation *per se*, rather a bubble of destruction that itself expanded, billowing outward with a tremendous sonic burst. The massive creatures, still expanding, were compressed violently underneath it, disassembling and splintering under its wave. The weight of the shockwave flattened them, fracturing their bones and reducing them to putty beneath it.

Somewhere up in the skies, a tremendous roar sounded, followed by massive detonations and gunfire bursts. We entered into the Hoover building and threw ourselves into the center of a room and waited.

And then, rising in a swell beneath our feet, the sound of a massive collision thundered through the ground.

Falling from the heavens, a hideous alien body plunged to the Capitol Reflecting Pool beyond the lawn in front of the United States Capitol building. Whether by chance or aim, it didn't matter; it was dead, and the ground exploded in a splintering shock as the collision shook the very ground. Water sprayed up like a geyser high into the air.

And then…silence.

The drone gorgons were still out there.

Poor Capra. Poor Miguel. And where was my son-in-law? Where was Camjet?

My daughter cried softly into my shirt amidst the rubble. We looked around. Something stank. To our dismay, a dead gorgon carcass lay ten feet from where we were, having plunged through a ground floor window after being hammered by SPAAGs, or Vulcans, or the fighters above. We didn't know, and we didn't care, as long as it was dead.

The three of us just stared at each other through our masks, all eyes wide and ringed with fear. We were cut off from communication and had no way of finding out about Osaka…DC…or anywhere else on the planet.

The General radioed me. "Go ahead, Everett. We're in the Hoover building."

"Sir, I'm afraid I have some bad news."

"You better not tell me it's my son-in-law or Shipley. Please say they're alive, General." Janine stifled a cry.

"They're alive, sir, or at least I heard them on Channel 8. But a soldier here – name's Grantham – says Foxy went looking for you and the First Lady and First Daughter. He ran to the White House rubble and was last seen rappelling down the shaft after that thing took off. I'm afraid Lieutenant Shipley went with him, sir. They've switched off their radios, presumably because they know they're AWOL."

I sighed heavily and swore. And then I leaned my head back against the wall and knew precisely what I had to do.

Purpose coursed through my veins.

20 | RESCUE

Friday, March 10th 2045 · 0820 hours

They were everywhere. No one could understand it.

We connected with the General. He and that gun – it seemed so much bigger now in the thick of battle – were roving back and forth throughout the Hoover building to ensure the safety of the troops and to keep them moving and firing. We had no way of knowing what kind of numbers remained. Our jets still roared through the air, though far less in number. Gorgons still swirled about, hunting and becoming the hunted. SPAAGs shot autonomously up into the sky, tracking the disgusting animals wherever they encountered them. They had been preprogrammed to avoid anything metallic or non-organic in the sky, and they were doing their job. The gorgons were still all over the place, flitting about high and low: marauders in search of their next kill. We were pinned down in here. And somewhere, out there, my son-in-law and his accomplice were bravely – meaning *foolishly* – attempting to rescue Janine, my wife, and myself.

The snipers had reported in on Channel 8. At least, two of them had. The other snipers had been detected and were killed off. Pease's body was nowhere to be found. The remaining snipers were bravely still fighting off the gorgs in the thick of the morning as the battle waxed furious.

All I knew was that I had one thing to do, and I was considering the ramifications of it. Andi would protest. Janine less so. The General would forbid it and invoke some kind of constitutional protection ordinance over me.

Nonetheless, I had to do what I had to do.

I had to go get Liam. For Janine. For Andi. For me.

He was only twenty-two years old. He was the father of my daughter's child, growing in her womb. The fact that he and Jet were now in dereliction of duty didn't matter so much to me. They thought we were trapped down in there. I would have done the same to rescue them. Hell, I was now *going to* do the same to rescue them.

I didn't have much time; I knew that. Sooner or later, they would find that they were cut off down there, and they'd have to make their long way back. What if there was a gorgon down there? What if the cavern caved in and they were entombed down in the remnants of the PEOC? What if they got trapped in that vomitous alien slime?

I had to go. We needed every soldier up here alive. We ourselves were in a darkened inner room of the building, and there was rubble strewn all through the corridor outside.

Windows were blown out, and specks of dust floated freely through the air on their wayward journey through gravity.

I was getting antsy. I had to act. Andi was sitting by my side. Janine was nervously pacing. "Alright," I said, standing up. "That's it."

"That's what?" Andi said, jerking awake. She had been slumbering on my shoulder.

"I'm going after Foxy and Jet." I paced over and picked up the M5 and Beretta I had grabbed in the Command Center.

Janine gasped. Andi immediately tensed, and her eyes widened. *"What?!* No, you most certainly are not!" She got up quickly and walked over to me, her eyes glinting. My wife stood in front of me, barring the way out of the room.

"Hon, move," I said. "We don't have time for this."

"Wrong. I don't have time for your cockamamie antics. You're the President of the United States; you're not Batman," she said, theatrically.

"All I'm missing is the cape and the cowl, hon," I said coolly, trying to defuse her protestations. "That kid out there belongs to our daughter, and that's his child in her womb. And the man with him helped save our entire planet the first time around. I have to warn them down there."

"Warn them of what? Vance, they're soldiers. *Soldiers!* They can take care of themselves. That's what they're trained for!" she railed at me.

"So was I, hon. I was a Navy SEAL, remember? I was in the Air Force. I just lost my best friend today. I'm not losing Foxy or Jet."

She tilted her head. "Miguel?"

I sighed and bowed my head again. "Mayday over the Anacostia. His plane crashed."

Something in her softened.

"Hon, this is something I have to do," I insisted. "We just lost Darrell Austin. Peter Capra. Miguel. Evelyn Lynch could be dead. Thousands of good pilots have died. *Thousands.* That's just here! Countless more will have been lost in Osaka. Those things are still out there."

Her expression changed, and she nodded, with tears in her eyes. I was reaching her, but she wasn't ready to accept it. "Yes. Yes, I know, hon. Those things *are* out there. But you're the President! That's why you have *others* out there fighting battles so *you* don't need to. So you can be protected!"

I stared at her. "When have I ever had people fight my battles for me?" She bit her lip. "When have I ever wanted to simply be protected…instead of protecting?"

Andi paused, realizing she was desperately clutching the *now,* forsaking both my past and Liam's future. She looked over at Janine, who had been silently watching us. I knew where she stood. Now Andi did too.

She moved her eyes back to meet mine, mournfully. "You're a soldier," she breathed.

"I'm a soldier," I said, flicking up an eyebrow. "I belong out there, hon. You've always known that."

Andi didn't say anything. The First Lady, my beautiful bride, just took a deep, exhausted breath and stared into my eyes.

Eventually she looked up at me and came close. "Bring them back," she muttered faintly, and then she kissed me deeply, running her hands up and down my back. My heart traveled back to Wednesday night, making love to my wife. Through all the smoke, the dust, and the fatigue, I could still smell the intoxicating scent of her hair as she clung to me.

Without another word, the First Lady tore herself away from me and ran out, weeping. Janine watched her, and then slowly approached me. "Thank you," she quietly whispered. I took my daughter close to me and wrapped my arms around her.

"Carson's not gonna like this," I said.

She nodded.

"I need your help."

•   •   •   •   •

"Everett, could you come in here, please?" I hailed him. He strode into our room from a window, where he was monitoring the gorgons outside.

I directed him to the window at the far end of our room. My daughter nodded to him and then walked out and down the hall. The General approached me and then stopped. "Sir?"

"Everett, come have a look at this. Is that a Vulcan firing on one of our jets over there?"

"What?" he asked incredulously. I waved him to the window and then stepped aside as he peered out. "Where? I don't see any-"

My SEAL training kicked in. I wrapped my left arm around Carson's neck. He began to struggle. "What the-"

I wrapped my right arm up over his head and cradled it, tilting it forward to maintain control. My left arm began to squeeze inward on the sides of his neck. Everett struggled and tried to grasp me and release himself from my clutches. He panted and gasped as my grip stayed firmly intact, cutting off oxygen to his brain.

At the same time, Janine started screaming down the hall. The soldiers in our corridor were alerted to her screams. "Hey, it's the First Daughter. Hang on, Mrs. Mayfield, we're coming!"

Janine's screaming was convincing enough to summon Andi. Eventually I heard my wife's voice in the fray, pleading with her daughter. "What is it? What!?"

The General's body grew limp, and he fell asleep, his brain deprived of oxygen. His fingernails had given my arms and hands quite the beating. He slumped to the floor, and I carefully lifted his rifle strap over his neck and hoisted it over my own shoulders. I grabbed his extra magazines as well, and stripped him of his vest and helmet with his camera and headlamp attached.

"I'm sorry, Everett. Please forgive me," I said, gently. And then I was off, racing out the room and down the hall, palms upraised as best as I could holding that massive rifle.

Here we go, Rosie. Here we go.

•　　•　　•　　•　　•

I was on my way now, darting through the shadows. Masked, armed, and dangerous, just like the old days. And I was in pursuit of someone I loved, just like the old days. *My beautiful bride.* I remembered the early days of our courtship as I pursued her, my heart intent on her being the one. I smiled in memory as dark and threatening shapes whizzed high in the morning sky overhead. I was much more visible now, but I knew how to keep to the shadows. And there were a lot of shadows in the shrapnel and burning debris all around.

My eyes checked every dark blur. My heart was thundering within me as my body came alive with memory of the battlefield. Tactical programming resumed within me. Intentionality played against my own nerves, fusing presidential considerations with guerilla warfare tactics. Both strove for mastery within me.

My senses were alive, and my nerves were steeled; after all, I had once journeyed ninety-three miles from Mammoth Cave to the Embassy Suites in Nashville to visit Miguel. I could certainly go just a few blocks.

I had still not heard from Miguel. How could I now? I was on a radio only. Presumably, if he had landed safely, he would be somewhere near where his plane went down by the river southeast of us.

Lynch couldn't reach me either, and she was undoubtedly still firing away. Last I heard, the ships were being assailed. Maybe they had sunk the Truman. Maybe not. I had no way of knowing.

It seemed that wherever the battle raged, the gorgons went straight for the masks of those who engaged them. They knew. Somehow, they knew! And somehow, they knew who I was and where my administration sat. But why? *How?* Were they always much more intelligent than we ever suspected? Did they have the power of speech? They thrived on a telepathic paralytic that would immobilize their prey. If they could telepathically project paralysis *into* a person's mind, were they also able to extract information *out* of their mind as well? Had they done it before? If so, to whom? Who would have been in close contact with a gorgon, close enough for them to get that kind of information from them? My thoughts were scattered and jumbled as I tried to decipher this new mystery.

Think. You were in IT. The gorgons inject a 'trojan horse' virus into our systems that paralyzes it, sending us into an unrecoverable physical version of a Windows Blue Screen of Death. At the same time or before that, their attack confiscates our credentials, our intel, our knowledge. *Talk about a brute force attack.* The freezing was to immobilize our defenses so they could take our knowledge, and, eventually, our bodies.

It seemed far-fetched, but was it possible? I'd have to consider it later. In two minutes, I had raced from the Hoover building up 15th Street Northwest and across the pavilion grounds, crossing onto E Street and under the tree cover of the Tecumseh Sherman Monument. My heart was pumping with adrenaline. I raced up East Executive Avenue, approaching Pennsylvania Avenue. The destroyed East Wing loomed up before me. I was just up there four days ago. I couldn't believe what had happened to it. The historic mansion – home to forty-five presidents – was demolished. A pile of grayish marble rubble littered the grounds, with the damage extending all the way to the west corridor. I could see the window of the Oval Office staring out at me, but the corridor that ran to it was destroyed.

My radio squawked. In my ear came the raspy growl of an angry General. "Mr. President, I forgive you for what you've done, but I must protest, sir. You're the President of the United States. As acting protective cover in lieu of the

Secret Service, I order you to return to the Hoover building. It's not safe out there."

"Everett, forgive me," I whispered. "You know I have to do this. I'll be back soon."

"And I want my gun ba-"

I switched off. A smile teased at the corner of my lips. Of course he wanted his gun.

•   •   •   •   •

I had to carefully thread my way up the rocks, grasping for purchase amongst such fragments of boulders as I could. But soon, I was over the precipice, and I could see the yawning hole below me. A few tethers had been attached around a large, cracked boulder near the top. Several nylon cables and carabiners extended from it and down into the cavernous pit below. Jet and Foxy had gone down there.

I hoped I wasn't too late. DN002 was lower down and to the south of the PEOC. That ooze was down there, sliding, slithering, filling up the Blockade. They could be stuck in it, or they were about to be. I grabbed the cables, attached the carabiners to my belt and vest, and wrapped them behind and under me, lowering myself down slowly.

It was a long, slow descent, but I eventually made it. I switched on my headlamp and peered around.

The radio. I hoped to God that they remembered what I told them as I pulled it out and switched to Channel 10. I didn't even have to start. As soon as I switched it over, I could hear Jet whispering urgently.

"Mr. President! Andi! Janine! Come in, do you read me?" he urged.

"Jet, Foxy, this is Vance, over."

It took a minute, but the familiar sound short came through on my radio, and Jet answered in a whisper. "Mr. President! Vance! Where are you, brother?" His voice sounded somewhat boxed-in. I could tell they were farther in and, perhaps, somewhere in the cavernous passageway connecting the PEOC and DN002. I had no idea what condition it was in, if it was nearly all caved in or what.

"I'm on my way to you. We escaped up through the Launch of 002. Most of us are in the Hoover building. Jet, is Foxy with you?"

"He's right here, sir."

"Do not advance. I say again; do not advance. Come back the way you guys came. There's a material down there that is toxic, like a sludge or something. Alien. Those giants sprang from it."

There was a pause. The silent sound of them considering this new development was palpable. "I don't see any, sir. Liquid form?"

"No. Almost like a sludge. Ooze. How far in are you? Come back, you two."

"You're all out?" Foxy had taken the radio from Jet, and his young voice rang through clearly. "Janine and Mrs. Cardona too?"

"*Yes*, Foxy. All of us. I'm ordering you to come back with me. C'mon, guys. There's no time. That's an order."

"10-4, returning," Foxy confirmed.

I hadn't traveled maybe twenty more feet toward them when I could make out dim headlamps heading my way, as faint will-o-the-wisps in the dark. Reminded me very much of Mammoth Cave. I breathed a sigh of relief as they drew near, and they raised their masks. I raised mine.

"Well, I see you're still running around in tunnels," I said accusingly, but my giveaway smile drew them in, and we embraced. "You guys okay?" I looked them up and down. "You won't find anything that way except for alien ooze and a beat-up Blockade with a lot of giant gorg skeletons. Everyone ran across the lawn to where you guys were. Looks like we all missed each other on the way."

Jet laughed. "Always the case. Ships passing in the night. Nice gun."

"It's on loan from the General. We were friends. Not sure about that anymore. Don't ask," I said, and then turned to Foxy. "You okay, father to my daughter's child?" I lectured, reminding him of his role. "Don't you ever do anything so foolhardy again!"

"Yessir, Mr. President, Vance, sir. Sorry, Dad," he said, and then he burst out laughing. He couldn't contain it. *Goofball.* I gave him a stern laugh, and he slowly stifled his own laughter. I sprang for him and wrapped my arms around my son-in-law.

"C'mon, you two. Let's get outta here. Masks on."

We returned the way we came, trudging back up the passageway. Morning light was streaming through the broken cavern that was the East Wing. It lit up rubble I hadn't seen before. It seemed peacefully quiet up above, and I wondered what the morning held for us all now that the mate and its evil spawn had been destroyed. I wondered how Osaka had fared. I wondered if Miguel was still alive. And most of all, I wondered if Andi and Janine were still okay in the Hoover Building.

We ascended the nylon cables as before, and I went first, slowly filtering out above the rubble. Jet followed me, and he and I took up cautionary positions with guns toward the sky as Foxy followed behind.

We had just begun to ascend the hill and climb over when three dark shapes flew down and posted up right in front of us. We all brandished our rifles, but Jet exclaimed, suddenly, "Whoa! Stop!"

I looked over at him in disbelief. "Stop?" I whined.

"Stop!" He repeated. "I've seen these before. These are babies, sir."

"Babies?"

"Yessir," he said, holding his palm at me and Foxy, having us wait behind him as he approached. "I saw these on the carrier. Foxy did too."

"He's right," Foxy breathed, no less ready to keep his gun trained on them.

I then remembered reading Jet's report from aboard the carrier, when the three juveniles appeared following the annihilation of the gorgons in China, North Korea, and Iran, as the carrier approached the funnel and the queen's nest. The juveniles there had tried to freeze him.

Jet cautiously approached the three hovering figures, staring at them. "Look, they're doing it again," he said.

"Doing what?" I glanced all around, hoping this wasn't some kind of distraction or diversion from a greater threat. "Jet, we gotta move. We're not safe here." I couldn't see any gorgons zipping across the sky, but that could change in a heartbeat. A few fighters streaked across the horizon, their afterburners ablaze.

The juveniles held Jet in their deadly gaze, foiled by his mask. He just stared back, seemingly transfixed. They were smaller than the rest, certainly, but they were jetting out that awful mist, though in smaller quantities than their adult counterparts. One of them hissed at him, but the others remained quiet. The center one, the largest of the three, moved inches closer, as if it was studying Jet.

And that's when it hit me. Beyond all doubt, I knew it was the truth. It was attempting to paralyze him, yes; but it was *scanning* him. *The telepathy!* Had Jet and some of the others who had been up close with a gorgon been the key this whole time? Quickly I thought back to all of the reports of his and others' encounters. Had the gorgons studied him in his revolt at the Methodist Church? Or in the tank on the way to Mammoth Cave? Had the juveniles studied him, gathering intelligence aboard the Harry S. Truman? Had the gorgon that Allison Trudy and Joseph Bassett captured studied them? Gorgons had also then *killed* Allison Trudy and Joseph Bassett, paralyzing them. Had those beasts extracted information from them as well? Memories… clues… stratagems… protocols? Had the berserker studied Wyatt Shipley as he lay dying? Gathering history, policies, locations? And what about all the others who had died, frozen there, as their lifeforce had been sucked from them and their muscles lost the will to live?

I felt certain of all of it. The gorgons paralyzed their victims telepathically. In so doing, they relayed their telepathy back to their queen in an unbroken signal, tied together like a hive mind. And the queen! She, out of self-preservation, then relayed her telepathy across the vast expanse of space, back to the TRAPPIST-1 system and her home planet. That was how the gorgons knew who I was and where I was located as a world ruler! It had to be!

Strike the shepherd, and the sheep will be scattered. It was the same thing we did to their queen, just in reverse.

It all made sense now. They learned of our plan, slowly deducing it over sixteen long years above ground, just as we all were surviving below ground and learning how to defend ourselves. They drove us underground while they raped our planet and took what they wanted.

This was how they conquered worlds. This was what they did. This was all *they did.*

This was the basis of their wretched and terrible diaspora throughout the universe, spawning new breeding grounds on more hospitable worlds, hatching their repulsive offspring and spreading their seed across the galaxy.

As with Occam's Razor, the simplest explanation tended to be the right one. And that truth was staring Jet in the face.

I had to stop him. I lunged forward and pulled him back, simultaneously calling Foxy. "Foxy, *shoot!*" He instantly gunned down two of them. Their lifeless bodies thudded to the rubble below us. The third reacted in surprise and zipped away, leaving only a trace of a dissipating greenish mist.

Jet shook his head and cleared his mind.

"Jet, you okay?" Foxy asked him.

"Yeah, I'm fine," he said. "Weak, but fine. That was worse than the first time. I think all three of 'em were doing it. Crap, I may hurl," he said weakly.

"Yeah, well, puke while you're running, because we're not safe yet. Move." I switched back to Channel 8. "Carson, Carson, come in, over. This is Cardona. Incoming with Shipley and Mayfield."

Jet obediently ran while vomiting.

The General came back over the radio shortly. "We see you, sir. Come back," he growled.

At that moment, we all heard a massive blast to the east and looked up in shock. It was almost as if the sunlight had faded behind a gargantuan shape that bathed everything beyond it in shadow. A monstrous howl met our ears. A terrible and mournful cry screamed heavenward over by the Capitol Building. We couldn't see over the Hoover Building or the trees, but we knew it was there. Once again, tremors ran through the earth as the whatever-it-was broke free of constraints and tore through the ground with a clamor that drove all other sound away in its horrible wake.

The spawn must have emerged through Blockade DN005 and seen the carcass of the giant mate lying there. It was enraged, howling with despair, with a thirst for vengeance that could not be slaked.

And then we saw it. Lurching up over the skyline, a massive shape tore skyward. It was bigger than the brood that had emerged from out of DN002. It was bigger than the queen that we had destroyed over the Atlantic. It was bigger than all of them, even the wicked mate from which it had sprung.

The spawn was colossal, bellowing as it went, tearing the sky around it with venom and fury.

"Mayday, mayday," shouted voices. "New target at the Capitol Building, repeat, new target at th-" The voice was cut off. Of course – DN005 was there. The corridor connecting DN002 and DN005 was small, but evidently big enough to hold one as it slithered through, worming its way from danger, until its girth demanded too much around itself for the corridor and the destination Blockade to hold. This one had escaped the blast that had destroyed its kin; now it was livid, scorched with rage, swollen and ballooned in girth, and *hungry.*

There it was! We could see it now, an abomination, slicing through the air in its malice. It was too big to ignore; within moments our fighters were on it, firing at it.

"Mouth of God," I muttered.

"Oh no," Jet uttered.

"What the heck is it?" Foxy asked, shielding his eyes from the glint of the rising sun. "Is it another queen?"

"I don't know," I answered, "and I don't care. Whatever it is, it won't be here long. You guys ready to do this?" The three of us looked at each other. Without a word, we were running, running, in the heat of our speed, as if we were tearing down the dark, silent passages of Mammoth Cave all over again. We sprinted down E Street, and before long we were roaring down Pennsylvania Avenue. We passed several confused troopers along the way, heading away from the Capitol. "Get to safety!" I yelled.

I called to the snipers as we ran. "Pease! Pease, come in, over!" There was no response. "Reynolds! Toole! Mitchell! Grant?" No response from any of them…until Toole finally spoke.

"President Cardona, that you? It's Toole, sir!" My thick New York accent must have given me away.

"Yeah, where are you at, kid?"

"Old Post Office Tower, man! *Did you see that thing?!*" he cried.

"We see it. We're on our way there now! I want you to lay down a suppressing fire and hold it at bay. Can you do that?"

"You crazy? That'll draw that thing to me!"

"No, but it'll keep it distracted looking for you. I need you! I have a plan."

"Man, I sure hope so!" he shouted.

The beast swirled overhead. We stopped at John Marshall Park by the General Meade statue. I turned to Shipley. "Jet," I said. "Do you trust me?"

"Implicitly, sir," he said, but he looked confused at the very notion of the question.

"Good. I want you to lure in a gorg to you."

He tilted his head at me and pulled back.

"Jet, I need you to trust me. By all means, keep your mask on. But don't engage it. Just let it get close to you."

"Okaaaaay…," he trailed off. "I'm not sure I understand, Mr. President."

"You don't need to. All I need you to do is to keep that thing occupied. Keep it busy. I want you to think of every single scenario you can from the past nineteen years. Everything you know militarily. *Everything.* Everything that you've ever been able to experience as a soldier. Any interaction you've had with the gorgs. All your knowledge of our Blockades. The memory of your brother. Of Ally. Of Joe. Of your dad. Dredge it all up, soldier - *all* of it. Can you do that, soldier? That's what they want!" I was screaming at him, panting furiously from our run.

Jet stared at me. He knew what I was asking of him. "Yes, I can, Vance," he said wearily. "You better be right about this."

"I'm right. Get on Channel 8. Go. Channel 8!"

Jet sprinted off, calling out and yelling, heading off south toward East Seaton Park. "Foxy," I said to him, "you stay here and get under cover. You zero that thing if it tries to go for Jet instead of freezing him first. You take it out first; you got me? And get back on Channel 8 yourself!"

"Yessir, Dad, sir," he said with a smile. He was in his element, jovial as ever, and sprinting off for cover. I did the same, raising my radio as I ran.

The beast flew overhead, zigzagging through the sky and knocking our fighters out of its path. They tumbled and crashed to the ground in flames. From far away I heard sniper fire, coming from Washington Union Station. Toole was firing repeatedly on the spawn, stinging it and harassing it. It had not yet zeroed him, however.

"General Carson, General Carson, come in, over?"

"Carson here."

"General! Listen up," I said. "I have a plan, but I can't reach Lynch on my radio. Is she still active? Can you reach her?"

"We actually re-established communication with her an hour ago, sir. She's bringing the ships into port. Gorgs are thinning out in number, and the remaining jets are heading east to join the fight in Osaka. What do you need, Mr. President?"

"Hold your radio up to whatever you're talking to her through! I know it's ghetto, but just do it!"

"Hold the walkie-talkie up to the com, sir?"

"You heard me, Everett!" I had reached cover and was crouching down now. I heard nothing for a moment. Carson presumably was connecting to Lynch and informing her of our unconventional approach to communication.

"Admiral Evelyn Lynch here."

"Lynch! It's me. Cardona. I'm in the field. Listen up, you ready?"

"Ready, sir."

"I've discovered something of the gorgons. We just need to hold it at bay. On my mark, I want you to launch a DTB at the Capitol Building, and keep me apprised of impact time. You got that?"

"That will level all the communications in the city and cause catastrophic damage to the Capitol, sir."

"Lynch, the city is already destroyed. Trust me in this. As your Commander in Chief, I'm ordering you to fire a DTB at Washington, DC. That's the only way out of this. Do you copy? Confirm," I ordered.

There was another awkward pause. "Affirmative, Mr. President. Preparing for launch now."

"Copy! Carson, keep me on the line, and get everyone back down into DN002, *now!* Radio all troops to get as far away from the Capitol as they can!"

"Affirmative, Mr. President. I sure hope you know what you're doing, sir," he growled.

"I don't have to hope. I know it," I said, and then I ran toward the spawn. It had settled back down onto the Capitol building, looking mournfully down at the carcass of the mate lying in the pool. It craned its neck high and barked into the sky: a horrible clarion call for its drones, summoning them to itself. Yet, only a few blocks away, a solitary dark shape plunged from the sky over East Seaton Park, ignoring the summons.

"Dad, Dad, a gorg's got Jet, over!" Foxy whispered.

"Roger, keep it in your sights, Foxy!"

If my hunch was right, that gorg wasn't going to return to the beast. It was going to stay right there and engage Jet. I could see him, a tiny figure there in the park, his hands up in defensive posture toward the gorg while it hovered in front of him, bobbing its neck. *Good*, I thought.

It's reading him. It can't project through that mask, but it can extract. Fine. Keep doing that.

I needed to buy them time.

Lynch came over the radio. "Two minutes until impact, Mr. President."

"Roger!" I whispered back. "Carson, how's it coming?"

"We're on our way there, Mr. President," he growled, panting, and then he barked orders to others to hurry up. "Move, get moving! Run! Sir, the First Lady and Daughter are right here with me. C'mon, people, move like you got a purpose!"

"Good. Keep moving."

Suddenly, the beast stiffened. It held its ground, still and stoic. The other gorgons did too. They were still incoming, surrounding it, fawning over it, swirling around it, slowly, ritualistically, almost…religiously. It looked like it was meditating, crouching there near the ground, unmoving and in a trance-like state.

"Sixty seconds until impact, sir," Lynch reported.

The gorgon in front of Jet growled and hissed, jetting out vapor, but it didn't move, nor did Jet. I watched it in disgust, and then glanced back at the Beast at the Capitol. It was almost as if they were communicating. It seemed to go on forever.

"Forty seconds, sir."

The Beast fluttered lightly, its long, trailing tentacles spasming reflexively, almost like it had gulped down a data stream of information, telepathically projected to it from the one that had zeroed Jet. Hypnotized and spellbound, the large one stood, motionless, linked telepathically to its drone.

It was so obvious now. How did we all miss this?

"Twenty seconds until impact, sir," Lynch reported. "Get out of there."

She was right. It was time.

It was all about timing. Always. I jumped out of my position and radioed to Foxy. "Now, Foxy, now! Take it out!" A single burst came from Foxy's vicinity, and the gorgon fell with shattered head and chest. Jet was released from its powerful gaze, working to penetrate his reflective mask, and he stumbled to the ground and vomited. "Foxy, help Jet! Get to safety!"

I turned and faced down Pennsylvania Avenue. The spawn lurched and spasmed, suddenly free of the connection, eyes focusing on its surroundings, searching.

Lynch's voice came through: "Thirteen. Twelve. Eleven."

I took aim and fired the General's beloved fifty-caliber weapon at the Beast. It convulsed with each shot.

"Ten. Nine."

I shot. *Boom. Boom. Boom.* The gun was deafening. A true bone-rattler. The beast hissed virulently, clutching itself, deadly dark green vapor swirling around it. The gorgons watched it in amazement, wondering what was happening to their leader.

"Eight. Seven."

Ten voluminous shots, and my ammo was spent. I dropped the gun, turned, and ran breathlessly. The beast saw me. Their vision was based on movement; we always knew that. Far away, it could see a tiny figure hurtling up Pennsylvania Avenue, back, back, up, up, up toward shelter. *Any* shelter.

"Six. Five. Four," Lynch warned.

My legs felt like lead at first, but they remembered their old strength and began to pump like there was no tomorrow, propelling me up Pennsylvania. Fighters roared overhead, away from the blast zone, but they couldn't outrun Vance Cardona.

"Three. Two. One. Impact," said my Fleet Admiral.

Behind me, a fireball ate up the Capitol Building. The Ulysses S. Grant memorial burst into dust. A horrifying sound enveloped everything and thrust me thirty feet beyond where I was, ballooning outward in fury and speed, thrusting all light, matter, and sound before it and away from it.

The *Dissonant Tidal Bomb* vaporized all lifeforms within three square blocks, but the sound within it persisted. The deafening high-pitched tone cascaded outward in all directions, compressing sensitive alien ears that were the only ones that could hear above forty thousand hertz.

Bone fragments, shrapnel, chunks of skin, and unidentifiable soft matter exploded, landing all around me. Alien debris rained down unimpeded from a thousand gorgons and their hideous, obliterated alpha.

I hit the pavement hard, rolled a few times, and then lay still, thinking about life and death, humans and aliens, while the dust drifted down around me. I pondered how mad the General would be that I had lost his gun, and chuckled.

In the tumult, I didn't know where Jet and Foxy were. I hoped they were okay. I wondered if all the troops had gotten out of harm's way before the blast. There was a ringing in my ears that did not subside.

The radio crackled and then eventually returned. "Direct hit, direct hit!" It was the first time I had ever heard Lynch scream. This matter-of-fact, no-bullshit woman lost her composure and succumbed to joy. "Took out the remaining ground contingent as well, Mr. President! We're scanning, but we're not hearing many more reports of them. Aerial defenders have orders in hand to pursue and destroy. Stand by for confirmation."

"Roger," I grunted painfully. "Standing by." Something hurt in my leg, and my stomach had been flattened once I landed, knocking the wind out of me. I rose to my feet and looked back. The Capitol Building was gone. In its place was a blackened, crumbled heap of demolished historical remnants. I shook my head. Had I made the right call? Who knows. I just wasn't ready to order the deaths of any more men. I had already done the hard thing.

History would judge me, whatever history remained to do so. The one small crumb of comfort was that that wasn't a nuke that Lynch had launched. It was a powerful DTB with a tremendous explosive charge. Coupled with munitions, it was certainly devastating, but a nuke would have been much deadlier.

"Liam Mayfield! Cameron Shipley?" I yelled weakly. There was no response. I coughed and couldn't form the names. My leg spasmed, and I looked down. A small shard of some flying wood chunk had flown through the air like a projectile and impaled me in my right hamstring.

I bit down hard on my vest and jerked it out of me, dropping it to the ground. The smoke swirled around me as I stumbled blearily back toward the White House. It was so quiet. Dimly I could make out the muted and muffled sporadic thunder of fighters roaring through the skies beyond, pursuing the remaining gorgs. Once more, we were having to root them out. Altogether better, however, than being eradicated a second time.

Smoke was everywhere.

My mind buzzed as I coughed and retched, and my ears still rang.

I suddenly heard footsteps, turning around slowly to face them. Out of the fog came two figures, slowly, one leaning over the other. "Thank God," I voiced. "Guys! Ya made it," I exclaimed, and then I laughed. "Guys!" Jet was obviously still nauseous, leaning on Foxy as they approached.

But then I stopped and squinted hard through the smoke. No! It was the reverse. Jet wasn't leaning on Foxy. Foxy was leaning on Jet, and he wasn't walking properly. A sudden unreasoning fear laid hold of me, and I gasped. I found myself stumbling toward them. Jet was coughing, and I could smell vomit, but he was otherwise okay. His shirt was missing, and his amulet necklace bounced clumsily against his bare chest. Foxy, on the other hand, was having trouble breathing, and was clearly delirious with pain. His arm hung limply at his side.

"What's the matter?" I asked. "What hit him?"

"I did, sir," Jet muttered, moaning apologetically. He had been crying, and his face was streaked with tears. "I- I just couldn't see straight after that gorg, sir. I'm sorry. I…I was nauseous and blinded. That gorg just…just pulled all of those memories to the surface, like I was back there again. And th-then Foxy just came running at me out of the fog. I thought it was another gorg. I picked up my gun and just…shot. I'm so sorry, Vance…"

My blood pressure shot up. "Where?! *Where* did you hit him, Jet, where?!"

"In the arm, sir. I wrapped it up with my shirt and put his coat back on him, but he lost a bunch of blood, sir. We gotta get him back!"

"Negative, we'll never make it, Jet!" I grabbed my radio. "General Carson, General Carson, come in!" I yelled.

"Carson here," he replied.

"We need a medic right away! Are there any choppers in the area?"

"Where are you?"

I looked up. "Old Post Office Tower. There should be room enough to land in the street."

"Standby," he said curtly.

"I'm so sorry, Mr. President," Jet apologized. His lip was quivering as I stripped Foxy's fatigues off of him. Foxy moaned and grimaced. Blood spatter covered his face. Under his jacket, Jet had ripped off his own shirt and applied it as a tourniquet on Foxy. Below that, Foxy's arm was covered in dried blood, the flesh turning purple.

"Jet, look at me. Don't worry. It's all good. And stop calling me Mr. President, or I'm gonna ram you with this angry bald head," I scolded him. "You got a tourniquet on him; that was the first step. We'll get a medic here ASAP, *Captain*." Jet looked at me, surprised. "I told you we'd see if you'd be promoted again." I winked at him, then I turned back to Foxy. "Although I may have to demote you once more just for shooting my son-in-law."

"Story of my life," Jet grunted.

"*Liam.* Liam Mayfield, can you hear me?" I asked Foxy, leaning over him.

Foxy's eyes fluttered, looking up at me blearily. "Hey, Dad."

I smiled. "Hey kid. You're gonna be okay. Just hang in there. Janine's comin.'"

"Medic inbound, Mr. President," the General said over the radio.

"Great. Thanks, Everett. We'll be here."

I looked over at Jet. "You both took a bullet today."

He looked at me quizzically.

"Foxy took a bullet from you. You took a mind bullet from that gorg."

He sighed heavily, looking down at Foxy. "Is he gonna make it, Vance? He's gotta make it."

"You hear that, Foxy?" I asked him. "You gotta make it. That's an order from the both of us."

Foxy looked at us sleepily. Then he looked at Jet and squinted, coughing and flicking up his eyebrows, trying to clear his vision. "Wait, so you shoot me in the arm, and I'm supposed to obey you? You know we're supposed to shoot at the *bad guys*, right, Jet?" And then he looked over at me. "Somebody needs more training."

A pained laugh burst out of Jet. I smiled at my son-in-law. "Yes, he does," I agreed, looking sidelong at Jet. "You know this guy shot himself in the leg once, right?"

"Yessir," Foxy breathed. "A little target practice might be a good idea."

"Yeah, let's get him to the range straightaway."

Jet shook his head and sighed, pinching the bridge of his nose. "You guys, man."

"Aw, look at him," mumbled Foxy. "Poor guy. I think we hurt his one feeling, Cap."

"Hey! That's *Mr. President* to you, kid," I scolded.

The sudden insistence upon my presidential title caught him off guard, and he squinted his eyes in confusion.

"I'm just kidding," I said, laughing. "I'm just-" I tried. "Never mind. Just shut up and heal," I said.

Jet chuckled again, and I did as well.

Foxy snickered softly, and then laid his head back and took a deep breath. He was covered in sweat, dust and blood. The sweat carved little dirty rivulets down his head and neck.

We all took that deep breath. Even the unfamiliar voices that now greeted us.

One came from the building just south of us. Out of the entrance emerged a familiar face. Toole strode out, brandishing his sniper rifle. He lifted up his mask and cheered for us as he approached.

But then I heard another voice behind us. I practically felt it as he approached. I turned and saw a thick figure ambling up 12th Street heading north. Aged muscles straining against gravity and time. It was a husky figure with solid guns for arms and tree trunks for legs. His thick Mexican accent preceded him as he called for us, and then he began to jog our way.

Miguel Monzon. My Chief of Staff, and my best friend. Here he came, his shoulder still in a sling. His face was red and puffy, and he was panting, but this septuagenarian still had it. I was so elated, I couldn't hold back the tears.

The love was everywhere, and we understood it.

21 | DELIVERANCE

Tuesday, June 6th 2045 · 9:15am

It would take a long time.

A *very long time indeed*, Miguel echoed me.

We would be rebuilding upon our rebuilding, and we had only just begun. The repair of our planet would take even longer. The craft would need to be destroyed once again. This time, the vote was to systematically dismantle it. We had had enough of nukes. *Fuggedaboutit,* I said when asked about that possibility. I had no clue how we would go about dismantling a hovering ship in our atmosphere, but demolition crews and scientists could knock their heads together and figure that one out. I had other concerns, such as repairing a battered country *again*.

Foxy's arm still troubled him on occasion, but he was improving. He had gotten to know Miguel increasingly well through his convalescence; indeed, Miguel himself slung Foxy over his shoulder and carried him back to the Hoover Building. They were now 'brothers in bullet wounds,' or *hermanos heridos de bala*, as Miguel put it. Fist bumps abounded between the two of them. My son-in-law was healing. He just turned twenty-three on May 18th and was making great inroads to recovery. The doctors said he should be well enough for service in another six months.

Once I got over the depressing irony that both of their wounds came not from gorgons but from their fellow humans, I could see more clearly. It would still take time before we would all stop shooting each other.

The *Tsar Bombas* had proven ineffective. And now, astronomers and scientists were analyzing the ripple effects of twenty-two hundred megatons of nuclear detonation in space. So far, they had not registered much adverse consequence, except for a slight modulation of our polar axis, and a celestial void that nudged every orbiting satellite far out of its original rotation. Only time would tell. Space was, after all, a vacuum. Time would reveal whether we had set ourselves in irreversible harm's way. For now, we had survived. The moon was another story; scans confirmed it had taken on a somewhat more 'ovular' shape due to the compression waves that hit it. We'd see how that would affect us in time.

Jet had returned to Blue Spring, Kentucky just a few weeks ago. Blockade DN436 had opened up and released civilians once more, and Christine and little Wyatt received a military escort back home. Their reunion must have been joyous indeed. I wasn't there to witness it, but Christine emailed me and thanked me herself. Jet must have given her my personal email address.

Something about Jet: he had appeared a little clouded since that day in DC. I didn't know what it was and couldn't put my finger on it, but something those gorgs did to him – *twice in one day, no less* – affected him. His mind seemed a bit clouded, and he repeated phrases here and there. I appointed him a government-sponsored physician and psychiatrist and set them both up with a house nearby in Blue Spring. He deserved it. That man took a few hits for the country and deserved more honor than he had ever been formally given. He carried much guilt – Rosie would have a thing or two to say about that – for losing his little brother and almost killing his new little brother. He was soaked in PTSD, and dredging all of that trauma back up to the surface for the encounter with the gorg was something I should have never asked him to do. The man had lived a turbulent life, loved and lost, and nearly lost again. I was so proud to serve alongside him. However, his time for release from the service had come. He was honorably discharged and returned home, deservedly so, to his wife and son. Someone told me that Asher Collins also retired and moved out there. That news warmed my heart: at least he'd have a flyboy buddy nearby. Jet received his promotion to Captain with dignity. He had earned it. This time it was official, and this time it would remain, regardless of his enlisted or delisted status.

The best news of all? He made it home in time to see little Wyatt take his first steps. That brought joy to my heart.

Janine's bump was getting *big*. She was now thirty-one weeks along and under the care of her obstetrician. That baby was undoubtedly a boy; her bump was too big for it not to be. I asked both of them if they had picked out any names, and they wouldn't tell us. Said it was a secret. I told them that as President, I had access to CIA equipment and could find out if I needed to. Neener just rolled her eyes and scoffed at my feeble threat.

General Everett Carson continued to serve and oversee the rebuilding of the Blockades at DN002 and DN005. The PEOC bunker was a different matter. As for those Blockades, Carson was the unofficial custodian of them, running back and forth down there like a phantom as he had done for so many years, ensuring the survival of his charges. He was a man of strength; well-regarded and feared wherever he went. People looked up to him. The war heroes like he, Jet, Foxy, Miguel, Evelyn, and pilot Asher Collins were put on pedestals and adored. Rightly so. And furthermore, Everett remained my friend, fortunately, despite the fact that I had lost his precious rifle. I assured him I would make quarterly repayments.

And as for Lynch, her place was the sea. She continued to command, and had gained international fame for almost single-handedly destroying two massive aliens spanning two wars. Her reputation preceded her. People knew not to mess with Lynch. In that way, she wasn't too much different from Neener. Last I heard, she was somewhere out over the Bering Strait chumming with the Russians and discussing the efficiency or inefficiency of *Tsar Bombas.* I wouldn't dare debate that no-nonsense brain of hers.

Jean Graham had been executed. China didn't waste any time. They imprisoned her, waited out the invasion, and then held their own tribunal post-haste. They opted for a firing squad; the TOD felt that would be deserving and just.

Graham didn't beg, and she offered no complaints. They reported that she dressed up for the occasion and asked to enjoy one final cigarette while they shot her. It was an odd request, but then again, Jean Graham was odd. She had truly descended into madness, and history was all too glad to forget that blemish. No one shed a tear at her loss. Rosie might have; she never counted anyone as ineligible for God's grace and redemption.

So, that debt to the TOD was finally settled. We were starting to receive our equipment back, as promised, and their debt to us was being equally settled. Speaking of the equipment, they never actually used it – *any* of it. At first I was incensed at having extradited Graham for no reason. Ultimately, however, justice had been served in both directions. I had to trust that all those things were now balanced in the name of justice.

Today, on this nineteenth anniversary of the gorgons' first arrival, I couldn't help but wonder as we started over for the second time. I wondered back to the very beginning, in 2026, when the gorgons came, reflecting upon the havoc they wreaked. *That telepathy.* I actually envied it. Not the predatorial projection side of it, paralyzing their prey; rather their ability to read the minds of others. That's how they knew how to attack. Where we'd be. How we'd respond. That's how they killed us all off so quickly.

If only we could harness that ability and use it for good. If only we all had that ability and could better understand one another. Not out of nefarious motive. Not out of sinister intent, but out of goodwill. If that were the case, perhaps we wouldn't all be so frozen in our own skin. Perhaps we'd be able to connect more deeply with one another and not assume the worst of our fellow man.

Perhaps we'd be able to heal.

•   •   •   •   •

Finally, on a sunny morning in June, 2045, my wife and I were sitting once more on the lawn of the White House, staring off east at the warm, amber sunrise. The sound of construction equipment behind us beeped their incessant mechanical sounds.

"We're gonna be grandparents soon, aren't we?" she said, resting her head on my right shoulder. Her hair swirled around us in the low wind that raced along the lawn.

"Yeah, we sure are, aren't we? Crazy," I said. "To think that scrawny mop top and our little girl are gonna make a tiny human."

"They already made it, ya know. It's just gotta arrive," she corrected me softly.

"True."

"What do you hope they name it?"

"Shaniqua."

"Stop it," she said, and elbowed me.

"Ow!" I protested. "Still sore!"

"Dude. That was three months ago," she whined, straightening up and looking right into my eyes accusingly.

"Yeah, well, you try being thrown fifty feet and landing on your old hairy chest."

"Hairy, huh?"

I looked down. "Well, you haven't waxed in a while."

Her eyes narrowed. "Are you *trying* to be obnoxious, or does it come naturally?"

"I'm trying," I said, followed by a pause, and she snorted and rested her head back on my shoulders. "And it comes naturally."

Andi giggled. "Yes, it does."

We didn't speak a word to each other for a bit. Just let the sunrise do the talking. The light streamed around us, man and wife, groom and bride, the union of two lives, which created more life on this planet. I thought back to that abhorrent abomination that vomited out all its swelling insta-giants into the bowels of the PEOC, grunting silently and shaking my head. The whole thing felt inevitable. But so was trust, just like Rosie said.

Andi sensed my body language. "What is it?"

"Just remembering."

"Remembering Jean Graham again, aren't you? You miss her."

"Stop it."

She giggled again.

"No, I don't need to remember back to '26, hon. Or '42. That's seared into my memory," I assured her. "No. I'm remembering the day I got confirmation of them coming back. We were sitting right here. Remember?"

She nodded. "Mm-hmm."

"You told me you were thankful for the fifteen percent of my day that you get to lay here with me, out of all the people in this world."

"I am thankful."

"Well, there's even more repair to do now, hon. That percentage is gonna have to drop by necessity," I said, sighing and looking back at the remnants of our demolished White House.

She moaned and frowned. But then she sat straight up and clenched her lip with a determined look.

"Ya know what? That's okay. It just means that I need to have a more *concentrated* gratitude for the even less that I have."

I smiled at her. "That's a great way to live. Here's to a more concentrated gratitude. *Be thankful for what you do have, not angry about what you don't,* right? That's something my dad used to say to me."

"Your dad was a very wise man."

"It runs in the family."

"Yes it does, wise guy."

I smiled at Andi. "I sure love you, First Lady Leandra Dempsey Cardona."

"And I love you, President Vance Brennan Cardona."

And with that, she pressed her lips into mine, and we enjoyed a passionate kiss that both time and presidential appointments had denied us much of over the past few weeks. It was a kiss of life that would've had Rosie's blessing, certainly.

And it had been a long time coming.

The war for the universe is over.
Visit dissonancetheseries.com for the whole saga.

Read all the books in the series, in chronological order:

Dissonance Volume Zero: Revelation
Dissonance Volume Up: Rising
Dissonance Volume I: Reality
Dissonance Volume II: Reckoning
Dissonance Volume III: Renegade
Dissonance Volume IV: Relentless

I AFTERWORD

What can I say? *This is where I've belonged.* Admittedly, and in all honesty, I left the door somewhat ajar at the end of *Dissonance Volume III: Renegade* with that craft still looming large over the north Atlantic Ocean. That was an inescapable omen left unchecked. It wouldn't just go away.

Could the gorgons return? Were there more up there in that ship? Would they send a distress signal to their home planet and request more gorgons to ravage Planet Earth? The possibilities were endless.

What would it mean for the end of *Dissonance Volume III: Renegade* if victory was shorn of gladness, and the protagonists were called upon to end this menace once more? Would that be like the beginning of Alien 3, rendering moot the triumphant escape at the end of Aliens? Would authoring this new book perhaps be overkill or a killjoy? Or would it be riveting and climactic once more? Alternatively, would it just go to show how relentless and survivable the human race is, even in the face of a second extinction level event?

Ultimately, those are questions that only the reader can answer. For myself, I know which stories motivate me, and it certainly wasn't out of any sort of commercial aim that I returned to Earth of 2042 and beyond. Rather, it was out of a desire to continue telling a story that has so utterly moved and compelled me.

I wish everyone would read this series. Not because I am anything even remotely akin to Tolkien, Collins, Asimov, Foster, Corey, Lu, King, Crichton, Grisham, Clancy, or others…but out of a profound heart swell that went into it. It has become the beating heart of my creativity, and has fueled my dreams and aspirations far beyond anything else I've ever created.

Dissonance is my signature authoring work, and I believe it always will be. I *love* this story and this series, and I've kept hammering away at the series because it has so much heart, so much tension, so much at stake, and so much thematic depth. I'm so grateful for where it has led me, and where it's taking me even now at the writing. Eventually, I will move on and *finally* get to "Forecast" – right, Roland? – but until that time, the Dissonance series has been where my heart belongs, and I'm so grateful to have been a sojourner in these post-apocalyptic lands for a year.

Thank you so much to my dear Lord and Savior Jesus Christ for giving me this series to write. For giving me the gumption, drive, and passion to write it nonstop, and to push so hard to get it out in so short a time. Thank you for equipping me with a fast mind, and even faster fingers. Thank you for blessing me with the ability to, as a friend once said, "be dropped into the middle of a desert and still find a way to make money." I'm so grateful for the gifts and talents you've equipped me with. I can claim no credit; they all belong to and came from you, and glory is yours because of them. THANK YOU, LORD. In Jesus' Name, AMEN.

This is the saga I was born to tell, and to see it materialize and take shape in book form has been nothing short of fundamentally satisfying. Each new chapter, each new character, each new iteration reaffirms in me the unquenchable truth that this is where I belong: in this world and with these characters. Until my fingers and mind give out, this is where I belong.

THANK YOU from the bottom of my heart for continuing to journey with me in this saga. From the bottom of my heart, thank you *SO MUCH!*

Thanks also to the indispensable Alan Roth, Vance Pease, Roland Kouhsen, Walker Armstrong, Tom Armstrong, Hook Vetas, Jonathan & Keegan Wellons, and Janine Graves for your help and partnership in lifting this series off the ground. I could not have done this without you. You have restored harmony to dissonance, and helped me write something hefty and rich.

And for you, my reader, thank you for taking part in my story. With everything that is in me, thank you for journeying with Andrew & Melissa, Jet, Rutty, Sissy, Foxy, Rosie, Miguel, Joe, Steph, Maureen, Trudy, Vance, Andi, Janine, Carson, Christine, Graham, and everyone else. They thank you as well. ☺ Except for Graham. She's dead.

With love and gratitude,

Aaron Ryan

I ABOUT THE AUTHOR

Award-winning and bestselling Christian author, speaker, panelist, workshop presenter and voice actor Aaron Ryan lives in Washington with his wife and two sons, along with Macy the dog, Winston and Tibbles the cats, and the finch named Fry.

He is the prolific author of the bestselling *Dissonance* 6-book alien invasion saga, the Christian dystopian fiction trilogies *The End* and *Carbon*, the *Talisman* trilogy, the sci-fi thrillers *Forecast, The Slide, The Phoenix Experiment, Blood Echoes* and *The Darkness Within,* the nonfiction books *You are my whole Earth: A Daddy's love for his Sons, You're Going Straight To Helen (In A Handbasket), God Is Not Santa,* and *A Lyrical Empirical Satirical Miracle,* six children's picture books, the business reference books *How to Successfully Self-Publish & Promote Your Self-Published Book* and *The Superhero Anomaly*, 6 business books on voiceovers penned under his former stage name (Joshua Alexander), as well as a previous fictional novel, *The Omega Room.*

When he was in second grade, he was tasked with writing a creative assignment: a fictional book. And thus, *The Electric Boy* was born: a simple novella full of intrigue, fantasy, and 7-year-old wits that electrified Aaron's desire to write. From that point forward, Aaron evolved into a creative soul that desired to create.

He enjoys the arts, media, music, performing, poetry, and being a daddy. In his lifetime he has been an author, voiceover artist, wedding videographer, stage performer, musician, producer, rock/pop artist, executive assistant, service manager, paperboy, CSR, poet, tech support, worship leader, and more. The diversity of his life experiences gives him a unique approach to business, life, ministry, faith, and entertainment.

Aaron's favorite author by far is J.R.R. Tolkien, but he also enjoys Suzanne Collins, James S.A. Corey, Michael Crichton, Marie Lu, Madeleine L'Engle, John Grisham, Tom Clancy, Tim Lebbon, Christopher Golden, C.S. Lewis, Stephen King and Dave Barry.

Aaron has always had a passion for storytelling. Visit his website at https://www.authoraaronryan.com, join his exclusive Facebook group at https://authoraaronryangroup.com, or check out his store at https://authoraaronryanstore.com.

Readers, feel free to check out the following links for further information on Aaron:

Subscribe to Aaron's blog for free giveaways, news and new releases at **authoraaronryan.com/blog**

Join the Author Aaron Ryan Facebook community at **facebook.com/groups/authoraaronryan**

Subscribe to Aaron's YouTube channel at **youtube.com/@authoraaronryan**

Check out Aaron's IMDB page at: **www.imdb.com/name/nm5976186/**

Visit Aaron's social media links to connect with him at **dot.cards/authoraaronryan**

Visit **dissonancetheseries.com** for information on the entire epic "Dissonance" saga, including the prequels, *Dissonance Volume Zero: Revelation*, and *Dissonance Volume Up: Rising.*

If you liked Aaron's book or the "Dissonance" saga, please visit the Amazon and Goodreads pages for this book and leave a positive review. Once it shows up, please email the screenshot of it to aaron@authoraaronryan.com for a discount on your next book purchase from him! Thank you so much. Reviews really do help a ton!

Visit his author website and enlist at the blog:

Subscribe to Author Aaron Ryan

Follow Aaron and connect on Social Media:

I ALSO BY THE AUTHOR

As Aaron Ryan:

Dissonance Volume I: Reality
Dissonance Volume II: Reckoning
Dissonance Volume III: Renegade
Dissonance Volume Zero: Revelation
Dissonance Volume Up: Rising
The Complete Dissonance Sci-Fi Alien Invasion Saga
The End: Alpha
The End: Omicron
The End: Omega
The Complete THE END Christian Dystopian Saga
Carbon Volume I: Programming
Carbon Volume II: Reformatting
Carbon Volume III: Rebooting
The Complete Carbon Series
Forecast
The Slide

The Phoenix Experiment
Blood Echoes
The Darkness Within
God is not Santa
You are my whole Earth: A Daddy's love for his Sons
A Lyrical Empirical Satirical Miracle
You're Going Straight To Helen (In A Handbasket)
Talisman: Subterfuge
Talisman: Nexus
Talisman: Halcyon
The Complete Talisman Series
The Ring of Truth
The Sword of Joy
The Book of Power
The Super Ordinary Heroes Series: Empathy
The Super Ordinary Heroes Series: The Invisibility Cape
The Super Ordinary Heroes Series: The Time-stopping Hug
The Superhero Anomaly
How to Successfully Self-Publish & Promote Your Independent Book
Reflections: A compilation of journals and poetry by Aaron Ryan
The Omega Room
Glimmerings

As former stage name Josh Alexander:

Voiceovers: A Super Business, A Super Life
Voiceovers: A Super Fun Pursuit
Voiceovers: A Super Responsibility
Running a Successful Voiceover Business
How do I get started in Voiceovers?
Five T's to Triumph: The Secrets to Getting Cast in Voiceovers

Easter Egg: if you liked *Dissonance*,
you're going to love *The Talisman* series
…and you just may recognize some *very* familiar names!